Chris Faraday

TRINE

ANGRY
ROBOT

ANGRY ROBOT
An imprint of Watkins Media Ltd

Unit 11, Shepperton House
89 Shepperton Road
London N1 3DF
UK

angryrobotbooks.com
twitter.com/angryrobotbooks
Third Time's the Trine

An Angry Robot paperback original, 2023

Cover by Kieryn Tyler
Edited by Robin Triggs and Alice Abrams
Set in Meridien

ISBN 978 1 91520 244 4
Ebook ISBN 978 1 91520 262 8

Printed and bound in the United Kingdom by TJ Books Limited

9 8 7 6 5 4 3 2 1

MIX
Paper from
responsible sources
FSC
www.fsc.org   FSC® C013056

The Gracious Gazette
Sunday, May 9, 1897

FIREBALL INSTILLS FEAR

WITNESSES to the fireball streaking across the nighttime heavens last Monday believe it was an omen of dark tidings.

Mr Charles Gibbons, manager of a farmstead on Lower Berman Road, said he was awakened by persistent neighing from the horses. He was walking to the barn to investigate when he heard an uncommon noise from above.

"I looked up and saw a dazzling burst of light as brilliant as the sun," Mr Gibbons proclaimed. "A band of vapors trailed behind it, in thrall to its power and heralding doom."

Indeed, the very next morning, a calf from his herd fell into a ravine, impaled itself on a fence post and perished.

"A sign of its evil," he said.

Miss Henrietta Angstadt, of Pear Street, was in her back yard when the luminous object appeared. She said it made a harsh sound like bacon strips sizzling and appeared to descend toward Copernian Ridge.

"It gave me such a scare that I took cover under the nearest roof, which happened to be the outhouse. When I emerged, everything seemed different. A mist hung low over the land and the shadows were ill-defined. Later, when sleep finally took me, I had the most peculiar of dreams, that something vile had entered the world, and that the future would be darkened by great trials and tribulations."

But Professor Robert Summersby, of the School of Natural Science at Pennsylvania State College, believes the fireball was a natural event, although quite rare.

"It was likely a meteor that survived its plunge to Earth," the professor stated.

He and his research assistant made the two-day trip to Gracious on horseback with the intent of searching the mountains for where it came down.

"If we can locate the meteorite, or even just fragments that survived the dramatic fall, its composition may answer important questions about the universe and our place within it," Professor Summersby said.

THE FIRST PART

ORJOS: *The discordant one is fatally compromised. Repressed pain has created narcissistic instability. His self-destructive behavior will continue unabated.*

SILSO: No doubt he is troubled. Yet he is not the tragic figure you suggest. Profundity resides within him.

ORJOS: *A lost cause. When confronted by the Pestilence, he will capitulate.*

SILSO: Hidden strengths may yet emerge.

ONE

The Mercy of Gracious, yeah yeah;
The strength of its bones, yeah yeah;
Forever calling, yeah yeah;
Its wanderers home.

The ridiculous song splashed Brad Van Reed like a bucket of slime, its abrupt recollection a consequence of geography. He was turning onto Rural Route 57A, the main road into Gracious, Pennsylvania.

A wanderer home.

It was a cool Friday steeped in sunshine, the air alive with scented breezes, peppermint and pine, as pleasant a late May afternoon as these mountains were likely to offer. He fought an urge to steer his old Ford pickup onto the shoulder, make a U-turn and accelerate in the opposite direction with the haste of a man being pursued by a starving T rex.

The Mercy of Gracious.
Yeah yeah.

The upbeat melody and on-the-nose lyrics had been composed in that prehistoric and overrated boomer era – the 1960s – by some Beatlemania-stricken local. "The Mercy of Gracious" had been given the seal of approval by the Gracious Chamber of Commerce and drilled into generations of elementary school victims by teachers dedicated to brainwashing young minds. The truth was, the town and its environs did *not* represent the center of the universe, something Brad eventually realized after growing to understand the manipulative nature of adults. An interstate-deprived town surrounded by wilderness on the edge of nowhere should *never* be mistaken for merciful.

The song triggered another unpleasant memory: his initial escape attempt from Gracious a decade ago. He'd been a fourteen year-old videogame junkie harboring a black attitude to match his goth-chic attire. During active-shooter drills at middle school, he sensed teachers and classmates watching him like a hawk, all convinced he was the kid most likely to get hold of an AK-47 and make the nightmare real.

Such hatefulness had never crossed Brad's mind, not then, not now. He'd been too proud and tough to show it, but their suspicions hurt, and left him feeling even more isolated. Then had come the night his aunt and uncle dragged him to a school-sponsored intervention, where an oblivious psychologist and a timid guidance counselor took turns spouting platitudes about learning to control his anger. That's when he'd decided to run away.

He hadn't thought it through. A no-nonsense cop – what other kind were there? – caught him at the town limits and hauled his ass back home. Uncle Zack threatened to drag said ass out to the garage and beat some sense into it with the old razor strop used on his own butt in less enlightened times. Aunt Nipa's pleas for a reduced sentence instead resulted in Brad being grounded for a week with no TV and confiscation of all things digital.

The iron fist, the velvet glove. Grim Uncle Zack, always ready to punish. Kindly Aunt Nipa, always lobbying for understanding. She meant well, but a week of enforced boredom hadn't exactly been a mild sanction. He'd rather have taken the beating.

"Shit!"

He slammed the brakes as three white-tailed deer, a doe and two fawns, darted out of the woods. The F-150 was too old to have anti-lock brakes and shuddered as it skidded to a halt. Another few feet and the trailing fawn would have been roadkill.

The trio raced into the trees beyond the opposite shoulder and vanished. Brad scanned the woods from where the animals had appeared, wary of stragglers. None were visible but something else was.

It dashed out of the woods from the same spot as the deer. Presumably a human male, it was short, barely five feet. From the neck down it was clad in some sort of camo-rubber outfit, fetishistic swirls of green and tan. But the headgear truly established its freak cred.

The boxy, tight-fitting wooden helmet looked to have been built by a carpenter unfamiliar with the straightedge. None of the angles were quite ninety degrees, giving the head a lopsided appearance. The helmet was open at the front, but the face was hidden by frosted goggles and a nose-mouth grill that would have made Hannibal Lecter envious.

The creature halted in front of Brad's truck. It seemed to glare at him, as if pissed off at having its deer pursuit interrupted. Raising a rock clutched in its fist, it smacked the rock down on his hood three times in rapid succession, then took off after its prey.

The hood bashing left new dents. The truck was decades beyond pristine, so they pretty much just complemented the dozens of other indentations. Still, someone messing with one of his possessions never failed to stir his anger. Brad considered chasing after Boxhead and giving him a serious ass-stomping.

He forced calm. It wasn't worth the effort. Besides, he was approaching Gracious, which had always been a magnet for the bizarre. Best to move on and consider Boxhead as just the town's latest incarnation of weirdness.

When he was in fourth grade, a deacon at the Methodist church suffered a breakdown and tried making his kids go to school in the nude. In high school, a popular cheerleader apparently forgot how to speak English and began babbling in an unknown language, which the local nerd colony suggested was a variant of Klingon. And only days before Brad's newsworthy getaway from Gracious two years ago, the reclusive Swanteri brothers, Hiram and Amos, abandoned their farm, purportedly to take up a feral existence in the wilderness out around Copernian Ridge.

The Mercy of Gracious. One fucked-up little town.

He depressed the gas pedal and continued his journey. A mile or so later, Route 57A looped around a series of bends between imposing tree-covered hills before emerging onto Lakamoxin Street, the town's main drag. Retail establishments fronted by angled parking spots and hungry meters were interspersed with row homes. He passed Moxie's Bar & Grill, which had always been the best downtown place to drink and eat and drink some more.

A block farther on was the Roberta Hotel, at five stories the tallest structure in town. Across from the Roberta was Majestic Beauty Salon & Bicycle Shop, run by a sixty-something husband and wife. Diego Rodriguez did hair and nails, Alondra Rodriguez, gears and spokes. The vacant lot beside their combo biz had been a Burger King until an unknown perp, reputedly hired by Moxie's, torched the restaurant and the chain elected not to rebuild.

Just beyond, Brad turned into the small lot for Fenstermacher's Emporium. The hardware-and-sundries retailer was decidedly old school and even more cramped inside than he remembered. Floorboards were spotted with throw rugs, their once-bright colors weathered to crap brown. Stuff – that was the polite word for it – was piled everywhere, crammed onto sagging shelves or suspended from wiry ceiling grapples.

Frying pans and house paints. Expensive solar panels and cheap tool sets. Lottery tickets, bargain-bin clothes and all sorts of vintage items, including a mint-in-box Commodore VIC-20 that aging proprietor Harry Fenstermacher insisted was a valuable antique. The computer fit with Harry's retail philosophy, which was to cater to all tastes by stocking at least one of every imaginable item, new and used. Some of the stuff had been here since Brad was a kid. There were no customers, another emporium hallmark. A Home Depot in Trevorport, fifteen miles south of Gracious, tended to vacuum up locals.

Harry sat behind a glass counter stocked with bins of hard candy. He was engrossed in a book on his favorite subject, World War II. A squealing tabletop fan begged to be put out of its misery.

"Hey," Brad called out.

Harry drooped his reading glasses to the tip of his nose and looked up. Brad felt like he was being scanned by a TSA agent. It wasn't the first time his appearance had prompted an optic pat-down. His ragged sweatshirt and jeans, ponytailed hair and tattoo of a coiled pit viper on his wrist were catnip for law-and-order types. Of course, Harry had other, more personal reasons for mistrusting Brad.

"Well, shit," the proprietor finally responded. His voice was Darth Vaderish, deep and solemn. "The prodigal son returns."

"Yeah yeah."

"Gracious doesn't deserve you."

"Coming back must be punishment for something I did in a previous life."

"More likely in this life," Harry said with an accusatory glare.

Brad had walked straight into that one. Ignoring the subtext, he pushed on, trying to maintain an air of politeness.

"How've you been, Harry?"

"Gettin' by. You?"

"Same."

"North Carolina treating you well?"

"It's not Gracious."

Harry didn't rise to the snark. "Family doing OK?"

"Haven't been out to the house yet."

The proprietor raised an eyebrow.

"I know, I'm an asshole."

"And who said people don't get smarter with age."

Brad offered a twisted smile.

"So, you figured to come in here first and get the lowdown?"

"Something like that. Aunt Nipa called, said Kristen's been having some problems." He didn't add that his aunt had practically begged him to come home.

"Uh-huh, heard about your sister a while back," Harry said.

"This was the earliest I could get away." That wasn't exactly true. It had taken Brad a good week to overcome his reluctance to get on the road. As departure day approached, his anxiety had gone through the roof. Drinking hadn't helped.

"You see my aunt and uncle lately?" he asked.

Harry shook his head. Brad absently toyed with the door of a pre-owned toaster oven, trying to work up to the question he'd really come here to ask. Instead, he detoured and related his encounter with Boxhead.

"Anyone else spot the freak?" he concluded.

Harry shook his head. "Been some new faces around town, though, including a pair of real nasty types. A big-ass skinhead. Gotta tip the scales at close to three hundred. He and his skinny pal got into a fight with Joseph at Moxie's the other night."

Pretty much everyone got into a fight at Moxie's. Brad had almost been arrested once for punching out some dickhead at the bar who'd called his sister retarded. Still, Joseph LeFevre had always seemed a peaceful sort. The old Creole had been a fixture around town for as long as anyone could remember, which meant he was about a zillion years past the age where he should be trading punches.

"There's also this creepy rich dude being driven around in a limo," Harry said. "Showed up recently. Nobody seems to know what he's up to."

Gracious didn't attract one-percenters. "Maybe looking to invest in the area? Bring back manufacturing?" When Brad left, the township had been trying to redevelop Eckenroth's, once the area's largest employer. The regional economy had taken a big hit when the owners received a generous tax-credit deal to move operations to a new facility in Georgia. The factory had been abandoned for years.

"I doubt he's looking to invest. But he did make some serious purchases from me." Harry darkened. "Unlike some others I could name."

It was a familiar complaint from Harry, directed at those who browsed at the emporium but purchased online.

"At least you're making money off him." *Quit stalling*, Brad chided himself. *Just ask him*. Instead...

"What did Moneybags buy?"

"All kinds of different stuff. A refurbished laptop, a box of jar candles. Even sold him that antique chamber pot I've had for ages."

Brad steeled himself and finally blurted it out. "How's your granddaughter?"

For a moment it seemed like Harry wasn't going to answer. Or worse, leap over the counter and punch Brad in the face.

"You two been keeping in touch?" the proprietor asked, his demeanor calm. "Phone calls? Texting?"

"Nope."

"No social media at all?"

He shook his head. "Ghosted her the day I left. Figured Felicity did the same to me."

"Sure as hell hope so."

"She home from college for the summer?"

"Yep."

"Working for her dad again at the bank?"

"Yep."

"Still hate me?"

Brad expected another yep but Harry hesitated. "I'd say she thinks of you more like a nasty virus she finally got vaccinated against."

"What went down between us... the wedding... all of it. Felicity didn't deserve that. I'm really sorry for what I did to her. For what it's worth."

"Ain't worth shit."

That was Brad's cue. He headed for the exit.

"Oh Brad, one other thing,"

He turned in the doorway.

"Don't mess with Felicity's head again. 'Cause if you do, I promise that some folks who actually care about her will fuck you up but good."

"Yeah yeah."

TWO

The house where Brad grew up after Mom died was ten miles west of town. The private lane angled off Heckmeyer's Road and curved through a forest of maples and black walnuts to terminate in a small clearing. An old Chevy Blazer was parked in front. The door of the separate garage was up, revealing Uncle Zack's pride and joy, a restored lime-green Plymouth Valiant that came off the assembly line in 1976, the US bicentennial year.

The three-story dwelling was pre-World War I. Clapboard siding, windows with shutters and an asphalt-shingled roof were standard for the region. But the mortared stone foundation dated to the 1700s, an earlier house having burned to the ground. A low picket fence on three sides separated a narrow strip of lawn from tree-smothered hillsides. Foliage crept right up to the fence, poised to overwhelm it should the zombie apocalypse ever put an end to weed whacking.

Brad turned around in the clearing so his truck was pointed back out the lane. A glance in the rearview mirror revealed no one emerging from the house to greet him. He imagined Aunt Nipa and Kristen wanting to do so but being restrained by Uncle Zack. His uncle had probably coached them not to let Brad know they were excited to have him home.

Stepping onto the porch, he noticed something odd. The side facing the garage sloped downward. By the end of the porch, it was a good six inches lower. And beyond, closer to the garage, a circular area bore fresh gravel. A large hole appeared to have been filled in recently.

The screen door sprang open disgorging Zack Manderbach. He was Mom's uncle, technically Brad and Kristen's great-uncle, although they'd never used the formal term. A bear of a man who'd turned eighty-one in March, he hobbled onto the porch with his unique walking stick, a twisted piece of lacquered hardwood. Having survived two tours in Vietnam with barely a scratch, he'd lost all the toes and a chunk of his left foot in an industrial accident a month before he was scheduled to retire from Clark's feed mill.

"Hey," Brad offered.

Uncle Zack grunted and held the door open. Brad slipped past.

The living room looked the same as when he'd left, a monument to retro. Rose-patterned wallpaper clashed with paisley-upholstered furniture. A squarish television was built into a cabinet, connected to a rooftop antenna that could access a grand total of four channels. Atop the cabinet was a DVD player vintage enough to still have a slot for VHS tapes. His aunt and uncle were also afflicted with an old-folks aversion to cell phones. Communication with the outside world was strictly via landline.

The locked gun cabinet mounted on the wall held two old hunting rifles and a pump-action shotgun. Their inherent masculinity was tempered by Aunt Nipa's handiwork, a set of doilies tethered to the glass door.

"Something to drink?" Uncle Zack asked. "Got iced tea or water."

"No thanks. Where are Kristen and Aunt Nipa?"

"Shopping. A woman from church drove them down to the mall in Trevorport. We didn't think you'd get here till tomorrow."

"Got off a day early."

His uncle settled into the recliner. Brad perched on the arm of the sofa closest to the door.

"Still working for that construction outfit in Charlotte?"

"Yeah," Brad said, gesturing toward the front picture window. "What's with the crooked porch?"

"Sinkhole formed under the corner of the house. Just happened a few days ago. Before that, another one opened up closer to the garage."

"Yeah, saw the fresh stones."

"Took three tons of 2A modified stone to plug it."

"Whole house isn't going to sink, is it?"

"Foundation's strong."

They were silent for a moment.

"Got a crew coming out next week," his uncle continued. "They're gonna jack up the edge of the house and fill in the second hole."

"Sounds like a plan."

More silence. Brad regretted arriving a day early. Dreams of escape were already percolating. He wished he hadn't promised to stay the whole weekend.

"When are you expecting them back?" he asked, checking his phone. There was another text from the girl he'd slept with last Saturday, asking why she hadn't heard from him. He deleted it.

"Should be soon," Uncle Zack said.

"Aunt Nipa wasn't real clear about what's going on with Kristen. Just said she's having some problems."

His uncle withdrew a paper from his shirt pocket and carefully unfolded it. "The psychiatrist wrote this down for us."

"She's seeing a shrink now?" Brad should have guessed but it still came as a surprise.

"Diagnosis is positive-symptom schizophrenia," Uncle Zack read from the paper. "Delusional thoughts with occasional hallucinations."

"She's having hallucinations?"

"Gonna let me finish?"

"Sorry, go ahead."

"Imaging studies negative. Screening for alcohol and drugs negative."

"Christ, she's only eleven years old. What the hell are they doing all that for?"

Uncle Zack glared.

"Look, this is a bit of a shock, OK?" Brad figured his sister was just having a more serious version of her anxiety bouts, which had plagued her at least since kindergarten. But those usually just left her emotionally tender for a few days. They always passed.

"The doc said they needed to rule out physical causes for her illness."

"I suppose that makes sense."

Uncle Zack continued reading. "Excessive fears related to specific areas within the home." He paused. "Unhealthy attraction to an inanimate object."

Brad didn't have to ask about that last one. The amulet. The damn thing should have been buried with their mom.

"So, the shrink has some kind of treatment plan?"

"She's considering putting Kristen on a mild antidepressant. Worried about going overboard with drugs on account of her age, though. We're supposed to take her back to the hospital next week. She thinks a team approach is the best option. Psychologist, social worker, nurse. So far, Medicaid's picking up the tab." Uncle Zack grimaced. "Bound to be deductibles, though. I'm guessing that when all is said and done, ain't gonna be cheap."

Brad wondered if his aunt had asked him home because they were having money problems. He had a few thousand in savings and would help if he could, but it wasn't like he was earning a fortune. His job was still bottom rung, a basic laborer. And construction projects tended to be erratic, which meant he spent a fair amount of time out of work.

"How's Kristen managing in school?"

"She's not. They said she was too disruptive to continue

regular classes. The district's paying for a part-time tutor for the rest of the school year so she won't fall too far behind. As for starting sixth grade in the fall...?" Uncle Zack trailed off with a shrug. "Who the hell knows?"

Kristen was whip-smart, one of the brightest kids in her class. Brad was sure she'd catch up no matter what happened.

He heard a vehicle and went to the window. An SUV pulled up. Aunt Nipa exited the front seat with two bags of groceries. Kristen hopped out of the back. The gray-haired woman behind the wheel did a three-point turn to head back out the lane, but paused as Aunt Nipa leaned in the driver's side to chat.

"Brad's here!" Kristen yelled, spotting his truck and dashing toward the porch. "I have to tell him about the shoo spots!"

"What's that about her shoes?" Brad wondered.

"Not what you wear on your feet, the other kind of shoo. You know, go away?"

Trust me, I'd like to.

"Just make sure you take it seriously," his uncle warned. "Else she gets really bent out of shape."

Kristen raced through the door. She brightened to a major-league smile at the sight of Brad and rushed into his arms.

"Hey kiddo! Great to see ya." He leaned over for the embrace. She hugged him super-tight, as if desperate for reassurance.

She finally broke away. He took a step back to take her all in. "Wow, you are getting to be a big girl. Definitely grown a bunch of inches since I last saw you."

It wasn't just her height. She had a more mature look about her even though she was clearly still preadolescent. Maybe it was the V-neck sweater and pants outfit, or the blond hair trimmed shorter than he remembered, or the serious way she seemed to be studying him. They'd Skyped over the past two years – holidays, her birthday, a few other occasions. But the changes hadn't been as noticeable onscreen.

"So kiddo, what have you been up to?"

She ignored the question. "Brad, are you going to sleep in your old room?"

"If that's OK with everybody."

"You just have to be careful in case you have to go to the bathroom late at night."

He grinned. "What's the matter, afraid I'll wet my bed?"

"Uh-uh. There's a shoo spot in the hallway right outside your door."

"Oh yeah, I heard something about those."

"Uncle Zack put masking tape around them to mark them off. You mustn't step past the tape. There's another shoo spot in the kitchen next to the refrigerator. And there's one in the back of the basement near the water heater." Kristen frowned. "At least I think that one's a shoo spot. There's something different about it. Something strange."

"Strange, huh?"

She nodded, oblivious to the irony. Brad struggled to hold back a grin. He couldn't help being amused at how utterly serious she looked.

"So exactly what are these shoo spots?"

She shrugged.

"You don't know?"

"Uh-uh."

"So what happens if I step on one."

"You mustn't," she whispered.

"How come?"

Kristen turned away, stared at the wall. She slipped a hand under her blouse, her fingers tracing the links of the silver necklace until they reached what hung from it out of sight. The amulet. Clutching the tiny triangle was something she did when anxious or afraid.

Brad heard the SUV driving off. A moment later Aunt Nipa entered. Uncle Zack got up from his chair and she handed him the shopping bags. He ferried them through the hallway, past the dining room entry and into the kitchen.

His aunt's jet-black hair, a dye job, was styled into bangs. She had a petite figure and was a foot shorter than his uncle. They'd always seemed an odd couple, and not just physically.

Aunt Nipa's cheeks widened with delight. She gave him a crushing hug.

"Missed you, boy!"

"Yeah, same here. Good to be home."

Her lopsided expression indicated that she knew he was fibbing about that last part.

Brad had just turned fourteen and Kristen was still a toddler when Mom died. His sister had been a precocious baby, already walking confidently by her first birthday. Aunt Nipa had served as a decent surrogate mother to them, doing her best to care for an infant and tame Brad's wilder instincts with plenty of affection and heart-to-heart talks. His teen years would have been even crazier without her steadying influence.

"I'm ordering pizza for supper from Arantino's," Aunt Nipa announced as Uncle Zack returned. "Sound good?"

Kristen wagged her head. "I want green peppers and sausage. But not the hot kind."

"They deliver this far from town now?" Brad asked.

"I give the boy an extra tip."

"Listen, I'll pay. My treat."

"*Sha*, Bradley Van Reed," his aunt scolded. Although having emigrated to the States some four decades ago after meeting Uncle Zack in Taiwan, she retained a few snippets of Mandarin Chinese, her native tongue. *Sha*, as Brad recalled, meant something like "foolish." It was one of her favorites, often used in conjunction with his uncle's full name.

"OK, deal," Brad said. "But let me take you all out for dinner tomorrow night."

"That sounds nice, doesn't it," she said, turning to Uncle Zack, whose expression suggested otherwise.

Kristen opened the roll-top desk beside the TV and withdrew

a box of crayons. "I'm going to color the tape around the shoo spot outside Brad's room. Just to be extra safe."

"That's a good idea, sweetie," Aunt Nipa said, forcing a smile.

His sister dashed off. Brad had a hunch he'd come home too late to do much good.

THREE

A couple slices of pizza and a Michelob hit the spot. Dinner-table conversation was subdued, the subject matter limited for Kristen's benefit. Still, his sister seemed pretty normal during the meal, talking about her tutor, whom she liked, and her homework, which mostly bored her because it was too easy.

In spite of the psych diagnosis and the shoo spots and all the rest of her weirdness, Brad wondered if she might just be going through some sort of phase. After all, he'd been pretty messed up at her age. Then again, he'd had a good excuse, whereas Kristen had enjoyed the good fortune of never having gotten to know their late father. Unless there was some genetic flaw that manifested as psycho behavior, crappy parenting on the paternal side was unlikely to have caused her troubles.

Brad couldn't resist inquiring about Felicity. He half expected his aunt and uncle's response to mirror Harry Fenstermacher's.

You abandoned your bride on your wedding day and ran away, he imagined Uncle Zack growling. *A bit late to be asking how she's doing.*

Over these past two years he'd made an effort not to think about Felicity Ann Bowman. It wasn't easy suppressing the emotions of having left town without warning, hours before he was due at the chapel. But now that he was back, she kept pop-tarting into his head, demanding acknowledgment.

His aunt and uncle didn't berate him. Instead, they traded wary looks and changed the subject. It seemed like they were hiding something, which naturally made him more curious.

After dinner, he helped Aunt Nipa clear the table, making space for Kristen to work on a social studies theme her tutor had assigned. He offered to help with the dishes but his aunt waved him off. Grabbing a second beer from the fridge, he wandered out to the front porch.

The air bore a pleasant chill. The sun had fallen behind the western hillside beyond the garage, casting early shadows. One swath fell on the newly graveled sinkhole. He wondered again if two depressions in the earth so close to one another indicated a large, hollowed-out space beneath the entire house. Despite Uncle Zack's contention that the foundation was strong, further subsidence might be in the cards. Or worse, total collapse.

The screen door opened. His uncle limped out. The bent floorboards creaked noisily as he eased himself onto the swing and posted his walking stick upright between his legs. The slatted bench was toward the side where the sinkhole had undercut the porch. But the swing was chained to a roof beam and remained level.

"You OK?" Brad asked, noting his uncle's pained grimace.

"Arthritis acting up. No big deal."

When Uncle Zack said it wasn't a big deal, the opposite was usually true. Although as gruff as ever, a certain hardness in his features had departed, leaving him with gaunt cheeks and dark circles under the eyes. His eight-plus decades on the planet included going to work at age eleven to help support his family, followed by his stint in the army. Those hardships had taken a toll.

"Nice evening," Brad ventured, leaning over the railing to gaze into the forests.

"Yep."

"Kristen wants to go to the library tomorrow. All right if I take her?"

His uncle nodded. "The two of you ought to spend time together. Considering you're only planning to stay the weekend."

Brad took an extra-long swig of beer.

"Dealing with your sister isn't getting any easier. Been especially hard on your aunt, way more so than she lets on. The two of us ain't spring chickens anymore. We could really use some help."

Brad had known this conversation was coming but hoped it could have waited. Like maybe until Sunday night when he was packing for the drive back to North Carolina.

"Wish I could stay, but I can't." He turned away to avoid Uncle Zack's scowl. "I've got a job down south. A life."

It wasn't much of one, he admitted. Long weekdays on construction sites when the work was available, evenings at his apartment downing brews in front of the TV. Friday and Saturday nights he usually went barhopping, on the prowl. Most of the women he hooked up with were as commitment phobic as he was and just wanted sex, which was more than fine with him. Occasionally he encountered one who thirsted for a relationship, like his most recent conquest, who kept texting him. He did his best to shut those down.

"Think I'll head for town," he said. "See what's going on at Moxie's."

There was a chance Felicity would make an appearance. Better to encounter her this evening with some alcohol in his system. Moxie's used to be their regular hangout. Then again, that might be good reason for her to avoid the bar. By now her grandfather Harry would have informed her that Brad was back in town.

"It's early yet," Uncle Zack said, motioning to the empty portion of the swing. "Why don't you sit a while."

Reluctantly, he took the proffered seat. His uncle wasted no time launching into the heart of the matter.

"OK, listen up. I know you've been hauling around a lot of crap and have a serious grudge against me. Maybe some of it's deserved. I was hard on you growing up, I know that. I just didn't want you to turn out like your father."

"Not much chance of that." As often as Brad repeated that phrase, he never quite managed to convince himself it was true.

"You're older and more mature now," his uncle continued. "Time to get past all that teenage crap. Your aunt and I always tried to do right by you and Kristen."

"I get that, Uncle Zack, really I do. And I know you're really worried about her and want me to stay and help."

"It's more than just being worried. There are things about your sister that aren't normal."

"I'd say pretty much everything going on with her fits that description."

"No, I mean things that aren't natural. How much do you know about the amulet?"

He shrugged. "Just what I've heard over the years. Maternal heirloom and all that. I know that the women in our family going back to Grandma Isabella have been obsessed with it. I remember Mom used to touch it all the time whenever something was bothering her. Kristen does the same thing. I always thought it was kind of unhealthy."

"Three generations," his uncle murmured. "I think the amulet is the real cause of Kristen's troubles. When your mother died, your aunt and I talked seriously about getting rid of it. But Janice's will was pretty clear. It was to be passed on to her daughter. So in spite of our reluctance, we followed your mom's instructions. Naturally, we waited until Kristen was bit older, past the baby stage of putting things in her mouth. But I swear, the moment we gave it to her, it was like giving heroin to an addict. She became as fixated on it as your mom and grandmother had been."

Brad remembered well. Throughout his teen years, Kristen hardly ever removed the amulet. She wore the necklace every damn day, slept with it nights. Pretty much the only time she took it off was when Aunt Nipa gave her a bath. Even then, she demanded it be kept within sight, on the shelf near the tub.

Still, he figured there was a reason for her attachment. "She probably has early unconscious memories of Mom wearing it. So in her mind she associates the good things about our mother with the amulet."

"Your aunt and I used to think the same thing. But there's something else going on. The amulet has powers. Unnatural powers."

Brad laughed. "What, you mean like the one ring from *Lord of the Rings*?"

His uncle stared blankly, not getting the reference. The few books he read were related to hunting and fishing. And his taste in movies skewed toward whatever Aunt Nipa liked to watch, usually romantic comedies from the 1950s.

"It's just a dumb little trinket, Uncle Zack. It hasn't got any evil powers."

"I never said evil. Although maybe it is, I don't know. Anyway, when Kristen was still pretty young, around five years old, we started talking about getting it away from her. Before she became even more obsessed.

"We knew she'd put up a hell of a fuss. But when she lost a baby tooth, your aunt got an idea. She told Kristen to put the tooth under her pillow for the tooth fairy. Late that night, when the two of you were asleep, we snuck into her room. I grabbed the tooth and your aunt left in its place a silver dollar and a bag of candy. We planned to tell her the tooth fairy had been extra generous in leaving her the gifts. But in exchange, it had taken the amulet, which it would put into safekeeping for her until she was older."

The idea sounded seriously dumb. And obviously hadn't worked.

"Let me guess, she woke up while you were trying to slip off the necklace and went ballistic."

"No. The thing is, we just couldn't do it. We couldn't take the amulet."

Brad nodded. "You were worried about her colossal freak-out."

"No, that's not what I mean. When I say we couldn't take the amulet, I'm speaking literally. We were *unable* to remove it."

An owl hooted its stuttering rhythm, breaking the hush of the evening wilderness. The sound gave Brad an uneasy feeling.

"I don't follow," he said. "What do you mean you couldn't remove it?"

"I tried first. Aunt Nipa gently lifted her head so I could undo the clasp. But something happened as I touched the necklace. I had a flashback to Vietnam, to the worst day of my life."

He turned away, stared ahead toward to where the lane disappeared into shadowed forest.

"We were defending a temporary base just south of the DMZ – the demilitarized zone. It came under mortar and rocket attack. My two best friends in the squad were ground zero for a shell. One got split in half, the other had his head torn off." Uncle Zack's voice fell to a whisper. "Worst day of my life."

Brad knew from Aunt Nipa that his uncle had gone through bad times in the war. But he'd never spoken about it before, at least not to his great-nephew.

"I'd had flashbacks before, nightmares. But most of them happened in the years following my discharge. Today they call it PTSD. Back then it was mostly undiagnosed. Anyway, I hadn't been affected by it in years, so I was surprised as hell to suddenly have those memories come flooding back. I jerked my hand away from the necklace. Kristen stirred and we held our breaths, thinking she was going to wake up.

"She didn't. We waited a few minutes and I tried again. This time when I touched the necklace, the flashback was stronger, even more intense. It was like I was back there in the jungle, seeing my buddies ripped to pieces, feeling the awfulness of watching them die all over again." His face contorted. "Nobody should have to endure something like that even once."

His fingers tightened on the arm of the bench, a death grip.

Brad wanted to say something comforting but couldn't find the words.

"I ran out of Kristen's bedroom. Your aunt followed. She asked me what was wrong. I couldn't tell her, couldn't even speak. Just stood there in the hallway, shaking. After a while, I calmed down. The bad memories fell back into that devil's pit where they normally live."

Uncle Zack went quiet for a time, again staring off into the distance. When he finally continued his voice was more subdued.

"Nipa suggested we try again. But I couldn't do it, couldn't go back in there. So she went by herself. I watched from the doorway as she lifted Kristen's head. As she was reaching for the necklace clasp, she jerked her hand away and came running out the door, looking like she'd seen a ghost. Much later, when we were calm enough to talk about it, she told me she'd had a flashback too, to the worst day of her childhood. It was right after World War II in Taiwan, a period known as the White Terror, when Chinese communist sympathizers were being rounded up, put in jail or worse. Nipa saw her parents murdered right in front of her."

Brad was riveted. That he'd never heard any of these stories about his aunt and uncle was as astonishing as the circumstances in which they were being revealed.

"One other thing happened that night. Just as we were about to close her door Kristen became agitated, like she was having a bad dream. She uttered these words over and over again in her sleep, 'The Trine. The Trine. The Trine.' Then she clutched the amulet, which seemed to calm her down, and said, 'It can't be taken, only given.'

"We didn't know what any of that stuff meant, didn't even know what that odd word was until your aunt looked it up. Trine means three, like in one third of a circle. It's also from astrology, something about the relative positions of the planets."

"The amulet is triangular shaped. Probably just a word she heard somewhere."

"Maybe."

"Did you ever ask her about what she said?"

"The next morning. She had no memory of it. But I'll tell you one thing. Your aunt and I never again considered trying to take the amulet from her."

Brad didn't believe in the supernatural. Yet clearly his uncle was telling the truth, or at least what he felt was the truth. In any case, it was plain to see that the incident had deeply affected him.

"How come you never told me about any of this?"

"Back when it happened, you were in high school. Remember what you were like at that age?"

He did. Not only rebellious but as prickly as a rabid porcupine.

"Anyway, thanks for telling me now."

Brad wasn't thankful, not one bit. However bizarre his uncle's story, at some level it represented another attempt to get him to stay in Gracious.

He downed the rest of his beer. "Gonna take a shower and get changed. Get ready for town."

Uncle Zack gave the faintest of nods before craning his attention back toward the encroaching dark.

FOUR

Joseph LeFevre had long ago mastered the art of keeping out of sight. He observed Kristen's house from halfway up the hillside behind the garage, motionless amid the undergrowth. He was far enough away that anyone randomly gazing through the twilight likely would catch only smears of his camo overcoat.

The child's brother had arrived unexpectedly today. A short time ago he'd ventured onto the porch with his uncle. Brad and Zack were engaged in intense conversation. The latter seemed to be doing most of the talking. Joseph remained too distant to make out his words. But he suspected they related to Kristen's woes.

Joseph felt sad for Kristen. He wished he could do something more meaningful than occasionally borrowing his landlady's old Nissan SUV, parking off-road and hiking the half mile to this observation post. It wasn't like secretly keeping an eye on her was likely to help. But he felt obligated to do it.

Kristen had been an unexpected addition to the family, born when Janice Van Reed had been in her mid-forties. He'd performed a similar duty for Janice before her tragic early death. Back then the family had been intact and living on Laurel Street, a cul-de-sac of modest cottages on the western edge of town that had seen better days. The Van Reed cottage had been pinched between a small playground and woodlands, the pleasant surroundings in contrast to the turmoil that must have been happening within those walls. Had Joseph known more at the time, he could have intervened. But perhaps it was better he hadn't. Interventions often had unintended consequences.

And prior to looking out for Janice, he'd kept an eye on *her* mother, Kristen's grandmother, Isabella. A far more rewarding task, yet in the end, infinitely painful. Isabella had been the love of Joseph's life.

The bittersweet memory induced a sigh. He'd spent far too many years without her. Isabella's absence, along with other trials, had taken their toll. The infirmities of an eighty-seven year-old body and too many decades removed from the touch of his true love often left Joseph contemplating the end of his time here on Earth. It was an event bearing down on him with the unstoppable fury of one of those steam locomotives of his youth.

Truth be told, he sometimes wished for it to be over. He couldn't imagine taking his own life, though, considering the renewed promise he'd made to Isabella as she lay dying of cancer in that hospice. On his final visit, he'd vowed to continue watching over Janice and any other future descendants who might someday bear the burden of the amulet, the first of the three parts of the Trine.

A hoot owl broke his concentration. Loud and insistent, it was close by, no more than a few trees away. The sound was territorial. The owl probably was calling for its mate.

As a young man, Joseph had dreamed of going on the road and experiencing the fullness of the world, like Jack Kerouac and his other heroes of the Beat Generation. But that destiny had forever passed him by at age twenty-eight, when he'd met Isabella. His universe had been transformed, for both better and worse.

And then there was the weapon to consider. Joseph didn't know anyone worthy of inheriting the second part of the Trine, which he'd had in his possession for more than half a century. That left a troubling question. What would become of it after he was gone?

Despite his commitment to Isabella, he doubted he was

doing much good by venturing out here from time to time and spying on Kristen from the wilderness. Such feeble efforts were unlikely to alter her fate. The universe had played a cruel trick by robbing her of a mother when she was still so young. If Joseph had learned anything since that monumental day in 1966 when he and Isabella had found the two parts and the meteorite on the far side of Copernian Ridge, it was that the amulet was too formidable to be under the sway of someone of such tender years. He'd heard rumors around town that Kristen was tilting into madness.

Equally concerning was the recent *siy nan*. At least Joseph thought it was a sign. Something dark and sinister had invaded the eidolon, the great dream forest into which he occasionally journeyed for guidance. A flying apparition, it swooped over those ethereal mountains like a malignant bird of prey. Because the eidolon was a mental projection of the Trine – at least that's what Joseph had come to believe – the apparition could represent the long-feared coming of the Pestilence.

There were troubles out here in the real world as well. Joseph wasn't certain if they too were *siy nan* and related to the eidolon apparition, or merely coincidence. Whatever the case, he'd sensed a disturbing evil in the two strangers who'd come to Moxie's the other night, even before their crude remarks directed at a table of young women. The mad cackling of the bigger man, a hulking skinhead with a huge belly, coupled with the fear on the women's faces had prompted Joseph to intervene.

In retrospect, laying his hand on the skinhead's arm – a gentle touch meant to suggest communication – had been unwise. He hadn't intended a confrontation. But in the eyes of the bartender, Little Moxie, Joseph was the instigator of what had happened next.

He hadn't been prepared for their swift attack. The skinhead knocked Joseph off the barstool with the swipe of his massive arm. His skinny companion with the straw cowboy hat and incongruous fanny pack kicked Joseph as he writhed on the floor. Little Moxie broke things up before Joseph was seriously injured, although he still felt the bruising around his midsection, and no doubt would for weeks or even months to come. At his age, his body no longer snapped back to equilibrium with the swiftness blessed upon the young.

Little Moxie had ordered the ruffians to leave. A few minutes later, after making sure they weren't waiting outside for an ambush, the bartender had ejected Joseph too.

Had he been carrying the weapon that evening, the fight's result would have been different. But he never took the second part outside except on those rare occasions when he intended to use it. Revealing its existence in any public venue would leave him facing too many questions he wasn't prepared to answer. Best in the long run he'd endured the beating instead.

Movement drew his attention back to the Manderbach house. Brad got up from the porch and went inside, leaving Zack alone and gazing solemnly into the trees.

Joseph didn't know what to make of the arrival of the brother, especially with the boy having been away from home for so long. Brad had been a tumultuous presence as far back as his early teens, the dark sheep of three generations of the family, seemingly on a mission to alienate the world. Joseph had never fully grasped the underlying reasons for his twisted character, although his selfish drunk of a father certainly had played a significant role. And then, with the untimely deaths of both his parents...

Perhaps Brad having been absent for two years had enabled him to transcend his upbringing. Then again, how much change was possible for a man who'd skipped town on the day of his wedding, leaving a heartbroken bride at the altar?

The appearance of the flying apparition within the eidolon and those two ugly men in the real world left Joseph with a quandary. If each of those incidents was indeed a *siy nan*, it could mean a direct threat to Kristen was building. The family would have to be warned.

Should he try talking to Brad? Make his concerns known to Zack and Nipa? Or perhaps reveal to Kristen herself the dark forces that might well be aligning against her?

No clear option presented itself.

His thoughts shifted to another concern. The sinkholes. The one between the house and garage had been filled in. Knowing Zack to be a diligent homeowner, the larger one tilting the porch no doubt soon would be addressed as well.

As a Creole child growing up in New Orleans, Joseph recalled hearing stories about the *gouffre* that often swallowed chunks of land in and around the city. But those sinkholes generally had clear causation: ground subsidence, due in part to sections of the city being located below sea level. Pennsylvania's geology and hydrology were different, as he'd learned after going online at the Gracious Community Library recently to research the matter.

Excessive moisture in the ground might have raised the water table high enough to eat away at the soft limestone deposits dotting the region. Still, it had been a mild winter in terms of snowfall and an unusually dry spring. That left a troubling alternative explanation.

Did the sinkholes have something to do with Kristen's fraught relationship with the amulet?

FIVE

Fridays were family nights at Moxie's Bar & Grill and the spacious dining room in the rear sounded full. From beyond the swinging doors came the hiss of chattering parents and squabbling kids.

Brad remained out front on a swivel stool at the U-shaped bar, nursing a Coors Light. Above the bar, a ceiling-mounted TV was tuned to a music channel, the speakers pumping out "Irreplaceable" as Beyoncé danced through a mansion.

Along one wall, young couples occupied vintage booths, the scarred tabletops heavily varnished, the vinyl seats haphazardly patched with utility tape. The opposite wall was caked with black-and-white photos of some pre-rock era when the tavern hosted dances. The men wore suits, the women swirling dresses, and everyone looked happy. Very weird.

A forty-something woman sat down three stools away from Brad and ordered a wine spritzer from Little Moxie, the bartender. Her gaudy lipstick and too-tight jeans suggested she was fueled for launch, rendezvous and docking.

He returned his gaze to Beyoncé but his mind drifted. Coming home had been a mistake. In North Carolina he had a simple routine – work, drink, sex – no unpleasant memories of his asshole father, nothing to trigger the heartless way he'd left Felicity and abandoned Kristen at an age when his presence might have helped with her craziness. And now there was that crap from Uncle Zack about the amulet.

Sometimes he wished he could take all his troubles, compress them into a ball and hurl it far away. The notion had occurred to him frequently over the years. He supposed such a thing had been a dream of humans for as long as they'd walked the earth… or at least the dreams of people like Brad, who always seemed buried in a trash heap of troubles. Maybe that was the real purpose of yoga masters and preachers and medicine men and all those other mystics throughout history. It wasn't about reaching a higher plane of existence. It was just about showing people a way to climb out of their personal landfills.

Taking a swig of beer to wash away such thoughts, he entertained switching to something harder. Straight shots of vodka had once been a fave. He'd celebrated his twenty-first birthday downing a row of them on this very barstool. Felicity had confiscated his keys and driven him home, a good deed he'd rewarded by vomiting into her Volvo's glove compartment while clawing for a breath mint. But tonight he intended staying sober. At least until he was certain she wasn't going to show.

Screwy as it was, he missed her. While away, the triumvirate of work-booze-sex had blurred those emotions. But now such feelings kept coming back into focus. It was more than just her natural sensuality. He missed her keen intelligence and her fascination with the sciences. Brad was reasonably bright, albeit a classic underachiever, according to teachers and guidance counselors. But Felicity was super-smart and left him in the dust, especially when it came to her fave, astronomy. Some nights he enjoyed simply listening to her talk about black holes or supernovas, not fully comprehending but nevertheless moved by her passion for the subject matter.

He'd admired her toughness, too. It wasn't like she was pure tomboy, although she did get a junior hunting license at age twelve and shot her first deer a year later. Grandpa Harry, a serious outdoorsman, had mentored her, and she knew way more about all that wilderness stuff than Brad was ever likely to learn. At school she'd played soccer and volleyball. After school she took self-defense courses and boxing lessons.

And then there was her dry sense of humor, the way she could juxtapose two ideas to elicit laughter. He recalled the time she'd read a clever essay in a high school English class that compared tweeting to peeing in 280-drip increments.

"Bradley Van Reed, I thought it was you."

The forty-something woman ambled over to him. Close up, her face revealed deep lines. He might have misjudged her age; she could have passed the big five-oh. He returned her smile while struggling with an ID.

"Fifth grade?" she hinted. "I've lost a little weight."

The memory came. She'd been his homeroom teacher at Gracious Elementary. 'Lost a little weight' was an understatement. She must have dropped a good hundred pounds.

"Mrs Rodriguez?"

"It's 'Miss' now. I've been divorced for a while. And since we're out of school and both adults, you can call me Carla."

Was she hitting on him? He wasn't sure. To be on the safe side, he mentioned he was planning to meet someone.

"Me too," she said, her smile expanding. "My new boyfriend."

"Cool."

"Mind a bit of company till he shows?"

He glanced at the door, hoping to spot Felicity entering. No such luck. He gestured to the adjacent stool and Carla slithered onto it.

"I heard you were back."

"News travels fast."

"Especially in Gracious. The smaller the town, the bigger its ears."

He nodded.

"I'm so sorry to hear about your sister. She's in my homeroom. Or was. I hope she's doing better."

"Hanging in there."

"Kristen's an extremely bright child. I'm confident she'll

come out the other end of whatever she's going through."

"That's the plan."

"How's she been sleeping? Any more of those night terrors?"

The question seemed too personal. Brad answered with a shrug.

"Sorry, I don't mean to pry. It's just that everyone at school is rooting for her. I had my students make get-well cards." Carla sighed. "It's a shame for someone so young to have to bear such a weight. I often used to tell her, 'Just give it up, Kristen. If you do, I'm sure you'll feel so much better.'"

"Give what up?"

"The amulet."

Brad frowned.

"Well, you must know about her disturbing fixation. In school she was constantly touching it, fondling it. Of course, many children latch onto objects. A doll, a toy, something they get overly attached to. But they're usually younger. And Kristen..." Carla sighed. "Her obsession always struck me as unhealthy."

Brad sensed someone behind them and turned. A towering man in a gray business suit, easily six foot three, leaned in. He gave Carla a quick, passionate kiss on the lips. He was slim below the waist, but above tapered into the impressive physique of someone who lifted weights. He stared down at Brad from behind mirrored shades, his expression indecipherable. Curly black hair suggested an African American ancestry. Yet his skin was vampire pale.

Carla made the introductions. "Brad Van Reed, Nidge Desoto."

They shook hands. Nidge's palm was massive, his grip iron.

"Let's go," Nidge ordered, taking Carla by the wrist and prying her from the barstool. "I'm hungry."

Carla threw Brad a parting nod as she allowed herself to be led toward the dining room. As the couple plowed through the swinging doors, Little Moxie wandered into

Brad's field of view. The bartender wasn't little and he wasn't young. He reminded Brad of some missing-link type, with ape arms that often politely but firmly guided rowdy drunks toward the door. His name served to distinguish him from his retired father, Big Moxie, who was thinner and scrawnier but a hell of a lot meaner when it came to ejecting noxious customers.

Little Moxie leaned over the bar. "You know that guy?"

"Carla's date? Just met him."

"Know who he works for?"

"Not the faintest."

"Sindle Vunn."

Little Moxie's look suggested further explanation was unnecessary. Brad's quizzical expression said otherwise.

"Sindle Vunn? The rich dude who suddenly popped into town?"

Brad nodded. Harry Fenstermacher had mentioned the creepy one-percenter being driven around in a limo.

"Some folks think he's a junior Trump, looking to buy properties at distressed values. Others say he's a Wall Street investment banker who got bored ripping people off. But I think he's one of those Silicon Valley gazillionaires. He was having dinner here last week and I overheard him talking about computer shit, like how to program robots to do special jobs. And you know what *that's* code for, don't you?"

"Give me a hint."

"Replacing all of us with machines and putting everyone out of work. And then guess who's gonna be behind the counter waiting on us when we go to the unemployment office to sign up for our checks?"

"More robots?"

"Damn right, more robots," Little Moxie snarled, lightly smacking his palm on the bar for emphasis. "And even more bucks in their pockets."

"And this Nidge, what exactly does he do for Moneybags?"

"His chauffeur." The bartender shook his head in disgust. "Sindle Vunn. Now what the hell kind of name is that?"

Brad was tempted to point out that the question was coming from someone who referred to himself as Little Moxie.

"And here's the thing, nobody knows shit about the guy. Can't find a trace of him online. Not a goddamn thing. But you can bet that somewhere along the way, he ripped off a busload of regular folks."

That prompted Little Moxie to launch into a whispered diatribe against the wealthy, which quickly expanded to other sorts he didn't like. His targets ranged from liberal politicians and monopolistic Internet providers to personal enemies like the pharmacy clerk slow at filling his prescriptions and the middle school coach who wouldn't start his grandson at point guard.

"World's going to hell, I'm tellin' ya. And this town? Good you got out when you did. There is some crazy shit goin' down around here."

Brad wanted to leave before the rant plumbed even more abysmal regions. But the "crazy shit" remark made him curious. Could Little Moxie be referring to Boxhead? He waited for a break between outgassings and jumped in with his tale of the morning encounter.

The bartender fell back a pace and scratched his forehead. "That's a new one on me. But at least your dude seems like a real person. Definitely not the case with Nowhere Man."

"Who?"

"Big sucker. Flies around the mountains at night. Saw him once a week or so ago when I was driving out along Rockbottom Road. Came soaring down over the trees, just above the canopy. Buzzed my Escalade. Ain't afraid to say it, scared the crap out of me."

"Some kind of large drone?"

"Weren't no drone. It was a person. With wings."

"Batman, maybe? One of the Avengers?"

"Yeah go ahead, joke about it, but I'm tellin' you, he's real. Or mostly real, because sometimes he'd kinda fade away and you could almost see right through him."

"Ghost Rider? The Spectre?"

Little Moxie ignored Brad's latest jibes. "And when you *could* see him proper… he's got no hair and his skin is all pockmarked and slimy, like he takes baths in motor oil. And he's got these clawed hands and the worst stink you can imagine. Had my window down and when the wind blew the right way, smelled his funky ass from twenty feet overhead."

"Uh-huh. Why's he called Nowhere Man?"

"Don't know, didn't do the naming. But I ain't the only one to be spotting him. He's buzzed a couple others, always at night." Little Moxie lowered his voice. "Some say he's a demon from beyond."

Brad imitated the tonal eccentricities of the theremin from those old monster movies and segued into a laugh. Little Moxie darkened.

"You ever see him for yourself you won't think it's so goddamn funny. And a flying demon ain't the only weird shit going on. What about your mom's grave?"

Brad frowned. "What about it?"

"You didn't hear? Thought Zack would've told you. Happened last week. Somebody dug her up."

"What!"

Before Brad could demand more information, Little Moxie spun toward the entrance and pointed an angry finger past Brad's face.

"Hey, don't even think about comin' in here!"

Brad turned. Joseph LeFevre stood in the doorway. He was as ancient and disheveled as Brad remembered. The scraggly uneven hair and beard were years overdue for scissors and razor. Age lines creased his dark skin. Liver spots dotted his hands. His familiar camo overcoat, worn year-round, was weathered and torn. Gracious boasted more than its fair share of oddballs, but in terms of longevity, Joseph had them beat by a mile.

"Forget it, Joseph," the bartender growled. "Not going to have you startin' more trouble. Those two assholes might have killed you. Can't afford to have people dying in here. Bad for business."

Brad figured Little Moxie was referring to the incident Harry Fenstermacher had mentioned. He wondered what had triggered the fight. Joseph had never been known as a brawler.

The old man stared intensely at Brad for a moment. Then he turned and shambled back out the door. A woman from one of the booths snared Little Moxie's attention and the bartender headed there to take her order.

Brad felt his anger stirring as he dwelt on what Little Moxie had revealed about his mother's grave. Why hadn't Uncle Zack and Aunt Nipa said anything? You'd think it was important enough to mention. What the hell else were they keeping from him?

He was suddenly too pissed to see Felicity tonight. That was presuming she even showed, which seemed unlikely at this point. Leaving half a glass of beer, he made for the exit. He was barely out the door when Joseph confronted him on the sidewalk.

"We need to talk."

Brad was in no mood. He held up his hand.

"Sorry Joseph, gotta go. Whatever's on your mind, don't have time for it right now."

He caught an odorous whiff as he slipped past Joseph. The dude was overdue for a shower. Last Brad had heard, he resided in one of those cheap rooms on the top floor of the Roberta Hotel. But maybe he was homeless now.

"Please," Joseph said. "It will only take a moment of your time."

Brad reached his truck but hesitated, recalling how well Joseph had treated him as a kid. Often when Mom brought him into town on their Saturday morning shopping trips, they'd encounter the old Creole at Fenstermacher's Emporium or the farmer's market or the library. Joseph would always chat with Mom, complimenting her on what a nice outfit she wore or telling her how fresh and vibrant she looked that day. Better yet, he'd usually have a small present for Brad. Maybe a candy bar or a bag of marbles or various books, including an old juvenile adventure novel from Joseph's youth called *Tom Swift and His Giant Telescope*. As ridiculously out of date as that book and some similar items had been, Brad had always appreciated the gifts. Years later, though, he'd wondered whether Joseph secretly had the hots for Mom and had been awkwardly trying to hit on her, reinforcing such efforts with gifts for her son.

"Your sister is in danger," Joseph warned. "I believe they've come here to take that which cannot be taken."

"What the hell are you talking about?"

"Kristen needs protection. Now that you're back, you must try keeping an eye on her as often as possible. She needs someone to watch over her, especially after dark when–"

"Whoa, enough! First of all, I don't want to hear all your weird shit. Got enough crap screwing up my life already. And besides, I'm only in town for the weekend."

"For your sister's benefit, you should consider staying longer."

"Not going to happen," he snapped. "Kristen's sick, she's getting professional help. End of story."

"She is not ill. She is a victim of–"

"Gotta go. Anything else, Joseph?"

The old man seemed about to respond when something across the street caught his eye. Brad turned and followed his gaze. A black limo was parked there, its rear window partway down. He could just make out a shadowy figure inside, watching them. Considering that limos in Gracious were as rare as vegans at the church barbecue, and that the chauffeur Nidge remained inside with Carla Rodriguez, the limo's occupant had to be the mysterious Sindle Vunn.

The window rolled up. Joseph turned and headed off down the street, leaving Brad with even more unsettled thoughts.

SIX

It was the same old crap with Uncle Zack, a tendency to keep important things from Brad, as if he couldn't be trusted to know the whole truth. That wasn't why he'd left town but certainly it had been a factor. OK, a small factor. The main reasons he'd wanted out was that life in Gracious had become too oppressive, and was threatening to become even more so when he married Felicity. Even though post-college job opportunities likely would have taken her elsewhere, she'd expressed the desire to return home eventually, and for the two of them raise a family together in Gracious.

Brad's sense of home was radically different. For one thing, he'd likely make a lousy parent, considering that his own father had been such a miserable drunken prick.

He shook his head, trying to banish such negative thoughts before they triggered his worst memories and an even deeper anger. Rehashing all that crap about his father was a waste of time. He forced his attention back to the issue at hand – Uncle Zack's deceitfulness.

Aunt Nipa was culpable too, for not making waves and blissfully going along with her husband's wishes. The obedient housewife, 1950s style. Still, he couldn't really be mad at her. She was a product of her time. But Uncle Zack... he didn't merit the same consideration.

Brad continued stewing as he guided the truck out of town and onto Heckmeyer's Road. Beyond his anger was the disturbing issue itself: the idea that someone had desecrated

Mom's grave. Plus, now there was Joseph's warning about Kristen being in danger. *I believe they've come here to take that which cannot be taken.* Was he referring to the amulet? It seemed likely. The words echoed Uncle Zack's tale from when he and Aunt Nipa had tried removing the tiny triangle from around Kristen's neck.

He sighed. *Two more days.* OK, maybe closer to two and a half days. But whatever the case, first thing Monday morning he intended to be on the road, heading back to North Carolina, back to an apartment, a job and an existence far from the troubling emotions and cascading mysteries that seemed to constitute life in Gracious.

He was a mile from the house when approaching headlights appeared around a bend on the lightly traveled road. As the vehicle flashed by, he had the distinct impression it was an old Volvo.

"Felicity?"

But what would she be doing way out here? Her family lived on the other side of town. Was she returning from his aunt and uncle's place? Had she gone there to see him?

He pulled onto the shoulder and checked the rearview mirror. The Volvo had come to a stop on the shoulder a couple hundred feet back. Its four-way flashers ignited.

Definitely Felicity.

He felt an unpleasant stirring in his guts. Before Little Moxie had dropped the bomb about Mom's grave, he'd been looking forward to seeing her, even though a reunion was liable to be something less than Hallmark ecstasy. At best, he expected her to ream him a new asshole.

But at the moment, he was focused on confronting Uncle Zack. An encounter with Felicity was best put off until tomorrow. He was tempted to step on the gas, hightail it out of the situation. He had a certain familiarity with such ploys.

The Volvo's door opened. A figure stepped from behind the wheel and walked toward him. Steeling himself, he grabbed a flashlight from the glove compartment and matched her approach stride for stride.

They stopped two yards apart. He kept the beam pointed down at the gravel shoulder, viewing her through its reflected light.

Felicity was as attractive as memory painted. The lithe body, the wavy auburn hair that just tickled her shoulders, the face that somehow combined tenderness with toughness. And those piercing green eyes, that in better times seemed able to look deep into him. But there was also something different about her too, something he couldn't put his finger on.

"Hello, Brad." There was no trace of animosity in the greeting, an encouraging sign.

"Hey."

"You're looking well."

"You too, Felicity. How's school going?"

"Good. Challenging."

"Still working on your master's degree?"

"Earned it in December. Going for my doctorate now at Penn State."

"Wow. That's cool. Congrats. Still astronomy?"

"Astrophysics."

Brad had been in some lame, avoid-the-subject conversations but this one put them all to shame. Time to get real.

"So, what are you doing out this way?"

"I went to see your aunt."

"Oh yeah? See her about what?"

She didn't answer. Translation: *None of your business*.

"I'm only back for a few days," he said. "We should get together."

"Why?"

There it was, the beginning of an awkward conversation that at the moment he definitely did not want to have.

Behind her, the Volvo's passenger door opened. Brad hadn't realized Felicity wasn't alone. He aimed his flashlight past her at the woman stepping from the car.

She looked to be Felicity's age but with a petite figure. Straight dark hair, pageboy styled, outlined a pixie face dominated by heavy black eyeglasses with circular frames. The glasses gave her a hipster vibe. She remained by the Volvo, unblinking in the splash of his beam.

"You OK, Felicity?" the woman called out.

"Fine."

Brad raised an inquiring eyebrow.

"That's Flick. She came home from school with me."

"Flick?"

"Uh-huh."

He suddenly realized what was different about Felicity. She had on stud earrings, some kind of jeweled design that glittered at the edges of his flashlight beam. She used to hate earrings, never wore them.

She started to turn back to the Volvo, hesitated. "I'll be at the library first thing tomorrow morning, doing some research. We should talk. If you want to stop by?"

"Yeah, sounds good. I was planning to take Kristen there anyway." He wondered if she already knew that from her conversation with Aunt Nipa.

Flick waited until Felicity reached the Volvo. The two of them got in at the same time. Doors slammed shut in tandem. Brad watched until the taillights disappeared before returning to his truck.

SEVEN

Kristen and Uncle Zack were in bed when Brad reached the house. Just as well. He didn't want his sister overhearing any discussions that might involve the amulet. Plus, anger over his uncle's lack of transparency could spill into a shouting match. Best they didn't go face-to-face until the morning. It would give him a chance to cool down. Or not.

Aunt Nipa was awake. She was always the better choice for a rational discussion anyway. And without Uncle Zack around, she'd be more inclined to talk freely.

She occupied his recliner, knitting what appeared to be either a scarf or some sort of hat. The TV was tuned to some reality show but the volume was cranked so low the host's words were barely perceptible.

"You're home early," Aunt Nipa offered. "Do you want some coffee?"

Brad scowled. "I'm not drunk."

"I wasn't implying that you are."

That was debatable. The coffee question was right out of Aunt Nipa's old playbook, the assumption being that he was likely to come home at night boozed up or high, or both. He'd always resented the subtle accusation. Never mind that she was almost always on the money.

"Sorry, didn't mean to snap," he said, taking a spot on the sofa. "Guess who I ran into on the way back?"

Aunt Nipa kept her eyes downward, working the needles, creating endless loops of yarn.

"I know it's none of my business," he continued when she didn't respond. "But I'm curious what you and Felicity were talking about."

"It was nothing terribly important."

"Did you meet her friend?"

"Yes, Flick. Emily Flickinger, a very nice young woman and extremely bright. Rather serendipitous they're together, considering their names."

"I don't follow."

"Flick pointed out that her nickname can also be a nickname for Felicity. Isn't that something?"

"Something, yeah."

"At any rate, I'm glad Felicity found a partner."

"Partner?"

"Uh-huh. As in lover. As in lesbian. Or is it more proper to say LGBTQ these days?"

Brad laughed at the absurdity of what she was telling him. "Felicity isn't gay."

Aunt Nipa finally looked up from her work. "I always thought you knew. I figured that was the real reason you called off the wedding and left town so suddenly."

"Wow, you are so totally wrong. I mean, hey, trust me, Felicity and I did it often enough." He forced another laugh but it came out hollow. "We had sex, Aunt Nipa. Lots and lots of sex."

"Uh-huh. So?"

"So I would have known."

"As I'm sure you also know, people are complicated. When I was a young girl in Taiwan, I encountered women and men who had those kinds of same-sex feelings. Back then, it was terribly forbidden, of course. They had to keep it strictly to themselves, pretend to be like everyone else, even get married to the opposite sex. Felicity always reminded me of them somehow."

Brad's anger stirred, heat-seeking the nearest target. "You're saying you realized she was gay back then? And you didn't tell me?"

"Don't you dare get mad at me, young man. You know darn well you wouldn't have listened to anything your uncle and I had to say on the subject, or on pretty much any subject."

She wasn't wrong. But Brad was still pissed off she hadn't told him. The more fundamental question was, how could he have been so oblivious? Yet maybe deep down he'd always known, or at least suspected. The two of them once spent a weekend in Philadelphia visiting Felicity's cousins, who'd taken them to a trendy nightclub. Brad wasn't much of a dancer but Felicity was, and she'd spent most of the evening on the dance floor with another woman. He recalled being envious, sensing the two of them shared something beyond his grasp. And there had been similar incidents over the years.

Screw it. Right now he had more important things on his mind. He'd see Felicity in the morning, deal with it then.

"So why were the two of them out here?" he demanded. "To tell you about their sex life?"

"Don't be silly. You remember that old chunk of rock I bought you when you were a kid? The one people thought might be from outer space?"

"Yeah. Was supposed to have come from the Copernian Ridge meteorite. What about it?"

"That's why Felicity stopped over. When she was home for the Christmas holidays, she'd asked to borrow it for some tests. Tonight she returned it."

The meteorite was part of local lore. Back in 1897, witnesses had seen it coming down somewhere around that ridge just beyond the northeast border of the county. Despite repeated searches, it had never been located, at least not officially. But then fragments supposedly taken from it showed up around town, for sale at exorbitant prices. After several were tested and pronounced counterfeits, the prices fell to rock bottom, so to speak. In later years the fakes were sold as cheap paperweights.

"Felicity confirmed your meteorite chunk was also a phony," his aunt said. "But I'd always figured that."

"Then why was she interested in testing it?"

"I don't know. Something to do with her astronomy studies?"

"Astrophysics."

Aunt Nipa returned to her knitting. Before there were any more distractions, Brad confronted her with the subject he'd originally wanted to talk about.

"I just heard about Mom's grave. What the hell, Aunt Nipa? Why didn't you or Uncle Zack tell me?"

"The cemetery paid for a new coffin and reburial. It didn't seem important enough to make a big fuss over."

"Not important enough?" His anger again peaked. The emotion was like one of those sine waves, endlessly oscillating. "You should have called and let me know."

"For what purpose? There was nothing you could have done about it." She shrugged. "It happened last week. It's in the past."

"What exactly happened?"

"Someone dug up the casket and pried open the lid. But Chief Wellstead said that the remains didn't appear to have been compromised in any way."

"Robin Wellstead? She's police chief now?"

"Since last year."

Brad remembered tangling with her back when she was just Officer Wellstead, the police department's first female hire, as well as its first African American. She'd had to put up with a lot of crap on both fronts from local bigots and other mouthpieces for the ignorant. Brad had resented her too, although not because she was black or a woman. Ten years ago, she was the one who'd caught him when he'd tried running away.

"Did they catch who did it?" he asked

"The chief says it's an ongoing investigation."

Something in his aunt's tone hinted she was being evasive.

"C'mon, Aunt Nipa, what aren't you telling me? You know I'm going to find out anyway."

"Chief Wellstead said that two men came to town a few weeks ago. A big skinhead and his smaller friend." Her face twisted into a scowl. "*Liumang.*"

The word meant hoodlums or hooligans or something of that sort. When Brad had been in high school, his aunt had often used it to describe some of the sketchy characters he hung with.

The two men were likely the same pair who'd fought with Joseph. But why would they dig up Mom's grave? A disturbing possibility occurred to him. Could they have been looking for the amulet, unaware it had been passed on to Kristen? But if so, why?

His fists tightened. If he ever ran into the bastards...

"Don't do anything rash," Aunt Nipa warned, reading his intentions. "The chief says these are very bad men with violent histories. She's trying to get evidence to build a case against them. Promise me you'll keep your distance and let the law handle it."

Brad nodded but wasn't sure it was a promise he could keep. In any case, there was nothing to be done about it tonight. He gave his aunt a goodnight kiss on the cheek and headed for the stairs. Although it was still early, it had been a long day. He needed to hit the sack.

"Brad?"

He stopped on the third step, turning to face her.

"I know it's hard for you. But try to be more... forgiving."

He fought back an urge to snap a retort, instead concealing his anger behind a tight smile.

"Oh, and be careful not to step on that shoo spot outside your room."

"If Kristen's asleep, what does it matter?"

"Be careful anyway."

EIGHT

Elrod stared into the campfire, intrigued by the roaring blaze. There were a whole lot of fucked up things in the world, but fire wasn't one of them. Fire was cool. Well, actually it wasn't cool, it was hot.

That was funny. He chuckled, then reminded himself to remember the line. That way he could run it through his head again in the future and have another laugh.

Almost as cool as the fire was the small headless fawn cooking over it on a steel spit roaster. The rod was held upright by tripods made from sawed branches.

"Is it almost ready?" he asked, trying not to sound whiny and petulant. That's what everybody always said he sounded like whenever he opened his mouth. Elrod couldn't help it. And goddamn, he could almost taste supper. He couldn't recall the last time he'd had fresh venison. Maybe he'd never had it?

He couldn't remember.

Double Bub stood to the side of the fire, occasionally rotating the spit so the meat got tenderized equally. The freak usually caught only small animals like squirrels or woodchucks, except for that time the three of them were passing through some midwestern town and a cocker spaniel in someone's backyard growled at Kyzer the wrong way, which pissed off the Kyze-Man so much that he growled back.

Double Bub, ever eager to please Kyzer, hopped out the back of their van while it was still moving, jumped the fence and snatched the little bitch. Elrod still couldn't figure how the freak moved so fast, or how he could see where he was going with that crooked box on his head and goggles so dark you could probably stare into the sun without frying your eyeballs. But after Kyzer strangled the dog, they'd had one fine-ass dinner that night, Double Bub sauteing the meat in his special garlic sauce.

Today, the freak had outdone himself by catching the fawn, which weren't no easy feat for a normal person, and Double Bub was about as far from normal as you could get. Elrod had gone hunting with him once, which was boring as shit, as they had to hide in some bushes and not move for hours until a woodchuck finally appeared and he lunged at it like a maniac. When it scuttled away, he chased after it and knocked it out with a rock. He'd apparently done the same with today's meal, dragging the unconscious fawn back here to the campsite. Double Bub had no qualms about doing his own killing but had brought it back alive as a gift to Kyzer, who'd promptly decapitated it with his trusty hatchet while Double Bub clapped and danced round in circles like a maniac. Elrod didn't begrudge the freak his little pleasures. Hell, if a dude was such a mess above the neck that he had to wear a box on his head so as not to scare the shit out of folks, he deserved occasional me time.

Elrod and Kyzer had met Double Bub a couple or three years back. He'd been living in a shack in an alley behind some seedy bar in Georgia where he worked as an off-the-books short-order cook, out of sight of customers, who'd probably throw up their lunches if they ever saw him without his headgear. Elrod had been in the alley for a smoke when he heard rustling from the shack, and that's when he'd peeked through the grimy window and got his first look-see. Figuring to show off his discovery, he'd raced back into the bar and dragged a bitching Kyzer away from his beer.

Elrod figured the Kyze-Man would burst into one of those crazy hyena laughs of his at the sight of Double Bub without his headgear. But that wasn't what happened. Instead, Kyzer got all kinds of serious and tried talking to the freak, which was useless as Double Bub could only manage grunts. But he wasn't a complete dummy and had learned to read and write, and by passing notes and using simple sign language, they'd managed to communicate. Elrod later figured Kyzer had a soft spot for Double Bub on account of having a younger brother who'd died in childhood from being born with no arms and legs, and a bunch of his internal organs on the outside.

The next thing Elrod knew, the Kyze-Man was inviting Double Bub to join them on the road. The three of them had been together ever since.

Double Bub's real name was Dudley Wallaker the Third. Elrod always wondered if his father and grandfather were walking nightmares too. If so, that was OK with Elrod, who wasn't exactly a poster boy for the all-American family either.

Noise from the surrounding forest drew Elrod's attention. A flashlight beam appeared, followed by the Kyze-Man himself, all three hundred pounds of him. Back when the two of them were in that shit stain of a high school, the football coaches tried to recruit Kyzer to play offensive tackle. He'd been considering it too, dreaming about Rose Bowl glory followed by bucket loads of NFL cash. But then he got caught selling weed to a bunch of entitled middle school brats and was expelled. Elrod had quit in protest and that's when the two of them stole their first car, a beamer, and headed out to see if the rest of the world was as fucked up as the one they were leaving. News flash – it was.

The Kyze-Man had gathered dead wood in a makeshift sling, and he threw all of it onto the fire. The flames leaped higher, scorching the fawn's underside. Had Double Bub's face been uncovered and capable of expressing normal emotions, Elrod imagined he'd have looked pissed. You don't mess around in the chef's kitchen when he's making dinner.

"How soon chow down?" Kyzer demanded.

Double Bub held up five fingers of his left hand, then raised the right one to display the middle finger. Kyzer didn't get angry, just unleashed one of those cackling laughs. Not for the first time, Elrod felt kinda jealous of their weirdo relationship. If Elrod ever gave the Kyze-Man the finger he'd get a whoopin' in return.

The three of them froze at the sound of an approaching vehicle, then relaxed when they recognized the hum of Sindle Vunn's limo. They couldn't see it but knew it was creeping up the dirt lane to park behind Kyzer's van, a few hundred feet from the campsite. Nidge treated the limo like it was his goddamn lover or something, always washing and polishing it. For all Elrod knew, he was screwing it in the tailpipe as well.

The engine shut off. Car doors slammed shut and fresh illumination pierced the trees. Sindle Vunn emerged first, carrying an electric lantern to light their way. Nidge, wearing a hefty backpack, followed.

The boss smiled that bright-ass smile of his as he entered the clearing. That smile always seemed to Elrod like it could light up a room better than any piddly-ass lantern. Yet he still found it creepy on account of the way he wore almost the same expression when he was pissed. You could never really tell what was going on with the guy under that Elvis pompadour.

Elrod had always liked Elvis even though the King had died long before he was born. But he'd always figured that if the last three letters of his own name had been *vis* instead of *rod*, and if he'd been able to sing, act and swivel his hips, and didn't have the urge to set stuff on fire all the time, he too could have gotten rich and been loved by millions of people.

Of course, nobody would ever mistake the boss for the King either, not with that tiny mouth and beady eyes. But he was a six-footer like Elvis, and it seemed like he had his shit together, which they said was the kind of vibe Elvis gave off when he was at the top. Plus, the boss always dressed classy, just like Elvis. No white costumes with fancy gold belts or any of that

Vegas crap, but those gray and black business suits always made him look sharp, which they sure as hell should, on account of supposedly costing $3,000 apiece. And, like Elvis, he was generous to his friends, always making sure the four of them had enough pocket money.

Elrod wasn't sure where the boss had gotten his bucks. Nidge once hinted he'd inherited a nest egg from his parents, then quadrupled it by investing in some Silicon Valley computer business that hit the big time. The computer part sounded right, on account of the boss always talking about robots and apps and shit like that. Supposedly, he'd gone by another name back then.

Sindle Vunn spread his arms in a welcoming a gesture. "My friends, you are indeed a sight for sore eyes!"

It had been a week since the five of them had been together. Even though the boss' compliments always sounded like flattering bullshit, they nevertheless made Elrod feel good. He smiled back.

"And Double Bub... indeed, the olfactory delights oozing from this magnificent feast surely would earn you a place among the world's finest chefs!"

The freak hopped up and down on his tippy toes, which was how someone with a horror-show face and screwed-up vocal cords displayed pleasure.

"Could use some wap," Kyzer said, coming right to the point as usual. But his tone was more respectful than the way he usually talked to Elrod and Double Bub.

"A fresh supply of the royal nectar will be forthcoming tomorrow," Sindle Vunn said. "Tonight, I'm afraid we will have to settle for fine dining."

It wasn't like they were going to argue. The boss was the only one who met with Nowhere Man in person. The rest of them didn't even know what he looked like, although the boss often said that, being a godlike entity, Nowhere Man wasn't bound by the rules governing appearance. Elrod figured that meant he was an ugly SOB, maybe even uglier than Double Bub.

Still, he didn't care what Nowhere Man looked like as long as the flow of wap kept coming. He wasn't jonesing yet, having taken his last remaining dose a few days ago. He could hold out till tomorrow. Still, he didn't want to think about what would happen if he was ever forced to go longer than that.

Nidge removed his backpack, unfolded a portable aluminum chair and placed it near the campfire. Sindle Vunn took off his jacket, brushed a speck of dirt from the sleeve and carefully hung it on the back of the chair before sitting down. Nidge squatted on the ground beside him. Why the chauffeur didn't carry a second chair for his own ass was just another of the question marks surrounding them.

Another mystery was why the boss was making them stay out here in the woods instead of at the cabins. True, the campsite was close to downtown Gracious, making it easy to pick up supplies. But if it rained, like it did a couple evenings ago, the three of them would have to sleep in the van, and being squeezed between squirmy Double Bub and farting Kyzer weren't much fun. Best of all would have been if they'd been allowed to stay at the nearby crack house, which had some beds, chairs and a comfy sofa. But the boss didn't want to take the chance of anyone following them there and messing up Nowhere Man's big plan.

"Nidge's seduction of the child's teacher went as anticipated," Sindle Vunn announced.

"Ya' do her?" Kyzer asked.

Nidge grunted.

"Any good?"

"Fuckable."

In many ways, Nidge and the Kyze-Man were two of a kind. Neither of them spoke more than a handful of words a day and both of them were big and mean. They both liked killing, although they used different methods. Kyzer was old school, preferred beating people with his fists or using the hatchet he carried on his belt.

Although Nidge had been an Army combat engineer trained in demolition, Elrod knew that he preferred killing up close and personal with his ivory-handled garrote. Elrod had never understood the preference. Blowing things up and burning things down were sort of kissing cousins, and although he preferred the latter, he surely could see the attraction of rigging explosives and seeing stuff fly into pieces. But instead, Nidge liked choking people. Elrod supposed there was no accounting for taste.

He always thought it would be cool if Kyzer and Nidge faced off in the ring for guts and glory. They could advertise the fight as "The Skinhead versus the Chauffeur," or maybe "Hatchet Man versus Demolition Dude." It would be one awesome wrestling match, a battle of two mean and hungry dinofuckers.

Sindle Vunn went on. "Nidge has confirmed through the teacher that the child possesses what Nowhere Man desires. Had this information been acquired earlier, the unfortunate incident of the mother's disinterment could have been avoided."

He threw Elrod and Kyzer a reprimanding look, causing the Kyze-Man to run a hand across his shaved skull, which he did when someone criticized him and he wasn't in a position to kick their ass. Elrod had no choice but to keep his mouth shut as well, even though he felt they'd been raked over the coals enough already for the fuck-up. How the hell were the two of them supposed to know the dead bitch hadn't been buried with the amulet, without digging her up? She was the only clue they'd been given when the boss sent them to Gracious as advance men to gather intel. It had seemed the sensible thing to do. Plus, there'd been the possibility she'd been buried with gold or diamonds or other jewelry they could pilfer. But that idea was also a bust. Her bony corpse held nothing of value.

The boss's main criticism was that their actions could have alerted the child's guardians, the aunt and uncle. Conceivably, they could have gone on the run with Kristen to keep her safe. Fortunately, that hadn't happened. No harm, no foul, the way Elrod figured.

"When we make our move?" Kyzer asked.

"I fully expect that Nowhere Man will issue authorization very soon."

Elrod looked forward to it. They hadn't seen action in a while. There'd been the fight with that old man in the bar, and although it had been fun kicking his ass after Kyzer dropped him, it wasn't the kind of satisfaction you got from killing. It was months since they'd done that, well before they'd hooked up with the boss. The "fearsome threesome" – that's what Kyzer sometimes called them – had done a home invasion in some shitty little Indiana town. It had been a real hoot, especially when Double Bub took off his headgear and the family screamed in horror. Even better had been the final act, setting the place on fire with the family still inside.

Double Bub signaled dinner was ready and handed out the plates. He carved generous slabs of the deer meat and slathered them onto a large serving dish. Elrod's mouth was watering as he sat on the ground beside Kyzer and watched Double Bub fork the slices onto their plates, all except for Nidge, who apparently had eaten earlier in town.

Elrod retrieved his personal utensils from his fanny pack. He was desperate to dig into the venison. But they always had to wait for the boss to give one of his stupid invocations.

"We thank this four-legged fauna for its sacrifice to our abiding hunger."

Elrod removed his straw cowboy hat and held it over his heart. It always seemed the proper thing to do during a blessing, like what you did at a football game when they played the national anthem.

"And we give thanks to its two-legged brethren, especially

those who will soon join it in the great beyond so that the rapture of Nowhere Man may spread across the land."

"Amen to that!" Elrod yelled, not understanding all that rapture stuff, nor the reason Nowhere Man wanted the amulet in the first place. That kind of shit was above his pay grade. As long as Nowhere Man kept supplying them with wap, or the royal nectar or whatever the hell you wanted to call it, Elrod would do whatever was asked.

"Bon appetit," Sindle Vunn said, his cheeks spreading into a smile.

NINE

Brad bolted awake to his sister's piercing screams. Lunging from bed he dashed into the hallway, remembering at the last instant to sidestep Kristen's shoo spot. The six-foot-long rectangle was just outside his door. She'd used her crayons to neatly color its masking-tape perimeter with alternating red and yellow safety stripes. Since arriving, he'd been trying to ignore the obvious conclusion that the three shoo spots had the dimensions of coffins.

A baseboard nightlight provided enough illumination to reach the back of the house. He flung open her door. Kristen stood by the window gazing into the darkness, consumed by a torrent of shrieks. The necklace dangled on the outside of her pajama top. Her hand clutched the amulet.

He spun her away from the window, cradled her in his arms. The screams stopped as if cut off by a switch. But shudders continued coursing through her.

"Just a nightmare," he soothed, holding her tight.

He sensed movement behind him. His aunt and uncle appeared in the doorway in nightclothes, faces pale with concern. Uncle Zack looked ready to say something. Aunt Nipa gripped his arm, urging silence.

"Go back to bed," Brad said. "I'll stay until she calms down."

Aunt Nipa mouthed *thank you*. They retreated into the hallway, gently closed the door.

Kristen's shudders relented. Brad released her. She continued her iron grip on the amulet.

"Out there," she said, pointing through the window. "I saw it."

The psychiatrist's report had mentioned hallucinations. "You think you saw something. But it was just your imagination."

"No, I saw it."

"People wake up sometimes and think they see things. It's just their minds playing tricks on them." He'd experienced it a few times himself after getting wasted on various drug-and-booze combos.

She shook her head. "No, Brad. It was out there!"

He looked into the darkness. The tree line behind the house was silhouetted by a low-hanging half-moon.

"When I woke up, I saw it watching me. Sometimes it would fade away but then get solid again. It flew away when I screamed."

A chill touched Brad as he recalled the bartender's story about Nowhere Man. He was going to ask Kristen for a more detailed description but reconsidered. Her response would do neither of them any good. Better to just soothe her into falling back to sleep.

He pulled down the shade and closed the curtains. "Hop back into bed."

"You'll stay with me?"

"Uh-huh."

"You have to keep watching the window in case it comes back."

"Absolutely. Don't worry, nothing's getting past me."

She looked skeptical. But she got under the covers anyway and pulled an old blanket decorated with Disney's *Frozen* characters up to her waist.

"Brad?"

"Uh-huh?"

"You didn't step on the shoo spot, did you?"

"No way, I was super careful. Oh and hey, I like the way you marked the tape with your crayons. Makes it easier to see."

She thought about that for a moment. "I'm going to color the other shoo spots as soon as I get up tomorrow."

"Good idea. Now close your eyes. And try not to think of bad things."

He moved a pile of books from her desk chair to the floor, positioned the chair beside her bed and sat. She gazed at him blankly. He responded with an encouraging smile.

Her eyes blinked and finally closed. Her fingers loosened their death grip and fell away from the amulet. He leaned forward to gaze at it more closely.

Cast in the shape of an equilateral triangle, the sticks were about an inch long and slightly overlapped at the ends. They were neither identical nor perfectly linear, having subtle bends and imperfections, like tiny twigs. The amulet's hue complemented the silver necklace but was duller, closer to pewter gray.

Kristen had once allowed him – reluctantly – to take it off the necklace and cup it in his hand. He'd been struck by its weightless feel, figuring it must be made of aluminum or some other ultralight metal. Yet that contradicted a story he'd heard as a kid about his grandmother, Isabella, who in the 1960s had taken it to a jeweler to be evaluated.

Supposedly, the jeweler was astonished at its lack of mass, and initially believed it was cast from some specialized aviation alloy. But when the man accidentally ran the amulet across his display counter, it put such a deep scratch in the glass that he had to have the whole panel replaced. The jeweler claimed it had a hardness at least equivalent to that of a diamond. He'd asked to keep it a few days for a more detailed examination, but Grandma Isabella apparently had gotten nervous by then and just wanted out of there, even after the man offered to buy it for three grand – serious money in that era.

Grandma Isabella had died before Kristen was born, when Brad was only two. He had no memories of her. Mom had never said how she'd come across the triangle, at least not to him. But he'd overheard his mother once mention to Aunt Nipa that Isabella had found it while hiking in the mountains.

Kristen asleep looked so peaceful and untroubled, and Brad had a sudden urge to touch the amulet. Not to take it but just to see if there was a repeat of what had happened to Uncle Zack and Aunt Nipa. Surely the notion he'd be overwhelmed by bad memories was ludicrous. His aunt's and uncle's experiences were likely based on the overwhelming guilt they'd felt for trying to steal something that didn't belong to them. He knew something about guilt, an emotion as powerful as a tornado. It could stay with you for years, whipping through your head and spreading all sorts of turmoil, which is why he consciously tried never dwelling on it.

He leaned closer, extended a forefinger toward the amulet. But he stopped inches away.

What am I afraid of?

He brushed his finger against the triangle before he could talk himself out of it. His body tensed, anticipating being bowled over by some heavy metal crapfest.

Nothing happened. At least, nothing scary. Touching the amulet hadn't slammed him with any bad memories. Then again, his intentions weren't hostile. He wasn't trying to take the amulet from her.

An impression of a color came over him, however, a shade of green as vivid as spring grass. The color pulsated in his head for a moment, leaving him with the familiar idea that had surfaced earlier at the bar: the notion of taking all his troubles, squeezing them into a ball and hurling the ball far away. It was at once tantalizing and childishly absurd. And to contain everything messed up in his life, the ball would have to be about the size of the Grand Canyon.

An odd question occurred. What if something that wasn't alive attempted to take the amulet from his sister? Could a robot, for instance, be programmed to take that which can't be taken? Equally odd, what if someone who had no bad memories tried to confiscate it?

He shook his head. The latter notion was absurd. Everyone in the world was screwed up in some way, shape or form. Besides, the amulet was just a simple trinket, nothing magical. His sister was a mixed-up kid suffering from bad dreams and hallucinations. Little Moxie's Nowhere Man was the byproduct of a bartender overindulging in his products.

He stood up and tried to shake off the entire evening of batty ideas. As he was about to exit Kristen's room, he heard the whisper of his mother's voice in his head.

Find the third part.

It wasn't the first time Mom's phantom words had come to him over the years, usually dispensing some kind of advice or instructions. *Take out the trash. Be attentive at school today. Time for bed.* The utterances usually occurred when he was tired or preoccupied, and echoed actual things she'd said to him as a child. But this was different.

Find the third part. What the hell did that mean? Did it have something to do with that word Kristen had used when Aunt Nipa and Uncle Zack attempted to take the amulet from her? Trine?

He could speculate all night and be no closer to a rational answer. Pulling Kristen's blanket up to her neck to cloak the amulet, he retreated from her room.

TEN

Gracious Community Library's regal bearing distinguished it from the town's other structures. It had been built in the mid-nineteenth century as the municipal building, back when the town had its own mayor, council and police department. Consolidation in the 1970s dissolved the borough, robbing Gracious of governmental independence and making it part of the surrounding township, which was headquartered in a newer subdivision five miles east of town. Only the library remained onsite.

Brad headed up the wide granite steps and held open the heavy door for Kristen. The library's interior complemented its elegant facade. Aisles ran perpendicular to the front checkout counter beneath a high ceiling. Chandeliers hung from long chains, their original incandescent lamps replaced with modern LED bulbs.

The library had just opened and they appeared to be the only patrons. A woman with narrow lips and a shock of white hair stood behind the counter. Brad didn't recognize her.

"Is Felicity Bowman here?" he asked.

"And you are?"

"Brad Van Reed."

Judging by her venomous scowl, Brad may as well have answered, "Satan's BFF."

"Felicity is occupied," the woman said curtly, returning her attention to a pile of books on a wheeled cart.

"She knows I'm coming."

"I was not informed she was expecting company."

And who the hell are you? Her social secretary?

Kristen tugged at his arm. "I want to look at the YA books."

"Go ahead."

"Come with me."

He could practically feel the librarian's glare on his back as he followed Kristen into the aisles. There was no sign of Felicity, but she'd mentioned doing research so she could be in the basement. That's where the older and more valuable items were kept.

He'd deleted Felicity's phone number two years ago but eliminating it from memory hadn't proved as simple. At the moment, that was a fortunate thing. He punched in the digits. She picked up on the third ring.

"I'm in the tombs," she said, skipping any hint of pleasantries. "Come on down."

"Not sure the Nazi at the counter will allow it."

"Mrs Cloppenhauser is a good friend of Grandpa Harry. She's just trying to be protective. Let me talk to her."

"Hang on."

He told Kristen where he was going. She lowered a book she was paging through and frowned.

"You'll be OK," he assured her. "Just hang loose. I'll be back in a few minutes. All right?"

She glanced around warily but muttered, "All right."

Brad headed back toward the counter before Kristen could mount an argument. She'd seemed fine at breakfast and hadn't mentioned last night's drama. He recalled suffering nightmares at her age too. They were no big deal, just part of growing up. They weren't a sign of mental illness or anything weirder.

He'd been telling himself that all morning.

At the counter he handed the librarian his phone. She adopted a fresh scowl as she listened to Felicity.

"Dear, are you sure you'll be safe alone down there with someone like him?"

"I'm standing right here," Brad muttered.

Whatever Felicity said in response heightened the librarian's displeasure. The call ended and she returned his phone. He wouldn't have been surprised if she'd made the sign of the cross and doused him with holy water.

"The door is just behind aisle four," she instructed.

"I know where it is." He couldn't resist a parting shot. "Oh hey, you've been enormously helpful."

The tombs was the nickname for the basement because of its original use as the borough's police department. The back part still housed the original jail cells. The library had received a grant years ago to upgrade the front area – formerly cop offices – to American Library Association conservation standards. That included temperature and humidity control as well as fire protection. Brad knew such details only because Felicity once persuaded him to read a paper she'd written about it for twelfth-grade English. She'd always had a thing for libraries.

He opened the old steel door with its barred window and headed down the concrete steps. At the bottom were two doors. The right one led to the upgraded section.

A shot of cool dry air touched his face as he entered the conservation room. Modern shelving contrasted with refurbished oak desks, the latter deep enough to house spacious map drawers.

Felicity was leaning over a work table, studying a large topographical map and snapping photos of it with her phone. The yellowing paper suggested the map was old. She was dressed the way women dressed when they wanted to camouflage even the slightest hint of their sexuality. He figured the baggy sweatshirt, loose jeans and scruffy Reeboks were meant for him, a not-so-subtle reminder of her unavailability.

"Hey," he offered, instinctively tugging down his sweatshirt sleeve to cover the viper tattoo on his left wrist. He'd gotten it not long after leaving town for reasons he could only recall as having something to do with a night of binge drinking. Felicity hated snakes. Whether that had figured into his rationale for getting the tat, he couldn't have said.

"Hey," she retorted, giving him a sideways glance before returning her attention to the map.

"So, what are you researching?"

"Remember the Copernian Ridge meteorite?"

Brad nodded. "Aunt Nipa said you returned my old chunk last night. Another fake, right."

"Just like all the others I've managed to test. But I wanted to be sure."

"Why the interest? Something to do with your doctorate studies?"

"More like a side project, although if I get good results, I'll fold it into my dissertation. It's related to something I came across in an antiques store near the university. An old notebook from 1897, by a grad student who worked for a Professor Summersby. The prof was with the School of Natural Science, back when Penn State University was known as Pennsylvania State College.

"Summersby heard about the meteorite and came to Gracious to search for it. He brought along this grad student as his research assistant. According to Summersby's official report, they never found anything. However, the two of them weren't together most of the time. They searched separately to cover more ground."

"Makes sense."

She straightened and brushed a strand of hair from her face. He'd always enjoyed letting his fingers stroke that wavy mass.

"But according to the student's notebook, after several days of exploring the area, Summersby abruptly insisted they call off the search and return to the college. He claimed the reason was because his toothaches had grown too severe. Seems he had really bad teeth and was frequently in pain from them.

"The student suspected it was more than dental problems. Summersby began acting very strangely. He became increasingly secretive and paranoid. Not long after returning to school, he resigned his position and moved out of the area. After that, there's no trace of what happened to him."

"Probably not hard to pull a disappearing act back then," Brad pointed out. "Pre-Internet and all that."

"You're right. And the web has its limits when you're trying to track down people who lived more than a century ago. But here's the interesting thing. The grad student speculated that Summersby might have found the meteorite and wanted to keep the discovery to himself."

"Why would he do that?"

Felicity shrugged. "Maybe there was something about it that he thought would be valuable. Possibly it contained gemstones. Space peridot, black diamonds, something along those lines."

"Is that common?"

"Not really. But let's assume for a moment that for whatever reason, Summersby did find the meteorite and wanted to keep it secret. The grad student left some clues to the area he searched as well as where Summersby was planning to search." She gestured to the table. "This is a USGS map – US Geological Survey – of Copernian Ridge. It's from that same era."

"Aren't these online?"

"Most are. But they tend to be smaller, the details compressed. Plus, many of the digital versions were modified and updated over the years as new data became available. I wanted to see the original, full-sized one, the one printed back then, the one Summersby and his student likely used. They may even have come to the local library and looked at this very copy. Anyway, I'm trying to make an educated guess of their search grids."

"But if Summersby did find the meteorite, wouldn't he have taken it with him?"

"Possibly. But there's a fair chance it was found in an isolated area and was too big to move very far. If so, he may have chipped away pieces for analysis, maybe pieces he presumed valuable. And even if he did take the whole thing there still should be evidence of where it landed."

Brad nodded. "So you're checking the supposed fragments that people acquired back then, hoping that one of them turns out to be authentic."

"Yeah. But so far I'm batting oh for nine. Every one I've found and tested turned out to be a fake."

As fascinating as her quest sounded, it also struck Brad as something of a wild goose chase. There had been a number of unsuccessful searches for the Copernian Ridge meteorite over the years, including several organized by various college and university astronomy departments. What made Felicity think she'd succeed where so many others had failed?

She read his skepticism. "Yeah, I know, the whole thing's kind of a shot in the dark. I can't really explain it, but I have a hunch there's something important about that meteorite. And we've got a big advantage over all previous search efforts. First thing in the morning we're heading into those mountains for our initial look around."

"We?"

"Flick and I."

Brad gave what he thought was a nonjudgmental nod.

"We've been together since last summer," she said, leaning back over the map to snap more photos. "Actually, we recently got engaged."

He couldn't hide his surprise. "You're going to get married... the two of you?"

"Yes, the two of us. That's how it usually works."

"No, I know that. What I mean is..." He let the sentence trail off. He didn't know what he meant. Probably best to stop talking now.

"We haven't told a lot of people yet about the engagement so don't spread it around."

"No problem. Congratulations."

"Thanks. I'm pretty confident my second trip to the altar will have a better outcome."

Brad ignored the barb but realized it gave him an opening to say what he'd wanted to say to her for the past two years. "Felicity, I never told you how sorry I am for what happened... the way things went down. To this day I don't exactly know why I split. I just know that I panicked. I couldn't see the two of us being together... not like that, not forever. Bottom line, I was a class-A jerk. A total freaking asshole."

She craned her head toward him, met his gaze. "I was pretty hurt when it happened. And incredibly mad at you for a long time."

He was about to offer further repentance but Felicity raised her hand, cutting him off.

"But then I realized it was the best thing that could have occurred. It helped me acknowledge my real feelings. You ditching me turned out to be a blessing in disguise."

"I'm glad. I mean, not about the way it went down, obviously, but–"

"No, I get it. The thing is, even when you proposed and I said yes, I had serious misgivings. The two of us... it was more a matter of inertia than love. I think we both knew in our hearts it wasn't right, wasn't real. Problem was, I couldn't openly admit it. Thankfully, you came to your senses first." She paused. "Still, your timing could have been better. The day of our wedding? Really?"

"I know. Unforgivable."

She stared for a long moment, then offered a wry smile. "You've changed."

Brad didn't think so. But he nodded anyway. They gazed at one another, silent for a moment. She returned her attention to the map.

"I'm making a grid based on what I believe was Summersby's search area. Flick and I rented a house here for the summer so I can work for my dad again as a teller down at the bank. But that still leaves us with a decent amount of free time, especially on weekends."

Brad was glad the conversation had shifted away from the personal. "So what's your big advantage over previous searches?"

"Lidar."

He'd heard the term but wasn't overly familiar with the technology. "Something to do with self-driving cars, right?"

"Light detection and ranging. And yes, it's used for self-driving vehicles as well as for other things, such as high-res aerial mapping. For our purposes, last month we arranged for a series of overflights of what we deemed to be the primary target area. A small plane equipped with a lidar unit and a couple of technicians to operate it. They made multiple passes across the region over the space of several days, each time scanning the forested mountains below with millions of laser pulses. Another group of techs took the raw lidar data, ran it through filtering algorithms and ultimately interpolated it into usable 3D maps. Bottom line, the data provided us with a number of anomalous locations. Any one of them could be the site of the meteorite hit."

"Sounds complicated. And expensive. How'd you get your school to pay for it?"

"They didn't." She paused. "Flick is covering all our expenses."

Brad arched his eyebrows.

"Yeah, she's rich. Paying for the house rental too. Family money. Way more than she could ever spend in a life–"

A deep rumbling shook the room, followed by what sounded like a muffled explosion.

They raced out into the corridor. Puffs of brown smoke and dust jetted out from beneath the other door, the one leading to the old jail. Brad's first thought was for his sister. He dashed toward the steps and was surprised to see her standing at the top.

"Kristen! Are you OK?"

She didn't answer, just stared down at him with a blank expression.

"Kristen? Answer me."

Mrs Cloppenhauser appeared behind her, wide-eyed. "Goodness, what was that?"

"Not sure," Brad said. "But you'd better get my sister and everyone else outside. And call the fire department."

The librarian gripped the back of Kristen's shoulders and guided her away. Brad turned back to the impacted door. The worst of the dust cloud had relented, leaving the portion of the cement floor in front of it coated with a fine layer of dirt.

He gripped the knob, then glanced over at Felicity. She nodded approval. He whipped open the door.

The old jail's central corridor was flanked by three cells on either side. At least that's how Brad remembered it from Felicity giving him a tour years ago. Now, the entire corridor and the two nearest cells were gone, having fallen into a gaping hole. It looked at least ten feet in diameter. With Felicity beside him, he inched toward the edge, careful not to step too close. The perimeter could be unstable.

Rubble from the collapse was heaped about fifteen feet below. Chunks of concrete and sections of iron bars from the jail cells were nestled amid the debris. A rusty pipe protruded like a flagpole, its other end still connected to an upended toilet, the porcelain bowl cracked in two.

"Wow," Felicity uttered.

"Yeah."

"We should get out of here. More of it could collapse."

Brad nodded.

"Must have been a sinkhole," she said.

"Yeah. Must have been."

ELEVEN

Brad stood with Kristen outside the library. A small crowd had gathered, drawn by the fire engines and other emergency vehicles haphazardly strewn along the block. The cops had set up a perimeter to keep people back, bright yellow police tape wrapped around trees. The building didn't look unstable. But fire department personnel remained inside, checking things out.

Kristen tugged his arm. "Brad?"

"Uh-huh?"

"Does Fenstermacher's Emporium sell that yellow tape?"

"I don't know. Why would you need...?"

He trailed off, the answer obvious.

"Kiddo, your shoo spots are already well-marked."

"I could pay for the tape. I've been saving my allowance."

"Keep saving it."

He ignored Kristen's sour look, his attention drawn to Felicity emerging from the back seat of Chief Wellstead's 4x4, where the chief had been interviewing her. Flick was waiting. Brad watched the couple converse quietly before heading off down the block, hand in hand. They hopped into a Jeep Grand Cherokee that looked brand new or close to it. He reminded himself he had no right to be jealous, even while acknowledging an uncomfortable sensation at seeing Felicity being affectionate with someone else.

As he watched the SUV drive off, the chief approached. Robin Wellstead remained as attractive as she was when she'd first joined the department. When Brad wasn't much older than Kristen, he and some of the boys he hung with would ogle her when she passed, referring to her in giggling whispers as "Officer Well-Stacked." They'd brag to one another about what they'd do to her if she ever arrested them. Of course, it was all just puerile nonsense. Back then, none of them were doing anything to anybody, let alone to a grown woman carrying a badge and a gun.

The night she'd caught Brad as he was trying to run away, Robin Wellstead used the drive back to his aunt and uncle's to administer a scared-straight lecture. It had been intense, and he recalled practically shrinking into the caged back seat of her cruiser while trying to retreat from her harsh words and wagging finger. But then she'd surprised him by offering to help if he ever needed it, even if it was just having someone to talk to about his problems. She'd even given him a card with her home phone scrawled on the back, which he probably still had in the depths of his old wallet. No wonder she'd risen through the ranks to head up the police department. She was good cop/bad cop all rolled into one.

Chief Wellstead smiled at his sister. "Honey, are you OK?"

Kristen wagged her head.

"And you?" the chief asked, turning to Brad with a less inviting expression.

"I'm fine."

"Felicity filled me in on the details of what happened. Anything you want to add?"

"I'm sure she covered everything. Do they know what caused the collapse?"

"Not yet. The inside walls weren't damaged, so it doesn't appear to have been a bomb. The investigation will probably take a while, maybe weeks. Unfortunately, the library will have to stay closed until the engineers are sure there's no further danger."

"I work construction now, down in North Carolina."

"I heard." She smiled faintly. "Are you offering to help do repairs?"

"No no. I just wanted to throw out an idea about how it might have happened. Years ago, when the place was still being used as a jail, the old pipes could have rusted out and leaked. The water would have been turned off by the time the library took over but over the years could have eaten away at the subsurface. And then one day, *boom*. The floor collapses. It's a pretty common cause of sinkholes."

"That's an interesting theory," she said.

Brad didn't believe a word of it. He wasn't ready to entertain what increasingly seemed like the real cause, the common denominator between the sinkhole in the library and the pair at Uncle Zack's, neither of which seemed as large as this one. He gazed at Kristen, a part of him wanting to ask if she was somehow responsible for the collapses. The very idea was totally bonkers. Still, another part of him didn't want to hear her answer.

"How long are you staying in Gracious?" the chief asked.

"Not long."

No matter what was going on with Kristen, whether or not there was some unnatural explanation for all the weirdness, Brad was more convinced than ever that there was nothing he could do to help. The faster he left town, the better for one and all. Uncle Zack had said they had another appointment for Kristen at the hospital in a few days. Modern medicine was her best shot. The doctors would prescribe something stronger than the mild antidepressant they already had her on. She'd eventually get well.

Brad wanted to ask the chief about the desecration of his mother's grave. But a fireman caught her attention and she headed away. He turned back to Kristen, realizing she'd left his side. He spotted her approaching two spectators near the police tape. The young woman had braided red hair and wore a tie-dyed skirt. The little boy sitting on the grass beside her was making soaring motions with a Batman action figure. He looked about four. The similar hair color suggested they were mother and son.

The woman turned her head in profile. Brad recognized her. Sue Lynn Everett. She'd been in his year at school but had moved away from Gracious right after graduation. He'd had a secret crush on her in seventh grade, as did a hefty percentage of the boys in his class.

Kristen tapped Sue Lynn's shoulder to gain her attention. She responded with a friendly smile and leaned over to hear what his sister had to say. Brad was too far away to catch Kristen's words. But whatever they were, Sue Lynn lurched upright with a frightened gasp. She grabbed hold of the boy and scurried away, glancing back over her shoulder as if to assure herself that an eleven year-old monster wasn't in hot pursuit.

"What the hell did you say to her?" Brad demanded as Kristen ambled back in his direction. She was fingering the amulet but looked nonchalant.

"Nothing."

"Don't give me that crap. I'm serious!"

"Can we go to the emporium now?"

"No, we can't go to the emporium!" He grabbed her shoulders, spun her to face him. "Now tell me what you said to Sue Lynn and why it freaked her out."

"I told her it's not safe for her and Brandon to shelter in place. That's her little boy's name. They should go somewhere else."

Brad frowned. The "shelter in place" phrase was right out of the Covid-19 playbook.

"Kristen, that virus isn't a big problem anymore. And why would you say something like that?"

"Because." She tried to pull free of him. He tightened his grip.

"You must have said something more than that to freak her out like that."

Another shrug.

"Answer me, goddamn it!"

"Fine," she said defiantly, stretching out the word to make it sound like two syllables. "I told her it's coming for Brandon's best friend. It's going to fly into Brandon's bedroom and carry his friend away and make him do bad things."

"What the fu–! He chopped off the word, knowing how Aunt Nipa felt about swearing around Kristen. "What the hell's the matter with you! Why would you say something like that?"

"Because she wouldn't listen when I said she should take Brandon somewhere else before it comes."

There was no mystery as to what "it" was. Kristen's airborne creature, Little Moxie's Nowhere Man. But, whether real or imaginary, his sister should know better than to utter something so callous.

Fury overwhelmed him. He grabbed her by the arm and dragged her across the parking lot.

"That hurts!" she whined. "Let go."

"Too bad."

His deepest rage, one he'd been trying to keep buried since arriving, erupted to the surface. It was a rage he experienced all too often, and that always left him feeling pissed off at everybody and everything. He realized that by directing the anger at multiple targets – the world in general – he was able to avoid its true source.

But this time he couldn't keep the rage dispersed and generalized. This time the source came attached to it, inseparable.

Brad had been eleven – Kristen's age – the first time his father, on one of his drinking binges, urged that they wrestle on the living room floor. In the beginning, the roughhousing had been fun, the kind of dad-son bonding he'd longed for as they took turns pinning one another to the carpet amid laughter. He was too naive to question that his father might have ulterior motives, or wonder why Mom was never around during what seemed like those fun impromptu bouts.

At first, he ignored that his father's hand occasionally would brush against his crotch. But then those touches started increasing, until finally one evening his father grabbed hold of Brad's junk while trying to kiss him on the lips. Frantic, he'd pulled free of the groping fingers and booze-stained mouth and ran to his room, hiding in the closet for the rest of the night.

The following morning, his father, sober, apologized and promised it would never happen again. He begged Brad not to say anything to his mother, alternating the pleas with warnings that if she found out, the family unit would be shattered forever.

Despite Brad's silence about the abuse and the fact that his father kept the promise and never tried touching him again, the "family unit" continued on a relentless path toward disintegration. His father started drinking even more. Arguments with Mom that devolved into screaming matches became the norm. On one particularly nasty afternoon at the house, his father had come at her with raised fists and savage threats, backing off only when Kristen erupted into tears from her playpen.

And then came that awful night when a sobbing Aunt Nipa informed Brad of the crash. He'd later learned from the accident report that his father's souped-up Chevy Camaro had been doing in excess of 110 miles per hour when it left the road and went head-on into a tree. His parents died instantly. Suicide-murder was suspected but never proved.

Over the days that followed, turbulent emotions had cascaded through Brad. Awful enough having both parents die, but Mom was by far the greater loss. She was the one he could always count on. The day of their funerals signified the beginning of his periodic bouts of rage at the selfish asshole who'd taken her from him. He'd even considered changing his last name from Van Reed back to Manderbach, Mom's maiden name. Ultimately, he decided it would be too much of a hassle.

Brad released Kristen's arm when they reached the parking

lot. Whipping open the passenger door, he snarled at her to get in the truck. When she didn't move fast enough, he grabbed the back of her shoulders and thrust her up into the seat.

"Stop it, Brad!"

"Shut up! Put your seat belt on!"

He didn't wait for her to do it, ramming the accelerator and exiting the lot in a swirl of tire smoke. His return to Gracious had been a colossal mistake, one of the worst he'd ever made. He'd been here less than twenty-four hours and already he was wading through endless bullshit.

A whack job of a sister addicted to a bizarre amulet... weird sinkholes... Boxhead... Nowhere Man... the desecration of Mom's grave... Joseph's cryptic warning... Flick and Felicity...

It was all too much. No way was he going to wait until Monday to get the hell out of town. First thing tomorrow, he'd be on the road and heading south, putting as much distance as possible between Brad Van Reed and The Mercy of Gracious.

TWELVE

Joseph paced his fifth-floor room at the Roberta Hotel in an agitated state, consumed by worry. It was dark out but he hadn't turned on the lights. The streetlamp outside his window provided enough illumination to keep him from bumping into things.

The place wasn't much – kitchenette, bed, bureau and a tattered chair facing a small TV he rarely watched. Down the hall was a bathroom shared with the floor's other tenants. Water pressure was abysmal. The tub took forever to fill and the shower nozzle rarely exceeded a piss stream, so he didn't wash often. That was OK, though. He didn't think he smelled.

What did stink was falling behind on the rent. His meager social security checks, earned in his younger days mostly from low-paying jobs – janitor, handyman, gas station attendant – weren't keeping pace with inflation. The only reason he hadn't been evicted was because he'd helped the Roberta's owner and landlady, Mrs Jastrzembski, out of a jam. Her ex-husband had returned to town a few years ago and had been stalking her. Joseph paid the scoundrel a late-night visit with the weapon and persuaded him that Gracious wasn't a good fit. For that good deed, Mrs Jastrzembski cut him slack on the rent and occasionally lent him her SUV for his spying trips out to Kristen's.

His agitation and worry had been building since last night when her brother had brushed off Joseph's warnings about the threat to his sister. It seemed clear that Brad remained as self-centered as ever, unwilling to look beyond his own needs and desires.

Equally worrisome was this morning's collapse at the old jail. Joseph was more certain than ever that Kristen was creating the sinkholes. It was unlikely that she realized that her strained relationship with the amulet was somehow responsible.

Still, why were her powers manifesting in such an odd way? From those brief glorious years he'd had with Isabella, he'd gained some knowledge about the first part. But neither Isabella, nor as far as Joseph knew, her daughter Janice, had ever caused actual physical disturbances. According to Isabella, the amulet's sole power was its capacity to produce visions, allowing its bearer to catch glimpses of people, places or incidents from other times. Most visions seemed of the future, of things yet to happen. Occasionally they revealed aspects from the past. Few of them were crystal clear, however. More often they possessed a vagueness, a choppiness that made it difficult to use them to make accurate predictions.

Was there something about Kristen that made her powers fundamentally different from those of her mother and grandmother?

Joseph stopped pacing. He couldn't answer such questions. But maybe Silso Orjos Sohn, the bizarre entity he'd dubbed SOS, could. Kneeling, he stuck his hand under the TV stand, feeling for the hidden latch he'd installed years ago. A gentle tug opened a set of floorboards. He reached into the hidden compartment and retrieved a trash bag. It held two objects, the crumpled steel chain gave the bag its weight. The other object was so light it might as well have been composed of air.

He peeked out of his room into the hall. No one was around. With bag in hand he exited, locking the door behind him, and proceeded to the fire door at the back of the hall. Four flights of dimly lit stairs spiraled downward. He chose the ascending steps, a short flight that accessed the top of the building through a steel hatch.

Joseph pushed it open and stepped up onto the roof. There was a chill in the early evening air, and he tightened his coat collar. Once summer came, a few of the younger tenants would venture up here to sunbathe. But this time of year, Joseph rarely encountered anyone, particularly after dark.

Best to be safe, however. Closing the hatch, he withdrew the chain from the bag. He looped it through the handle and coiled the chain around a nearby vent pipe. Should someone ascend the stairs, they wouldn't be able to open the hatch. That would give Joseph enough time to return to the world, undo the chain and explain to the intruder that he wanted to take in some fresh night air undisturbed. No matter that the excuse was flimsy. His reputation as the local oddball would likely carry the day.

He made his way across the graveled asphalt to the rear of the building. Sitting on the all-weather rug he kept up here, he propped his back against the parapet, reached into the trash bag and withdrew the second object. He could just as easily do this in his room. But he preferred the open air.

The seemingly weightless triangle was the identical shape and configuration as Kristen's amulet. The main difference was its size. Whereas each of the three sticks composing the first part of the Trine were a mere inch or so in length, the second of the three parts had sides about ten times as long. As with the smaller version, the ends of the sticks slightly overlapped.

A quick appraisal might suggest the sticks were made from grayish tree branches glued together. Nothing could be further from the truth. Although the triangle might be mistaken for wood, no earthly fire could affect it. Orjos of SOS had once told him a legend about the second part of the Trine, that it had been tempered within the heart of the universe's hottest sun, rendering it forever a kinsman of flame. Of course, one had to take tales related by that particular version of SOS with a certain degree of skepticism.

Gripping one of the sticks around its middle, Joseph extended the weapon in front of him and cleared his mind of extraneous thoughts. The Trine glowed an intense shade of red, as if suddenly thrust into a raging fire. Having performed the trick countless times over the years, the effect wasn't unexpected. Closing his eyes, he prepared to cross over.

Joseph suspected other gateways existed into the eidolon. But this was the only one he knew. He released the triangle and it hung before him, suspended in midair by some force beyond his comprehension. Although he'd never understood the source of its powers, he'd long ago learned to use them to do his bidding.

The weapon began spinning. Its rotation wasn't simple like that of a wheel. Instead, it spun in three dimensions, like some fantastic crimson gyroscope. Picking up speed, it twirled faster and faster until the three burning sticks disappeared into a blurred sphere. Moments later, the sphere transformed into an opening, a wide black hole wreathed in blazing red sparks.

Joseph either fell into the hole or it enshrouded him – he was never exactly sure how the transition occurred. A harsh crackling filled his ears, like that of a raging campfire. It was followed by a flash of light so blinding it seemed to momentarily glow from within every crevice of his body.

The sensory barrage ended. He'd crossed over to the eidolon. The weapon remained afloat in front of him but was now motionless, merely a plain triangle again.

He stood on a dirt path, surrounded by a great wilderness basking under the bluish glow of a full moon. As always, it was night, with the moon low on the horizon. The forest canopy filtered the moonlight in odd ways, creating geometric patterns on the path: squares and rectangles, octagons and hexagons, pentagrams and triangles. Joseph sensed veiled meaning in the shapes, as if some giant hand had scrawled a secret language across the landscape. Much of the eidolon seemed to be like that, full of cryptic symbols, hidden significance and mystifying intentions.

Was there a reason that the range of distant mountains refused to draw closer no matter how long and far he walked?

That the large golden berries drooping from bushes were impossible to detach no matter how hard he pulled? That his footprints in the dirt disappeared with each new step? Answers to those and similar questions continued to elude him despite all his visits to the eidolon since that life-altering year, 1966. That's when it had all begun, on a breezy day when he and Isabella had hiked into the wilderness of Copernian Ridge for one of their trysts. Instead, they'd stumbled upon the first two parts of the Trine and the remnants of the meteorite, forever altering their lives.

Joseph extended an arm toward the second part. Ever obedient, the triangle leaped into his hand. He headed in the direction of the moon, knowing it was the only sure landmark for navigating here. The path itself changed from visit to visit, winding more to the right one time, more to the left the next, yet always gently ascending. He didn't own a phone but had once borrowed his landlady's and tried using its GPS and call functions in the eidolon. A wasted effort. This realm tolerated no earthly technologies.

Joseph kept his attention focused straight ahead as he walked. Creatures roamed these woods, mostly humanoid-shaped, some big, others small, united by a fierce antagonism to interlopers. Silso and Orjos, SOS's two talkative and diametrically opposed heads, referred to them as *the venting*.

Always when Joseph came here, he sensed he was being observed by the venting. Mostly they stayed out of sight. On occasion, he caught a glimpse of their shadowy forms slinking through the foliage. Rarely did they venture near enough for him to make out their features clearly. Even when he did, it was as if he was looking at something not fully *there*, something better glimpsed through peripheral vision rather than direct eyesight.

Long ago on his first trip to the eidolon he'd wandered off the path to investigate a moaning sound like an animal in torment. Despite the forest growing thicker and less hospitable the farther from the path he went, he'd pushed on, driven by curiosity, the impetuousness of his younger self and an urge to help a creature in pain. Eventually the woods became so dense he could barely navigate between the trees.

Just as he'd squeezed between two gnarled maples to where the moaning originated, a squid-like thing had leaped down on him, a mass of slapping tentacles, angry and malignant. Like the other venting, it was hard to see, even at such close range. He'd been tempted to use the weapon to repel the creature, but some instinct warned against revealing its powers. Instead, he'd batted it away with his hands and beat a fast retreat back to the sanctuary of the path.

The incident had served to make him acutely aware of the eidolon's dangers and he'd never ventured off the path again. A subsequent conversation with Orjos affirmed his decision not to wield the weapon in the eidolon, that to do so could serve to attract more of the venting. Even so, over the past few years he sensed that the venting's numbers were increasing. Where once he'd glimpsed two or three of them amid the trees, these days he might get the impression of dozens, even hundreds.

"Good evening, Joseph."

The familiar voice was sweet and lyrical, yet not readily identified as male or female. It called out to him from the small clearing up ahead, where the path terminated on the crest of the hill. It was Silso, friendliest and most helpful of three-headed SOS, although that wasn't really saying much. Silso's conjoined siblings, Orjos and Sohn, were asleep, their heads hanging limply.

"Good evening, Silso," he said, bowing slightly as a sign of respect. The head possessed an indefinable quality that had always struck him as regal, as if it was some visiting king or queen from a distant throne.

The triplet of heads sprouted from SOS's thick neck and were symmetrically arrayed, 120 degrees apart from one another. The neck functioned like some impossible revolving tray, rotating whichever head was awake to face him. A white gown began at the base of the neck and cascaded outward to form a conical shape that descended all the way to the ground, completely hiding SOS's arms, legs and sex organs – if it indeed had any.

"You are troubled," Silso said.

The conjoined heads resembled one another. All had wavy black hair, the fierce ultramarine eyes of a deep ocean and the dark skin of his own Creole ancestry. It was impossible to determine their genders. At times, Silso seemed female and Orjos male, or at least they betrayed faint characteristics of feminine and masculine. Then on a subsequent visit they might give off an opposite sensibility, with Silso leaning toward male and Orjos female. The third head, Sohn, never changed, yet its features rendered it even more challenging to make a determination of sex. Joseph suspected that his own notions of gender held no meaning here. His perceptions, like the eidolon's shifting landmarks, were yet another example of the realm's fluidity.

"I am troubled," Joseph admitted. He'd only ever seen one sibling awake at a time. Mostly it was Silso or Orjos. On the rare occasion when Sohn was running the show, it didn't speak, just stared at Joseph with an expression that he took for either profound wisdom or utter befuddlement.

"More so than usual," Silso said. "You worry about the child."

"Yes."

"She faces the most terrible of trials."

Hearing it said aloud induced a sickening feeling in the pit of his stomach.

"But you already know this. So, bearer of the second part, why have you really come?"

"There have been new developments." He brought Silso up to date on the latest happenings in the real world, in Gracious. The ominous appearance of Sindle Vunn. Tangling with those cruel men at the bar. Brad's return. The mysterious sinkholes.

Maybe Silso already knew about all those things. It was hard to determine just how much of the real world SOS was capable of perusing.

"The amulet cannot be taken," Silso said after he'd finished. Repeating the obvious tended to characterize many of their conversations. It was as if after each of his visits Silso forgot elements of what they'd discussed previously.

"But it can be given," Joseph pointed out.

"Nowhere Man will attempt to take the first part. It must remain with the child."

"Who's Nowhere Man?"

"A recent designation for the Pestilence."

Joseph wondered if the name had some connection to the old Beatles song. The idea wasn't worth pursuing. He had more important concerns.

Years prior to Kristen inheriting the amulet, Silso had expressed the same idea in reference to Janice, that the first part must remain with her. And before that, with Isabella. However, neither Silso nor Orjos had ever conveyed such beliefs about the second part, that Joseph must always be its bearer. As for the mysterious third part of the Trine, neither of the heads would discuss its whereabouts or its capabilities no matter how hard he pressed them.

"Kristen is too young," Joseph said, hoping there was some other way, that the child could somehow be convinced to pass the amulet on to a new bearer, a person older and more mature. "It appears that it may literally be driving her insane."

"The first part must remain with the child," Silso repeated.

Joseph wondered if Kristen ever came to the eidolon. Isabella claimed not to be able to do so using the amulet, and had adamantly refused his offers to attempt accompanying him here using the second part. Presumably, Janice also had been unable to make the journey. But Kristen... clearly there was something different about her. He'd never seen her here but that didn't prove anything. In the past he'd asked, but Silso and Orjos had refused to comment.

"Time is running out for Kristen, isn't it?" he asked glumly.

"Time is always running out, yet continues to flow into the future and into the past."

That was less than helpful. "How long does she have?"

"An indeterminate amount."

He contained his frustration. "Silso, I could really use some specific direction here."

"Intervene."

"How?"

"Intervene."

Either Silso didn't want to or wasn't able to provide specifics, which was fairly typical. But right now he needed something more. He had to be careful, though. If he pushed too hard, the head would fall into silence and their encounter would be over. Orjos's conversations could be equally enigmatic, endlessly thwarting Joseph's desire for clear explanations.

"There are various means of intervention," he stated, figuring it was an indirect way of requesting clarification.

"The brother."

The other two heads seemed to move ever-so-slightly, as if nodding in agreement. But Joseph wasn't sure. Maybe he'd imagined it.

"You're talking about Brad. I've already tried involving him. Waste of time."

"Seek him where he is not expected to be."

"What does that mean?"

"The first part must remain with the child."

"Yes, you've made that clear. Brad isn't the sort of person who is concerned about others. I've tried alerting him to the danger facing Kristen but–"

"Tell him the truth, about what connects the two of you."

Joseph grimaced. "I can't. I vowed to Isabella I'd never do that."

"Tell him the truth."

The truth. He tried futilely to wrench the very idea from awareness before it could lodge itself and bring up a host of painful memories. After so many decades, it wasn't just a matter of breaking an ancient promise. Outright fear was now part of the equation. He couldn't imagine, after all these years, how Brad and Kristen would react if they learned he was the one who'd gotten their grandmother pregnant, that their mother Janice was his biological daughter…

…that they were his grandchildren.

Besides, forever meant forever, which was the only way of thinking about the vow he'd made to Isabella long after the hard realities of that era forced them apart. Admittedly, he hadn't been entirely robbed of familial pleasures over the decades. Watching from afar as Janice grew into a fine young woman, and later the mother of two wonderful children, had brought a certain satisfaction.

When Brad was a still a boy, Joseph used to make sure he ran into mother and son when they came downtown for Saturday morning shopping. He relished those encounters, knowing he was buoying Janice's spirits by making complimentary remarks about the family. Even better was seeing Brad's face light up when Joseph gave him a candy treat or a book or some other trifle he just happened to have on him. Bringing joy to his grandson often raised his own spirits, making him look forward to the following weekend when he'd arrange for another "accidental" run-in. And back then, before Brad hit his tumultuous teen years and went all morbid, Joseph even had entertained hopes that the boy would become a worthy heir to the second part of the Trine.

"Vow or no vow, you must do what is right," Silso said, drawing Joseph's attention back into the great dream forest. "Seek out the brother. The child is beyond your direct help."

Those last words sent a chill through him. Before he could respond, Silso whipped its head to the left. Joseph followed its gaze. He saw nothing but the dense forest surrounding the clearing. Yet he had the impression that a large troop of the venting were moving closer.

"What about the sinkholes?" he asked. "I sense that Kristen is responsible. Yet neither Isabella nor Janice ever hinted of or displayed such an ability. Can you tell me anything about them?"

Silso's eyes closed. The head drooped into slumber. SOS scurried from the clearing, its conical form gliding smoothly, as if its motion wasn't the byproduct of legs or feet but of wheels or treads or some other fantastic form of locomotion. The three-headed entity quickly disappeared into the woods. He heard the rustling of branches and had the impression the venting were being forced to step aside to allow SOS safe passage. A moment later there was only silence.

Something prompted Joseph to look up. He saw it immediately, the airborne apparition that must have inspired SOS's swift exit. It swooped across one of the distant mountain ranges. As with his previous sightings, it was too far away to make out clearly. The best description he could manage was that it was a large humanoid figure with a set of wings sprouting from its back. The wings flapped occasionally, but the creature mainly appeared to be riding air currents.

On recent visits to the eidolon, he'd asked Silso and Orjos about the apparition, whether it indeed was the Pestilence. Both heads had been even less responsive than usual, evading most of his questions on the subject, although Silso did admit that the creature was responsible for the venting's growing numbers. And Orjos had given the ominous warning that the creature was growing more powerful and soon might be able to cross over into the real world.

The apparition dove toward a ridge and disappeared from view. A bone-deep dread came over Joseph, the same feeling he'd experienced during previous sightings. He no longer doubted it was a *siy nan*, and that it indeed was the Pestilence.

Intervene. That's what Silso wanted him to do. But how?

And despite Silso's words, Kristen somehow had to be warned. As for Brad – Silso's suggestion notwithstanding – trying to involve him still seemed like a wasted effort, particularly after that brushoff Joseph had received outside Moxie's. And revealing the truth about the siblings' ancestry...

That was a bridge Joseph had no desire to cross.

There was another possibility. He could ask to borrow Mrs Jastrzembski's SUV and drive out to the Manderbach house this evening. No more hiding in the woods and spying on Kristen though. It was time for a frank discussion.

But then he recalled Mrs Jastrzembski mentioning that she was going out of town Saturday. Joseph wasn't about to make the miles-long hike to the Manderbach home at night. By the time he got there they'd be in bed, and rousing them from slumber to say what he needed to say would likely get him ejected from the house by way of Zack's boot heel.

His thoughts turned to a more sensible option. The Manderbachs attended the Lutheran church in town with Kristen. They rarely missed Sunday morning services. Perhaps tomorrow they'd even persuade Brad to join them.

In any case, Joseph would wait until after services and approach Zack and Nipa in the parking lot, out of Kristen's earshot. He'd tell them the whole story, or at least as much of it as he'd been intending to relate to Brad. He had to convince them that Kristen was in mortal danger. He wouldn't mention the eidolon, which likely would suggest he'd taken one too many leaps beyond sanity. Even so, the conversation would be challenging.

But they had to be made to understand. He needed to persuade them to come up with a plan to safeguard their great-niece... Joseph's granddaughter. If such a plan indeed was possible.

THIRTEEN

Brad felt bad about his awful behavior toward Kristen. An hour or so after returning from the library he'd apologized to her. By then, enough time had passed for his anger to return to its default state, medium simmer. Kristen seemed to accept how regretful he was. Still, she'd refused to talk further about her warning to Sue Lynn and spent the rest of the afternoon alone in her room.

Uncle Zack and Aunt Nipa, having heard about the sinkhole collapse in the library basement, quizzed Brad about it.

"Just a random event," he'd told them. "I'm sure it has nothing to do with the sinkholes here at the house."

They accepted his explanation without comment although he sensed a certain puzzlement over why he'd felt the need to utter it. He wasn't sure either.

As promised, Brad took them to dinner that evening, at Moxie's. After last night he would have preferred another restaurant but Aunt Nipa really liked one of the chef's specialties, salmon with creamed asparagus. It was a quiet dinner, everyone in their own little world. Several of his aunt and uncle's friends came by their table to offer greetings, most of which were brief and inordinately polite. He had the impression they took pity on Zack and Nipa for having to raise such a troubled child as Kristen, not to mention the shame of having a wedding absconder in the family.

One of the women said something supportive to Aunt Nipa about needing to maintain a positive attitude, then turned to Brad.

"I'm sure everyone is really glad to have you back."

"Just trying to do whatever I can to help," Brad replied, forcing a smile. His response caused Uncle Zack to unleash a dismissive grunt.

"Screw you!" Brad said, glaring at his uncle.

The insult blasted across the restaurant. Heads turned toward them from adjacent tables, expressions ranging from curious to reproachful. The woman retreated.

"Sorry," Brad muttered under his breath, sensing everyone gradually turning their attention away. He hadn't told his aunt and uncle he was cutting his visit short and would be leaving first thing in the morning. But given his past history, he figured Uncle Zack suspected and had seen fit to out his hypocrisy.

The four of them skipped dessert. There seemed to be a mutual feeling of wanting to get home as soon as possible, even Kristen, who'd had a sweet tooth for Moxie's peanut butter ice cream. His aunt and uncle dutifully thanked Brad for treating them to dinner and urged Kristen to do the same. She did so but with a formality more befitting a total stranger.

It was obvious she was still sore at him over this morning's incident at the library. But he remained angry at her as well. Kristen's warning to Sue Lynn and Brandon about the kidnapping of her son's best friend was just so callous, so unlike her. Brad had to keep reminding himself that his sister was ill, wasn't fully responsible for what spouted from her messed-up head.

They got home around nine. It was almost dark. Uncle Zack planted himself in the recliner and turned on the TV. Aunt Nipa suggested Kristen go to bed but she insisted on staying up, and disappeared into the kitchen with a drawing pad. His aunt didn't push the issue.

Brad headed for his room and began packing. Best to wait until the last possible moment to divulge his escape plan to minimize flare-ups. He figured to break the news just as they were getting ready for church. For Aunt Nipa especially,

Sunday services had always proved comforting. The emotional security of the church would help all three of them accept his decision. It was the perfect time.

After packing, he flopped on the bed and checked his messages. Nothing consequential. There were several from a guy he knew from the construction company who was big into jock humor. He was always sending stupid texts, most barely worth a chuckle. There was a mass email from his supervisor, informing the crew that permits for the new site had been approved and that they all were to report for work Monday morning. That was good news and reinforced his rationale for leaving ahead of schedule. He'd make the leisurely drive back to North Carolina tomorrow, reach his apartment early enough for a solid night's rest and be ready to jump back into work and a normal routine.

He went back downstairs. Aunt Nipa was on the sofa knitting. The TV remained on but Uncle Zack was asleep on the recliner, fitfully snoring. In the kitchen, Kristen was at the table working on a drawing. She came alert when Brad strode past.

"Watch out for the–"

"I know, the shoo spot. Don't worry, not going to step on it." She'd been issuing the warning whenever he entered the kitchen.

He glanced down at the forbidden zone. Like the shoo spot outside his bedroom, it had been outlined in masking tape and distinguished further by Kristen's red and yellow safety stripes. He hadn't ventured into the basement since yesterday to check the third shoo spot near the water heater, the one Kristen claimed was different than the others. But he assumed it too had been given the crayon treatment.

He snared a Michelob from the fridge, figuring to open it later in the privacy of his room. But as he turned to exit the kitchen he hesitated, plagued by self-reproach over his latest plan to escape Gracious.

"What are you drawing?" he asked, moving behind Kristen.

She reacted by turning the paper over so he couldn't see it.

"C'mon, kiddo, not even going to show me? Even if it's a picture of me looking like the ogre from *Shrek* I can take it, honest."

"It's not from *Shrek*," she whispered.

"Listen, I still feel bad about losing my temper today. There's a lot of things going on in my life that… well, they really don't have anything to do with you. When you said those things to Sue Lynn, I know you thought you were just trying to help her. Kristen, I'm really *really* sorry."

She considered his words for a moment then flipped over the paper, revealing the drawing. It was done with colored pencils and revealed an artistry he hadn't known she possessed.

Five figures colored in browns and grays stood ominously to one side. A sense of uneasiness came over him as he realized the smallest of the quintet had a lopsided box for a head. On the opposite side, a man and a girl were holding hands. Between the sets of figures were three triangles nested within one another. The tiny, innermost one was green – obviously the amulet. The middle one was red. The outer triangle was white but not drawn as solid lines like the others. Instead, it was diaphanous and cloud-like, as if to suggest it wasn't real or existed in some ethereal state. Was it supposed to represent the third part of the Trine?

The drawing featured an additional element he'd initially overlooked. Hovering above the five figures was what he'd taken for an amorphous black smudge. But looking closer, he sensed it had form. With a little stretch of the imagination, it could represent a winged figure. Nowhere Man?

Brad's first urge was to say goodnight and return to his room. He didn't want to know what the elements of the drawing meant. Yet another part of him couldn't be contained.

"That's supposed to be us, right?" he asked, pointing to the man and girl.

"Uh-huh."

"And those other figures?"

"Bad men," she whispered.

"And the triangles?"

"The three parts of the Trine."

"And what does the Trine do?"

Kristen shrugged.

"Your amulet is the first part, right? Do you happen to know where the other two parts are?"

She turned away, either unable or unwilling to provide further details. Outside, a breeze set the back porch wind chimes crooning an offbeat melody. Farther from the house, Brad heard the agitated air rippling through the forest.

He changed his mind about the beer and returned the unopened bottle to the fridge. A small cabinet beside the stove held a better option: Uncle Zack's liquor stash. His aunt and uncle weren't big drinkers. The modest selection was for holidays or the rare occasions when they had company over.

He found a nearly full bottle of Prairie Organic Vodka on the top shelf. Plopping ice cubes in a large Pepsi glass, he poured the vodka almost to the brim. He debated whether to take the bottle with him but decided it wasn't necessary. He could always return for a refill.

He left the kitchen without another word to Kristen, drink in hand. Passing through the living room he sensed Aunt Nipa staring as he headed for the stairs.

"Have you decided yet?" she asked.

"Decided?"

"About going to church with us in the morning?"

It was at least the third time she'd asked. He repeated his earlier answer.

"Let me sleep on it."

Reaching the second-floor hallway, he had an impish urge to stomp all over Kristen's shoo spot and see what would happen. Instead, he took a big gulp of vodka and navigated around the forbidden area to his room.

Closing the door, he sat at his old desk and plopped the glass nearby. He stared at the fake meteorite chunk, which Aunt Nipa had returned to its familiar place at the edge of his bureau. Dark gray, it was the size of a baseball, but with a jagged surface marred by darker protrusions. He was reminded of his aunt giving it to him when he was a boy, and how excited he'd been when she related the story of how it might be a real piece of the Copernian Ridge meteorite. It wasn't, of course. And now it also reminded him of Felicity.

Enough, he told himself. Time to stop dwelling on all the crap in his life.

He retreated into his phone, played a series of YouTube shorts. The first was a puppy and a kitten playfully wrestling in a flower garden. Additional videos followed, each accompanied by a vodka chaser.

Horizons compressed. Worries shrank. Brad knew he was as close to feeling good as he was likely to get.

FOURTEEN

Elrod lay on his back by the remnants of the campfire, a hand jammed down the front of his pants, vigorously spanking Sergeant Apone. But tonight the sarge was playing hard to get, resisting Elrod's spirited efforts to transform from a flaccid flea flicker into a downfield touchdown.

He'd told himself the reason he couldn't get it up was because he was hungry. But after interrupting his efforts to raid the van's ice chest and wolf down some odd-tasting venison bologna Double Bub had prepared from last night's feast, that excuse went kaput. It was no use lying to himself. The reason the sarge couldn't reach the goal line was more fundamental.

I need wap.

"Where fuck is he?" Kyzer bitched, a shadowy figure pacing in the dim light of a stationary lantern, their only illumination. The Kyze-Man had been stomping around the clearing in tight circles for the better part of an hour, his own desperation for wap manifesting as relentless movement.

Double Bub was no more immune to the craving. The freak was cocooned in his sleeping bag, nestled against the ashes from last night's deer roast. But the bag writhed and heaved. It reminded Elrod of a giant worm trying to twist free from the beak of some monstrous bird.

Kyzer continued cursing, his boots raising dust clouds as they stomped the dirt. He almost kicked Double Bub's headgear, which was lying on the ground beside the sleeping bag. When the freak zippered up, it was pretty much the only time he took off helmet, goggles and grille.

Elrod gave up on the sarge and removed the wad of tissues from his pants. Jacking off was one of the few ways of distracting himself from wap lust, and at the moment it was letting him down in a big way. He used to be able to go four or five days between hits but now withdrawal symptoms began after less than forty-eight hours. His flesh tingled as if tiny insects crawled on it. Palms and forehead were sweaty, as if caught in a Mississippi heat wave. As bad as the physical symptoms was the anxiety. It reminded him of what he'd endured as a child when his whore of a mother chased him around the trailer park with a hickory switch.

He checked his watch again. Almost eleven. Sindle Vunn had said he'd return hours ago. Shit, what if something had happened to him? What if he wasn't coming and there'd be no wap?

The thought was too awful to contemplate.

"Goddamn motherfuck!" Kyzer growled, continuing to circle the clearing and punish the earth with the heels of his size-thirteen shitkickers.

Elrod needed a change of scenery. He made for the woods but inadvertently crossed in front of Kyzer.

"Where fuck you going?

"Take a piss," Elrod lied.

"Why not here?"

'Cause I'm shy, he wanted to say, but swallowed the words on account it being the sort of smart-ass remark that could provoke the Kyze-Man into slapping him upside the head. And that was under normal conditions when Kyzer wasn't caught up in the wap lust.

Using his phone's flashlight to see, Elrod scurried through the trees to the fire lane and hopped into the back of the van. Kyzer had built a hidden compartment under the floor to hide their weapons and other illicit stuff. It was big enough to hold Elrod's newest and most cherished possession.

Kneeling on the floor, he peeled back the carpet to reveal the compartment. He yanked on the recessed handle and the detachable lid popped free. Nestled among Sindle Vunn's Glock and a bunch of portable cell phone jammers was a hard-shell suitcase. Elrod undid the snaplocks and popped the lid. Just the mere sight of what lay within spiked his excitement. For a few wonderful moments, wap lust retreated.

The compact twin metal canisters, bound together with nylon webbing, were encased in a bed of foam rubber padding. The canisters' stem valves had been drilled out and a thick rubber hose inserted in the openings to connect them. A second hose was attached to the bottom of one tank and terminated in a two-foot length of black anodized pipe. Welded to the business end of the pipe barrel was a propane torch head with a trigger handle.

Elrod ran a hand across the tanks, massaging the cool metal. The boss had given him the flamethrower a few days ago, explaining that although homemade, it was a product of professional workmanship, and used high-grade napalm with a polystyrene thickener. Elrod had made his first flamethrower back in middle school using a discarded fire extinguisher filled with gasoline. But this unit was miles beyond such amateur efforts.

He'd been so overcome with emotion at the unexpected gift that he'd found himself fighting back tears of joy. The boss was hardcore all right, but at times he had a heart of pure gold.

Elrod had tried out the flamethrower a couple times to get a feel for it, firing a few short bursts into the campfire. He'd been careful not to overdo it and waste precious fuel, which was only good enough for a forty-second sustained burn. Still, there was more than enough left in the tank for an additional test before he went hog wild with it later, during what promised to be a special night.

He froze. A vehicle was approaching. So far they hadn't been bothered by any strangers out here, but there was always a first time. Maybe some kids looking for an isolated spot to get high. Or some diligent fire inspector in search of illegal flamethrowers…

Relief washed through him as he recognized the limo's soothing purr. He re-latched the suitcase and replaced the hidden compartment's lid. By the time Nidge eased to a stop, Elrod was outside the van, leaning against the rear doors in what he hoped would be mistaken for a casual pose. Still, it took all his willpower to keep still and not show Sindle Vunn just how bad he was jonesing for a hit.

"Hey boss," he greeted the pair as they stepped from the limo. "How goes it? Nice night, huh? Kyzer and Double Bub were getting worried that you weren't coming, but not me though, on account of I always know you're a man of your word and do the right thing." He realized he was babbling nervously and tried to slow down. "Anyhow, I came out here to get away from them for a while. Maybe grab a smoke."

"You're not a smoker," Nidge pointed out.

Elrod grimaced. He'd screwed up with that smoking remark. What a dumbass thing to say. Sometimes, even when the wap lust wasn't upon him, the weirdest shit popped from his mouth. He giggled to cover up the mistake.

Sindle Vunn flashed a smile and headed toward the camp. He was dressed in an expensive-looking suit as usual. But instead of a dress shirt and tie, he wore a black turtleneck. More suitable for tonight's work, Elrod figured.

Nidge mouthed the word *moron* at Elrod as they trailed the boss. The insult didn't bother Elrod. He was used to people saying he was stupid and calling him names. What did bother him was that the chauffeur looked none the worse for wear. For whatever reason, Nidge seemed able to go longer than the rest of them between hits. Or maybe the boss had already given him a dose. There were certainly advantages to being a chauffeur.

Double Bub was out of his sleeping bag with headgear back

on as they entered the clearing. He stood beside Kyzer, the pair of them trying to keep still and not let on how badly they needed fixes. The boss wasn't fooled.

"I do apologize for leaving the three of you in such a state. It certainly was not intentional. We had further work to do at the crack house, installing security measures and readying it for Nowhere Man's arrival. Naturally, we mortals need to make allowances when seeking his largesse. And alas, he will not be joining us on tonight's escapade. Another important duty draws his attention."

Don't care, just wap us. Elrod lined up beside Kyzer and Double Bub. Fearsome threesome indeed! They no doubt looked exactly like what they were, a trio of rattled junkies.

"I bring additional good news," the boss said. "Not only has our esteemed savior provided what you desire, but he has deemed the importance of tonight's events worthy of a bonus. Therefore, each of you will be provided a double dose. One hit now and the other when we're ready to depart on our mission."

Elrod was thrilled. Two wap hits in the space of a couple hours. By the time he strapped on the flamethrower he'd be on fire!

He giggled with the notion.

The boss nodded to Nidge, who removed a small cardboard box from his pocket. Popping the lid revealed eight silvery metal vials topped with corks, each about the size of a thimble. Elrod felt himself bouncing from foot to foot with anticipation.

Give it! Give it! Give it!

Nidge removed his own two doses, leaving six for the rest of them. Sindle Vunn required wap too but, according to Nidge, always took his hits "straight from the source," from Nowhere Man himself. Elrod wondered how that worked but the details weren't something the boss felt like sharing. However, Nidge hinted that such direct hits of the royal nectar were far more potent, and that after each dose, the boss experienced a spirit-transforming, I-see-Jesus-in-the-sky high.

Nidge extended the box. Elrod and Double Bub lunged forward at the same instant but Kyzer grabbed them by the backs of their necks and yanked them away from the prize. The Kyze-Man didn't like being last. He snatched two vials, popped the cork of one and swallowed the contents.

Elrod shoved in front of Double Bub, determined to be second. Twisting out the cork he stared for a moment at the syrupy black goo. It had a sweet fragrance, some kind of spicy smell that always reminded him of Christmastime. He downed it in a single gulp. Too bad the taste didn't match the smell – more like sour milk. Small price to pay for the instant warm feeling in his chest. At his very first wap months ago, it had taken several minutes to feel the effects.

Elrod's anxiety retreated. Withdrawal symptoms vanished. As a bonus he was able to peer deeper into the surrounding woods. He spotted a rabbit nibbling on a plant, a squirrel racing up a tree. As Sindle Vunn explained it, the freshly wapped were briefly capable of enhanced eyesight, as if they were wearing night-vision binoculars. That should come in handy for this evening's work.

Wap's most pleasurable sensation was making him feel like he was part of something bigger than himself, something awesome. He supposed it was how people felt when they got caught up in a religion or sensed that life had some deeper purpose, things he'd never experienced prior to taking hits of the drug. Maybe that's why the boss was always referring to Nowhere Man as their savior, and how very soon the whole world would come around to his ways.

Before that could happen, however, some serious hatchet work needed doing, as Kyzer put it. There were those who would resist being united, resist the new religion. And the worst enemies of all were those somehow connected to the child's amulet.

Elrod looked at Kyzer, Nidge and Double Bub, and somehow realized they were experiencing similar thoughts and emotions. Wap made their common essences recognizable to one another, drew them together. There was pleasure in that, pleasure in knowing that the four of them – plus Sindle Vunn in his special way – were ready to kill in the name of the savior.

FIFTEEN

Brad came alert, listening for what might have interrupted slumber. It was still dark. His bedroom window was ajar. A wavering breeze slipped through the curtains, conveying the peculiar harmonies of the wind chimes.

He glanced at the wall clock. Nearly four-thirty. Even early risers like his aunt and uncle should still be asleep. Had someone's nighttime bathroom visit awakened Brad? Maybe a herd of deer scampering through the woods, their spindly legs convulsing dry foliage?

His headache was a third possibility. He became acutely aware of it as he sat up in bed. Returning to the kitchen for that vodka refill had been a mistake. He didn't know how many shots those two glasses he'd downed contained. But clearly a number that was not a tribute to good health.

Trying to go back to sleep would be futile. The prospect of lying here until daylight held little appeal, not with a throbbing skull and a host of concerns he'd temporarily drowned with the vodka. Doing his best to ignore the headache, he rolled out of bed and slipped into jeans, sweatshirt and boots.

He drew his phone from the charger. There was a single email, again from the girl he'd slept with last weekend. Reiterating what a good time they'd had, she'd accentuated the point with an attached photo of herself sitting on a wooden fence in front of a pasture. Her smile was engaging, and it prompted him to recall what a pleasant time he'd had in her company, even before they'd retreated to his apartment for sex.

A sound of distant high-pitched laughter interrupted his reminiscence. Was that what had awakened him? Easing open the door, he slipped quietly into the hallway, intending to make his way downstairs.

The laughter came again. It was creepy, not reflective of joy or amusement. More like the cackling of something malicious, something predatory. He assumed it was coming from the TV. Maybe Uncle Zack had fallen asleep in the recliner with the set still on.

It sounded a third time, louder. Brad frowned. Its clarity indicated something beyond the living room's bandwidth-addled television speakers.

Stepping around the shoo spot, he tiptoed toward the staircase, guided only by the nightlight. He didn't want to turn on the hallway fixture. If it was an intruder, he didn't want to alert them. Easing halfway down the staircase, he peered into the living room. Moonlight penetrated the gauze curtains, providing enough illumination to reveal that the recliner was deserted and the TV off.

He froze at a new sound – creaking footsteps. Someone was walking across the lopsided front porch. A set of moving shadows passed by the window. A chill went through Brad. *Two of them.*

He debated what to do. Making a run for the gun cabinet was tempting. But with a child in the house, his and aunt and uncle were super cautious and kept the key elsewhere. He could break the glass and grab Uncle Zack's pump-action 12-gauge. But then he'd have to scramble to locate a box of shells, possibly in one of the nearby drawers but maybe in another room. The time it would take to carry out those tasks and load the shotgun rendered the idea impractical.

A better option was his uncle's old service revolver, a Smith & Wesson .45. Aunt Nipa had bought him a fancy gun safe for it with a combination lock. The secured weapon was kept in their bedroom dresser.

As he turned to tiptoe back up the stairs there was yet another disturbance, this one coming from the kitchen. Someone outside was rattling the back door, as if trying to open it. It couldn't be the shadowy figures on the front porch. They wouldn't have had the time to circle around back.

More than two of them.

The sound of shattering glass, again from the kitchen. Brad abandoned caution and raced up the steps. Pounding on his aunt and uncle's door, he flung it open and lunged into their room. Aunt Nipa sat up in bed, her moonlit face pale and startled. Uncle Zack stirred but didn't awaken.

"Someone's trying to break in!" Brad hissed, shaking his uncle by the shoulder.

"What the hell!" Uncle Zack's groan dissolved as Brad's grim expression registered.

"Someone's trying to break in," he repeated with greater urgency.

His uncle came alert and swiveled out of bed. Stepping into slippers, he opened the top drawer of the dresser, withdrew the gun case and punched in the lock code.

"At least three of them," Brad said. "Front and back. They broke a window."

Kristen screamed.

Brad bolted from the bedroom and raced to the back of the house. Before he reached his sister's door it sprang open. Kristen appeared in the portal in rose-petal pajamas and slippers, clutching the amulet. Her mouth was agape, her eyes wide with terror.

"They're here for me," she said. Her voice was weirdly calm, in stark contrast to her horrified expression.

Whatever doubts Brad had been entertaining about the authenticity of Kristen's weird behavior dissolved in that instant. Her strange fears, her wild claims... she'd been right all along. They were here for her. They were here for the amulet.

"C'mon." He reached out his hand. She didn't move.

"Kristen, we have to go!"

He grabbed her by the wrist, dragged her toward his aunt and uncle's room. As they reached the door, Uncle Zack emerged, revolver in one hand, walking stick in the other. With a glance at Brad and Kristen he headed for the stairs. Aunt Nipa followed, her hand on his back. Whether for her own comfort or to steady him, Brad couldn't say.

"Be careful," she whispered.

Uncle Zack reached the landing. He halted, listening intently for any noises downstairs. For the moment it was quiet. But that breaking glass suggested that the intruders might already be inside.

Aunt Nipa turned to Brad. "I tried calling for help. The phone is dead."

Another chill went through Brad. The intruders must have cut the landline.

He couldn't imagine the cops getting here in time to stop whatever was going to happen. Still, her idea wasn't without merit. Maybe a cruiser was patrolling in the area. Brad punched 9-1-1 into his cellphone.

Nothing happened. He checked the signal strength meter. The sloping icon was all the way down, indicating no service. That shouldn't be possible. He'd been getting service throughout the house since he'd arrived. A more ominous sense of foreboding ripped into him. The intruders must be using some kind of signal-jamming device. Whatever was happening was the result of careful planning.

He shook his head at Aunt Nipa, indicating his phone was out too. They were on their own.

He needed a weapon. He regretted not making a try for the shotgun when he'd had the chance. Maybe they could still reach the gun cabinet.

A weapon came to Brad out of the blue in the form of the walking stick. Uncle Zack handed it back to Aunt Nipa. His uncle had realized it would be easier for him to navigate the stairs by clutching the banister railing, keeping his other hand free to wield the gun. Brad snatched the walking stick from his aunt's fingers.

"Stay here," Uncle Zack hissed at them. He inched his way down the steps. Brad ignored the order, staying right on his tail. There were no fresh noises, no indications of anything out of the ordinary.

"Keys to the gun cabinet?" Brad whispered.

"In our room. Nipa keeps 'em in a vase. Back shelf of the closet. Shells and bullets are there too."

Too time-consuming. He'd have to make do with the walking stick. Its thick handle made for a decent club.

From the kitchen came a crackling sound. It sounded like someone walking across broken glass.

"Who's there!" Uncle Zack bellowed, rushing down the rest of the steps with all the speed he could muster. Reaching the living room, he limped toward the kitchen with the revolver held high.

Brad headed the other direction. He slid back the front door deadbolt and whipped open the door, ready to beat off the intruders with the makeshift club.

The porch was deserted. There was no one in sight for as far as he could see in the dark. His truck and his uncle's Chevy Blazer appeared undisturbed.

He closed the door and latched the deadbolt, then scurried down the hallway. He reached Uncle Zack and they entered the kitchen. The back door was ajar, a hole punched through its window. Glass fragments littered the floor. But no intruders.

Uncle Zack pulled the door wide open and stepped onto the small back porch.

"Nobody out here," he muttered. "Maybe just asshole kids."

"I don't think so. I think they came for the amu–"

A gunshot blew out another chunk of glass from the door window. Uncle Zack grunted and fell back against Brad, clutching his left side.

"Fuckers!" his uncle hollered. He raised the revolver and fired three wild shots into the darkness.

Brad yanked him back inside and kicked the door shut. He dragged Uncle Zack away from the window, eased him onto the floor with his back against the refrigerator. Grabbing a dishrag from a magnet hook on the side of the fridge, he pressed it against the wound. His uncle winced in pain.

"Goddamn! Shouldn't have fallen for that trick."

"Trick?" Brad asked, kneeling beside him to examine the puncture. The bullet had entered far enough to the side that it shouldn't have hit any major organs.

"Old Vietcong tactic. Breach the perimeter, then retreat and take potshots at whoever comes to check it out."

A creaking noise. From above. Someone had climbed onto the back porch roof. From there they'd be able to reach the window to Kristen's bedroom. His uncle arrived at the same realization.

"Go!" he hissed, shoving the revolver into Brad's hand.

"Keep pressure on the wound."

Brad laid the walking stick on the floor within Uncle Zack's reach. Steeling himself, he dashed toward the hallway, aware that for a few seconds he was exposed to the gunman out in the darkness.

No shots came. But he felt no sense of relief. One or more of the intruders may have reached Kristen's window from the porch roof.

He dashed through the living room, aiming the gun at the front windows, ready to fire at any shadows. No targets. Panic hit when he reached the bottom of the staircase. Aunt Nipa and Kristen weren't at the top where he and Uncle Zack had left them.

Brad bounded up the steps two at a time, lunged into upstairs hallway. *Deserted.* The door to Kristen's bedroom was closed. It had been open only minutes ago.

Heart pounding, trying to keep the gun barrel steady, he eased along the hallway toward his sister's room.

The first door he passed was also shut. It led to the attic. Had Aunt Nipa heard someone climbing through Kristen's window and retreated up there with his sister in tow? Hopefully not. Once in the attic they'd be trapped. The only way out was through the small window, with a long straight drop to the ground.

"Kristen?" he whispered. "Aunt Nipa?"

"In here."

It was his aunt's voice, coming from her bedroom. He swung the door open. The two of them were huddled in front of the closet. Aunt Nipa was clenching Kristen's palm. His sister's other hand was wrapped tightly around the amulet.

"Was that gunfire?" Aunt Nipa's face was etched in fear. "Is Zack OK."

"He'll be all right." Brad had no idea if that was true. But he had to remain positive.

"We heard noises from Kristen's room. I think someone may have come through her window."

"The two of you stay put," Brad urged. "I'm going to get my keys. The four of us are getting out of here in my truck."

She gave a frightened nod. Brad backed out the door and crossed the hallway to his own room, unconcerned that he was stepping through the shoo spot. He grabbed his car keys and wallet from the dresser and returned to the hall. Not taking his eyes off Kristen's door, he backed up toward his aunt's bedroom.

He heard a door open behind him. The bathroom. Before he could whirl around, a hard object cracked the back of his skull, throwing him forward. The revolver flew from his hand as he sprawled face down onto the floor.

He rolled onto his back, fighting dizziness. Two men hovered over him. One was smiling, and incongruously garbed in a tailored gray suit, polished shoes and a black turtleneck. Brad instinctively knew he was the man from the limo, the mysterious Sindle Vunn. He carried a handgun. From the way he was holding it by the barrel, it had been the weapon used to knock Brad down.

The other man was a brute with a shaved head and a cruel expression. He had to be the skinhead who'd fought with old Joseph at Moxie's, and who with his companion had dug up Mom's coffin.

Brad glanced at the revolver, which had landed a few feet away. Sindle Vunn took note and kicked the gun farther down the hall.

"Watch him, Kyzer."

Fighting wooziness, Brad tried to stand up. The skinhead grabbed his ankles and lifted them off the floor. Brad kicked but couldn't break his grip. Trapped in that awkward position, he watched helplessly as Sindle Vunn opened his aunt's door. Aunt Nipa and Kristen shrieked as he pushed them out into the hallway. Still wearing that incongruous smile, he grabbed Kristen's wrist and squeezed.

"Show it to me."

His fist tightened. Kristen cried out.

"Let her go!" Brad yelled.

Aunt Nipa clawed at the compressing hand. Sindle Vunn smashed her across the forehead with the gun butt. She fell, landing on her back within the taped outline of the shoo spot, unmoving.

"Bastards!" Brad kicked madly, trying to break the iron grip on his ankles.

The pain became too much for his sister. She was forced to open her fingers. Sindle Vunn quickly pulled his hands away, wary of touching the amulet. He stared at it, longing in his eyes. Kyzer, keeping Brad helplessly suspended, turned to look as well.

Brad caught a glance, and again experienced a quick impression of a vivid, pulsating shade of green. As before, the color was accompanied by that tantalizing idea – more absurd than ever under the circumstances – of somehow compressing all his troubles into a ball and hurling it far away.

Sindle Vunn grabbed Kristen around the waist and threw her over his shoulder. She started screaming. Her captor withdrew a stubby purple syringe from his pocket, removed the plastic sleeve and jabbed the needle into Kristen's butt through her pajamas. She released one more sustained scream before abruptly going silent and limp.

Kyzer dragged Brad feet-first toward the stairs. And then Brad was bouncing down the steps like a sack of dirty laundry, frantically trying to keep his head high enough to avoid slamming the tops of the risers. He managed that feat but his upper back and shoulders took a beating. Twice he grabbed hold of the handrail uprights, briefly interrupting his descent. Each time, Kyzer yanked him forward with such force that it felt as if his arms would tear from their sockets.

Nearing the bottom, he went airborne. He tried wrenching his hands behind his neck to cushion the blow of his head slamming the living room's hardwood floor. He was an instant too late. He hit with a resounding crack. A wave of blackness overwhelmed him.

Even though momentarily blind, he heard two gunshots from upstairs. A sickening feeling touched home.

"In here," came another male voice from the kitchen. Kyzer dragged Brad through the hallway. He was still too stunned to even think about resisting. His eyesight was returning but his fast-moving surroundings remained little more than a blur.

Carpeted hallway gave way to cool linoleum. The brutal ride ended. But Kyzer kept his feet elevated.

His vision cleared. The sight that greeted him was horrifying. Nidge, the chauffeur, stood in front of the refrigerator. Dressed in black like some vampirish ninja, he was holding Uncle Zack upright from behind by an ivory-handled garrote wrapped around the neck. Uncle Zack's eyes were closed. His head hung limply.

No... no...

Nidge released the strangling wire. Uncle Zack crumpled to

the floor, landing within the confines of the shoo spot beside the refrigerator. Brad knew he was dead.

"Bastards."

The word emerged as a whisper, lacking emphasis. It was all he could manage in his weakened state. Kyzer, amused by his feebleness, released a series of chirping, hyena-like laughs.

Brad caught movement by the open door and realized there was yet another intruder. Standing in the portal was Boxhead, the freakish thing that had chased the deer past his truck yesterday. That incident now seemed like it had occurred a lifetime ago.

Boxhead was bouncing softly from foot to foot, a weird sort of dance. He reminded Brad of a young child just learning to move his body to musical rhythms.

The floor vibrated as footsteps approached from behind. He craned his neck and gained an upside-down view of Sindle Vunn hovering over him. Kristen was still draped across his shoulder. Brad could only hope that she was just unconscious and not...

His mind refused to complete the thought.

Kyzer gave a twisted smile and motioned to Uncle Zack's body. "Hey boss. Lookee what Nidge got."

"Good catch," Sindle Vunn offered. "But I suggest the three of you finish up with a modicum of haste. Elrod is not known for his self-restraint. He is most eager to play his part in the festivities."

"Let my sister go," Brad pleaded. "Just take the amulet and leave."

Sindle Vunn stared down at him with faux sympathy. "Unfortunately, the situation is somewhat more complicated. Alas, one does not simply take that which cannot be taken."

Sindle Vunn turned toward the living room. But he hesitated at the table, spotting Kristen's drawing. He gazed at it for a long moment before returning his attention to Brad.

"It appears your sibling may be quite the clairvoyant. Our

master has a passing interest in the other two parts of the Trine as well. Would you happen to know their whereabouts?"

Brad's anger surged. "If I knew, I wouldn't tell you!"

"Hmm... no matter. All in good time."

Sindle Vunn left with his prize. Moments later, Brad heard the front door opening and closing.

Kristen's gone. Uncle Zack's dead. He didn't know what had happened to Aunt Nipa but those gunshots suggested the worst. A crippling pain rose up inside him. It would have overwhelmed him were he not about to suffer an equally grim fate.

His despondence reached rock bottom. But then some innate survival sense ignited and he kicked his legs with abandon, trying to break free of those fleshy tethers around his ankles. Kyzer responded by lifting Brad completely off the floor and dangling him upside down.

"Fuck you all!" Brad hollered.

"Boy got spunk," Nidge said, his face devoid of emotion.

More of Brad's physical strength returned. Even in such an ungainly position, he arched his body at the waist and pummeled his fists into Kyzer's massive thighs. The skinhead released peals of high-pitched laughter. Brad glimpsed Boxhead from the corner of his eye, increasing the tempo of his childish dance.

Brad aimed his punches higher. One of them connected with the crotch of his tormentor, who let out a pained grunt. Kyzer retaliated by whirling in a circle and spinning Brad around, quickly elevating him until he was four feet up, horizontal to the floor. He felt as if he was in some deranged version of the kids' game where you swung a bucket of water in a circular motion fast enough that the liquid didn't spill out. But in this case, he was the bucket.

After three or four revolutions Brad was feeling dizzy. Even in his condition he realized the worst was yet to come.

Kyzer released his ankles. Brad flew through the air. The

inevitable crash came swiftly. The back of his shoulders hit first, against the edge of the refrigerator. He dropped like a stone, landed with his legs sprawled across Uncle Zack's body. Pain shot up and down his spine.

He managed to roll over. The effort brought new agonies, this time potent enough to force him to cry out.

Kyzer came toward him, fresh malice in his eyes. "More hurt's a-comin'!" But the skinhead halted and spun toward the hallway. Whatever had snared his attention drew Nidge and Boxhead in that direction as well.

A strange whooshing sound filled the house, followed by loud crackling noises. Brad couldn't identify the source.

"What the fuck!" Kyzer hollered.

Nidge looked disgusted. "Never give a halfwit a flamethrower."

And then Brad saw it, an airborne mass of congealed fire, intertwined tongues of red and yellow, palpitating as if alive. The tongue of flame shot into the edge of the kitchen from the hallway, forcing the three intruders to leap from its path. A wave of heat cascaded from it.

Boxhead lunged out the back door, running for his life. Kyzer whipped out his phone, tapped a number. He listened then shoved the phone angrily back in his pocket.

"The jammer is still on," Nidge said calmly.

"No shit, Sherlock! Where fuck you leave it?"

The chauffeur gestured toward the fiery hallway. "Living room."

"Fuckin' Elrod!" Kyzer screamed. "I'll kill that fanny-packin' asshole!"

Nidge raced out the back door. Kyzer gazed down at Brad as if considering what to do next, maybe disappointed he couldn't finish his sadistic games. Another tongue of flame shot into the kitchen. That was enough for the skinhead. He bolted after Nidge out into the darkness.

Brad crawled on hands and knees toward the hallway,

trying to ignore multiple pains erupting along his back. His only chance was reaching the front of the house. Flames or no flames, going out the back door would again put him at the mercy of his tormentors.

The kitchen tablecloth and cabinets above the sink were already on fire. Gray smoke rose to the ceiling. Brad crawled past the table. A shower of sparks landed on his back. He batted them away but one landed on the bare flesh beneath his collar. With his other pains, he hardly felt the burn.

Other sparks touched down on the windowsill. The shade and the curtains erupted into flames. The conflagration spread quickly to the surrounding wallpaper.

He reached the portal to the hallway, peered around the corner. The front of the living room was a sheet of fire but the hallway wasn't as bad. Hot spots punctuated the walls, collateral damage from the flamethrower that had blasted the length of the corridor. Most of the ruin had been inflicted upon the flamethrower's farthest target, the kitchen.

He had to move. The front and back of the house weren't escape options, but he might be able to climb out the dining room window. If he got lucky, the intruders weren't watching that side of the house. Struggling to his feet, he grabbed a tea towel off the rack and soaked it under the sink. Pasting it across his mouth and nose, he staggered down the hallway.

He reached the entryway to the dining room. No flames... yet. He could make it to the window and get out.

He hesitated, his thoughts turning to Aunt Nipa. She was probably dead. But maybe not. Maybe she was just injured.

Funnels of smoke poured up the staircase. He'd never make it to the second floor.

He had to try.

He sprinted to the steps and grabbed hold of the railing. It was hot but not unbearably so. Holding his breath against the smoke, he made his way up to the second floor.

Aunt Nipa remained where she'd fallen, on the shoo spot

outside his bedroom. Two red splotches stained the front of her pajamas over her heart and belly. Gunshot wounds. She was gone.

Grief would have to come later – the fire was spreading fast. He rushed back to the staircase. The lower steps were barely visible through the dense smoke but he saw enough to know that the living room was now an inferno. Going downstairs was no longer possible. Nor was climbing out the window at the end of the hallway. It was ringed in flame. Even as he looked on, the glass shattered, strewing fiery shards into the hallway

The back window in Kristen's room was the best remaining option. The doorway to the attic was closer but climbing higher in a burning building didn't seem like the wisest plan.

He ran to her closed door, hesitated. In the movies, he'd seen what happened when someone opened a door into a room that was on fire. The flames instantly leaped free of their cage, feeding on the fresh oxygen and consuming the supporting actor or actress who'd pulled such a boneheaded move.

Flames rose up the staircase. The smoke burned his eyes. His lungs were about to burst from holding his breath. He had no choice but to exhale.

Drawing a breath ushered in a blend of air and agony. He dropped the damp tea towel, retching and coughing from the inhaled smoke. Out of options, he whipped open Kristen's door. No fire.

Smoke from the hallway swept past him, sucked into the bedroom by a draft. Behind him, the flames surged along the hallway, consuming carpet and wallpaper. The baseboard nightlight threw sparks, its plastic shield crumpling under the intense heat. The fire reached the shoo spot. Aunt Nipa's robe ignited.

He spun away, dashed through Kristen's room, fighting the urge to cough, knowing it would only suck more noxious vapors into his lungs. Waves of heat blasted his back.

Now or never.

Shielding his face with crossed arms, he crashed through her window. He landed upright on the back porch roof amid a spray of fragmented glass and splintered wood. The roof sloped downward. He was moving too fast to stop. He shot off the edge, arms flailing in an instinctive yet useless attempt to slow his fall.

It was seven or eight feet to the ground. He'd made the jump as a teen, on those nights he'd been restricted to his room and needed to be somewhere else. Muscle memory took over. Boot toes impacted first. He let his knees bend, absorbing the shock. Momentum carried him into a forward somersault.

He hopped to his feet. He was free of the fire. No time to savor it. The urge to cough remained but he couldn't risk it. Sindle Vunn and his gang weren't in view but they could still be nearby. If they heard him hacking away…

Keep moving. The forested hill behind the house was his only recourse. He sprinted across the mowed grass, leaped the low fence and plunged into the woods. Adrenaline and fear kept physical and mental anguish contained, but just barely.

He gazed behind him. The house was an inferno, sheets of fire erupting into the night skies. Loud crackling filled the air as more and more of the building succumbed. He released his breath, coughed loudly. The blaze was louder. No one should be able to hear him. Still, he had to keep moving. Terror at what his captors would do if they found him bolstered willpower.

He ran farther into the woods. The blaze illuminated his course until the ground leveled off. Soon, forest night enveloped him.

He reached for his phone, intending to use its flashlight. But the phone was gone. It must have fallen out of his pocket while he was being dragged, or maybe when he'd somersaulted upon jumping from the roof.

Faint moonlight and skies aglow from the fire revealed the contours of an opening in the trees up ahead. It must be a small clearing. He'd stop there, cough until he was all coughed out. Just a few more feet...

His legs tread air, unhinged from earthly connection. What he'd assumed to be a clearing was nothing of the sort. It was an anomaly in the forest, a narrow but steep depression. Even as he was plunging down into it a part of him wondered whether it was another of Kristen's sinkholes.

Boots touched ground. But he was on a steep downhill slope and couldn't decelerate. He had just enough time to register the shadowy branch in his path before it smashed into his upper forehead.

The world exploded into coruscating stars. And then he was falling again, this time into a darkness more profound than the most pitch-black night.

THE SECOND PART

SILSO: The discordant one will soon enter the eidolon. We should do whatever we can to help him.

ORJOS: *No, we should turn him away. Let the venting have their way with him.*

SILSO: You still refuse to perceive his depths.

ORJOS: *And you refuse to perceive the darkness that engulfs him. Better he suffer a merciful death than attempt to confront the Pestilence.*

SIXTEEN

Felicity Bowman hadn't been enthusiastic about waking up at five am. She was more of a slink-from-bed-around-nine sort, a chronotype that had proved challenging throughout much of her schooling, what with the rest of the world believing education was best earned through early morning classes. Today, the start of a long-anticipated enterprise provided incentive for getting up. Still, thank goodness for coffee.

She drew another sip from her "Astronomy Lover" travel mug and glanced at Flick behind the wheel, comfortably alert to the winding two-lane road they were traversing. That Flick didn't require heavy doses of liquefied caffeine in the morning was another way she and her fiancée were different. Melding their bio clocks had been a challenge in the year they'd been dating, particularly during the last six months living as a couple. Adjusting to another person's routine was par for the course in any dedicated relationship. Eventually, they'd work it out. The sheer rightness of being in one another's company would make it so.

I feel you feel I.

Out of context, the phrase sounded silly, something a stranger might perceive as overly sentimental. Not that either of them would ever use it in public. They'd adopted the expression in the earliest weeks of their relationship. Felicity wasn't even sure which one of them had uttered it first. Sometimes she thought it was Flick's creation, at other times, her own. Whatever the origin, it had come to symbolize the essence of what they had together, a connection as grounded as it was transcendent.

A smile touched Felicity's face. It was one of those smiles that burst out on occasion when all the important things in her world seemed to be going in the right direction.

Flick had made a solid case for getting on the road as early as possible. The lidar survey had revealed scores of ground-level anomalies, which they'd narrowed down to five likely sites where the Copernian Ridge meteorite could have impacted. Flick, working on a dual mathematics doctorate in statistics and operations research, had written an app correlating the overflight data with historical accounts of eyewitnesses, as well as with Felicity's educated guesses about the 1897 search parameters of Professor Summersby and his grad student. Results from the app prioritized the five sites. They'd selected the three most probable ones as today's targets.

Site A was within three-quarters of a mile of the nearest spot they could park. That wasn't too bad, considering that Sites B and C would require lengthier hikes through dense wilderness. Still, Flick was convinced that with their early start, they'd be able to reach all three targets and perform proper evaluations before it started getting dark. Should they not locate the meteorite today, they'd return next weekend to explore the two remaining locations.

Flick had bought the new Jeep Grand Cherokee only weeks ago specifically for this effort. Even though Felicity's father was president of a small local bank and made a good living, she and her siblings had been raised to value a dollar. Not touching savings accounts, avoiding buying on credit wherever possible and being especially cautious about large expenditures were family mantras. Flick came from a different tradition. Felicity admitted to occasional envy of what seemed her near-bottomless trust fund. But they'd vowed never to let their wealth differential become a source of contention. Besides, the

Jeep was way more comfortable than Felicity's old Volvo, and more suitable for these mountains.

They'd been traveling for a good forty-five minutes. Gracious and Copernian Ridge were relatively close via straight-line mileage, but the roads winding around these peaks, ridges and narrow valleys were another story. There were hairpins galore. Ten odometer miles might be consumed to reach a location half that distance as the crow flies.

It was a gorgeous morning, in the low seventies, and with no rain in the forecast. Dawn had crept across the mountains. The skies were fierce blue and nearly cloudless. Felicity's window was down. She leaned out occasionally, air-blasting her face and drawing in pleasant scents of honeysuckle and pine.

Flick kept her eyes straight ahead. She took it easy on the curves, aware from mapping their route that more than a few of them started out deceptively gradual before morphing into wicked hairpins. Felicity had come to appreciate her careful driving style after spending those years with Brad behind the wheel. She wouldn't describe him as reckless. Still, he often displayed a heavy foot on the accelerator when making turns, prompting any front-seat passengers to grab the dash and hang on.

"Anything new on the fire?" Flick asked.

Felicity undid the Velcro flap on a pocket of her hiking vest and scooped out her phone. They'd heard the alarms just as they were leaving the house. By the time they were ten minutes out, two clusters of fire trucks and ambulances had flashed past, the second one from an engine company in an adjacent township. That suggested it was a serious blaze. She'd been checking regional news sites every ten minutes or so. Thus far there had been no reports.

And there wouldn't be any for a while, she realized, at least none capable of being accessed. Her phone showed no bars – they'd gone beyond the footprints of regional cell towers. The signal loss wasn't unanticipated. It was likely they'd remain out of range for the rest of the day. Navigating to the three sites would be done with Flick's GPS receiver, which had direct satellite access.

"I'd give you one to three it's that abandoned factory," Flick said. Although she never placed bets, she was always estimating odds. The habit wasn't surprising. Flick's parents had made the better part of their fortune creating online casinos.

"You mean Eckenroth's?"

"Is that the big one at the far end of Denton Street?"

"Uh-huh."

"Looks like a fire hazard just waiting for vandals to torch. What'd they make?"

"High-end porcelain products. Building tiles, bathroom fittings, dinnerware. They had these elaborate showrooms in the basement and an outlet store. Generations of locals went there to check out the latest trends in home décor." Felicity smiled with a memory. "When I was a kid, my mom used to take me there."

"Your mom," Flick murmured, slowing to a crawl to navigate a hairpin.

Felicity immediately regretted her last words, and the topic was abandoned by mutual silent agreement. Discussing Felicity's conservative family was awkward. The two of them had had a number of discussions about the chilly reception Flick had received when Felicity brought her home for the first time over the Christmas holidays. Things hadn't improved since then, especially now that the two of them were back in Gracious for the summer and living together.

Felicity's mother had always been accepting of homosexuality and what she referred to as "those sorts of variant lifestyles." Just not in her daughter's case, as it turned out. Mom also believed Flick was spoiled and haughty because of her wealth, which simply wasn't true.

Her father also perceived their relationship through a warped lens. He believed that Felicity had "gone gay" in reaction to Brad dumping her at the altar. Sooner or later, he reasoned, she'd return to her senses and start liking boys again. Not Brad, of course. Far more disturbing to her parents than a lesbian relationship would be one that allowed *him* back. Even Grandpa Harry, more open-minded and accepting of Felicity's choices than the rest of the family, became apoplectic when Brad was mentioned. Apparently they'd had a run-in at the emporium the other day, with Grandpa warning Brad of dire consequences should he attempt reinserting himself into Felicity's life.

The threat was unnecessary. Flick was her soulmate. The sheer rightness of their feelings for one another immunized them against any and all interlopers. Still, they hadn't yet told Felicity's family or her close friends they were engaged, which was a minor point of contention between them. Flick wanted to be totally upfront about the situation. Felicity figured it was better to bring her family up to speed little by little. She remained confident they'd come around eventually. Maybe after a decade or two and some grandkids to spoil.

She reached over and gently stroked Flick's arm. Her fiancée smiled. Simple touching devoid of expectation was another pleasurable aspect of their relationship, something rarely possible with Brad. He'd usually been unable to distinguish between a desire for closeness and a come-on for sex.

Yet despite a plethora of character flaws, even his deplorable actions on their wedding day, Felicity still found reasons to care for Brad as a person. Those feelings were best kept to herself. Neither Flick nor her own family would understand. She continued to want what was best for him and hoped someday he'd be able to transcend his troubled childhood.

I feel you feel I.

If only he could experience that kind of love. If only he could awaken from the emotional slumber that kept the deeper and more meaningful aspects of the world at bay.

SEVENTEEN

Wavering shafts of sunlight penetrated the canopy, dodging branches, twigs and floppy emerald leaves, spreading warmth. Brad sensed it was morning. He felt at peace amid the chirps of wilderness awakening. The cool hard earth pressing against his back reminded him of a camping trip Mom had taken him on. He couldn't recall exactly when, but hoped they could do it again soon.

Consciousness ascended. Mom was gone. She'd died years ago. He longed to cling to her memory, longed to return to her sanctuary, where the world felt free and alive and ripe with possibility. He couldn't hold on. The fantasy floated away, buffeted by currents immune to his will.

Full awakening brought devastating images, a condensed replay of last night, each memory more horrific than the last. The attack on the house. Uncle Zack... Aunt Nipa... the fire...

Kristen.

He struggled to his feet. Dull throbbing pains cascaded up and down his back. His upper forehead ached. He touched the spot and winced. The bruise on his head was the size of a grape, the hair camouflaging it; stiff, dry and coated in a sandy material. He dislodged a speck of it with his finger, held it up to his face. Dried blood.

He had to call the police. Kristen could still be alive. Those men wanted the amulet. *The Trine... It can't be taken, only given.* He recalled the story Uncle Zack had told of when he and Aunt Nipa had tried to remove it from her while she was asleep, and of how those bad memories had overwhelmed them. But his aunt and uncle would never have hurt Kristen to get her to surrender the amulet, whereas her captors...

He shuddered and reached for his phone, then remembered he'd lost it. The only option was returning to the house. By now, someone must have seen the flames and called the fire department. They likely would still be on-scene.

He climbed out of the steep-walled pit he'd fallen into. The dense growth, including the tree he'd slammed, revealed that nature had created the depression long ago. It wasn't one of Kristen's sinkholes.

Reaching level ground, he started back. But all too soon, the realization came that he'd been walking too long. He should have reached the house by now. The canopy was thick, the sun still too low on the horizon, depriving him of a precise reference point to determine what direction he should be heading. Had he run farther than he imagined last night?

He plodded through the undergrowth for another ten minutes before admitting the obvious. Somehow, he must have gotten turned around. Instead of walking toward the house he'd likely ventured deeper into the forest.

I don't know where I'm at or where I'm going. A feeling of desperation came over him.

Even weirder, it was starting to get dark. Was a storm coming? Halting, he gazed upward at the occasional breaks in the canopy. The darkness was arriving with alarming speed, and storm clouds didn't appear to be the cause. But it couldn't be night already. That made no sense. He would have had to have been asleep for something like fifteen-plus hours. Granted, that branch had given him a solid whack on the head. He could have suffered a concussion. Still, it was hard to grasp that he'd been unconscious for an entire day, and that he'd mistaken sunrise for sunset.

Suddenly the skies were pitch black, night coming on with impossible swiftness. Weirder still, a full moon appeared, low on the horizon, its bluish light bathing the wilderness. But the moon had been only half-full this weekend. And the quality of the trees themselves seemed to have changed although he couldn't have said exactly how. Maybe it was the way the canopy filtered the moonlight to form geometric patterns on the ground, everything from triangles and squares to pentagrams and octagons.

He was on a dirt path that wound gently upward in the direction of that intense moon. Before he could consider what it all meant, he sensed he wasn't alone. There was movement in the surrounding trees, all around him. Whatever they were, they were drawing closer.

I'm still out cold. It's just a strange dream.

Dream or not, he picked up his pace on the ascending path. He sensed a clearing up ahead at the crest, intuited he'd be safer there. But the flurry of movement solidified into figures moving in parallel with him amid the trees. Most seemed to be human or of humanoid shape, yet a few were bizarrely different, alien. Problem was, he couldn't say exactly what any of them were because he couldn't actually *see* them. The harder he tried gazing upon any particular one, the more indistinct and shapeless it became. Only by not looking directly at them was he able to discern they were there, which made no sense. Some unnatural force interfered with the process of clear visual identification.

He had the impression they were of various sizes as well, and that they moved with different gaits. Some were upright and stiff-legged, others hunched over. Some pranced madly like children on sugar highs while others shambled along, dragging one foot after the other. But he sensed a commonality. They were united by their intentions.

They wanted to cause him harm.

Panic overtook him. He ran, trying to reach that clearing up ahead at the top of the hill. But somehow in his haste he found himself stumbling off the path and deeper into their midst. They surrounded him, closed in.

The first ones reached him, arms groping. At the moment of their touch, he experienced a barrage of anger and loneliness, inadequacy and disgust, other dark emotions as well. It was like slamming into a wall of gloom and pessimism. It left him feeling that everything was hopeless.

He fought against the despair and tried pulling away from the groping appendages. But more clusters of them attacked him from behind and from the sides. Spectral fingers grasped at his neck, trying to choke him. He flailed vainly at the hands even while acknowledging that fighting was useless, that life itself was wretched and not worth carrying on. The only sounds he heard were his own frantic shouts.

And then a fiery red staff was whipping through the air, smashing into their ranks, sending them tumbling away like bowling pins in some nightmarish alley. The wielder of the staff came into view and astonishment momentarily eclipsed Brad's fear and despair. It was Joseph. Yet somehow he no longer appeared ancient and decrepit even though the age lines on his brow were clearly visible and his cruddy attire marked him as the same person Brad had encountered at Moxie's. It was the way he moved, a vitality suggesting the strength and determination of unbridled youth.

Joseph's glowing staff arced with fierce conviction, crashing into what Brad sensed were the heads and bodies of the faceless enemy. And then he was free and the horde was in retreat, vanishing back into the cover of the enveloping woods. He dropped to his knees, his body aching from bruises, punches and swats. His neck hurt from their attempted strangulation.

"How did you get here?" Joseph demanded, glaring down at him.

Brad couldn't think straight. Nothing made sense. This place... the old man playing superhero... it was all too surreal. He gazed at the staff in Joseph's hand. The reddish glow was gone, rendering it pewter gray. It had tiny bends and imperfections, like a skinny tree branch. The texture reminded him of a larger version of Kristen's amulet.

"How did you get here?" Joseph repeated, his annoyance increasing.

"I don't even know where here is! I ran from the fire, got knocked out. Woke up and it's light out. Then suddenly it's dark again and those freaks are all over my ass. Where am I? What is this place? What's happening?"

His questions produced only a skeptical look on the weather-beaten face.

"What the hell's going on, Joseph? What were those things? They seem like people. But I couldn't see them clearly. And when they touched me..." He stopped, not wanting to dwell further on that bombardment of despair and negativity that had coursed through him.

"They are not people. They are the venting."

"The what?"

The ancient face softened into a grudging nod. He seemed finally to accept Brad's confusion as genuine.

"The venting. Malignant creatures. Mostly humanoid in form but not always. I don't know what they represent. They are part of the eidolon."

"The eidolon?"

"This place. Another realm or dimension, separate and different from the real world. Where is your sister? Did you make the crossing with her?"

"They took Kristen. I think they're going to... hurt her. Make her give them the amulet."

"Who took her?"

Brad gave a quick recap of the attack, choking back agonies as he spoke of his aunt and uncle being murdered. When he finished, Joseph stared grimly up at the dark skies, as if searching for something.

"We need to return," he said finally.

"Return?"

"To the world. Do you know how?"

"Do I look like I goddamn know how?" Now that he seemed momentarily safe, Brad's anger surged.

"We'll have to try going together." Joseph hesitated. "I've only ever done it alone. It could be dangerous for you."

"Is there a choice?" He couldn't imagine having to stay here, not with those things on the loose.

Joseph raised the staff above his head. It snapped into the shape of a triangle. Amid all the madness, the transformation in and of itself wasn't the surprise. It was the fact that the staff had become a near exact version of the amulet, but significantly larger.

"What is that thing?"

"The second part of the Trine." As if anticipating Brad's next question, he added, "Your sister's amulet is the first part."

"How did you make it transform like that? Why do they want Kristen's amulet?"

"No more questions, not now. The venting could return, and in vaster numbers." He again turned his gaze skyward. "Worse, their master could come. We need to leave quickly."

Joseph closed his eyes and extended the triangle in front of him. It started glowing again, quickly reaching a fiery scarlet hue. He released it and it hung in the air, defying gravity. Like some mad gyroscope, it began spinning in three dimensions. Faster and faster it twirled until its very shape morphed into a blurred sphere, which then became a black hole enveloped in red sparks.

Brad felt himself falling into the hole. Either that or the hole itself was enveloping him. Violent crackling noises filled his head, eliciting painful memories of the burning house. There was a burst of confusing white light, so vivid that it seemed to emanate from within his body.

The aural-visual assault terminated. It was daylight again. They were still surrounded by wilderness but it was the right and proper forest, where he'd been walking before somehow crossing over into that hellish realm. The natural scents of the woods seemed more intense now that he was back. He might have found them more pleasing were it not for his proximity to Joseph, whose BO was as daunting as ever.

The triangle hung suspended in midair a few feet away. It was no longer aglow. Joseph grabbed the weapon-slash-interdimensional-portal and holstered it somewhere within his bulky overcoat.

"I don't suppose you have a phone tucked in there?" Brad asked.

"You suppose correctly."

"How about water?"

Joseph retrieved a plastic bottle from a pocket. Brad opened the nipple top, threw back his head and squirted. The water felt good trickling down his throat. He took two more big squirts before handing it back.

"Which way to the house?" he asked. "I kind of lost my bearings out here."

"Your house burned to the ground. Besides, it's not where we need to go."

"We?"

"Do you want to save your sister?"

"Of course."

"Then you need to come with me."

Joseph headed off into the trees, apparently secure in his sense of direction.

"So where *are* we going?"

No response. Brad hesitated a moment then followed.

EIGHTEEN

Joseph was tiring from the trek but forced himself to continue at a brisk pace. There was no need to glance back to make sure Brad was keeping up. He was a noisy hiker, unaccustomed to moving through woodlands with stealth. Had Joseph been around throughout Brad's youth like a proper grandfather, the boy would have been taught wilderness savvy, as well as being provided with a host of survival skills that might have made for a very different sort of…

He waylaid the thought before it could assume a deeper foothold. Shoulda-coulda-woulda – the bane of living in the moment. You had to deal with the real world on its own terms, not as you hoped it might be or might have been.

At least Brad's stream of questions had run dry for the moment. Joseph had encouraged that condition by giving the same reply to each one.

"No time to waste on chit-chat," he would say. "Your sister's life is at stake."

Which inevitably drew snarky retorts, such as…

"What's the matter, dude, can't walk and talk at the same time?"

Multitasking wasn't Joseph's issue. He had no idea what to do once they made it back to town. He needed time to think, and to do so quietly, without constant interruptions. The trek was better spent contemplating options. Those men could have taken Kristen anywhere and he hadn't so much as a clue how to find her. It seemed mostly a matter of luck that he'd run into Brad and rescued him from the eidolon.

And then there were Silso's final chilling words to consider. *The child is beyond your direct help.*

Awakening early this morning, he'd headed to the Apex Eatery, a retro fifties diner clad in stainless steel less than a block from his apartment. He'd intended to have his usual leisurely Sunday breakfast before ambling over to the Lutheran church after services let out to have that frank discussion with Zack and Nipa.

His plan had taken an instant nosedive. Everyone at the diner was talking about the big fire in the wee hours. Somehow, Joseph had slept through the racket of emergency vehicles streaking through town. When Donna, the venerable waitress and Apex fixture, mentioned that the fire had been at the Manderbachs, Joseph held back a sense of panic. Hitching a ride out there in the bed of the pickup truck of three teen boys eager to gawk at the destruction, he'd stood with a small crowd behind a perimeter of police tape, watching firemen probe the smoldering rubble. The mortared stone walls remained but the wood-framed upper floors had collapsed into a massive heap. The garage and Zack's and Brad's vehicles were intact, having been far enough from the inferno.

Joseph's feelings sank further as the first two bodies were removed. The stretchers were covered in white sheets. Although neither victim appeared to be a child of Kristen's years, the gaggle of firemen remained hard at work sifting through the wreckage. A backhoe lent by a local construction firm arrived to help dislodge the heavier debris. Whispers cycled through the crowd that the bodies of the two younger family members would soon be uncovered.

"No way this was accidental," he heard a fireman mutter. That arson was suspected came as no surprise. Upon arriving, Joseph had detected a faint stink reminiscent of gasoline. A Vietnam War vet in the crowd, a man from Zack's VFW post, mentioned it smelled like napalm.

Joseph cursed his own foolishness for waiting until this morning to approach the Manderbachs. He should have come straight out here following last night's visit to the great dream forest. Silso had instructed him to intervene. The urgency hadn't been apparent but he should have realized it anyway. Intervene *now*, not later, was what was meant. Had he heeded words left unspoken, he might have been able to prevent this tragedy.

Reporters and a TV news crew arrived at the scene, prompting Chief of Police Robin Wellstead to issue a statement. The two bodies removed from the house would require autopsies for identification, she announced, dodging further questions as to who the victims might be or whether others were known to be buried under the rubble.

Joseph maintained realistic hope Kristen had survived. Whoever had done this surely had come for the amulet. And because the Trine could only be given, not taken, there was a good chance the child had been kidnapped. He'd initially held out no such expectations for her brother. But then he recalled Silso's puzzling words about Brad.

Seek him where he is not expected to be.

The elusive meaning of the phrase abruptly seemed clear. The one place Brad absolutely wouldn't be expected to be was the eidolon. How he could have gotten there remained a mystery. As far as Joseph knew, only someone in possession of the second part of the Trine could make the crossing. But could Kristen somehow have been responsible? Could there be more going on with the amulet than he was aware? Had she escaped into the eidolon and brought Brad with her?

Retreating from the gawking crowd, Joseph had slipped into the woods. Once far enough from the house and enveloped by wilderness, he'd used the second part to create an opening and enter the eidolon. As usual, he found himself upon the winding path amid darkness. Reaching the top of the hill, he encountered SOS in the clearing. This time, imperious, cynical

Orjos was awake, and conjoined heads Silso and Sohn drooped in slumber.

The encounter had been brief, with Joseph as usual begging for some crumb of a clue that might help him find Brad. But instead, Orjos ended up telling him something that shook him to the core. Before he could try eliciting more details about Orjos' stunning revelation, muffled shouts came from the trees. He'd instinctively known it was Brad and raced off to help. Transforming the triangle into a staff – a useful configuration for battle – he'd plunged into the thickening foliage to the source of the commotion.

Brad was surrounded by the venting. They looked to be trying to kill him. And if he was slain here, he'd be dead in the real world as well. At least, that's what Silso and Orjos often hinted.

Joseph waded into the venting, his fury conveyed to the weapon, enabling it to clear a path and knock the creatures away from Brad. Abandoning his prohibition against using the weapon in the eidolon could end up having dire repercussions, increase the venting's numbers even more. But extraordinary circumstances dictated extraordinary actions. He had to save his grandson.

"This is far enough!" Brad growled, drawing Joseph's attention back to the present and the hilly woodland they traversed. "I'm not taking one more goddamn step until you tell me what's going on!"

Joseph halted. Brad sat on the mossy end of a fallen tree. His fists were tightened, his face ripe with frustration.

"Your sister needs our help. We shouldn't waste time by–"

"Yeah yeah. I get that. But no more silent treatment."

Joseph was about to launch further exhortations about how following his instructions gave them the best chance of saving Kristen. Brad beat him to the punch.

"Start talking. Where have they taken my sister?"

"At this moment, I don't know exactly where she is."

"But you have a way to find out."

Joseph didn't respond. Brad's anger flared. "You have no idea, do you? Then why the hell should I keep following you? Besides, I heard a car in the distance. I have a pretty good idea where we are." He pointed at a nest of evergreens rising gently to the north. "I'm guessing Heckmeyer's Road is just over that hill. I can get back to Gracious on my own from here."

"And what will you do when you get there?"

"What else, find those pricks. I figure they don't know I survived. No reason for anyone to suspect they were responsible for what happened, right? So, there's a good chance one or more of them might be hanging around town."

"And if you should find them, what then?"

"Make 'em tell me where Kristen is, then kill the motherfuckers!" Brad drew a deep breath as if trying to calm down, as if knowing how deranged he sounded. "I'll let the law deal with them. Tell Chief Wellstead everything that's happened and let her arrest them."

"Involving the cops isn't wise."

"Why not?"

"It would only complicate matters." Joseph had suffered a few run-ins with the police, going all the way back to his teen years. The encounters had never ended well. "And it's doubtful those men would allow themselves to be captured. Even if they were, they wouldn't surrender Kristen. The one they serve has too much power over them."

"And who might that be? Also, how do you know all this shit? Either way, you gotta come clean. Tell me what's going on or I'm outta here!"

Joseph considered his demands. They made sense. And there was another factor to consider, something that had occurred to him while saving Brad in the eidolon.

For a long time, Joseph had tried ignoring the question of what might happen to the second part of the Trine after he died. Should it fall into the hands of someone with bad intentions, the world could suffer terribly. Brad had led a troubled and tormented life but it had never turned him into a bad person. Insensitive maybe, but not deliberately cruel, although Felicity Bowman might well have a different take on that. Still, having done some growing up, at least to an extent, Brad seemed to have shed some of the darkness that had enveloped him as a teen. And after what had happened, he now had more than enough incentive to confront those who'd kidnapped his sister and murdered his aunt and uncle.

Could it be destiny that Joseph had encountered Brad under such distressing circumstances? At long last, was there a viable heir to the second part of the Trine? Someone to relieve him of its burden?

NINETEEN

Brad was bluffing about leaving Joseph and heading out on his own. But he figured Joseph wouldn't know that, at least not for certain. The old man was firmly entrenched in all the weirdness that had been happening. Bottom line, he represented the best chance of finding Kristen. No way was Brad going to allow them to part ways.

Joseph gazed at him for a long moment. Finally, he sat on the log beside Brad.

"Not so close. You stink to high heaven."

Joseph seemed surprised, as if unaware his odor would frighten skunks. But instead of moving to the opposite end of the log and creating a decent stink gap, he reached into his coat and withdrew a worn leather pouch.

"You're killing me here," Brad said, making an exaggerated pinch of his nostrils.

"Medicine," Joseph explained, trickling a teaspoon of fine sandy powder from the pouch into his callused palm. Scooping up a handful of moist earth from beneath the tree, he rubbed it into the powder, creating a chalky paste.

Brad glared. "You expect me to swallow that crap?"

"Of course not."

Before Brad could think to object, Joseph smacked the wad of paste against the forehead bruise peeking out from beneath his hairline.

"Oww, goddammit! What the hell!"

"It will help with the pain."

"Newsflash, it hurts *more*."

"Give it a moment."

"Don't need your medicine man bullshit, Joseph. Oh, and FYI, they stopped treating wounds with bacteria-coated mud about two centuries ago. Now get the hell away from me!"

Joseph complied, moving to the far end of the log.

Wincing, Brad resisted an urge to clean off the damp clump sticking to his bruise. But curiously, the worst of the pain had subsided. Maybe the old man had some kind of healing powers. If true, Brad wasn't about to tell him so. Instead...

"Just hope I'm not going to get an infection from that crap."

"You won't. Do you have other bruises?" Joseph extended his palm, which still held a smear of the paste.

"Not a chance."

Joseph skimmed off the remaining paste from his hand against the log. He asked again how Brad had come to be in the eidolon.

"I told you, I haven't the faintest idea. One second I'm here, next second I'm there."

Joseph went silent as if mulling over his answer. Brad had about a million questions but focused on the overriding one.

"So how do we save Kristen? I'm guessing she doesn't have a lot of time. So you'd best just give me the short version."

"There is no short version. Still, I don't believe they'll do anything to Kristen just yet."

"How can you know that?"

Joseph gazed up at the sky through a break in the canopy. "Those men who took her, they won't act against Kristen on their own. They'll wait for their master. I don't believe he's yet crossed into our world. He'll likely want to be there for any attempt to remove the prize from her possession."

"The amulet can't be taken, only given," Brad murmured. "Is that also true for your weapon?"

"I don't believe so. At least I've never been given evidence to suggest that the rule applies to the second and third parts of the Trine."

"And what is the third part?" Not that he really understood what the first two parts were. But the question seemed particularly worth asking. The other night in Kristen's bedroom his mother's voice had told him to find it.

"The third part is hidden. Or lost. Or maybe it was never here." Joseph shrugged. "I just don't know."

"Well, no way does Kristen give up the amulet." An appalling thought occurred; he could barely get the words out. "Does that mean they'll... you know... hurt her?"

Joseph shook his head. "She would have to give it up of her own free will and not be under any sort of duress. Their master is shrewd, however. He doubtless has a plan to get it from her."

"So just who is this son of a bitch?"

"The Pestilence. He is also known as Nowhere Man."

"That's the same flying creature Kristen claimed to have seen."

Joseph frowned. "Did your sister say when and where this occurred?"

"Friday night. Right outside her bedroom window."

"If that's true, then he's already able to cross over into our world."

"Little Moxie saw him too. That's where I first heard the name. He said Nowhere Man buzzed his Escalade. Called him a demon from beyond. And they both said he fades away sometimes, like he's partly a ghost."

"It may be that he cannot yet exist fully within our world. Possibly he can only venture here for short periods." Joseph frowned. "How did Little Moxie know to call him by that name?"

Brad sensed the question was rhetorical but answered anyway. "He didn't say. What does it matter how he knew the goddamn name?"

"Because I only ever experienced it within the confines of the eidolon."

"Experienced it how?"

Joseph didn't reply. He got up from the log, anxiously pacing back and forth. After a time, he apparently reached a conclusion and calmed down.

"The attack on your house occurred just before dawn. Even if Nowhere Man now has the ability to cross over, I believe he still needs to avoid the light of day. I don't believe he'll make an appearance again until it's dark. We should have until then to find Kristen."

"What, he's like some kind of vampire?"

"It's more like his essence is shrouded in gloom. That's something I sensed about him in the eidolon. Even though there he's solid and substantial, not ghost-like at all."

Joseph's assumptions sounded pretty vague. Brad wondered if it might be just wishful thinking. Still, better to take an encouraging point of view and believe time was on their side and they had until nightfall.

"So why does Nowhere Man want Kristen's amulet?"

"He ultimately seeks all three parts."

"Sindle Vunn said that at the house. But the way he said it, the amulet was what was really important."

"And I'm not sure why that is. I only know that he intends perverting the first part to his will. He seems to lust for power, dominion over others. I believe the amulet is somehow key to achieving that. Conversely, perhaps the three parts can stop him from achieving it."

"So if that's true, he wants the three parts so they can't be used against him."

Joseph shrugged. "Again, it's a possibility."

"OK, so tell me more about this eidolon?"

"The great dream forest. It's believed to be a projection of the three parts of the Trine." Joseph resumed his seat at the far end of the log.

"Sure as hell didn't feel like a dream when those things were kicking my butt. Just where are you getting your information from?"

"From the eidolon. Which ultimately means, of course, that my knowledge emanates from the Trine itself."

"And what exactly is the Trine?"

"I don't know."

Brad grimaced. He couldn't tell whether the old man was deliberately holding back or was only capable of speaking in circles.

"My knowledge of the Trine is obviously incomplete. I know certain things about my weapon and the amulet. But I've never been able to figure out what the Trine's ultimate purpose might be. I don't even know if it has an overall purpose."

"So the second part, your weapon, how does it work? How'd you go all Gandalf on those creatures, the venting?"

"I wish I could give you a precise answer. I can't."

"Of course you can't," Brad muttered, allowing his frustration to shine through.

"I'm not trying to be cryptic. The best I can explain it is that the second part of the Trine is like a living thing. When you touch it, you feel its essence deep inside you. By manipulating that essence to undertake a specific action, the Trine's physical aspect – the triangle itself – assumes the configuration necessary to carry out your will. Does that make sense?"

"Sort of. And the amulet?"

"It has a very different capability. My understanding is that the first part might be thought of as the proverbial crystal ball. It enables its bearer to glimpse bits of the future, or sometimes the past, see people, places and things that don't yet exist or happened long ago. Often those visions have a strong emotional component, a personal connection."

Brad recalled Aunt Nipa and Uncle Zack landing in Kristen's shoo spots. Yet his sister had also warned him not to step within those borders. That suggested her visions of the future remained vague. She'd known someone was going to die in those locations. She just hadn't known who or when.

"The amulet may have other powers as well," Joseph continued.

"Like causing bad memories in someone trying to take it without permission? Or causing sinkholes?"

"The bad memories, yes. I believe that's a defense mechanism of sorts. As to the sinkholes… I'm not sure."

"So where did you get your part from?"

Joseph seemed hesitant.

"I still might do this on my own," Brad warned.

"I found the Trine nearly sixty years ago. In 1966. We were hiking in the mountains, on the far side of Copernian Ridge."

"We?"

Another pause. Then…

"I was with a young lady."

"Getting it on, huh?"

Joseph ignored the inference. "We wanted to be alone. Really alone. Far from the critical eyes of townspeople. My Creole background… it didn't exactly endear me with the locals. My auntie and her boyfriend brought me up to Gracious from New Orleans when I was just a nipper. He'd been offered a job in a local mill. But he soon quit and took off for greener pastures. Auntie and I… we didn't have an easy time of it. Gracious was rife with small-town prejudices back then."

"Still is."

"But far worse in those days. The idea of a local girl going out with a man not from around here, let alone a long-haired hippie whose skin was less than lily white…" He trailed off, a flash of anger warping his features. "Anyway, the two parts literally came to us. A short time later, we found the meteorite. Or at least part of it."

"The Copernian Ridge meteorite? That has something to do with the Trine?"

Joseph stared into the distance as his reminiscence

unfurled. "It was a beautiful spring day, around this time of year. We drove out early that morning for a picnic in the mountains and ended up on the remnants of what seemed to be an old Indian trail. We came to a perfect spot, a tiny clearing nestled amid towering pines. We could hear the winds shrieking through the treetops. But in the clearing it was calm, peaceful." A smile came over him. "We'd brought along ham and cheese sandwiches, a bag of Utz potato chips and a bottle of Boone's Farm apple wine. We ate and drank. We smoked a little pot. After a while, we lay down on a blanket and made love..."

He trailed off, lost in the memory.

"And then what happened?" Brad quizzed, trying to push past the nostalgia detour.

"We slept for a time, most of the afternoon in fact. When we awoke, the two parts of the Trine were floating above us in the clearing. As if by instinct, without really understanding what I was doing or why, I grabbed the weapon out of the air. My lady friend did the same with the amulet. In some unfathomable way, we immediately sensed their powers, and that they were called the Trine, and that there existed a third part. We also had the impression that the two parts chose us to be their respective caretakers."

"Wait a minute, Joseph. Aunt Nipa said that my Grandma Isabella found the amulet while hiking in the mountains. So she's the lady friend you're talking about?"

An unreadable expression came over Joseph. He turned away.

"Son of a bitch! She is, isn't she? You and my grandmother hooked up." Brad didn't know how to feel about it. The whole notion was just too weird.

"We were only together a short time. Little more than a fling. Isabella soon went her own way. Later she married Bernard, your grandfather."

Brad wondered if other members of his family knew about

their long-ago relationship. If his mother had been aware of it, she'd never said anything, at least not to him. He'd never known his maternal grandfather. Bernard had died young, years before he was born. A familiar anger surfaced. It was that same old crap with his family, being kept in the dark about everything. A chill spread over him as he realized the only family he had left was Kristen.

Joseph went on. "After a time, Isabella and I started hiking back to my van. But only a short distance from the clearing, something drew us off the trail. To this day, I couldn't say what it was. A rustling of branches, an odd smell, a feeling…

"Whatever the impetus, we waded into denser woodlands. We hadn't gone very far when we came across a conical depression in the earth. It was a few yards wide and maybe five feet at its deepest. At the bottom of the depression were broken clumps of a darker stony material. It looked notably different from the surrounding rocks. We knew it had to be remnants of the famed Copernian Ridge meteorite.

"Some of the stones had unusual edges, angles that couldn't have occurred by accident. Isabella and I started fitting them together, like pieces of a three-dimensional jigsaw puzzle. We realized they must have formed the outer shell of some spherical object made up of interlocking triangular faces. Although pieces of the shell were missing, we estimated the object contained within the meteor would have measured five or six inches in diameter."

Brad held up his hand. "Whoa! We're talking space aliens here, some kind of hi-tech thing from outer space?"

"So it seemed. Part of the meteorite must have shattered upon impact. Whatever the missing object was, it certainly wasn't natural."

"Summersby," Brad blurted out, recalling what Felicity had told him about the Penn State professor and his grad student who'd come to Gracious to search for the meteorite. "He might have found this object and taken it with him."

Brad detailed what he'd learned from yesterday morning's conversation with Felicity at the library. Joseph's surprised expression indicated he was hearing it all for the first time.

"So according to the student, this Professor Summersby became secretive and paranoid. And then he resigned his position at the university and disappeared."

"Yeah. What do you think it means?"

"I'm not sure," Joseph said. "Maybe the object's uniqueness made him greedy, made him imagine great fame and fortune when he eventually revealed it to the world."

"Which obviously never happened. Do you think maybe he took the third part of the Trine?"

"I suppose it's possible."

"So, the three parts must have been contained inside the meteorite as well, right? Or, inside this spherical object that was inside the meteorite."

"Isabella and I suspected as much, despite the second part being larger than the object's diameter. Nevertheless, the meteorite, the missing object and the Trine are somehow all connected. Further investigations led us nowhere. Yet looking back at those events all these years later, I've always wondered whether the Trine actually drew us there that day. That it meant for Isabella and I to find the two parts."

"You make it sound like the Trine's consciously alive."

"Perhaps it is."

Brad revealed his mother's ethereal voice instructing him to find the third part. Joseph was surprised.

"Did she give you any specific clues as to how?"

He shook his head. "Maybe bringing the first two parts together reveals the location of the third part?"

"Isabella and I thought of that. Early on we tried all sorts of experiments meant to unite the two parts. But nothing ever came of them."

A fresh worry touched Brad. "Felicity and her friend were planning to head out early this morning to search for the meteorite. You think if they come upon it they'll be putting themselves in danger?"

"I wouldn't see how. Isabella and I returned to the site several times in those first weeks and searched the whole area for clues. After we broke up, I went back a number of times on my own." He shook his head. "I found nothing. And remember, there have been many searches for the meteorite since 1897. The isolated location makes it unlikely Felicity and her friend will discover it."

Brad wasn't so sure. Those lidar flyovers Felicity arranged could make the difference. "What about the meteorite fragments? Where are they now?"

"Isabella and I left them at the site. We were becoming aware of the powers we'd been endowed with, and felt it best to keep the entirety of our discovery secret. Returning to Gracious with those fragments would have sparked too many questions. The less that was known, the safer we'd be."

"And you kept the Trine a secret all this time."

Joseph nodded. "I believe Isabella did too, at least until your mother was old enough to understand."

They went silent for a time. Brad suddenly recalled what had happened yesterday outside the library after the basement collapse.

"Kristen approached this woman I knew from school. Sue Lynn Everett. She had her little boy with her, Brandon. Kristen tried to warn her about something bad that was going to happen. Now I'm thinking that she must have had another vision from the amulet."

"What was the warning?"

"Something about it not being safe for them to shelter in place. Kristen told Sue Lynn it's coming for Brandon's BFF. 'It' must have referred to Nowhere Man."

"Kristen knows this boy and his best friend?"

"I don't think so."

"Where does the family live?"

"Not sure. But Sue Lynn used to be all over social media. If I can get online, shouldn't be hard to track her down. But then what? Stake out their house, wait for Nowhere Man to show?"

An odd expression came over Joseph. Was it fear? Was he afraid of a confrontation with Nowhere Man?

"We should talk to this Sue Lynn," Joseph said. "See if there's some connection we don't know about. We also need to check with Little Moxie, learn where he heard the name Nowhere Man."

Brad felt invigorated. There were finally concrete actions they could take. It wasn't much but it was a start. But he realized there was another problem.

"The more I think about it, the more I figure I can't just go waltzing into Gracious. The cops will have a shitload of questions about what happened."

"And it's very possible they won't believe you, even without bringing the Trine into it."

"Not believe me or worse." His rep around town was more than enough to cast suspicion on him. He was sure he could ultimately convince Chief Wellstead of his innocence and prod her into searching for the real culprits. But such an effort also would eat up precious time.

"We'll have to be cautious, especially closer to town." Joseph rose from the log. "For starters, you might want to practice hiking more quietly."

Brad gave a grudging nod as they resumed the trek. But almost immediately, he shoved a branch from his path and allowed it to swing back with a noticeable crack. Joseph turned and glared.

But Brad had more important things on his mind than moving with ninja stealth. Despite Joseph's belief that Kristen was safe until dark, he couldn't stop worrying about her. What if the old man was wrong?

And then there was his anger, never far from the surface and now smoldering from a new source: being kept in the dark about Joseph having dated Grandma Isabella. Joseph claimed their relationship was short-term, little more than a fling, and that his grandmother and grandfather had later tied the knot. Still, it was easy to imagine things happening somewhat differently. Brad could have ended up with Joseph as his grandfather.

He suddenly recalled those childhood encounters with Joseph during shopping trips with Mom. Joseph had always gone out of his way to be extra nice, chatting with them and bearing gifts for Brad. Did he feel a duty to the family because of the Trine? Or was it something more than that?

Brad didn't like the direction of his thoughts. He forced concentration back on the wilderness obstructions. Better to dodge clumps of undergrowth and watch for whipping branches than entertain absurd scenarios.

TWENTY

Felicity formed her hands into a stirrup to allow Flick a foothold, then pushed her up the side of the short rock face. The petite woman scrabbled for a grip on the upper edge, sending a spray of loose stones and dirt down on Felicity. A pebble landed in her mouth.

"Almost there," Flick said, grunting from the exertion. "Just a bit more."

Felicity spit out the pebble and pushed harder.

"OK, I'm up!"

Flick's weight dissolved as she reached the top and crawled onto the clearing above. They were at Site B, having made the longer hike here after their first target was a bust. The circular depression in the earth at Site A, so promising in the lidar data as an impact crater, turned out to be a natural sinkhole. It probably was the result of subsidence in the region's karst topography. Felicity wondered if the same kind of soluble limestone had accounted for yesterday's collapse at the library.

Flick headed inward from the cliff and out of view. After a long silence, Felicity called up to her.

"Anything?"

"No meteorite, no signs of an impact. But definitely something unwholesome up here."

"What do you mean?"

In lieu of clarification, a rigged length of rope dangled over the cliff. Felicity took hold, planted her feet against the cliff and walked up its face. Flick helped her climb over the edge.

They stood in a tree-shrouded clearing that was devoid of undergrowth except for a few patchy spots of grass. Flick had knotted the rope into a bowline looped around the trunk of a white pine. About five yards in from the cliff was the beginning of a steep hill, and a few yards up it, the mouth of a small cave. A conglomeration of jagged rocks and pebbles were scattered at the base of the hill. The rubble appeared to have come from the front of the cave, as if some animal had clawed at the opening over the years, chipping away to enlarge it for easier entry. The diameter looked just sufficient for a person to crawl through.

The angle of the cave entrance and the dense overhanging foliage had made it undetectable from overhead. The lidar survey spotted the rubble and made an algorithmic assumption, warranting further investigation.

But neither the cave itself nor the fact it appeared deliberately enlarged had inspired Flick's "unwholesome" remark. It was the foul odor permeating the air.

"Nasty," Flick said.

"Like something died." Felicity had gone hunting with her father and Grandpa Harry as a teen, and more than once had come across dead animals well into the putrefaction stage. The odor was similar yet not precisely the same. Some other smell was mixed in, something sweeter and not so altogether unpleasant. Steeling herself, she took a hearty sniff, hoping to identify the secondary scent.

Big mistake. She doubled over, fighting nausea and dizziness. She clenched Flick's shoulder to maintain her balance.

"Don't take a deep breath," she warned. "That is one powerful stink."

Flick's curiosity overcame the caveat. She threw back her head and sniffed for all she was worth. Either her sense of smell was more limited or she was simply immune to such foul odors.

"Christmassy," Flick announced. "Underneath the death

stink, at any rate. Some kind of spice, I think. Reminds me of the holidays."

The clues connected the dots for Felicity. "It's cloves." Her mother was into decorative candles. Every December she added clove-scented ones to her traditional windowsill decorations. And there was something else familiar about the fragrance, something she'd read about recently. She couldn't place the memory.

Flick approached the cave. "What do you think, an animal den? A bear, maybe? It could have caught some smaller critter for lunch and left the carcass inside to rot."

"I don't think so." Felicity reached into a vest pocket for a surgical mask. She always carried one as a precaution since the coronavirus pandemic. She pinched the nose wire tightly, hoping to reduce the smell. It helped somewhat.

"The opening is too narrow for anything larger than a cub," she added. "And I think Mama Bear would discourage her cubs from exploring a cave that she couldn't fit into."

Flick removed her backpack and retrieved her flashlight. "I'm going to check it out."

"I don't think that's a good idea." The impact of the foul odor was sending admonitions straight into Felicity's brain. Something that smelled this bad probably should be avoided if possible. "Best to let it be. Besides, if we leave now, we'll have a good head start hiking to Site C."

Flick checked her watch. "We're actually a full hour ahead of schedule." She'd drawn up an hourly itinerary for the day, calculating how long to spend at each of the three target locations. "While we're here, might as well see what's what. It's just possible this cave was never entered in all of history."

"Something's been inside," Felicity reminded her, gesturing to the rubble at the base of the hill.

"But if it was just an animal enlarging its den, we could still be the first human explorers." She grinned. "That means we'd also get to name it. Does 'Felicity Caverns' sound too ostentatious?"

"Actually, too modest. How about 'Felicity *Grand* Caverns."

"That works."

Joking about it or not, Felicity still thought going inside was a bad idea. Flick had a tendency to push the envelope at times. It was actually one of the things Felicity liked about her, so she kept silent and followed her up the hill. Flick knelt and shined her flashlight into the darkness.

"It gets wider inside. I can see maybe fifteen feet or so. It appears to bend to the left and descend."

This close, the odor was even stronger. Felicity took out a handkerchief and tied it over the surgical mask. The combination worked – she could hardly smell anything. She also could barely breathe.

Flick ducked low, ready to crawl in.

"Wait," Felicity said. "You should be rigged."

"Not necessary."

"In case I have to pull you out."

Flick chuckled. "I love it when you worry about me."

"I'm not worried about you. I'm worried about me having to crawl into that stink-hole to rescue your ass."

Felicity took out her own rope, looped it through a pair of carabiners on Flick's belt and secured it with a knot. She played the rope out slowly as her partner squirmed through the tunnel.

"I'm at the bend," Flick called. "The drop isn't too bad. No more than a thirty-degree angle. And plenty wide enough. Not much chance of getting stuck."

"Good to hear," Felicity said, retrieving her own flashlight. She spotlighted Flick's kicking legs as they disappeared downward around the bend. All that remained visible was the glimmer of her retreating beam.

"It's opening up even more… a level gallery… a good twenty feet wide… at least twice that in length." Her voice was muffled but still discernible. "The stench is a lot stronger in here… Must be the source of… Wait! There's something at the far end."

Felicity tensed. "You OK?"

"So much for getting to name the cave. Someone's been here. There's an object and it looks manufactured. Some kind of complex polyhedron. Diameter of maybe five or six inches. Can only see about the upper third of it. The bottom portion appears to be embedded in a piece of rock... whoa!"

"What?"

"Holy shit! I think that rock might be our meteorite! The outer surface has definite signs of atmospheric smoothing. It matches some of those photos we looked at. Initial guess is that it's at least partly made of iron."

Felicity felt her excitement building as well. The element was commonly found in meteorites. "Can you carry it out?"

"Gonna snap some pictures first."

Felicity tried to contain herself. She had a load of questions. If it was the Copernian Ridge meteorite, had it landed nearby? If so, why were there no signs of an impact crater in the immediate area. How did it get inside the cave? Most importantly, what was the embedded object?

"OK, I photo-documented from multiple angles. I'm going to try picking it up..." There was a long pause. "No can do. I can move it but only a little. Would definitely need your help getting it out of here."

"Can you separate the object from the rock?"

"Not a chance, it's jammed in tight. I could use my rock hammer–"

"No no, don't do that. You might damage it. Removal should be done with fine tools in a lab environment."

"You're right."

Felicity had another idea. "I'm coming in. We can haul the whole thing out of there together. Maybe we can rig a rope around it or use some other method to increase leverage–"

"Wait!" Flick yelled. "Be quiet. I hear something moving around in here. I think it's right above me–"

A gurgling scream erupted from the cave. Before Felicity

could react, the rope was yanked violently into the cave. Had she been gripping it tightly, the polyester fibers might have burned her palms.

"Flick! Are you OK?"

No answer.

Felicity dropped to her belly and squeezed through the opening. She'd crawled half the distance to the downward bend when Flick responded. Her tone was frantic.

"Don't come in! I'm coming out!"

"Are you–"

"I'm coming out!"

Felicity started retreating. Her progress was slow. It wasn't easy crawling backward in such a confined space. She'd only gone halfway to entrance when Flick lunged up from the bend. She was moving fast, her features contorted by panic. Her flashlight was gone.

"Hurry up!" Flick screeched, quickly squirming to Felicity's position. "Move your ass!"

When Felicity couldn't wiggle backwards fast enough, Flick grabbed her shoulders and shoved.

"Stop pushing me, it's not helping. I'm going as fast as I can!"

"Go faster!"

Felicity's feet reached the opening. She scrambled out. Flick dove over the top of her and rolled down the hill.

"Get away from the entrance!" her partner screamed.

Felicity lunged from the cave, scrambled down the hill on hands and knees. Flick reached level ground first and roared to her feet, her eight-inch Bowie knife out of its belt holster. She'd bought the knife, carabiners and most of her other gear specifically for their search effort. The blade likely hadn't been unsheathed until now.

"What was it!" Felicity hissed. "What did you see?"

"Shh! Listen!"

Flick was waving the knife back and forth, her attention

riveted to the opening. Felicity heard nothing out of the ordinary, only the distant chirping of birds and a faint wind scouring the treetops.

"I don't think it followed me," Flick said. She was breathing hard, body still on high alert.

"What didn't follow you? What happened in there?"

"Something big… it came down from the ceiling, hit me from behind. I jerked forward… tripped… fell…"

Felicity laid a hand on Flick's back, comforting her. Her muscles were all tensed up. Shudders passed between her shoulder blades.

"You're safe now," Felicity soothed.

"I dropped my flashlight. Never got a clear look at it. Don't know what it was."

"A swarm of bats maybe?"

Flick considered it for a moment then wagged her head, as if eager to accept the idea. "Yeah, bats. That's what it must have been. A big-ass swarm of them. Must have dropped down on me all at once."

"They often hang from cave ceilings," Felicity said, continuing to gently rub her back. "You probably disturbed them." She gazed at the entrance. There was no sign of movement. "They're not likely to fly outside until after dark."

"Yeah, makes sense. Good to know." Flick slipped the knife back into the belt sheath but kept her fingers on the hilt and anxious eyes on the cave.

"How'd you find your way out without the light?" Felicity asked.

"It stayed on after I dropped it. Just enough illumination to reveal the entry shaft." She gave a nervous laugh. "No way I'm going back in there for a lost flashlight. The bats can have it."

Felicity frowned. "You've got something on your lower lip."
"What is it?"

"I don't know. Some kind of black goo."

Flick extended her tongue.

"No, don't lick it!"

"Too late. I think a bit of it got sprayed in my mouth right after that thing… those bats… came down on me. Pretty sure I accidentally swallowed some." Fear came over her. "Do bats spray people with poisonous venom?"

"Not that I know of. Worst case, a bite can carry rabies. You weren't bitten, were you?"

Flick checked by pawing at the exposed flesh on her arms, neck and face. She shook her head.

"You should be OK then." Felicity adopted an encouraging expression, not wishing to consider the consequences of her appraisal being wrong.

Flick gingerly licked the inside of her mouth with the tip of her tongue. She made a yucky expression and spit. "Kind of tastes like sour milk."

"Stop sampling it. Wash out your mouth."

"Yeah, sorry." Flick retrieved her water bottle, rinsed and spit three times. Felicity undid the handkerchief wrap from her own face and gently wiped the remaining residue from Flick's lip. It was syrupy but came off easily. She sniffed at the stained fabric.

"Smell," she urged, extending the hankie.

Flick's eyes widened as she inhaled. "Cloves. Didn't notice the scent until now. Must have had too much adrenaline pumping."

"That would do it. You said you snapped some pictures?"

"Oh, yeah." Flick took out her phone and accessed the first photo. The object protruding from the top of the rock was composed of identical triangular faces. They had an orange-brown coloration. Thin darker lines separated the triangular shapes.

"My god," Felicity whispered.

"Hell yes, my god! If this is the meteorite, and if that object was inside when it came down… We may have just discovered evidence of an extraterrestrial intelligence!"

Felicity felt her own excitement cascading. But she immediately tamped it down, forced a semblance of calm. As incredible as the discovery seemed, it was important to stay rational and view things from a scientific perspective. That meant bringing a healthy degree of skepticism to the table. For all they knew, it was some kind of nerdish hoax. Or an elaborate public sculpture by some secretive artist, like that metal monolith that showed up in the Utah desert years ago.

"We need to get back to Gracious," Felicity said. "Regroup, analyze our options. Put together a larger expedition. The meteorite impact site must be close to here. And we'll need to have some extra hands to help us move the rock out of the cave–"

"No! We need to keep all of this secret! If not, there's going to be a stampede out here."

"I'm aware of that. I'm only talking about recruiting a few people I know and trust." She frowned when she realized Brad was the first name that popped into her head.

Flick scrolled through the photos to the tightest view of the object, pinching the screen to zoom in. "Freaking incredible!"

Questions bubbled through Felicity, nearly overwhelming her attempt to remain rational. If the object indeed turned out to be real and was the product of some alien technology, what was its purpose? How did it get enclosed inside a meteorite and why? Had it been traveling through space for millions of years before randomly impacting the Earth? Or was it some kind of probe, deliberately sent?

"I took a course in computational geometry two summers ago," Flick said. "Wanted to bulk up on grad credits. We studied polyhedral shapes. Can't be positive until we're able to get online. But if I'm remembering correctly, and if the buried portion adheres to the sphericality suggested by the visible segment, then I'm thinking it might be a geometric shape known as a pentakis dodecahedron."

Felicity was thankful Flick had calmed down and was again

thinking logically. "Next time we come here, we might want to plan on arriving just before nightfall. There's a good chance the bats will be flying out after dark to forage for insects."

"Yeah, good idea," Flick said, continuing to cast wary glances at the cave mouth. "Wait for them to fly away."

TWENTY-ONE

Joseph delicately parted a cluster of branches and made his way past while continuing to reveal what he knew about Nowhere Man. "I don't believe he's aware I have the second part of the Trine. If he was, it's likely he'd have sent his minions after me as well."

Brad had fallen into a stealthy hiking rhythm by observing the old man's careful ways. Of course, the fact they were conversing tended to negate any advantages of a quiet passage through the forest.

"Good to know, Joseph. But that's not what I asked you."

"In answer to your question – do I have anything to eat? – I would point out there is food everywhere in the forest. You need only grab it as you pass."

"What food?"

"Berries. Edible grasses. Wood maggots."

"Yummy. I was thinking more along the lines of a Big Mac."

The old man stopped beside a shriveled pine and withdrew his water bottle. He took a swig and offered it to Brad.

"I said *hungry*, not thirsty."

Joseph continued on. Brad followed, trying to ignore his growling stomach. It seemed like they'd been hiking for hours. "Shouldn't we be getting close to Gracious by now?"

"We're taking a slight detour."

"A detour? Why? Major tree construction up ahead?"

Joseph ignored the quip and pointed to the rising terrain before them. "It should be just over this hill."

"What should be over the hill?"

"Recreational facilities."

"Can hardly await," Brad muttered.

They reached the top. A new and more pervasive sound was added to the background hum of forest birds and insects.

"Is that a waterfall?

Joseph retrieved an ancient piece of buckskin from his coat. Carefully unwrapping the soft leather, he revealed four slabs of beef jerky.

Brad glared. "You've had food all along? You've been holding out on me?"

"These are emergency rations."

"Starving isn't considered an emergency?"

"A person can easily survive a week or more without eating." Joseph paused. "But there is a limit to how long one can go without water or endure childish whining."

"Screw you." Brad snatched two pieces of jerky. Joseph rewrapped the rest and returned the buckskin to his coat.

"Not bad," Brad said, biting off half a slab and tooth-wrestling with the salty fare. "Make it yourself? Kill a cow with that fancy weapon? Cure the meat in some smokehouse out here in the boonies?"

"The clerk at the Seven-Eleven may have details on the snack's origin."

Brad resisted a comeback. Getting food in him was improving his mood. Slightly.

They descended the hill and came upon the "recreational facilities." A fast-flowing brook swirled around half-submerged rocks. The water was clear and shallow, maybe two or three feet at its deepest. The banks were layered in dark moss and fairly steep. Upstream a few yards was the waterfall, a two-stage cascade over a jumble of boulders, about eight feet high in total. The tree canopy shadowed most of the area. A cool breeze coming off the stream provided a welcome respite from the morning's increasing humidity.

Joseph halted at the edge of the bank just above the moss line and gazed down at the gurgling waters. When he showed no signs of emerging from that solemn stance, Brad grew impatient.

"OK Joseph, yes, it's very pretty. But now that you've had your detour, we should get back on track."

The old man removed his coat and threw it over the branch of a maple sapling. The weapon was revealed, fastened to a makeshift hook sewn into the liner. Brad stared at it, fascinated. But curiosity turned to a scowl as Joseph slipped off his pants, socks and boots. His exposed arms and legs were bony and discolored. White briefs and a sleeveless T-shirt appeared to date from the dawn of clothing.

"Seriously? You're going to take a bath?"

"Shower, actually." Cautiously descending the bank's slippery moss, he waded into the stream.

"Unbelievable."

Moving upstream, Joseph turned and backed into the waterfall. An enthusiastic whoop followed as the cold spray blasted him.

"Dammit, we're wasting time!"

"You have been complaining rather vigorously about my body odor."

"Yeah, well I put up with it this long, can do it a while longer. And in case you've forgotten, Kristen is the priority here."

"The water is invigorating. You should try it."

"Not in the mood."

"It might soothe your injuries and quell your anger."

"I don't want to be soothed and quelled!"

Joseph responded by turning away from Brad and planting himself on a large boulder at the waterfall's edge. Ducking his head under the cascade, he ran his fingers through his scraggly hair and scrubbed.

"Hey, want me to fetch you shampoo and conditioner?"

If Joseph heard the taunt over the waterfall's noise he didn't react. Brad was attempting to come up with another snarky remark when the triangle again snared his attention. Seeing that Joseph's back was still to him, he moved toward it.

Close up, the second part of the Trine didn't seem all that mysterious. The only enigma was how those overlapping ends held together. There weren't any hinges in the corners, at least none he could spot. But maybe they were too small and mounted on the insides of the sticks. Of course, hinges wouldn't explain how the triangle had turned into a fiery staff and later, a burning hole that allowed them to transit out of another dimension.

He extended a hand to touch it but hesitated. Joseph might get pissed off. Or something weird might happen, like the triangle transforming into a staff, which this time might decide to beat the crap out of him. Still, he'd handled his sister's amulet without any ill effects. And, like then, he wasn't trying to steal or possess the second part of the Trine. He was simply trying to satisfy his curiosity.

Screw it.

Joseph was still turned away. Brad gingerly closed his fist around one of the sticks.

The triangle fell apart.

The two sticks not in his grip fell and plopped in the mud on the edge of the stream bank. For a moment they were motionless. Then, as if possessing a life of their own, they started rolling toward the water.

"Shit!"

Brad lunged, trying to grab the runaway pair. But they were already beyond his reach. They splashed into the stream, floated away in the swift current.

His boots touched the slippery moss and his feet went out from under him. He landed on his back and slid down the bank feet first. He tried digging in with his heels but he was moving too fast, and the bottom of the bank was nearly vertical.

His boots finally caught hold of a protruding slab of rock.

But the sudden stop vaulted him upright, then into a forward somersault. He splashed into the stream headfirst.

Spluttering, he erupted from under the surface. He was soaked through and through. And the water...

"Jesus, it's freezing!"

Joseph turned from his perch at the cascade, regarded Brad with amusement. "Change your mind about bathing?"

Brad realized he was still clutching the single stick beneath the water. With growing panic, he scanned for the other two. But either they'd been swept downstream around the nearest bend or had become waterlogged and sank.

"Uh, listen Joseph, I kinda had a little accident. The thing is–"

"Lift the stick you're still holding out of the stream. Extend it in front of you."

Joseph didn't sound pissed, a good sign. Brad followed his instructions.

"Now raise your arm toward the sky. Keep looking at the stick."

He felt silly but did it anyway.

"The power of the Trine is ultimately the power of your beliefs. Nothing more, nothing less. Touch its essence. Let it wash over you."

Brad tried. But he didn't feel any essence. All he felt washing over him was the chilly water, which was causing his drenched clothes to stick in uncomfortable places.

"Imagine the second part of the Trine as a living entity with whom you're conducting a trade. You are giving it something, your belief. In exchange, it is giving you its power."

The directives sounded like a bunch of New Age nonsense. "Got news for you, pal. Whatever you think is supposed to be happening ain't."

"You must allow yourself to feel it. Feel its vitality, its lifeblood."

"The only thing I feel is goddamned ridiculous!"

Joseph sighed. "You are not entirely to blame for your cynical attitude. It seems to be an outgrowth of the pessimism that plagues so many of your generation."

"Hey, don't give me that generation-gap crap. You old fuckers left us a shitty world to deal with."

"The world is, and always will be, what you make of it."

"Gee, get that from the back of a cereal box?"

Anger flashed on Joseph's face. "Do you want to save your sister or not?"

"Of course I do."

"Then start by concentrating on that, believing in it."

Brad pictured Kristen in his mind. Even if those men hadn't physically hurt her, they could be trying to make her afraid or somehow trick her into surrendering the amulet. It was terrifying just thinking about what might be happening to her, and he'd been deliberately avoiding such dark thoughts. Yet beneath his own fears and ever-present anger he sensed a more fundamental emotion. Although he hadn't exactly been the supportive brother over the years, he cared deeply about Kristen.

The stick in his hand seemed to twitch. At first he thought it was a muscle spasm. But it happened again, then a third time.

"Good," Joseph said, striding out from under the waterfall and smoothing back his wet hair. "As you awaken so does the Trine."

Brad felt encouraged. "OK, now what?"

"What do you want to happen?"

"I want to find the two sticks that floated away."

"Then imagine the second part reforming in your hand. Plant a picture in your head of it happening."

It was easier to follow Joseph's suggestion without looking. He closed his eyes. For a moment nothing happened. Then the stick jerked violently, as if something was trying to yank it from his grip. He heard erratic splashing, distinct from the swirling eddies from submerged rocks. For a moment he thought the sound was due to Joseph approaching. But then he realized it came from downstream, the opposite direction.

Brad opened his eyes. The two missing sticks were making their way toward him, working against the current, rotating on their axes and paddling the surface as if gripped by invisible hands. When they closed to within a few yards they leaped out of the water. Airborne and spinning like helicopter blades, they tumbled toward the stick in his hand.

With an explosive crack, the three sticks snapped together. Their sudden realignment into a triangle sent quivers radiating through his hand, then up his arm and out across his chest. For a moment, the second part of the Trine assumed a faint reddish glow. As the color faded, the quivering sensation did as well. But left in its wake was a kind of crackling energy. The energy seemed to flow through him, as strangely gratifying as it was indescribable.

"Awesome," he whispered. "I feel it."

Once again, his mother's voice reverberated through him.

Find the third part.

"How do I do that?" he wondered, directing his words at the surrounding trees.

"How *did* you do that," Joseph corrected, misunderstanding the focus of his question.

The energy faded, leaving Brad with a sense of accomplishment. He still wasn't sure how he'd done what he'd done, not exactly. The rejoining of the sticks had something to do with his concern for Kristen. Yet there remained a gulf between the act itself and his understanding of it. Still, no denying the result. A simple conviction to bring the sticks together had brought a strange capability within his grasp.

TWENTY-TWO

Joseph was pleased at Brad's accomplishment, but kept his expression neutral. This was a delicate moment. Show too much encouragement and Brad's ego might overwhelm his achievement, ultimately helping no one. Better to display a mask of indifference, let things develop further before recognizing the possibility that his grandson might be a suitable heir to the second part of the Trine. It also wouldn't do any good to reveal that the sticks breaking apart had been Joseph's doing, a test to gauge Brad's suitability.

Joseph made his way up the bank and retrieved his clothes from the sapling. Brad clambered out of the water too, his gaze fixated on the clutched triangle. A covetous tremor infected his words.

"That was incredible! It's like I could feel its power running through me."

Joseph began dressing.

"You can make it do anything, can't you?"

"Within reason."

In truth, Joseph didn't know the extent of its powers, or even what other configurations it was capable of being transformed into. He'd used its default triangular shape to enter the eidolon, only transforming it into a staff when requiring a weapon. And considering he'd possessed the second part for close to six decades, using it for fights occurred rarely.

Besides wading into the venting to save Brad, the last time he'd willed it into a staff was when confronting his landlady's vile stalker of an ex. In that instance and a few similar situations over the years, he'd made sure his adversary was drunk, high or so marginalized that no one would believe a tale about being assaulted by an unnatural weapon. If word of the second part's existence became public, it would bring only endless trouble.

He finished dressing and extended his palm to Brad. "May I have it back, please?"

There was a moment's hesitation, not unexpected. Joseph envisioned Brad's thoughts. With such a weapon he could find Kristen and destroy those who'd taken her.

"Of course you can have it back. After all, it was given to you." His smile looked forced.

"It seems to lack the first part's defensive capability, the way the amulet protects its rightful bearer from thievery. Therefore, the bearer of the second part must be forever wary. They must remain cognizant of their own darkest impulses and never allow themselves to be consumed by lust for its power." He uttered the words to gauge their impact. But Brad already had turned away.

Donning his coat, he sequestered the weapon inside and continued the trek, heading downstream parallel to the bank. Brad followed a few paces behind. His stealth had improved, Joseph was pleased to note. As a bonus, there were no further complaints, about his wet clothing or whatever.

They hiked another mile, arriving at a spot where the brook narrowed and the banks grew less steep. Joseph motioned it was the place to cross. In tandem they leaped easily to the other side. Leaving the stream behind, they came upon a trail that wound its way up a gentle hill. The density of the forest dwindled as they ascended, the trees growing farther apart, the clumped undergrowth giving way to open areas. Big patches of sky became visible through the thinning canopy.

They reached the top of the hill, a transitory point between the wilderness behind them and the beginnings of civilization spread out below. They were on the far western outskirts of Gracious.

"We should be extra cautious from here on out to make sure no one spots you," Joseph said.

"Yeah," Brad muttered, glaring at him. "Was there a reason you brought me this way?"

"I'm sorry. I forgot this is where you used to live."

Joseph hadn't forgotten. He'd guided them here deliberately. It was another test of sorts, this one meant to prompt Brad into recalling the unpleasantness of his younger years. Forcing him to acknowledge his past might serve to awaken the more honest and enduring self that Joseph hoped existed beneath intemperate layers of anger and pain. Such acknowledgment would go a long way toward showing him that Brad indeed was the worthy heir.

TWENTY-THREE

The two of them remained hidden from view, just inside the tree line. Downhill, maybe a hundred yards from their position, was the rundown park Brad had frequented as a child. It wasn't much: a tot lot, a pair of swing sets for older kids and an unenclosed basketball court. The latter had so many areas of eroded asphalt that it was impossible to play anything approaching a skilled game. Two preteen boys were dodging the dips and holes anyway, shooting hoops. Otherwise, the area was deserted.

Brad gazed across the park to Laurel Street, which terminated in a cul-de-sac. He was surprised to realize something was missing: the home where he'd been raised.

"Where are the cottages?" Five of them used to ring the cul-de-sac. Technically they were small houses, but everyone always referred to them as cottages. Brad had lived in the middle one.

"They were falling apart," Joseph said. "Attracting vagrants and wildlife. The township declared them unfit for habitation. The few remaining residents were relocated and the structures demolished."

"Good riddance."

The words emerged caked in bitterness. Admittedly, Brad still retained some good memories of growing up here. Still, every one of those recollections was now tainted. He recalled how hopeful he'd been that a cold alcoholic father was finally attempting to connect with a lonely son through those playful wrestling matches. But after realizing he'd merely been the target of a predator grooming his victim for more insidious abuse, those hopes had departed. It had made him wary of all long-term relationships. He could see a direct line from his father's exploitation to his wedding day escape.

That betrayal had fucked up his life, fucked up his whole family. He thought about his mother, about what a truly wonderful and caring person she'd been. How had she ended up marrying such an asshole? Hadn't the amulet somehow warned her what he was really like beneath that layer of surface charm?

Then he remembered. The amulet hadn't come into Mom's possession until years after their marriage. It hadn't been passed to her until Grandma Isabella's death in 2003.

A disturbing notion occurred. Had Mom been able to sense shoo spots the same way Kristen did? When she'd gotten into the car with his father on that fateful night, had she somehow known that both of them were going to die in a suicidal crash?

He grimaced. *It's in the past, don't think about it. Stay focused on doing what needs to be done to save Kristen.*

Joseph was watching him curiously. Brad forced a shrug. "Just going down memory lane, thinking about when I lived here. And yeah, I know, a complete waste of time."

"Not always."

Brad changed the subject. "I've been wondering about some stuff. What if those pricks threaten to hurt someone Kristen cares about in order to convince her to give up the amulet? Would that still be considered handing it over by her own free will?"

"A good question. I don't know the answer. From what you've told me about last night though, I suspect their original intent was to kidnap you as well. Possibly for just that reason."

Brad had considered that as well. The fire and his close escape from it may have saved him from a more agonizing destiny, being tortured in front of his sister.

There was no upside to dwelling on such things. "OK, moving on. If they do try taking the amulet from Kristen, they get bombarded with bad memories, right?"

Joseph nodded.

"But what if they just ignore what's happening in their heads? What if they somehow repress all their painful memories. Just push on through the hurt and take the amulet from her?"

"I'm told such a scenario is unlikely."

"You're *told?* Told by whom?"

Joseph hesitated. Brad had the feeling he'd made an unintended revelation.

"C'mon, Joseph, out with it. Is there a person in the eidolon you actually talk to?"

"There is. Although calling it a person stretches the definition of the word. More like an entity."

"This entity have a name?"

"Silso Orjos Sohn."

"Sounds like a drug for hemorrhoids."

"SOS for short."

"Male or female?"

"Both. Or neither. Its gender is unclear. In addition, SOS has three heads."

"Seriously?"

Joseph shrugged. "The great dream forest is a place of abstractions, of symbols."

"Maybe so, but that is still massively freaky."

"I suppose over the years I've become acclimated to its strangeness."

"Can't you go back into the eidolon and just ask this SOS for help in finding Kristen?"

"SOS doesn't function like that. Only two of the heads, Silso and Orjos, ever speak to me. And they generally avoid direct assistance."

"Why?"

Another shrug. "I've entertained the possibility that it's

because they want me to do the work, figure things out on my own."

"So SOS just gives you hints and clues."

"Something like that."

Brad returned to his original line of questioning.

"What if those men somehow did manage to get the amulet from Kristen against her will? For the sake of argument, what would happen then?"

Joseph turned his gaze skyward. He seemed to study a cluster of puffy cumulus clouds. "I don't know. Isabella and I came to suspect that in the event of such circumstances, the first part of the Trine might simply disappear, literally vanish into thin air. Based on the seemingly magical way the two parts originally came to us, it seems a reasonable assumption. Perhaps it would then reappear elsewhere and seek out someone new to wield it."

"Which Nowhere Man wouldn't want to risk happening."

Joseph nodded and withdrew the buckskin from under his coat, offering up the rest of the beef jerky. "This should hold you over until I return."

Brad took one of the two remaining slabs. Joseph pointed to the cul-de-sac where the cottages had stood. "Make your way over to the woods behind Laurel Street. I'll pick you up over there."

"What if your landlady's away again or she doesn't want to lend you her SUV and phone?"

"I'll improvise."

Joseph started making his way down the hill toward the park.

"Maybe I should tag along. I could keep out of sight."

Brad's proposal was met with a wry expression.

"OK, dumb idea. It's just that I'm not too crazy about hanging around out here."

"You'll be fine."

"Yeah, I'll be fine." *I'll just sit under a tree behind where my house once stood and bathe in glorious memories.*

TWENTY-FOUR

Felicity was increasingly concerned about Flick's anxiety. Whatever was bothering her had escalated during the hike back from the cave to where they'd left the Jeep at the edge of the road. Flick had insisted on stopping every few minutes to rest, yet the breaks didn't seem the result of tiredness or physical infirmity. She would sit cross-legged on the ground, staring off into space, not talking, absorbed in some private world she declined to share. The return trek already had taken them three times longer than their hike out to Site B.

At first, Felicity chalked it up to Flick still being freaked out by what had happened at the cave. But on each occasion, after Felicity's insistent prompting got them moving again, Flick would look back in the direction they'd come. Felicity eventually concluded those glances weren't based on some fear they were being followed. The real reason was creepier.

Flick didn't *want* to leave. It was as if some mysterious force was drawing her attention back there, back to the cave. Attempts to get her to talk about it were met by shrugs and silence.

They'd had enough excitement for one day. Felicity insisted they cancel the trek to Site C, which would be added to next weekend's agenda. Despite the momentous discovery at Site B of the meteorite and its intriguing geometric object, solid reasons remained for sticking to their original checklist. For one thing, they still hadn't found where the meteorite had landed. It could be at one of the other sites pegged by the lidar.

They finally reached the Jeep. Flick handed Felicity the key fob.

"I don't feel like driving."

"Sure, no problem." Felicity was glad for the offer. In her fiancée's distracted condition, she shouldn't be behind the wheel.

They threw their backpacks in the cargo area. But Flick didn't hop into the passenger seat. She just stood there, staring back at the spot they'd emerged from the trees with a kind of pensive yearning.

"Hey, you're going to be OK." Felicity tried bolstering the soothing words with a gentle back rub. Flick jerked away as if touched by a hot iron.

"Sorry," Flick muttered, avoiding eye contact. "I'm a little… off."

"Hey, don't sweat it. We just need to get away from here. Get back to town, get ourselves cleaned up. Have a glass of wine and relax."

Felicity didn't mention she'd come up with a different plan. She intended driving them straight to Gracious Health at the eastern edge of town. It was a well-furnished med center, less than a full-blown hospital but more than a rural clinic. Reticence over informing Flick of her decision was based on what she suspected would be strong objections. Flick had a mild phobia of doctors anyway and avoided them unless absolutely necessary. That, coupled with her present condition…

In any event, Felicity would wait until they were pulling into the med center's parking lot to deal with any protestations.

Her handkerchief contained a sample of the syrupy black goo Flick believed she'd swallowed. By now Felicity had little doubt it was toxic, some kind of poison or venom from the bats that likely was inducing bizarre neurological effects. Hopefully, the sample was intact enough for a lab to analyze and come up with an antidote.

"We really should get going," Felicity urged, trying to draw Flick out of her latest daze.

"I suppose so." Her tone didn't sound convincing but she finally climbed into the Jeep. Felicity started the engine and quickly pulled out, not wanting to give her any opportunities to reconsider.

They'd gone less than a mile when Flick jerked her head toward the passenger-side window, as if something in the forest had caught her attention. She grabbed hold of the dash, a veritable death grip.

"Stop!"

"Why?"

"Just stop! Right here, right now."

Felicity slowed to a crawl but didn't pull over. "First tell me what's going on."

Flick took a long moment to respond. Felicity had the feeling she was trying to come up with a believable excuse.

"I need to throw up."

Felicity still hesitated. Flick became agitated, pounded her fists on the dash.

"Stop the goddamn car!"

Felicity pulled over. They were on a slight downhill section of the two-lane road, and it lacked much of a shoulder between the asphalt and an imposing tangle of woodlands. An approaching vehicle cresting the hill behind them at speed hopefully would spot the Jeep in time to swerve or brake.

Flick hopped out. She turned away and bent over. Felicity couldn't tell if she was vomiting, suffering the dry heaves or just pretending to be ill. She finally straightened and faced the Jeep. Her eyes were pinched, her cheeks pale.

"You should drink some water," Felicity advised, checking her phone, hoping they somehow were passing through a region with coverage. This latest incident had increased her unease to the point where she felt Flick might require emergency care. Summoning and rendezvousing with an ambulance seemed a better option than driving to the med center. It ultimately might not save them any time, but the

EMTs would be able to check her vitals and maybe offer some sort of immediate treatment.

The idea was a nonstarter. Her phone still had no bars.

"My water bottle's in my backpack," Flick said.

Felicity pressed the button on the dash, popping the rear hatch. Flick scooped out her backpack. But instead of opening it to retrieve the bottle, she slung the pack across her shoulder and dashed off into the woods.

"What the...!"

Felicity leaped out of the Jeep, locked it with the key fob and took off after her. The trees were pinched tightly together and the undergrowth thick. She could only catch sporadic glimpses of Flick up ahead. Her partner was running with frantic abandon, as if her life depended on it.

"What are you doing?" Felicity hollered. "Come back!"

No response.

"Flick, listen to me, please! I think you're sick. That stuff that got in your mouth, it must be toxic in some way. You've been poisoned. We need to get back to Gracious so you can be treated."

The trees abruptly parted. Felicity intersected a dirt path, just wide enough for a vehicle. Foliage overhanging it from both sides suggested it was an old fire lane, rarely if ever used.

Flick had turned left onto the lane and was a good thirty yards ahead. Moments later she disappeared around a sharp bend. By the time Felicity reached the spot there was no sign of her.

"Flick! Where are you? Talk to me!"

She jogged along the lane, scanning the enveloping woods on both sides, periodically calling out. She'd proceeded a ways when the crackling of dry branches being pushed aside emanated from the trees to her right. Felicity spun toward the noise with a sense of relief but was startled to realize it wasn't Flick.

Two grizzled old men stepped out onto the lane. They were garbed in raggedy jeans. Their plaid shirts were torn and faded, the fabric stained beyond salvation. Faces were swamped by thick unkempt beards. Their matching ginger hair, shoulder-length and untamed, suggested they were blood relatives. The taller one held an ancient, double-barreled shotgun. Thankfully, it remained pointed at the ground.

A cluster of red flags waved in Felicity's head. There was a wildness about the men that called for extreme caution. She forced herself to remain calm and offered a friendly smile.

"Hi. You guys surprised me. I'm looking for a friend of mine."

"Private property," the one with the shotgun said, his tone icy and off-putting.

"Sorry, just want to find my friend."

"No friends here. Get lost."

"I can't, not until I find her. The thing is, I believe she swallowed poison. She really needs help."

"It's not poison."

It was Flick's voice, emanating from the woods behind the men. Felicity sighed with relief as her partner emerged onto the lane.

"Oh my god, you had me so worried." She took a step forward but the men moved to block her path. The shorter one swept aside his hanging shirttail, revealing a belt-holstered revolver. His companion raised the shotgun. It was now aimed at Felicity's kneecaps.

"You need to leave," Flick said. Her voice was distant, her demeanor that of a stranger. She squeezed herself between the men as if they were her bodyguards. Felicity was too stunned to move.

"Now, bitch!" the taller man yelled. Spittle sprayed from his mouth as he raised the shotgun to Felicity's belly. The shorter one drew his revolver, waved it erratically in her direction.

"OK, OK! I'm going." She extended her open palms, a gesture of surrender, and backed away slowly. She fought an urge to turn and run, worried the action might give the men an excuse to shoot her in the back. Better to keep facing them with hands up. She recalled the advice her father gave to his bank employees in the event of an armed holdup. *Don't stare directly at the robber. Don't make any sudden moves. Keep your hands in sight at all times.*

Felicity followed those edicts while backing up, until she was safely around the bend. Once they were out of view, she leaned over, gripped her knees and squeezed, preventing her body from doing what it wanted to do: quaking in fear from a close escape from a life-threatening situation. Several slow deep breaths calmed her down.

She straightened, debating her next move. Back to the Jeep, of course, but after that, what? Drive until she got within range of a cell tower, then call for help?

The men had aimed guns at her, made a direct threat. That should be more than enough to involve the police. She was certain they'd been lying about trespassing on private property. The entire tract encompassing Copernian Ridge was owned by the state. There was zero chance it had been subdivided and acreage sold off to private parties.

Trying her best not to worry about Flick and whatever was prompting her insane behavior, Felicity hustled back to the spot where she'd encountered the lane. As she reentered the woods, something about the two men caused her to recall the week leading up to her aborted wedding.

The memory popped into her head. She knew who they were. The Swanteri brothers.

Farmers Hiram and Amos Swanteri had abruptly abandoned their homestead, which had been in their family for five generations. Rumor had it the bachelors had taken up feral lifestyles. Occasional witnesses claimed to have spotted them in the wilderness around Copernian Ridge. Their radical metamorphosis had captivated Gracious, even attracting regional coverage by TV and news outlets, as well as assorted blogs fixated on outlandish happenings. Local interest had peaked after less than a week, however. The Swanteri brothers' story had been superseded by a more sensational abandonment that Sunday, when Brad left Felicity standing alone at the altar.

Hiram was the elder brother, the one with the shotgun. The fact she now knew their names only brought more questions. What had caused Flick to join up with such unhinged characters? It appeared she knew them, but how could that be possible? And even if she'd somehow encountered them previously, how could she have known they were close by? Yet her sudden demand that Felicity pull over seemed to indicate she'd been expecting a rendezvous at that spot.

No answers were apparent. Felicity was certain of one thing, however. Flick needed help, and fast. Out in these woods, in the company of two men who were just as whacked out as she was... the odds would rapidly diminish for a positive outcome. And she had a gut feeling that the longer Flick's poisoning was allowed to go untreated, the worse it would become.

She reached the road and got into the Jeep. Based on the original drive to Site B, she guessed it would be nearly half an hour before she got within range of a cell tower and could call for help. Then she'd have to convince the police it truly was an emergency, and that a threat had been made on her life.

She knew Robin Wellstead through her father. If she could reach the chief directly, things might be expedited. But more than likely Felicity's call would be processed by one of her officers. Most of them were male and, even in this day and age, afflicted with a residue of sexism, especially toward the LGBTQ community. She could already imagine a lengthy conversation trying to persuade some macho male cop how dire the situation was, that it wasn't just a squabble between a couple of lesbians blown out of proportion.

And even if and when she did finally make her case, it might be another hour or more by the time help was dispatched and arrived here. Who knew where Flick and the Swanteris might have gone by then? Unless a full-blown search party was sent – highly unlikely – it could take forever to track her down in the vast expanse of these mountains.

Felicity sat behind the wheel, mulling over other options. She could call Brad. He'd certainly assist with a search. Her parents were too far away to help, out of the country on vacation. Grandpa Harry was around, and he might be able to recruit a bunch of his friends. If he convinced enough people, an effective hunt could be launched.

She grimaced, rapidly losing faith in the whole idea. It left her with the same problem as calling the police. Any kind of search, whether with one or two cops or a small army of family and friends, would take precious time to organize. Not to mention they'd be looking for a pair of armed men who might have no qualms about gunning them down at first sight.

Another option entered awareness. Earlier in the week, Felicity had revealed their exploration plans to Grandpa Harry. He was a longtime hunter and the most wilderness savvy of anyone in her family, and he'd insisted she take sensible precautions.

"There are black bears up on that ridge," he'd warned. "Maybe other kinds of predators too."

She hadn't asked what other kinds he was referring to, but something in his voice cued her that he just might be talking about the human variety. Had he known more than he was letting on about the Swanteri brothers?

Her initial response to his warning had been to playfully call him a worrywart. But he'd persisted and eventually convinced her that what he was proposing made sense.

Felicity reached a decision. Moving the Jeep a bit farther down the hill to where the shoulder was wider and it was completely off the road, she got out and retrieved her backpack from the cargo area. Tucked away at the bottom under packets of survival rations, was the handgun Grandpa Harry had loaned her. Flick was a gun-control advocate, although not hardcore about it. Still, that's why Felicity hadn't mentioned she was bringing along a weapon.

She drew the 9 mm Beretta from its worn leather holster, made sure the safety switch was on and snapped in one of the two fifteen-round magazines he'd supplied. She was no stranger to firearms in general or this gun in particular. Grandpa Harry had often taken her hunting as a teen and taught her to shoot with various firearms, including the Beretta.

She looped the holster through her belt so the gun hung on her right, easy to draw with her shooting hand. Her hunting knife was sheathed on her left hip. Donning the backpack, she locked the Jeep, took three steps toward the woods and halted.

What am I doing? This is nuts.

She was about to pursue two armed whack jobs, by herself, in isolated terrain, and with no way to call for assistance should things go bad – which they very likely could. Not only did she have to track down Flick and the men, she had to figure out a way of convincing her reluctant partner to come to her senses and accompany Felicity to the med center. Calling the cops or enlisting family and friends might not be the best options, but they were certainly a hell of a lot more sensible than what she was about to attempt.

Yet time was running out for Flick, of that Felicity was sure. Something bad was going to happen to her, something even worse than what had occurred already.

I feel you feel I.

The mantra reinvigorated her. She would find Flick. She would save her. It didn't matter how challenging and dangerous the task was, it had to be done. It was the only way.

TWENTY-FIVE

Brad sensed hours had gone by since Joseph's departure. Finally, he saw a shabby blue Nissan cruising up Laurel Street. He slipped from the bushes where he'd been hiding and waited impatiently for the SUV to curl around the cul-de-sac, which it did with agonizing slowness. Age or infrequency behind the wheel seemed to have rendered Joseph an excessively cautious driver.

Brad scampered across the gravel lot to the curb, aware he was crossing sacred ground. He'd spent his first fourteen years in the home that once had stood on the very spot where he tread. While waiting for the ride, his thoughts inevitably had drifted into nostalgia mode.

Yet, surprisingly, the miseries heaped upon the family by his father didn't dominate his reminiscing. Plenty of bad things had happened in that cottage but plenty of good ones as well. Foremost among them, Kristen had been born.

One memory in particular had stood out. She'd been about six months old, and he'd been babysitting while their parents were away for the evening. He'd scooped her from her crib, laid her on her back on that threadbare excuse for a rug in front of the TV and watched with fascination as those tiny arms and legs wiggled ferociously in an attempt to roll over onto her stomach. Her triumphant smile when she finally succeeded seemed to radiate from one end of the room to the other.

"Good girl!" he'd exclaimed, lifting her above his head and spinning them round and round. Her smile had brightened further, finally dissolving into a contagious round of giggles.

"Go back there," Joseph instructed, nodding toward the rear seat.

"I can hunker down up front," he argued.

"Safer in the back. More room for you to stretch out too."

"Any word on Kristen?"

"Nothing on her whereabouts."

Brad opened the rear door and squirmed across the seat, keeping below the window line. Discarded food wrappers and other trash squished beneath him. At least his wet clothing had mostly dried during the wait. Nevertheless, he felt grungy and in need of a change.

"What took you so long?" he demanded.

"I fished around for news. The fire department finished going through the wreckage for bodies. It's been officially announced the two of you are missing. The police issued a statewide amber alert for Kristen." He paused. "There's been talk that you were somehow responsible for starting the fire, and that you kidnapped your own sister."

"That is goddamn ridiculous!"

"Of course it is. But apparently you were seen outside the library yesterday morning being abusive toward her and shoving her into your truck. And last night at Moxie's, a number of patrons witnessed you getting into a fight with your uncle."

"Jesus Christ! It wasn't a fight! It was just a few words over something he did. And with Kristen at the library, yeah, I might have lost it for a second or two. But I didn't hurt her, not really. And later I apologized. Everything was cool between us and..."

He trailed off. The accusations were total bullshit. But given his less-than-stellar reputation around town, he could see how people might consider him the prime suspect. There was nothing to be gained by dwelling on it. Nevertheless, it was more vital than ever that he stay out of sight.

"There's more," Joseph said. "Something else happened last

night, apparently around the same time as the attack on your home. I ran into an EMS worker, a man I've known since he was a youngster. I helped his brother out of a jam once. He told me his ambulance was called out to help a little boy traumatized by a strange theft. Something crashed right through the screened window of his third-story bedroom and–"

"Sue Lynn's son, Brandon." There was no doubt in Brad's mind. Kristen's warning had been accurate, same as her earlier premonitions regarding the shoo spots. "It was Nowhere Man, wasn't it."

"Undoubtedly. That probably explains why he didn't participate in the attack on your house. The theft of the boy's robot somehow must be equally important to his plans."

"A robot? That's Brandon's BFF?"

"Apparently the boy has serious developmental issues. His parents bought the robot for him in order to foster improved emotional and cognitive skills. The boy wasn't harmed physically although he received quite the fright. He was so devastated by the loss of what he perceives as his best friend that he had to be sedated."

Brad gave a thoughtful nod, then remembered Joseph couldn't see the gesture. He tried not to imagine the terror such a young child must have experienced encountering such a creature. At least when Kristen had first seen Nowhere Man, she'd been older and better able to process her fright. And her rock-solid belief in the amulet was always there to help her through times of crisis. He could only hope its presence was sustaining her now.

"But why snatch a four year-old's robot toy?" he wondered.

"That's the $64,000 question, isn't it. For now, the police and the parents have agreed to keep the incident out of the public eye. Apparently, the robot is far more than a simple toy. The father is some kind of computer researcher. The robot is an expensive, highly advanced prototype with customizable features."

Joseph put the old Nissan in gear and pulled out. Brad

sensed them circling the rest of the cul-de-sac and heading back down Laurel Street.

Sue Lynn presumably would have revealed to the police Kristen's warning outside the library. Considering all the other signs pointing to Brad as the villain, he'd probably be considered a suspect in the robot theft as well.

Murder. Arson. Kidnapping. From the standpoint of the authorities, he could very well be public enemy number one.

"Did you get that phone from your landlady?"

Joseph extended an older model iPhone over the seat back along with a caveat. "Don't try to contact anyone."

"Yeah yeah, got it." Still, Brad was tempted to text Felicity, warn her that she might be putting herself in danger searching for the meteorite. But even if she was within cell phone range, a text likely would prompt additional questions from her. Worse, Felicity might feel compelled to involve the cops even if he warned against it.

For the time being he gave up on the idea. Felicity was on her own. He settled for checking news sites and local blogs for any updates on the fire. But there was nothing online beyond what Joseph already had told him.

"So what next?"

"Little Moxie's house," Joseph said. "I need to learn where he first heard the name Nowhere Man."

"Why not just call him?"

"We haven't always seen eye to eye. I believe he might be more amenable in person."

Brad scrunched further down on the back seat as the SUV reached an intersection and turned onto Eberhausen Avenue. From his low perspective, he could just make out the uppermost floor of row homes on the south side of the block. He still couldn't fathom the importance of Joseph's puzzlement over how someone first heard the name or how it possibly could help them rescue Kristen. But for the moment, he couldn't think of any logical alternatives.

A feeling of despondency set in. It was already early afternoon and they were no closer to finding his sister.

Joseph pulled up to a stop sign. He chucked a white paper bag into the back seat. "You need to keep your strength up."

It was takeout from the Apex Eatery. The bag held a tuna sandwich, tortilla chips and a 16-ounce plastic bottle of Clover Farms Icy Tea.

He muttered thanks. The beef jerky had helped, but he remained monumentally hungry. Devouring the new food and guzzling the beverage provided much needed nourishment. But nothing more, nothing that might lift his hopes.

TWENTY-SIX

Little Moxie and his wife lived in a spacious old rancher adjacent to that newer subdivision where the governmental offices were located. Joseph eased the SUV to a halt at the end of their long driveway.

"Garage doors are up but his Escalade's gone," Joseph announced. "His wife's car isn't here either."

Brad, supine on the back seat, hadn't been expecting much from the visit. But he experienced disappointment anyway. It already seemed like a wasted effort, bringing them no closer to finding Kristen. He started to rise.

"No, stay down. We're close to the township complex."

"How close?"

"You can see police headquarters from Little Moxie's side porch."

"Wonderful. So why are we still here?"

"Big Moxie might be around and know his son's whereabouts. He lives with them now."

"Since when?" The last Brad had heard, Big Moxie had a place on Lakamoxin Street in Gracious, within walking distance of the Bar & Grill.

"He had a hunting accident last December. Got shot. In a wheelchair, permanently from what I hear. Had to sell his own place and move in with the kid."

"I still say this is a waste of–"

"Shh," Joseph urged. "He just came out the front door. He's motoring down the porch ramp, coming our way."

Joseph got out of the vehicle. The SUV's windows were lowered, and the two men were close enough for Brad to eavesdrop.

"Joseph LeFevre, you old Creole buttwipe. What brings your sorry ass out here?"

Wheelchair-bound or not, Big Moxie's gravelly tone and insult-laden phrasing hadn't changed. Before he'd retired from a long career bartending, Brad recalled that there were few individuals, organizations or institutions he wouldn't trash. Often to their faces, and in the most colorfully insensitive language imaginable, a trait that obviously had been passed on to Little Moxie. Uncle Zack used to say the tavern portion of the Bar & Grill was where you went for a cold beer and a hot insult.

"I need to talk to Little M," Joseph said. "Expecting him back soon?"

"Not till tonight. Drove over to Wilkes-Barre, supposedly to set up a deal with a new beer distributor. But it's just an excuse to blow his wad at the casino."

"Got a phone number?"

"Sure. But trust me, he won't answer when he's at the blackjack table or feedin' the slots."

"Candice with him?"

"Are you kidding? She hates that gambling shit. Down in Delaware, visiting her folks."

"I suppose you heard about the fire," Joseph said.

"Yeah. Hell of a thing. Zack Manderbach always had a broomstick up his butt but he was a straight shooter. Nipa too." There was long pause. "They find the kids yet?"

"Not that I know."

"I hear those shake-a-dick cops are lookin' at Brad for torching the place. He was always a wild son of a bitch, but no way do I see him wasting his own family. Moron cops. Most of 'em can't tell the difference between a fudgesicle and a fartsicle."

"Brad would never hurt his own," Joseph agreed.

"So whaddya want with Little M?"

Joseph seemed to hesitate, prompting Big Moxie to growl, "What's going on, is it a fuckin' state secret?"

"No, just curious about something I heard your boy mention the other day. A wild story about a flying creature buzzing his Escalade."

"You mean Nowhere Man."

"Right. I believe that's what he called it."

"You see the sucker too?"

Brad imagined Joseph shaking his head no in response. "But I've been hearing stories."

"Same here," Big Moxie said. "Little M wasn't the only one to have a close encounter. Frankie Bonaduce's nephew and his girlfriend were parked out at Gunther Lake one night when it flew right past their windshield. Soared almost down to the water before taking off again. Said it kept fading in and out of view like it was a ghost." Big Moxie unleashed a bawdy chuckle. "Heard it scared 'em so bad they gave up tryin' to do the boner bounce."

"Where did Little M ever come up with such a crazy name?"

"Yours truly."

"No shit. Where'd you hear it?"

"Remember the Swanteri Brothers? Went off the grid a couple years back?"

"Sure."

"Well, one night last November, not long before that sorry excuse for a hunter mistook me for venison and put a Winchester 270 slug through my spine, I was with some guys up on Copernian Ridge. Deer spotting. Ran into Amos Swanteri, the younger brother. Looked like the Wild Man of Borneo reincarnated. Drunk as a skunk too. Amos never did have much going for him in the brains department. Slow as molasses. I always took him for a retard, or whatever the PC fuckin' term is for that sort these days.

"Anyways, Amos starts ranting that we're trespassing, that

we was on Nowhere Man's land and that if we didn't leave right away, Nowhere Man was going to fly out of his cave and come swooping down on us. And then we'd all get goo-shooted and become his slaves forever."

"What's goo-shooted?"

"No idea. We let Amos carry on for a while, sounding more and more whacked. He finally got so pissed that we weren't leaving that he started fumbling for his sidearm. But like I said, he was wasted and we was all packin' and drew faster. It was three against one, which was enough to finally yank the scuzz bucket out of his brain fog and realize he'd better let it go. Last we saw of him he was slinkin' back into the woods, muttering that Nowhere Man was a powerful demon from beyond, and that someday he was going to get all of us but good."

"And he said this Nowhere Man lives in a cave up on Copernian Ridge?"

"Sure did."

"Where exactly were you spotlighting?"

"Parked at the edge of the old Baisley fire lane. Hoofed in a ways."

"Can you be more precise?"

"I don't know, maybe went in a mile or so." Big Moxie's tone changed to annoyance. "Why do you wanna know all this crap? Not writing your memoirs, I'm guessing."

"Just curious."

"Ahh, I get it. You're going after that flying goo-shooter, ain't ya?"

Joseph responded with a dismissive grunt. "Why on earth would I do something like that?"

"Hey, first of all, I know you too well. Haven't forgotten the old days. Back around '52 or '53 when we was in junior high, back when it didn't take much to get you riled. I can still see you ambushing those four older guys. Called 'em *tèt zozo* or some shit like that. All they did was insult your auntie, but you beat the crap out of them with a bat."

"I remember."

"Put one of 'em in the hospital."

"Two of them," Joseph corrected.

Big Moxie laughed. "Yeah, you were a righteous badass. Cops don't like that sort, especially when their skin ain't white enough. They stomped your ass pretty good, didn't they?"

"Even before they threw me in a cell." Joseph paused, as if remembering. "Took me out behind the jail. Used brass knuckles and belts."

"Pricks. Lucky for them you wasn't packin' your nasty voodoo stick back then."

"My what?"

There was a long silence. Brad imagined they were staring one another down. He had to restrain himself from peeking over the window lip.

"C'mon, Joseph. I told you about Nowhere Man, least you can do is tell me one of your precious little secrets. You think I don't know about that weapon of yours? Shit man, I worked behind that bar for more than fifty years. Got a gander at every fuckin' secret this township has to hide.

"Let me tell ya, I listened to more than a few losers with a load on, sittin' on those stools, pourin' out their woe-be-me stories about tangling with you in some dark alley or deserted hallway or lonely place out in the sticks. Every last one of 'em said you cleaned their clocks. Not that they weren't asswipes and probably deserved it. But they all said you took 'em down with this fiery staff that glowed like the devil hisself."

"And you believe a bunch of drunks?"

"Sure as hell do. Hear a crazy story once, easy to dismiss. Hear the same story a bunch of times from different mouths over the space of half a century and you're bound to become a true believer."

"You've got the wrong idea," Joseph said. "Way back in the day, I maybe hit someone once with a burning stick from a campfire. You know how these things get all blown out of proportion. Stories grow into legends. People love to pump things up."

Big Moxie wasn't buying it. "I'm thinkin' that *you're* thinkin' that this Nowhere Man had something to do with what happened to the Manderbachs. That's why you're going after him, ain't it? See whose voodoo is more powerful. Challenge him mano a mano."

"You're barking up the wrong tree."

"You think he's got the Van Reed kids?"

"I have to go. Take care of yourself. Give my regards to Little M and Candice."

Brad heard Joseph approaching, walking swiftly. But Big Moxie wasn't letting it go.

"Hell, Joseph, what's the point of lying about this crap now? We're just two old codgers circling the drain. I get that you might have good reason for not telling a soul about what really happened with Isabella, why you'd wanna take that secret to your grave. But this weapon of yours... c'mon, do a show-and-tell for an old friend. I want some of that voodoo magic keeping me company when I give this world the final finger and go down for the dirt nap."

Joseph hopped into the SUV, hit the starter button. Big Moxie was still talking as they pulled out. His last words were lost in a rumble of engine noise.

"Copernian Ridge is our best shot," Joseph said, trying to contain irritation. "I know the abandoned fire trail he mentioned. It's in the general vicinity of where the meteorite landed. That cave must be nearby."

Brad barely heard what he was saying, his head suddenly fixated elsewhere. "What did he mean about not telling a soul about what really happened with Isabella, taking that secret to your grave?"

"Just a lot of nonsense."

"Didn't sound that way. Sounded like something really important."

Joseph hit the gas hard. The Nissan nailed a bump at the bottom of the driveway. Old shock absorbers caused Brad to feel the bounce to his bones. It almost jarred him off the back seat.

His earlier suspicions about Joseph and his grandmother, the ones he'd tried to tamp down, swept through him with a vengeance. He bolted upright.

"Stay down!" Joseph hissed.

"No, goddamn it, not until you tell me what Big Moxie meant."

"It's nothing."

"Stop the fucking car!"

Joseph accelerated. Brad wrenched open the door, threatening to jump out as they slowed for a curve.

"Someone will see you!"

"Let 'em! I'm tired of your bullshit. Either level with me right now or I am fucking gone!"

Joseph completed the turn, pulled to a stop on the shoulder. A field of sweet corn flanked one side of the road. On the other side was a pasture, a tractor meandering across it in the distance. There was no one close by, but just up ahead was a row of McMansions built in the heady days leading to the '08 housing bubble collapse. Some were vacant and others only half-finished. A handful were occupied, however. If Brad tried walking past them there was a good chance he'd be seen, not to mention being spotted by any passing vehicles. But he was too enraged to care.

"No more goddamn secrets, Joseph! I need to know the truth."

"All right." The aged voice bled resignation. "Close the door and lie back down."

"And then?"

"I'll tell you everything."

TWENTY-SEVEN

Joseph had known this moment was coming, even before his last eidolon encounter with SOS. Silso had been clear about what he needed to do.

Tell him the truth.

He'd been avoiding it, and not just since yesterday. He'd been avoiding it most of his life, pincered between his vow to Isabella and gut-clenching fear about how Brad and Kristen might react.

The truth.

He gazed into the rearview mirror. Brad had closed the door and returned to his supine position, out of sight. Joseph considered driving to a more isolated location. But fury sweltered in that back seat, too raw to endure a long drive.

"Now Joseph! I'm waiting!"

He shut off the engine, drew a deep breath and began. "It's what you already suspect. Isabella... Bernard... They got married. They raised your mom. But Bernard... he wasn't the one who got her pregnant."

Joseph felt his fingers tightening on the steering wheel, tensing for a vicious eruption from the back seat. But Brad didn't utter a word or make a sound. The only disturbance came from outside, a small truck passing them from the opposite direction. The driver barely gave the Nissan a glance.

"Isabella said it happened the day we made love out there at the ridge, the day we found the two parts of the Trine. The moment she told me about the baby I proposed to her. It wasn't just a matter of doing the honorable thing. I wanted very much to marry her. She wanted it too, or at least a part of her did. I told her we could run away together, maybe back down south to New Orleans or out to San Francisco, places where a white woman and a Creole man with a baby wouldn't stand out as much. Like I said, back then, in a small town like Gracious, a marriage like ours..." He shook his head. "It wasn't going to happen.

"Isabella's parents, they were churchgoers, very religious, very conservative. They gave her an ultimatum. Ditch me, or be permanently cut off from them. She was five years younger, only twenty-three and still living at home. A part of her couldn't imagine not seeing her folks anymore, especially with a baby on the way. And leaving the town where she'd been born and raised... Even though she knew in her heart we were meant to be together, that we were bound not only by our love but by the two parts of the Trine, she couldn't do it."

A lump rose in Joseph's throat. The last time he'd uttered such words aloud he'd been speaking them to Isabella. It had been the day she told him it was over, that they needed to break up, that it would be best for her if no one knew he was the father.

"An unpleasant choice for anyone to have to make. But Isabella did what she felt she had to do. She'd known Bernard since high school. He'd always been a suitor. I don't think she loved him, at least not in the beginning. But as time went on, I believe real feelings grew between them."

While the intimacy between us slowly died. As we came to know one another only by the guise of friendship.

"She started going out with Bernard within days of our breakup. It was a practical choice. She wanted to lessen any suspicions about who the baby's father was, make the timeline seem reasonable, so that it could have been Bernard who'd gotten her pregnant. She told him the truth, of course. He was a good man and went along with it. And he raised Janice like she was his own flesh and blood."

But she wasn't. She was my *daughter.*

"Isabella and I stayed in contact, of course. Met casually in public places on occasion. Traded stories on what we were learning about the amulet and the weapon."

Did you ever imagine how hard that was for me, seeing you holding that baby in your arms? So much I wanted to talk about besides the parts of the Trine and what secrets they held. So many other things I wanted to say…

Joseph released the wheel, slumped forward. He should have been relieved to finally admit the truth. But he felt only misery at having stirred to life what he'd long struggled to keep buried.

Brad finally reacted. His voice was tightly controlled, the words strung together in an awkward cadence.

"How could you… not tell us… that… you're… our grandfather."

"Isabella made me promise. She knew Janice would someday inherit the first part. I think she also sensed your mother would have a hard life, a complicated life. Maybe she foresaw such a future by means of the amulet. Or maybe it was just some kind of maternal instinct. In any case, she didn't want yet another burden laid upon her daughter. She never told Janice the truth. She didn't want her growing up wondering who her real father was."

"Uncle Zack… Aunt Nipa… did they know?"

"I'm not sure. But your uncle, being Isabella's brother… He was only a year younger and they were very close back then. She confided in him on various matters." Joseph shrugged. "She may have told him."

"How did Big Moxie find out?"

"Just like he said, half a century of being a keen listener behind that bar. At some point he must have heard enough rumors about Bernard not being the real father to put two and two together."

"Who else knew?"

"I don't know."

"Who the fuck else!"

The veneer had cracked. Joseph suspected the damage was beyond repairable, at least by him.

He started the engine. "We should get you some hiking clothes and pick up a few supplies. Can't risk going to the emporium. Harry would certainly be curious about why I need such gear. We'll have to drive to the Home Depot in Trevorport and–"

"Just fuckin' get on with it!"

Joseph pulled out. Silso's last words again echoed in some deep recess.

The child is beyond your direct help. He wondered if that applied to Brad as well.

TWENTY-EIGHT

Elrod wasn't jonesing for another wap hit, but at the moment he sure could use one anyway. The weird shit with the child would mess with anybody's head, even a normal person's. And he knew enough about himself to know that he and normal had never been drinking buddies.

Guarding Kristen Van Reed all by himself made for some hair-raising shit. He hadn't been this anxious since those older kids had thrown him into that trailer park cesspool to see if the crap was thick enough to float on, and it wasn't, and he went under and almost drowned. A vial of the royal nectar might have calmed his nerves, but Sindle Vunn said he wouldn't get another dose until after dark when Nowhere Man was supposed to appear, live and in person. Until then, Elrod was on his own.

Of course, he wasn't actually alone. Kyzer was here in the cabin with him. Not that the Kyze-Man's presence would do Elrod any good if the demon child suddenly decided she was tired of being locked up in the back room and turned herself into an avenging angel, like the one from that movie he'd seen as a kid that had scared him so bad he'd wet his pants. He imagined her smashing through the cheap plywood door and coming at him, all fire and fury, lightning bolts shooting from her head and melting his face.

"Fuck!" Just thinking about that shit was nearly enough to put him into a panic, especially knowing what she'd done to Kyzer. He could hardly take it anymore, just sitting here at the rickety picnic table, drumming his fingers against the wooden planks to keep his hands busy. He'd tried jacking off earlier to reduce his anxiety, but Sergeant Apone was also freaked out and refused to hold up his end of the deal.

Enough of this sitting-around crap. Elrod bolted to his feet and began pacing around the table and benches. You would have thought the boss would have arranged to have some fun stuff brought to the hideout to help them relax a bit, like maybe a flatscreen and some DVDs. But then he remembered the place was too far out in the sticks to have electricity.

OK then, so how about a laptop with some games on it, battery fully charged, hours of fun ahead, anything to take his mind off demon child. But no, Elrod didn't even have that much. The battery in his phone had run down. And it wasn't like the cabin itself was much to look at. There were no decorations, not so much as a shred of wallpaper, like the kind he'd had as a kid in that dumpy trailer. He'd stare at those flower patterns in his bedroom to take his mind to another place, especially when his mom and one of her tricks were screaming at one another in the next room on account of one of them feeling ripped off.

The hideout was so primitive it didn't even have glass windows, just poorly fitted screens. He'd been swatting all day at flying insects that managed to sneak through. Daniel fuckin' Boone probably had nicer digs when he was growing up back in 1492, or whatever the hell the date was.

The cabin had mostly been built by those whacko Swanteri brothers, although Elrod and Kyzer had hauled the wood framing and plywood out here in the van. That had been one bitch of a job, countless trips carrying lumber and shit through the forest.

A moan drew Elrod's attention to the corner. Kyzer remained huddled there, legs drawn up, arms folded over his chest, looking like some giant scared bunny rabbit. When the boss saw what had happened to the Kyze-Man, he'd calmly told the rest of them not to worry, promising the effects would be short-term and that Kyzer would make a full recovery. But it sure as hell didn't look that way to Elrod. Shudders continued racking Kyzer's body, and his face was still pinched and drawn. His forehead was covered in bruises and dried blood from where he'd tried hurting himself.

Elrod stopped pacing in front of him. "What the fuck were you thinking, asshole!" He was tempted to give him a kick for added emphasis. Had the Kyze-Man been his old self, even just talking at him in such a way would have earned Elrod a beatdown. He couldn't deny feeling good about having the upper hand for a change. Still, he'd much rather have his friend back, all snarly and pissy and slapping him upside the head. That's pretty much what had happened last night after they'd returned to the van as the Manderbach house burned in the distance.

"Shit-for-brains cretin!" Kyzer had screamed. "We were still inside there!"

Elrod shielded his head from the worst of the backhanders while trying to come up with acceptable reasons for firing the flamethrower a tad early.

"Wasn't my fault. I saw the boss come out the front door with the little girl. I figured y'all had gone out the back door."

"Why the fuck would we go out the back when the van's parked closer to the front!"

"Exercise?"

That earned an extra hard slap, which he managed to partially deflect with his forearm. He'd tried another excuse on for size.

"My finger slipped and the trigger got jammed wide open." It was super lame too, but better than the truth, that he'd hadn't really been sure whether they were still in the house. And once he'd opened up and that beautiful stream of fire was lighting up the skies, no way would he have been able to stop until every last bit of glorious napalm was drained from the tank.

Kyzer had muttered something under his breath, either tired of pounding on him or else knowing they needed to make themselves scarce before the fire company and cops arrived.

By the time the five of them drove all the way out here to the cabins it was dawn. The boss had carefully laid the unconscious child on the cot prepared for her in the back room, drawing a blanket up over her pajamas like a doting parent. He even left a water bottle and an unopened box of Nabisco Wheat Thins by her side in case she was hungry, as well as an antique chamber pot and a roll of toilet paper in case she had to go. Man, she was getting treated better than Elrod. His bathroom was the surrounding woods.

"We'll wait until she awakens before attempting to procure the amulet," Sindle Vunn explained, gazing pointedly at Elrod and Kyzer, as if they needed extra-special reminding.

"Why fuck not just rip goddamn thing off her neck?" Kyzer demanded. "What's the little brat gonna do?"

"Again, not a recommended course of action."

The boss stayed cool and calm as he always did when the Kyze-Man was in one of his pissy moods. Elrod figured Kyzer was still hot under the collar about that little mix-up with the flamethrower.

"We don't know exactly what will happen," the boss continued. "What we do know is that the amulet cannot be taken, only given."

"Ain't afraid of no dumb piece of jewelry," Kyzer growled.

The boss stared at Kyzer for a long moment, reconsidering. "Of course, the prohibition remains somewhat theoretical. Even Nowhere Man doesn't know exactly what might occur. If a person actually made the attempt and succeeded in capturing the prize, well…"

"Well what?" Kyzer demanded.

"Such a bold act certainly would earn that individual the most heartfelt of plaudits. Perhaps even a generous reward."

"What kinda reward?"

"I cannot say for certain. I am not privy to our savior's thoughts. But off the top of my head, I'm thinking that such a bold initiative could earn such an individual, at the very least, additional doses of wap."

Elrod could tell that the boss was trying to goad Kyzer into doing it. Nidge and Double Bub were watching closely, and Elrod had a hunch they were aware of what was going on too. Had Kyzer not been so irritated, he likely would have sniffed out the setup as well.

But he was and he didn't. Instead, the Kyze-Man favored all of them with a dismissive sneer. Then he yanked Kristen's blanket down to her waist and grabbed hold of the necklace, intending to rip the amulet from her neck.

Instead he froze, his fist clamped around the silver chain. Slowly, he turned toward them. He had the oddest expression, like he was expecting something really unpleasant to happen, like maybe he'd just swallowed a grenade and was waiting for the inevitable detonation.

His face dissolved into terror. He let out a scream so loud and piercing that Elrod lunged backward in panic, slamming his shoulder blades painfully against the wall.

Kyzer released the necklace. The amulet flopped back against the child's pajamas. He started spinning in circles, shrieking as if that exploded grenade inside him was napalm and was burning his guts to a crisp. Mad with agony, he shoved past them and stumbled back into the main room.

Rushing to the edge of the picnic table, he laid the hand that had grabbed the necklace palm down on the wood. Whipping out his hatchet, he swung it toward his exposed wrist, intending to chop off his hand. But at the last instant, some part of him must have realized that this wasn't exactly the greatest idea. Instead, he impaled the blade deep into the wood, inches from his fingers.

"Ah-dah-mah-dah-mah!" he hollered, the nonsense words trailed with another piercing scream. Hunching over the table, he bashed his forehead against the boards. The thud was so loud it reverberated through the room.

He did it again and again, battering his skull against that unyielding wood. Nidge took a step forward to intervene but the boss grabbed his arm.

"Better we see this through."

They didn't have long to wait. Nine violent head butts did the trick. Kyzer bolted in preparation for the tenth, but instead fell backward onto the floor, unconscious before he hit. Nidge and Double Bub dragged him to the corner, which is where he'd been ever since, still all kinds of messed up, alternating between totally conked out and half-awake. Every so often he'd release a moan that sounded like a hound dog with its paw caught in a bear trap.

A loud rap sounded from the other side of the cabin's interior door. Elrod was so startled he almost jumped out of his pants.

"What do you want?" He tried keeping a nervous quiver out of his voice while stepping as far from the portal as possible.

"Where's my brother?" Kristen demanded, not sounding at all like a prisoner, more like someone who might shoot laser beams out of her eyes, which would pierce the flimsy wood and burn straight into his head.

"I don't know where your brother is." Elrod wasn't about to tell her that her brother was almost certainly a pile of ashes, let alone that *he* was the one who'd burned down their house.

She went silent. Elrod stood rock still, his attention fixed on the door. It was secured by the padlock, to which Sindle Vunn had the only key, probably because he didn't trust the rest of them not to do something stupid. Kyzer being a case in point.

Elrod again wished he wasn't the only guard, at least the only conscious one. The boss and Nidge had left hours ago for the crack house to rendezvous with someone they referred to as Wolfie, who apparently was an important part of the plan. Double Bub had stuck around for a while before donning his headgear and trooping out into the wilderness, presumably to hunt supper.

Make sure the child is not left unguarded, even for a moment. The boss had issued the order to Elrod in his gravest voice, which meant there'd be hell to pay if he was to set foot outside the cabin.

Kristen spoke again. "You should let me go. Then you should leave this place too."

"Why?" he asked. "It's kinda nice in here." The instant the words left his lips he realized what a dumbass thing it was to say. But having a conversation with demon child was unsettling. It was messing up his brain-mouth connection, which happened a lot when he got anxious.

"It is *not* nice," she snapped, sounding so utterly sure of herself. "The room you're in is really dangerous."

"Is not." It was a pretty lame comeback. He was on a roll. But he was curious about what she meant. "Why is it dangerous?"

"It has a bunch of shoo spots."

Elrod frowned, not knowing what to make of that. Shoe spots? He gazed down at the planked floorboards. Sure enough, she was right. There were footprints visible in the dust and dirt that had accumulated or been dragged in. Many of the prints overlapped, and not just where the five of them had tread. The Swanteris, who lived in the cabin next door, had been in here enough to leave plenty of their own markings.

"You're right," Elrod admitted. "I see the shoe spots."

"You do?" She sounded surprised.

"Yep, I sure do." He wondered how she'd known the floor out here was dirty, since she'd been unconscious when brought to the cabin and had never actually viewed the larger space. And why did she think a dirty floor was dangerous? Was she worried someone might slip and fall?

Maybe Elrod was overthinking it. She was a girl, and girls more than boys tended to like things clean. His mother had drummed that into him even though she was a real slob.

An idea popped into his head. "Hey, you know what I'm gonna do? I'm gonna clean up out here. I'm gonna get rid of all those nasty shoe spots. I'll make it so nice you could eat right off the floor."

She didn't answer. Elrod took that as a good sign. He couldn't let her out of the locked room, of course. Even if he had the key, he wasn't about to open that door, not without a running head start. Which didn't make sense, as how could he open the door and get a running head start at the same time?

In any case, he could still do nice things for her. A little favor might go a long way in preventing her from doing whatever she'd done to Kyzer, making him want to bash his head until he knocked himself out. If she wanted the floor swept, that much he could do.

Then he realized he had a problem. He didn't have a broom. There was a brush and dustpan in the van but that was parked pretty far away, not to mention he dared not leave the cabin.

He looked around. Bits of refuse was scattered everywhere: fast-food wrappers, beer and soda cans, a jagged piece of thin cardboard... Yes! That would work as a dustpan. But he still needed something to sweep with. He opened his fanny pack and there it was, his toothbrush.

"I'm getting started right now," he called out.

Still no response. But he figured if she was unhappy with what he was doing, she'd say something. Starting catty-corner from Kyzer, he got down on his hands and knees. It wasn't exactly the fastest way to sweep a floor. But the toothbrush and cardboard worked just fine. Besides, it wasn't like he had anything better to do.

TWENTY-NINE

Felicity had been making her way through the woods for nearly an hour. The going was slow. She was capable of a faster pace, and the trek would have been easier had she kept to the fire lane. But that would have left her in the open, and she wasn't about to let the Swanteri brothers surprise her again.

On those hunting trips as a teen, Grandpa Harry had taught her to move with stealth through wilderness. Taking her time enabled her to use the full breadth of her senses to scan for threats. A distant sound, an unfamiliar smell – either was enough to prompt hesitation. She constantly pivoted her head, scanning the dense trees and foliage on both sides but keeping her primary focus forward. *Try to see at least twenty yards in front of you*, she recalled Grandpa advising.

She'd maintained a course parallel to the fire lane until reaching the spot she'd been ambushed, employing what tracking skills she'd acquired on those hunting trips. She looked for obvious signs of spoor. Tracking humans was not all that different from tracking forest animals. Footprints, broken twigs, bent leaves – all might indicate the direction from which the brothers had come, and presumably the direction they'd taken Flick.

The canopy was thick, illumination sparse at ground level. She used her flashlight to scan, keeping the beam aimed downward and her hand wrapped around the barrel head to prevent the light from being seen from a distance.

It was possible they'd proceeded farther along the lane, which rendered any search effort significantly more challenging. Still, this was the area where they'd emerged from the trees. It was a good hunch that somewhere in the vicinity she'd find evidence of a trail.

For a long time she found nothing. She was close to becoming disheartened when she finally came upon a trace of human passage. It was about a dozen yards from the spot where the brothers had appeared. The spoor was on the edge of a protruding slab of limestone. It was transfer – material someone's foot had picked up. The individual had scraped the damp soil from their boot onto the rock, leaving the faint impression of a tread.

Probing deeper into the underbrush she came across more boot prints. They were substantially larger than Flick's shoe size and thus likely male. Dropping to her hands and knees she employed sideheading, another trick Grandpa Harry had taught her. Keeping low to the ground with the flashlight, she twisted her head sideways to get a better angle on potential tracks that might be indiscernible from an overhead view.

The tactic worked. The flashlight beam revealed numerous tracks, including several smaller imprints she was certain belonged to Flick. Staying low, she crawled another ten yards or so in her prey's direction of travel, far enough to verify that the trio were moving on a set course. She seemed to be on a trail, but so rudimentary that in places it vanished entirely. Resuming an upright stance, she checked her compass heading. North-northeast. Using the compass as a guide, she resumed the trek, periodically dropping back down onto hands and knees to check for prints in case they changed direction.

Occasional breezes touched her face, their direction working in her favor. She was upwind of her prey, which meant the brothers likely wouldn't catch her scent. Still, they'd been living in the wild long enough that their sense of smell may have grown unusually keen. Countering that assumption, however, was their attire and overall appearance. They might well be unable to detect anything beyond their own stink. Odds were, she'd be able to sniff them before they sniffed her.

She checked her phone from time to time. She wasn't expecting to see any signal bars so wasn't surprised by their absence. Making a call wasn't a priority at the moment. She was using the phone to access those old USGS maps she'd snapped closeups of yesterday at the library.

She found the series of photos covering the area she was trekking through. The first one showed the fire lane, which intersected the road not far from where she'd parked the Jeep. The lane gently zig-zagged for nearly three miles before terminating at a higher elevation, at a fire tower. Newer maps she'd perused at Penn State showed no tower. Likely it had been abandoned long ago in favor of the more advanced technology for detecting remote forest blazes: satellites.

The trail she followed led gradually uphill and on a slight yet steady angle away from the fire lane. According to the best estimate of her current position, going by the compass and a feel for how much distance she'd covered, she was three-eighths of a mile from the lane. The photo showed nothing consequential ahead, just more elevation contour lines indicating that the land sloped gently upward.

She accessed the subsequent photo, which covered the adjacent map section. The contour lines were much the same except for an area directly ahead. Hachure lines – small tick marks pointing inward on the sweeping contour lines – indicated a depression ring. The area it encompassed sloped downward, forming a shallow bowl. She estimated the ring's diameter at 150 yards.

She recalled that the lidar survey had tagged the depression ring as an anomaly because of insufficient data. A statistically significant percentage of the laser pulses hadn't reached ground level. More advanced versions of lidar, such as those used by the military, offered superior analytics. But she and Flick had made do with what was available at a more reasonable cost, which also had limited the number of aerial passes. Flick, generous with her trust fund, would have spent the extra money. But at a certain point, Felicity had started feeling like she was being exploitative and had reigned in the expenditure.

The conclusion about the depression ring was that it was extremely overgrown. An unusually dense canopy interfered with the laser targeting. However, the site had been eliminated from primary consideration as a meteorite crater. The bowl was more ovoid than round, with random bulges along its perimeter suggesting natural ground subsidence rather than extraterrestrial impact. Then again, algorithmic bias could sometimes render such analyses problematic. Translation: anything was possible.

It seemed as if Flick and her captors – Felicity refused to consider them anything other than that – were headed directly for the depression ring. Still, they might pass through or around it toward a more distant destination.

She reached the crest of a small rise and came across a different sort of spoor. The thimble-sized aluminum vial was dirty, making it impossible to determine whether it had been discarded recently or had been nestled in the dirt for a long time. Lying nearby was a small cork, a perfect fit. Shining her light into the vial revealed the inside was stained black. Taking a whiff confirmed her suspicions. Cloves. The vial had contained the same black goo that had contaminated Flick.

Some other aspect of the fragrance was overly familiar. The elusive memory from outside the cave popped into her head. The grad student's notebook, which had served as her inspiration for this entire ill-fated quest. Professor Summersby had suffered from severe toothaches, which had been his rationale for calling off the search. As an aside, the student had written that Summersby always carried bottles of clove oil, a common remedy for tooth pain back then.

Felicity had no idea what it might mean but sensed there was some connection. She tucked vial and cork in her backpack. They might serve as additional samples for lab analysis.

Male voices, up ahead. Ducking low, Felicity undid the strap securing the holstered Beretta.

The voices were approaching. She drew the gun, knelt into a two-handed firing stance. She strained to hear what they were saying but could only make out a smattering of words. The first voice said something about "Nowhere Man." A reference to the old Beatles song? Then a second voice whined a complaint, something about "these patrols a waste of time."

It was definitely the Swanteris. She considered backtracking, putting more distance between them. But as they drew closer, she was able to get a bearing. They weren't coming directly toward her but seemed to be on a roughly parallel course.

She glimpsed them through the foliage, twenty-five yards away and heading back toward the lane. They were moving swiftly, suggesting they traversed a more regularly used trail. They came close enough for her to make out a chunk of conversation.

"Which one would you do?" Amos Swanteri asked. "The big one or the little one?"

"Don't even be thinkin' that shit," Hiram answered in an angry tone. "Those bitches ain't for us."

"But what if they was for us?"

"Beat your meat, will ya? Get that shit outta your head."

"I'd do the little girl and have the big girl watch."

"Shut it, fool!"

And then they were gone. Felicity waited until she was certain they were far enough away before getting to her feet and holstering the gun. But now she had a dilemma. Turn around and follow them on the presumed trail, or continue on their original course. Flick obviously wasn't with them, which suggested they'd left her at wherever the trail terminated. But there was no guarantee that was the case. Maybe Flick was someplace else entirely and they were heading to join her.

Either option was guesswork. Felicity took only a moment to decide. She'd stay on the original course, follow their spoor.

Although the brothers were now behind her and presumably putting more distance between them, she remained cautious. New worries intruded. Amos' reference to a big girl and a little girl was inherently disturbing. One of the girls must be Flick. But what else had those scumbags been up to? Was Flick the "big girl?" If so, had they kidnapped a child?

She pressed on. The ground before her leveled out, then began descending. She'd arrived at the edge of the depression ring. Down below, a few dozen yards away, was a primitive cabin enveloped in shadows. There was no sign of activity.

The reason for the substandard lidar results of the area and its inherent gloom became apparent. It wasn't just the densely packed maples and oaks, some rooted close to the cabin, others leaning inward from the ring's perimeter to provide extra shrouding. The entire canopy appeared to be cloaked in an additional layer of foliage. It was as if giant hands had draped a heavy green blanket over everything.

She squatted behind a cluster of bushes and retrieved low-light binoculars from the backpack. The cabin was crudely built using plywood sheets, with a pitched roof covered in tar paper. None of it seemed weathered, suggesting recent construction. The front side had a closed door, the longer side a small window. The window had no glass, just a screen. She estimated the cabin's overall dimensions at twenty feet deep, ten feet wide.

She trained the binoculars upward. The green blanket enveloping the area was artificial, a series of synthetic nets onto which leafy branches had been woven. She could make out spots along the perimeter where the netting was attached to the crowns of trees with short lengths of rope. However bizarre, there was only one logical conclusion. Someone had wanted the area camouflaged so thoroughly that, even in winter, it would be nearly impenetrable to aerial surveillance.

Felicity had read about extreme survivalists, determined not only to live far from civilization but paranoid about Big Brother spying on them. The Swanteris likely fit the bill. Still, a hell of a lot of work had gone into such a massive camouflage installation. Many of the trees were over a hundred feet tall. She had a hard time envisioning the brothers doing it all on their own. Had they hired professional tree climbers? Either that or found someone with *wings.*

Reining in her fantasies, she put away the binoculars and pondered her next move. There was a fair chance Flick was in the cabin, presumably alone. That still left Felicity with a big problem: how to convince her she'd been poisoned and needed medical assistance. Flick's actions indicated she wasn't likely to be swayed by rational explanations.

I may have to subdue her.

It wasn't the first time the thought had crossed Felicity's mind since setting out. From a practical standpoint, she knew such an onerous task was doable. Flick was in good shape but she was petite, and didn't have Felicity's physical prowess developed through years of sports and hunting.

But assuming she did subdue her fiancée, what then? Bind and gag her? Drag her back to the Jeep, likely kicking and protesting the entire way? The prospect was unappealing on so many levels.

One step at a time, she told herself.

She made her way cautiously toward the cabin, approaching directly from the front so as not to be spotted from the side window. Reaching the door, she leaned her ear against it, listening for signs of activity. At one point she thought she heard a soft moan but couldn't be sure. It might have come from outside, maybe a breeze disturbing branches.

The door didn't have an exterior lock, just a crude wooden handle serving to open and close it. She considered whipping open the door and barging in, gun in hand. It was the quickest course of action. But maybe not the smartest. It might be bolted from the inside. If so, she'd instantly alert any occupants to her presence.

She crept along the side of the cabin until she was just below the window. Now she definitely heard moans emanating from the other side of the screen. Just as she was about to stand and risk a quick look, peripheral vision caught sight of another structure. The second cabin was about thirty yards away. It was smaller but of similar construction, with the same type of gabled tar-paper roof and door-window arrangement. However, the exterior plywood was darkened from exposure to the elements. It had been here a lot longer.

She returned her attention to the window. Taking a deep breath, she popped up and gazed through the screen. The interior was illuminated by a battery-powered lantern on a picnic table and a second screened window across from her. Three rolled up sleeping bags were propped along the opposite wall. The table and its benches were the only furniture. A hatchet was buried in the table's dark wood.

She froze. In the back corner, on his knees facing away from her, was a skinny man with a fanny pack and a straw cowboy hat. It took her a moment to realize what he was doing: sweeping the floor. But instead of a dustpan and brush, he was performing the chore with a slab of cardboard and a toothbrush, periodically emptying the refuse into his fanny pack.

WTF?

Along the back wall was an interior door made from a single sheet of plywood. Judging by the cabin's dimensions, the second room was only five feet deep. The door had a shiny new latch with a padlock. Was Flick being kept in there?

She heard the moaning again. It wasn't Flick. Definitely a male voice, probably out of her view in the front corner. She backed away from the window, worried Toothbrush Man might turn and spot her. She inched her way around the perimeter to the far side, confirmed that the door and two windows were the only ways in.

She made her way to the second cabin. Peeking through a window, there was just enough light to reveal a single room with a more lived-in appearance. There was a small table, a pair of cots with rumpled blankets, several cabinets and a set of shelves crammed with boxed and canned foodstuffs. She crossed to the opposite window to confirm the cabin was vacant.

What now?

If Flick indeed was being held in that locked room in the first cabin, only one clear option presented itself. Felicity hadn't spotted an inside lock on the front door. She should be able to storm in and take the occupants by surprise. Keeping them covered with the Beretta, she'd force Toothbrush Man to unlock the interior door. Things might get hairy but she figured she could handle it.

Rustling noises issued from the trees behind her. She drew the Beretta and whirled.

"Flick!"

Her fiancée was approaching from the direction of the second cabin. She halted a few yards away. She had that same distant look, her eyes pinched, her features pale. She seemed to be gazing right through Felicity.

"Listen to me," Felicity said, keeping her voice low. "You've been poisoned but you're going to be all right. We need to get you to the clinic so they can give you an antidote. Do you understand what I'm saying?"

There was the faintest of nods. Encouraged, Felicity gently took hold of Flick's hand. She didn't resist.

"We're going back to the Jeep. But we have to be real quiet, OK?"

"OK," Flick whispered.

Felicity let out a sigh of relief. It appeared she was getting through to her. Holstering the gun, she tugged gently on Flick's arm, urging her to follow. But they hadn't gone more than a few yards when Felicity felt something stab into the side of her neck.

She whirled, astonished to see Flick holding a stubby purple syringe.

"What have you done? What was in… that… needle…?"

Felicity's mind swam. Dizziness came over her. She needed to sit down. Before she could attempt it, her legs buckled. She felt her left shoulder slamming the ground. There was no pain, just a smothering fog.

THIRTY

Brad seethed during the ride out to Copernian Ridge. Left briefly alone while Joseph shopped at Home Depot, at one point he found himself pounding the Nissan's back seat cushions in a fit of apoplectic rage. He managed to bring himself under control only when a frightened elderly woman scurried past the window.

Joseph returned with a pair of flashlights and other hiking gear, as well as fresh clothes for Brad: cargo pants and a plaid shirt. They were a decent fit but he wasn't about to offer thanks. He'd shut down all Joseph's attempts at apologizing for having been, in the asshole's own words, "an absentee grandfather." The phrase characterized a relative who forgot your birthday or never took you to the movies, not someone who'd cut himself out of your life for twenty-four fucking years.

Traffic thinned considerably once they were away from the store. Brad felt confident enough he wouldn't be spotted and sat up in the back seat for the rest of the journey, meeting Joseph's occasional mirror glances with murderous scowls. Only by concentrating on finding his sister was he able to convince himself not to abandon the selfish jerk and go solo. Besides, he'd likely need Joseph's weapon to wrench Kristen away from Sindle Vunn and those scumbags.

Joseph might have answers to important questions as well. Restraining his anger, Brad broached the one that had been puzzling him since Big Moxie's.

"Nowhere Man lives in this cave, right. But he also crosses

over from the eidolon. I don't get it. He's both places at the same time?"

Joseph's voice was tranquil and solemn, as if not wanting to risk a tone that might freshly stir Brad's anger.

"It is confusing. But I now believe his physical body originated in our world, that he was once human."

"Summersby."

"In all likelihood. But some part of him – the essence of his spirit, if you will – exists within the eidolon."

"Doesn't make much goddamn sense."

Joseph didn't respond. Brad went silent too. As they neared their destination, they came upon a Jeep Grand Cherokee parked on the shoulder.

"Pull over," Brad ordered. He hopped out before the Nissan even stopped moving and confirmed it was same vehicle Flick had been driving yesterday at the library. Felicity's "Astronomy Lover" travel mug in the cup holder was the giveaway. He'd been with her years ago when she'd bought it during a trip to State College.

That Felicity and her girlfriend – *fiancée*, he corrected himself – were out here as well remained troubling. But there wasn't anything he could do about it. Besides, unlike Kristen, Felicity was grown up and could take care of herself. But the thought provided no comfort, only fresh worry.

A half mile past the Jeep they reached the spot where abandoned Baisley fire lane intersected the road. The lane was badly overgrown, yet not so much that it prevented access. Joseph examined the overlapping tire tracks in the dirt, concluded they were recent and made by two vehicles. Judging by the fresh dirt on the macadam, he believed that one vehicle had departed back in the direction of Gracious.

"A larger tire with an asymmetrical tread pattern," he explained. "Possibly a limousine."

Brad acknowledged the assessment with a grunt. Rather than risk driving the Nissan into the lane, Joseph headed up the road another quarter mile and parked off road beneath a stand of black walnut trees. Better to hike back than risk encountering another vehicle or alerting Kristen's kidnappers to their approach.

They reached the lane and entered, Joseph leading as usual. Brad wished he had a gun. But it was doubtful he could have acquired one legally, and trying to track down and make a deal with one of the less-than-savory types he'd once hung with who had access to illicit firearms would waste even more time.

They came upon an old van, nearly as battered and dented as Brad's F-150. It was perpendicular to the lane, backed into a makeshift parking spot under the trees. Approaching cautiously, Joseph peered through the windows.

"Empty," Joseph whispered.

Brad tried the doors. Locked. They scanned the surrounding trees, alert for movement.

"You think it's them?"

Joseph shrugged and examined the overlapping tread impressions. It appeared as if the second vehicle, the limo, had driven farther along the lane then turned around and came back out again.

They located a rudimentary trail near the van that snaked through the trees and heavy undergrowth. Boot prints were clearly visible. Multiple individuals had been using the trail to move back and forth between the lane and wherever it led.

"Remember, move with stealth," Joseph advised as he eased onto the trail.

Brad resisted a sarcastic comeback. "Is this going toward where you found the meteorite?"

"No, away from it."

"Then we're probably heading away from Nowhere Man's cave too."

"Finding that cave would be like finding a needle in a haystack. Seeking out his minions is the wiser tactic."

Brad admitted it made sense. Yet again he got the impression that confronting Nowhere Man was something Joseph was determined to avoid.

They proceeded along the trail. Brad tried staying upbeat but for all they knew, the van and the tracks belonged to innocent hikers. And if it was the limo that had departed, Kristen might well be imprisoned in some basement a hundred miles away.

Joseph froze, held up his hand. Brad stopped and listened intently, trying to discern what might have spooked him. Then he heard it, the sound of an approaching vehicle. It sounded like it was behind them, back on the lane.

"The limo?"

"Could be," Joseph said.

The sound intensified then faded. The vehicle had driven past where the van was parked. It was heading deeper into the forest. Brad wondered if they should return to the lane and follow it. But Joseph indicated they should keep moving forward. Besides, there was a fair chance the trail was a shortcut to the same destination as the limo.

They hiked for another quarter mile or so, until Joseph again halted abruptly and raised his hand for silence. He spent a good thirty seconds imitating a statue before relaxing and continuing on.

"What was that all about?" Brad whispered.

"I'm not sure. For a moment I had the impression someone was out there, maybe tracking us and–"

A blur leaped out of the trees, slammed into Joseph with enough force to bowl him over.

Boxhead!

Everything happened too fast for Brad to react. Joseph landed on his back in a bramble of prickly vines. Boxhead leaped atop him, smashing a rock down on the side of his forehead.

Brad recovered his wits and lunged at the creature. But Boxhead was preternaturally swift. Vaulting off Joseph, the creature twisted toward Brad and raised its arm, ready to bash the rock into skull number two. They eyed one another from several paces away, a brief stalemate. Then Boxhead attacked.

But this time Brad was ready. A lifetime of fights in school, at Moxie's and in some North Carolina bars weren't for naught. He waited until the last moment, then lunged to the side and hammered his fist into Boxhead's stomach. The creature groaned and fell to its knees. The rock slipped from its grasp. Brad moved swiftly behind him, kicked the back of his right thigh hard enough to knock the creature face down in the dirt.

Brad whipped his attention toward Joseph. The head wound was nasty, blood streaming from it, smearing his face and pooling over his eyes. He was unconscious. Or worse.

Boxhead struggled to his feet, clutching his guts. Brad noticed the pouch slung over his shoulder, the tails of two dead squirrels protruding. It appeared he'd been hunting, the animals possibly dinner.

Brad reached under Joseph's coat and withdrew the second part of the Trine. Boxhead jerked backward, the sight of it clearly spooking him. Turning, he dashed away on the trail, in the direction they'd been heading. Even limping from Brad's kick, he moved with impressive speed.

Brad lowered the triangle and returned his attention to Joseph. He had a pulse. Wiping the blood from the craggy face and eyes with a handkerchief, he opened the first aid kit thoughtfully purchased during the Home Depot stop. He pressed a piece of dry gauze against Joseph's head wound until the worst of the bleeding stopped. Discarding the blood-soaked fabric, he cleaned the area as best he could with antiseptic wipes and placed an absorbent compress over the wound, binding it in place with strips of adhesive tape.

Joseph remained motionless throughout. Brad stared down at him, willing him to wake up. He didn't stir.

Think, Brad! Don't just sit here like a dipshit.

Right now, Boxhead was surely on his way back to wherever he'd come from. The rest of his gang likely were there as well.

And maybe Kristen. Remaining here with Joseph in the hopes he'd soon awaken made no sense. Eventually, Boxhead would return, and likely with reinforcements. If Brad was going to confront them, better to do it somewhere else, away from the unconscious Joseph.

"Sorry, old man. I can't stay. You're on your own."

Propping the first aid kit on Joseph's chest, Brad positioned his limp hands atop it. If he woke up, it would be right there, handy for self-treatment. If not...

Picking up the second part of the Trine, he charged after Boxhead.

THIRTY-ONE

Elrod had cleaned nearly half the floor with his toothbrush when Kyzer popped out of his brain fog and started yelling at him.

"Why the fuck you sweeping like that?" he demanded.

Elrod tried explaining but Kyzer cut him off. "Idiot! Put the goddamn toothbrush away. Tell me what happened since."

"Since you tried to take the amulet? Well, you went kinda nuts and–"

"Shut up! I remember that part."

"You were in some deep shit."

"Shut your goddamn mouth!" Kyzer warned. "We never talking about that stuff, not ever. Got it? Bring it up again and I'll beat your ass to molasses. I want to know what happened while I was… gone. And why the fuck you cleaning the floor like a retard?"

Elrod was secretly pleased to have his old friend back. But just as he was beginning to fill Kyzer in on what he'd missed and explaining about the shoe spots, that hipster girl with the big eyeglasses strolled into the cabin. She'd arrived earlier in the company of the Swanteri brothers.

She had a stupid name – Flick – but that wasn't the real reason he disliked her. There was a haughtiness about her, as if she was better than him, and he already had the Kyze-Man for putdowns. He didn't need to be lorded over by some mousy little thing with tits, thank you very much. Plus, the boss had taken her for a private meeting in the other cabin, and when they returned, they were chatting like BFFs. That didn't seem fair. She was brand new to their group and already getting special treatment. The boss never took Elrod anywhere for private meetings.

"I need your help carrying a body," Flick said, making it sound like an order, not a request.

"Dead body?" Kyzer wondered, intrigued.

"Unconscious."

"Why the fuck help you?"

"We serve the same master."

"So what?" Kyzer challenged, wrenching his hatchet from the table and returning it to its belt holster. He walked right up to her with his meanest look, planted his big belly against hers. It was classic Kyze-Man, using his bulk and nastiness to intimidate. Elrod hoped he gave her a good smackdown.

But Flick wasn't about to be bullied. Holding her ground, she reached into her pocket and withdrew a wad of bills and waved it in the air.

"Two hundred dollars to the one who helps me."

Kyzer snatched the bills from her hand. He counted them aloud – ten twenties – then nodded to Elrod.

"Stay here."

As Elrod registered disappointment that Kyzer had lucked into two hundred bucks instead of him, they heard noises outside. Kyzer reached for his hatchet but relaxed when he saw Sindle Vunn and Nidge emerging from the woods. The pair were approaching on one of the several trails that ultimately meandered back to the fire lane.

They breezed into the cabin, Nidge carrying a large corrugated box. He set it on the table.

"Is the child awake?" the boss asked. "The drug should have worn off by now."

Elrod wagged his head, trying to hide how sore he was at losing a payday to Kyzer.

"Excellent. Then I believe it's time for some frank dialogue."

He spoke the words super-loud, as if to make sure Kristen could hear from the other room.

Kyzer darkened, clearly wanting no part of another encounter with demon child. "Promised what's-her-face would help move a body," he said, gesturing to Flick.

Sindle Vunn frowned. "A body? Please explain."

"My girlfriend followed me here," Flick said. "I knocked her out with that needle you gave me for emergencies. I need help carrying her into the brothers' cabin."

"It would be wiser if you simply made sure she doesn't awaken."

"I know. That makes good sense." Flick hesitated. "I guess I'm not ready to do that. Not just yet."

The boss looked sympathetic. "I know how challenging it can be to unravel all the ties we have to our former lives. But the sooner you fully accept our savior and his gifts, the easier everything will become."

"I know. I just need a little more time."

"I'll do her," Kyzer offered.

"No, this is a task Flick needs to accomplish." The boss faced her. "What if Nowhere Man should give you a direct order? What if he should warn that disobedience would result in being forever deprived of wap?"

"That's different," Flick said, patting the hilt of her Bowie knife. "If it comes down to that, I'll cut her throat."

The boss gave an approving nod and turned to Kyzer. "Help Flick with her task. And should you prefer remaining at the other cabin until we conclude our business with the child, I would understand."

Kyzer, relieved, practically bolted out the door behind Flick. Nidge undid the box's flaps and withdrew a canvas tool pouch. Underneath was a larger object, about two feet high and enclosed in layers of bubble wrap. As the chauffeur unrolled the protective sheath, Elrod reminded himself to ask the boss if he could have the bubble wrap. He loved popping it on account of the sound it made, which reminded him of the crackling noises stuff made when it was being consumed in a fire.

Nidge completed the unveiling. Elrod was disappointed. He'd expected the object to be something cool, like maybe a new gaming console. Instead, it was a big doll, a plush red timber wolf sitting on its haunches.

"Allow me to introduce Wolfie," the boss announced with a smile. "Nidge, will you kindly fetch the child. And Elrod, please pick up Wolfie and set him down gently on the floor."

Elrod did as he was asked. The doll was heavier than it looked although nothing he couldn't handle.

"Thank you, Elrod," the doll said as its paws touched the floor.

Startled, he jerked away. "It... talks."

"Indeed," the boss said. "Wolfie is quite intelligent. And rather well-educated to boot."

"Good of you to say, and I appreciate the compliment." The doll's voice was reminiscent of a young boy's. "But like all of us here, I'm simply trying to do my best with whatever gifts I've been given."

Nidge unlocked the back room and motioned for Kristen to come out. She did so warily, her hand clutching the amulet.

"Hi, Kristen," the doll offered. "I'm Wolfie. I'm glad to see you're doing OK. I heard about what happened. I'm really sorry you had to go through all those troubles."

She frowned and took a step back. Elrod was glad to see he wasn't the only one unnerved by that babbling toy.

"Kristen, listen to me," the doll continued. "I know that you know the deal here. These men want the amulet. You don't want to give it up. And after what happened, believe me, I can absolutely understand your refusal."

"You're not real," she said.

"You know something, I get that a lot from people. But here's the truth. So help me god, I'm as real as you are."

The doll came off its haunches onto all fours and trotted back and forth in front of them.

"It moves just like a real animal," Elrod exclaimed.

"Of course I do. And Elrod, I'd be appreciative if you stopped calling me 'it.' That's kind of insulting, you know. How about instead, you try just calling me Wolfie."

"Sorry… Wolfie," Elrod whispered, feeling his face turning red. He hated when he blushed.

Wolfie stopped pacing and craned its head until their eyes met. "Hey Elrod, I'm sorry. I didn't mean to embarrass you. No need for you to feel bad. Let's just call it a misunderstanding between new friends."

"Thanks." Relief washed over Elrod. He wished that when he was growing up he'd had someone as nice as this to talk to.

Wolfie swiveled to Kristen. "Sweetie, I have to ask you to think about something for a moment. And I'd like for you to give it your honest attention. Can you do that for me?"

"You're not real," she said again. But this time she didn't look or sound nearly so convinced.

"We'll let that issue go for the moment. But here's the thing. I know just how attached you are to the amulet. I know that the very idea of giving it up is scary. But listen carefully to what I have to say. It's important. First of all, do you know what it means when someone says, 'Keep your eye on the big picture?'"

She gave a careful nod.

"Good. Then I want you to bear with me here and think about the big picture. And what I mean by that is, how the amulet fits into your entire life. Now I know it was a gift from your mother and I know it has very special powers. But can you honestly tell me that it's been a *good* thing? Don't you sometimes wish that the little triangle had never been given to you in the first place? Wouldn't your life be a heck of a lot easier if you didn't need to think and worry about the amulet all the time?"

She frowned. Wolfie went on.

"Come on, Kristen, be honest. Just tell me the truth. That's all I'm asking."

"Sometimes I think that," she admitted. "Sometimes I wish Mommy had never left it to me."

"Thank you, Kristen. I really appreciate your candor." Wolfie smiled. "Whoops, *candor*. That's kind of a big word. I'm not sure at your age you'd know what it means."

"I know what it means. It's like when you say something and deep down you really mean it."

"Very good! You know, you're a pretty smart girl. I know you haven't been in school lately because of the problems you've been having on account of the amulet. But I'll bet you're top of your class when you are there."

"I won the Brain Breaker contest last month."

"Really? That's great. I hope they gave you a prize or at least some kind of recognition."

"Uh-huh. I got to order pizza for the whole class."

"Whoa! That is so very cool."

Elrod wanted to tell Wolfie he'd won a prize once too, for having the best Halloween costume in third grade. But he figured the boss wouldn't like him interrupting.

"Kristen, can you do me a little favor?" Wolfie asked. "Can you show me the amulet? I just want to look at it."

She frowned.

"I just want to see what all the fuss is about."

She slowly opened her fist. Keeping the triangle nestled in her palm, she extended it toward him, but only a few inches.

"It's very pretty," Wolfie said, inching slowly forward. "May I touch it?"

Her attitude underwent a swift change. She clamped the amulet and backed away.

"Not even just a little touch?" Wolfie asked. "I promise I won't try to take it."

"No! You're just pretending to be friendly. You're bad like they are!"

"No he's not," Elrod muttered. He wanted to explain to her that Wolfie was really nice.

"Please, Kristen?" the doll implored. "Just a little touch."

"No!"

Sindle Vunn released an exaggerated sigh. "Wolfie, we gave it our best shot. But I'm afraid this isn't working. What do you think we should do now?"

Wolfie sighed. "I suppose we have to move to Plan B."

"If that's what you think is best."

The boss motioned to Nidge, who grabbed Kristen's arm and dragged her protesting across the room. Elrod watched in fascination as the boss withdrew the canister from his jacket that contained a bunch of those purple syringes. The child screamed as Nidge held her still and the boss stabbed her in the neck with one of the needles. Moments later she went limp. Nidge laid her face up on the table.

"Elrod, please set Wolfie beside her."

Getting that close to demon child wasn't Elrod's idea of a fun time. "Can't he jump up by himself?"

The boss arched his eyebrows. Knowing he had no choice, Elrod lifted Wolfie onto the table and quickly retreated. Wolfie drew wire cutters from the tool pouch with one of his front paws and crawled up onto Kristen's tummy. Clamping the blades onto her necklace, he squeezed the handles and sliced through the links. The amulet slid away from the severed necklace and plopped onto the table. It wasn't shiny like the chain. Yet as Elrod watched closely, it seemed to take on a faint greenish tint.

The boss sounded pleased. "The first part of the Trine is now yours, Wolfie. You are free to do with it whatever you like."

Wolfie stared at the amulet for a long moment, then placed it in Kristen's palm and gently closed her fingers around it. Climbing off her tummy, he assumed his original pose, sitting back on his haunches. Sindle Vunn scowled.

"Wolfie, why did you do that?"

There was no response. Wolfie just sat there, motionless. Elrod wondered if he felt bad about what he'd done, and wanted to make amends by returning the amulet to its rightful owner.

"Wolfie, quash override command, seven-axle-five-eight."

There was still no movement. Anger flashed on the boss' face and he looked in danger of losing his trademark Elvis cool. But he recovered fast and offered up a resigned smile.

"Remarkable. It would appear that the Trine's prohibition against being taken also extends into the electromechanical realm. Hours of reprogramming a wasted effort."

"Reprogramming?" It sounded to Elrod like the boss was saying Wolfie wasn't real. "What do you mean?"

Nidge snorted. "It's a robot, a computer with fake fur. Did you actually think it was alive?"

Elrod vehemently shook his head. Of course he hadn't thought it was alive, not really. He'd known from the beginning it was just a machine. The thing was, when Wolfie got to talking and saying nice things, you started believing he was something more than that.

The boss explained. "It was my idea and I truly thought it would work, and that it would simplify the acquisition of the first part. I asked Nowhere Man to procure Wolfie for us. I disengaged its cloud access, bypassed the default coding and introduced an app to carry out the task of acquiring the amulet. I was convinced the mnemonic core of an inorganic entity could not be weaponized against it."

Elrod thoughtfully wagged his head. It was often easier that way, pretending he understood what people were saying.

"Nowhere Man was skeptical but agreed to let me try. Alas, I was wrong. I comprehend my error now. No matter that Wolfie was a machine, he remained an extension of my beliefs. I programmed him to take the first part of the Trine. Therefore, it was the same as if I was reaching for the amulet." He paused. "One big difference, however. Adverse effects from touching the amulet were not suffered by yours truly but by Wolfie."

Elrod hoped Wolfie hadn't suffered too badly.

The boss gazed down at Kristen. "I should never have

doubted our savior's judgment in such matters. Ultimately it doesn't matter, of course. Now she is destined for a far more intense level of distress. Nowhere Man need not abide by earthly rules of what can and cannot be taken."

Elrod sure hoped that was true, and that the boss wasn't just saying it to make them feel better.

The front door whipped open. Double Bub barged in, looking all kinds of agitated. Hopping up and down like his feet were on fire, he pointed frantically toward the woods. Elrod stared where he was gesturing but didn't see anyone.

"Calm down," the boss urged. "Explain the problem."

Double Bub wagged his crate of a head and sat at the table, shoving the corrugated box out of his way. Producing a pencil and tablet he always carried, he began composing a note. He'd never win any speed-writing contests. He printed each letter with agonizing slowness. The boss looked on impatiently, then snatched the note before Double Bub finished. The boss read it and calmly turned to Elrod.

"It would appear that company may be coming. Get Kyzer."

"What should I tell him is hap–"

"Now, Elrod."

He knew that tone. Best to move his ass. But just as he was about to race out the door, a figure lunged from the woods. He was running toward them, full bore. Clutched in his hand was a triangle that looked for all the world like a larger version of the amulet. Elrod was simultaneously astonished and terrified to recognize the man from a photo Sindle Vunn had shown them.

"It's her brother! He's come back from the dead!"

THIRTY-TWO

Brad glimpsed a straw-hatted man with a fanny pack in the entrance. He ducked back into the cabin and slammed the door.

Don't hesitate, don't think about it. You have the weapon. You can't be stopped.

The silent pep talk solidified his purpose. Yet the triangle felt no different. There were none of those quivering sensations that had radiated through him at the stream. There was no red glow, no crackling energy.

Joseph's voice sounded in his head. *As you awaken so does the Trine.*

Invigorated by the words, he reached the door, wrenched it open and charged in. He froze. Kristen lay motionless on a picnic table, a large wolf doll beside her. Sindle Vunn hovered over his sister, a pistol pressed against her right temple. Farther into the room stood Boxhead and Nidge, and behind them, fearfully peeking out, the man with the hat. He had to be the one they'd called Elrod, the one who'd burned down the house.

Brad glared at Sindle Vunn, trying not to let the sickening feeling in his stomach migrate to his face. Raising the weapon, he willed it to come alive and reveal its incredible powers.

"Get away from her," he warned. "Now!"

"Put that thing down," Sindle Vunn said calmly, "or I'll make sure she never wakes up."

Brad's rage erupted. "Get away from her, motherfucker! I'll

tear you a new asshole! I'll send every one of you straight to fucking hell!"

His fury caused the other three men to back away. But Sindle Vunn held fast.

"Whatever you think you might achieve, I promise you won't do it before I pull this trigger."

Brad squeezed the stick in his hand, willed the second part to transform into a fiery staff that would knock away the gun. He tried recalling the exact sequence of events back at the stream. Closing his eyes, he took a forceful step toward Sindle Vunn.

I'm going to save you, Kristen. I swear I will.

He opened his eyes. Nothing. The triangle remained dormant. The gun barrel was still aimed at Kristen's head. He fought to contain growing panic.

Sindle Vunn grinned and faced the others. "Do you smell that?"

Elrod sniffed at the air. Frowning, he shook his head.

"It's fear. The scent oozes from him." The tormentor turned back to Brad. "Your sister and the amulet, they are joined. They are a unity of intent, complete unto itself. But you? You're just a loser holding a triangle. Frankly, it looks like one of those old-fashioned dinner bells used to summon the farm workers to the table. Is that your plan? Ring the bell and the yokels will come a-runnin'?"

Nidge laughed. Boxhead expressed amusement by hopping up and down. Sindle Vunn continued.

"It's actually rather sad and pathetic. Yes, the two of you are siblings. But clearly, you are not equal in your resolve. One of you is strong, determined. The other... so very weak."

Why isn't it working? What am I not doing that I did at the stream? What's different?

An answer came to him. The difference was Joseph. He wasn't here. His presence earlier had enabled Brad to feel the Trine's power, bring the sticks together. A more nauseating thought occurred. What if the incident back at the stream had nothing to do with Brad? What if Joseph had simply channeled his own power through him, using him like a trained animal. He wouldn't put it past that lying bastard of a grandfather to manipulate him like that.

I should have realized it earlier. I've been fooling myself. I never had any real control over the weapon.

"He's done," Sindle Vunn announced, turning to Nidge. "Kindly take away his dinner bell."

The chauffeur hesitated.

"Do it. He can't hurt you with it, at least not by means of any superhuman tricks."

Nidge sprinted across the cabin, surprisingly fast for a man that size. Brad swung the triangle at his head. The chauffeur raised his arm, deflecting the blow. The weapon hit his elbow, shattered. The three sticks clattered harmlessly to the floor.

Nidge's fist plowed into Brad's midsection. He doubled over, the wind knocked out of him. The next thing he knew, the chauffeur had him face down and was wrenching his arms behind his back. In seconds his wrists were bound by one of those heavy plastic zip ties.

Nidge rolled him onto his back. He glared up at his captors. Sindle Vunn holstered his pistol. It was the tiniest of consolations. For the moment, Kristen was not being threatened.

"We're leaving," Sindle Vunn announced, kicking the three sticks across the room, away from Brad. "Pick up the child."

"Back to Gracious?" Nidge asked, throwing Kristen over his shoulder.

Sindle Vunn nodded. "The drug will keep her unconscious at least until nightfall. When she awakens in the crack house it will be time for her to meet…" Trailing off, he smirked at Brad. "I believe you may know of whom I speak."

"Nowhere Man!" Elrod shouted with glee.

"Indeed. Double Bub, go to the other cabin and get the girl. Tell her she's returning to town with us."

The girl! Brad's heart pounded as fresh agony coursed

through him. Were they talking about Felicity? He writhed on the floor, trying to rip apart the cuffs even while knowing it was hopeless.

As Double Bub moved toward the door, Sindle Vunn had further words for him. "You and Kyzer will stay here. Just before dark, the two of you are to drive our prisoner back toward town. Once you're in cellphone range, have Kyzer call me. By then, our savior no doubt will have arrived and I'll be able to provide updated instructions." He smiled at Brad. "It's likely our spirited young friend will need to face a rather intense and disagreeable interrogation, so be sure he is not harmed in any significant way. No broken bones, that sort of thing."

Boxhead, whose name apparently was Double Bub, raised his arms and made an odd gesture, some kind of sign language. Sindle Vunn nodded with understanding.

"The brothers? When they return from their patrol, tell them they are to assist you and Kyzer with guard duty." He gave Brad a friendly wink. "I'm sure between the four of you he will prove manageable."

"What about me?" Elrod wondered, sounding hurt by being excluded from the plan.

"Hmm… I suppose you should come with us as well."

Elrod's features transformed to delight.

Nidge gestured to the sticks. "And that thing?"

"We'll bring it with us. I'm sure the savior will be quite pleased to acquire the second part of the Trine in such an effortless way."

"Why not bring the brother with us too?"

"Tempting. But I prefer we err on the side of caution. Best to keep him separated from the triangle for the time being. We wouldn't want him to make another feeble attempt to ring the dinner bell while we're on the road."

Double Bub exited. Sindle Vunn faced the man with the fanny pack.

"Elrod, would you do the honors and pick up the sticks? I'm quite sure they've been rendered completely harmless."

Elrod gazed warily, not wanting to touch them. But he did as he was told. Kneeling beside the closest one, he gingerly extended a hand. But just as his fingertip was about to make contact, the stick rolled away. Startled, he jerked upright and lunged backward.

"I didn't do that! It moved by itself."

"Maybe a breeze," Nidge said, not sounding convinced.

Brad wondered if he'd somehow unconsciously moved the stick. Maybe he'd been wrong about Joseph and he really did have some kind of real control over the second part. He forced himself to concentrate again, imagined the three sticks reforming into their natural shape. But nothing happened.

Sindle Vunn gazed back and forth between Brad's pinched face and the sticks. He seemed to be re-evaluating his plan.

"We'll also leave the sticks here for now," he concluded. "When Kyzer returns, I'd suggest moving dinner-bell boy to the other cabin. Put some distance between them to be on the safe side.

Elrod looked relieved that he didn't have to make another attempt to gather up the sticks. Brad watched helplessly as Nidge carried Kristen out the door. He noticed that his sister's right hand remained clenched. She must still have the amulet. That made sense. They wouldn't be bothering with her if they'd already gotten her to surrender it.

Elrod and Sindle Vunn exited, leaving the door open and Brad momentarily alone. He lifted his head from the floor. He could see the sticks, a mere six feet away. Double Bub and Kyzer would return in minutes or less. *Now or never.*

He closed his eyes, formed a mental image of the sticks reforming a triangle in his hand.

"I'm going to save you, Kristen." His voice sounded odd in the cabin's stillness. But maybe speaking aloud would bring the magic. "No matter where they take you, Kristen, no matter how far away, I'm coming for you."

He opened his eyes. Nothing. Not so much as a flutter of movement from the broken triangle.

He made another attempt, this time keeping his eyes open but uttering the words silently, in his head. The effort failed as well. Yet in the back of his mind, a hint of an idea struggled to take shape. Something to do with what had happened back at the stream. Something else that had been different besides Joseph's presence.

A more fundamental emotion.

It came to him in a rush. Storming into the cabin, every thought, every affirmation, had been about what he, Brad Van Reed, was going to do. His focus had been about making the power of the Trine come to *him* so that *he* could save Kristen. But when he'd drawn the sticks from the water and reassembled them, he hadn't been thinking about himself, what he could personally accomplish with the Trine. His thoughts – his feelings – had been attuned to how deeply he cared about his sister.

It wasn't about me. It was about her.

He tried recalling the nostalgic memories that flowed through him while waiting for Joseph at the site of their old house, like playing with Kristen as a baby. But instead, a more recent event popped into his head. It had happened two years ago, not long after he'd left town.

He'd been Skyping from North Carolina for his sister's ninth birthday. The conversation had begun stiff and formal, with Brad asking how school was going and Kristen dutifully thanking him for the Amazon gift card he'd sent. At the end of the call, she'd asked when he was coming home.

"I don't know. I need to stay down here for a while, get my head together."

"Couldn't you get your head together in Gracious?" she asked.

"Kind of tricky. I need some space, some distance."

Kristen thought about that for a moment. Then…

"Felicity told me about space and distance. She said that when you look out into space and see distant stars, you're actually looking backward in time. On account of the light leaving those stars a long time ago and having to travel real far to reach us."

Brad stiffened at the mention of his jilted bride. "Yeah, I guess that's true. What's your point?"

"Even if something's far away, the light is always coming."

He'd been impressed by the subtlety of her thoughts, and not for the first time imagined her as some wise old soul who just happened to be born into a child's body. But now, lying here handcuffed and helpless, an intense feeling inexplicably washed over him about what she'd expressed that day. *The light is always coming.* Somehow, those words encapsulated how much he cared for his sister.

Across the room, the sticks rolled toward one another, snapped back into a triangle.

Yes! He could feel its power. Heartened, he willed the triangle to rise from the floor. It elevated a few inches, hung there.

Now what?

Joseph's words returned, part of his counsel to Brad back at the stream. *What do you want to happen?*

"I want to get out of these handcuffs."

Plant a picture in your head of it happening.

He heard voices. But these weren't in his head, they were coming from outside. The others were returning. He had only seconds.

Arching his back, he squirmed to a sitting position. From there he was able to push off with his bound hands and launch himself onto his feet. He stared at the triangle, imagined it airborne.

"What the fuck?" someone shouted behind him.

Too late.

Brad twisted his head around. A man with shoulder-length hair and a wild beard stood in the doorway, holding a double-barreled shotgun. A shorter man, equally hairy and grungy, stood behind him. Even in their hirsute state, he recognized them as Hiram and Amos Swanteri.

Before Brad could formulate a thought for animating the weapon, Hiram flipped the shotgun around and swung the stock at him. Brad lunged sideways, dodging a blow to the head. But he couldn't avoid a shoulder hit that sent him stumbling sideways. Before he could regain his balance, Hiram's makeshift bat struck again, this time low, cracking the side of Brad's calf and knocking his feet out from under him. He banged the edge of the table on his way down and landed hard, once again on his back.

A swell of pains overwhelmed him. He couldn't focus. The room became a dark blur. When his vision cleared, he realized he must have drifted into unconsciousness for a few seconds. The door was closed and Hiram stood over him, the shotgun pressed into his guts. Kyzer and Double Bub were in the cabin as well, conferring with Amos Swanteri.

Brad angled his head toward the weapon. It was in pieces again, the three sticks motionless on the floor. He tried painting a picture in his head of it reforming. But between agonies coursing through his calf and shoulder, and the shotgun's twin muzzles shoved into his belly, he couldn't concentrate.

Amos was explaining to Kyzer what he'd seen when the brothers arrived. "It was all put together and floatin' in the air. I think he was doin' it. We gotta waste him."

"Ready anytime," Hiram growled, pressing the dual muzzles deeper into Brad's stomach.

"Boss said no," Kyzer warned. "Wants him alive. Savior wants him alive."

Hiram pulled back on the shotgun a few inches but didn't turn the barrels away.

"Take the sticks outside," Kyzer ordered. "Hide 'em somewhere where he can't see 'em."

"Don't take orders from you," Amos growled.

"Whazamatter, scared?"

"Hell no."

"Well then?"

"Screw you," Amos muttered, reaching down to grab the closest stick. It rolled away from his hand.

"Must not like your ass," Hiram taunted.

Amos got mad, made a grab for the second stick. It reacted by standing on end and slowly rotating like some kind of weird child's top. Amos hesitated.

"Just grab the fucker," Hiram snarled.

Amos tried. But as his hand was about to close around it, the stick shot straight up like a rocket. It cracked against the ceiling and stuck there, suspended like an icicle.

All eyes turned upward. Brad was as perplexed as his captors. He didn't know how he was doing whatever he was doing. Then he realized it didn't matter. Maybe he was eliciting some sort of unconscious control. Or maybe the weapon was acting on its own, protecting itself. Whatever the case, he needed to make that control deliberate, make it conscious.

Kyzer glared at Brad then whipped his attention to Hiram.

"Knock the fucker out!"

Hiram flipped the shotgun around, preparing to smash the stock down on Brad's head. Before he could carry through, the third stick leaped five feet off the floor. It tumbled end over end and hit Hiram across the face with a resounding smack.

Hiram yelped. The stick began circling his head like a moon orbiting a planet, moving faster and faster.

"Get away from me!" Hiram batted at it with the shotgun. But it dodged his onslaughts by speeding up or slowing down at the last possible instant.

The other two sticks took flight, tumbled haphazardly around the cabin like out-of-control drones. Amos drew his revolver, tried to get a bead on the closest one. The stick responded by going into orbit around his head. Amos fired blindly.

"Watch where the fuck you're aimin'!" Kyzer hollered as the shot passed within a foot of his head.

"Over here," Brad whispered. "Come to me."

But the sticks refused to obey. Instead, they froze in mid-flight and just hung there, dead in the air.

"No," Brad urged. "Come to me!"

They erupted to life, barrel-rolled toward one another. Grouped like a handful of darts, they shot away from Brad, toward the front door...

...which flew open with such force it tore right off its hinges. The door slammed hard against the floorboards. Joseph stormed into the cabin atop it, the sticks snapping into a triangle in his hand.

The weapon blazed, filling the cabin with a scarlet light so fierce it overwhelmed the illumination from the open door behind it. Red-hot embers streamed along the weapon's circumference, their hue complementing the blood-soaked bandage on Joseph's head and the fury in his eyes.

Hiram flipped the shotgun around, took aim at the intruder. The flaming triangle leaped from Joseph's hand and wrapped around the barrel. Like some impossible three-sided wrench, the sticks tightened, violently yanking the shotgun from Hiram's grip. The weapon flew across the room.

Amos frantically whipped his revolver toward Joseph and fired. He was too unsettled to take proper aim. The shot missed. He didn't get off a second one. The weapon transformed into a blazing spear. It shot across the cabin and impaled Amos's revolver, then lanced upward into his heart. It emerged out of his back in a spray of pulverized muscle and bone.

Hiram screeched as his brother toppled. He charged at Joseph. Brad swung his legs into Hiram's path, tripping him. Hiram slammed the floor.

Double Bub made a grab for the spear protruding from Amos. Before he could touch it, the weapon reformed into a squarish U-shape. The open end clamped onto Double Bub's neck and jerked upward, ripping goggles, grill and lopsided helmet from his head at the same time.

Brad gasped at the revealed face. Double Bub was a nightmare of cellular division gone horribly wrong. Two mismatched faces occupied a single countenance. There were two sets of eyes, two adjacent noses and twin earlobes on either side, one growing out of the other. The edges of the mouths were fused but not directly in line. One mouth was slightly lower, as if the two faces had grown at different rates. Misshapen skull bones at the crown protruded at nearly right angles, accounting for the squarish helmet, and the head was extra wide to accommodate the doubled sensory organs. He was literally his own twin brother.

Double Bub cloaked his face with his hands, as if embarrassed at being exposed. He dove through the nearest window but didn't make a clean getaway. His feet got tangled in the screening. Legs kicked madly, trying to tear free of the partition.

Kyzer whipped out his hatchet, lunging at Joseph. Hiram scrambled up from the floor, madness in his eyes, his wrath directed at Brad for tripping him. Drawing a serrated hunting knife, the remaining Swanteri brother attacked. Brad elevated his legs just in time and caught Hiram in the midsection, lifting him up and over. Hiram soared past his head and crashed to the floor a second time.

Joseph dodged Kyzer's hatchet blow. The weapon transformed back into a fiery spear. It lanced into the back of Kyzer's neck and twisted violently, nearly separating the head from the shoulders in a spume of crimson. Kyzer's body managed to stay upright for a moment before the knees buckled. Three hundred pounds, including the nearly decapitated head, crashed to the floor.

Hiram got to his feet again, started toward Brad. He gasped and abruptly halted. A mystified expression transformed into agony. The trio of burning sticks, having punctured his back, slowly sprouted from his chest in a triangular formation. Angry red flowers they seemed, signifiers of death.

Hiram grunted. His body spasmed. The sticks emerged fully, caked in clumps of flesh and pulpy internal matter, and leaving behind three bloody gaping holes. Hiram looked like he wanted to scream but could no longer manage such a complicated task. He fell over backward, landing with a dull thud. The sticks shot across the room and snapped into their default configuration in Joseph's hand.

The ferocity in Joseph's eyes lessened. The triangle seemed to dim correspondingly, its fury momentarily contained. Brad pried himself upright and turned away. Joseph's knife sliced through the cuffs, freeing him.

Noises emanated from the window. Double Bub's feet were still tangled in the screening. He kicked and twisted, frantic to break free. Fury returned to Joseph's face. The weapon again burned bright.

Brad reached the window first. Double Bub's arms clawed at the ground. Sensing their presence, he twisted his neck to gaze up at them. One set of eyes on the twinned face opened wide, shocked and afraid. The other set blinked rapidly, leaving Brad with the uncanny impression that the second countenance was fighting back tears.

Joseph raised the triangle to strike.

"No!" Brad grabbed his wrist, interrupting whatever deadly new transformation was intended. Pushing in front of Joseph, he untangled Double Bub's boots from the screen wire and shoved him all the way through the window.

Double Bub stared up at Brad for a moment. One face seemed thankful, the other perplexed by the unexpected display of mercy. The twinned mouths opened and closed, seemed to be trying to utter something. But no words emerged, only faint gurgling sounds.

The creature lunged to his feet and dashed off into the trees.

Joseph glared at Brad. But he knew he'd done the right

thing. Whatever horrible crimes Double Bub had committed, having to exist with such a cruel deformity demanded he be shown compassion. Or maybe Brad had been guided by a more subtle reason. Maybe his abrupt empathy centered on sometimes feeling that he too could have dueling perspectives emerging from a single body.

Joseph turned away and strode purposefully toward the exit. Footfalls reverberated as his boots trampled across the flattened door.

Brad gazed down at the three slain men. He imagined trying to explain to the authorities the level of violence that had been unleashed here and how it had occurred. Even though he knew there was just cause, such mutilated bodies doubtless would provoke the most intense questioning.

Joseph pivoted in the doorway, annoyed Brad wasn't following.

"Well, what are you waiting for?" he growled. "Let's go get your sister."

THE THIRD PART

SILSO: You were wrong about the discordant one. He is not fatally compromised. Were it true, would he have shown mercy to that malformed creature?

ORJOS: *His actions merely constitute a behavioral quirk. He will revert soon enough to his true character, at which time the Pestilence will be his undoing.*

SOHN: Judge not that which cannot be judged.

THIRTY-THREE

Leaving the cabin, Brad revealed what he'd overheard about Sindle Vunn and his thugs taking Kristen to a crack house in Gracious.

Joseph frowned. "Why would they go to such a place?"

"Don't know. But that's what he said."

In high school, Brad had been attuned to the drug scene and knew some of the regional dealers. Most didn't sell crack cocaine, however, meth being the more popular drug of the era. And he'd never heard of a house or apartment where crack was used or distributed. Of course, that didn't mean there wasn't one.

Joseph didn't seem to want to waste time puzzling over the matter. "Kristen's captors don't have much of a head start. Driving fast, we might be able to catch them."

Brad disagreed. Even if Mrs Jastrzembski's aged SUV could outrun the limo, a high-speed pursuit on a winding road probably wasn't in his sister's best interests. Besides, he wasn't ready to leave yet. Sindle Vunn had mentioned that "the girl" would accompany them. It was obvious he'd been referring to someone other than Kristen.

"There's a second cabin," he said. "It must be close."

Joseph scowled, annoyed at the delay. His attitude had undergone a profound change. Brad supposed that being attacked by Double Bub and nearly dying could be responsible for his foul mood. Still, he sensed it was more than that. A harshness had come to the forefront, a deep rage – qualities at odds with the man Brad had come to know throughout this extraordinary day. Or maybe those qualities had always been buried inside Joseph, consciously or unconsciously repressed. Maybe grandfather and grandson were more alike than he'd considered, both equally pissed off at the world.

He recalled what Big Moxie had said about the teenage Joseph, how he'd ambushed those four men for insulting his aunt, putting two of them in the hospital. *A righteous badass* had been Big Moxie's description. Brad could now attest to that. There'd been a savagery in Joseph's assault on Kyzer and the Swanteris. And had Brad not intervened, Joseph surely would have slain Double Bub.

A related thought occurred. Was the ferocity Joseph had unleashed in the cabin indicative of the second part of the Trine's true nature? Or was it more a reflection of Joseph's true nature?

Maybe a bit of both.

"Five minutes," Joseph grumbled. "If we don't find this other cabin by then, we go."

"Deal." Brad was torn over searching for Felicity while Kristen remained in peril. Despite that, he'd push the timetable if necessary. He couldn't leave here knowing Felicity might be nearby and also needing help.

He scanned the forests but couldn't see another structure. But there was the hint of a pathway along the left side of the cabin. Proceeding past the window, the one opposite from where Double Bub made his inglorious exit, he spotted the second cabin.

Joseph raced ahead of him, weapon at the ready. It might be a plain triangle again but Brad knew it could erupt into demonic fury at the first sign of a threat. He wasn't expecting any. Sindle Vunn's crew and the Swanteri brothers were accounted for, either dead or heading back to Gracious and the mysterious crack house. It was possible Double Bub would seek vengeance and circle back on them. But something in the creature's final expression – *expressions* – made that unlikely.

Joseph peered through the cabin's window, gestured all clear. Brad shoved open the door, his attention drawn by one of the cots. On it a blanket completely shrouded a motionless figure.

Joseph pushed past him and yanked off the blanket. It was Felicity. She was on her back, hands folded peacefully across her chest, like a corpse displayed in a funeral home. Her wrists and ankles were bound with zip ties. Joseph checked her neck for a pulse.

"Is she…?" Brad couldn't finish the sentence.

"She's alive." He shook her roughly but she didn't stir.

"Let's get her to her feet. She might snap out of it."

Joseph cut through her cuffs. Together they lifted Felicity from the cot, held her upright between them. Joseph shook her again and lightly slapped her face.

"Probably drugged," he concluded. "Lay her back down."

"We can't just leave her here."

"Yes we can."

Brad motioned to the cot. "We can use that as a stretcher."

"Bad idea. She'll slow us down."

"Are you going to help me or not?"

This time, Joseph made his displeasure known with a string of what Brad took to be Creole curses. But he helped Brad lower Felicity and strip off the cot's bedding. The legs were collapsible, and they secured Felicity to the aluminum frame with a length of rope from her backpack. Brad noticed she wore an empty sidearm holster and knife sheath. Her wristwatch, a rugged Timex owned for as long as he'd known her, was missing too.

He rooted through the backpack but found no gun, blade or watch. Her phone was on the floor. It had been smashed by someone's boot.

He strapped on her backpack. It had food, water and

other supplies that might come in handy. They picked up the makeshift stretcher and made their way toward the first cabin, with Joseph leading and Felicity positioned feet-first to lessen the amount of weight the older man would have to bear. Even so, Brad could tell the chore was going to be harder than anticipated, particularly for Joseph. He was already slowing as he struggled to keep the stretcher's front end elevated. Wielding the weapon might have provided him a burst of inner strength. But without its power, his physique reverted to its natural state, showcasing the impediments of his advanced years.

"Any chance you can turn that triangle into a medevac chopper," Brad quipped.

Joseph's response was a grunt.

"Listen, if you get tired, I can rig a rope around my shoulders and drag her on my own."

"I'll be all right."

But he wasn't. Joseph slowed even more. Just as they reached the first cabin, his strength abruptly failed. The front of the stretcher slipped from his grip, slamming to the ground and jarring Felicity.

Brad gently lowered his end. "All right, I got it from here." Retrieving the rest of the rope from the backpack, he was about to rig it to the frame when Felicity's arm shot out and grabbed his wrist.

"Where am I?" she demanded, sitting up. Her head whipped back and forth, her face etched with confusion. "What's going on? What are you two doing here?"

"Maybe you should lie back down for a minute," Brad suggested.

"Don't patronize me," she snapped, revealing a stubbornness he remembered as having surfaced more than a few times during their dating years. "Get this rope off my waist! And why are you wearing my backpack?"

Brad untied her and surrendered the pack. Felicity roared

to her feet, bombarding them with more questions. "Where's Flick? Why are you here? Why am I on a stretcher? Where were you taking me?"

Joseph's annoyed look and gestures indicated they should continue on and not waste even more time. But Brad knew Felicity well enough to realize she wouldn't budge without an explanation.

He started by detailing last night's events culminating in the fire. She hadn't known about Zack and Nipa's murders and Kristen's kidnapping. As her shock registered, Joseph continued walking, gesturing for them to follow while picking up the story. By the time they reached the trail, he'd given her a brief rundown of the amulet, the three parts of the Trine, the eidolon forest and Nowhere Man. Brad finished with a condensed version of the battle in the cabin between Sindle Vunn's armed thugs and Joseph's supernatural weapon, and the kidnappers' plan to take Kristen to a crack house somewhere in Gracious. By then, Felicity was regarding them as if they were some outlandish comedy duo setting her up for the big punchline.

"What a crock! What drugs are you on?"

"It's all true," Brad said.

"Bullshit!"

"You think I'd lie about something like this?"

She hesitated, then turned and stomped back toward the main cabin.

"You don't want to go in there," Brad warned.

Felicity ignored him and disappeared inside. She was gone for several minutes. When she emerged, her face was pale. She was carrying Hiram Swanteri's shotgun. Her belt sheath housed a knife taken from one of the men and the Timex was back on her wrist.

"There was a revolver too," she said, her voice eerily calm. "A .357 magnum – an old five-shot Charter Arms Bulldog. But it was unserviceable. Something melted the barrel."

She stared off into the trees, distracted.

"You going to be OK?" Brad asked.

"They have Flick, don't they."

"Seems likely."

Felicity rubbed the back of her neck. "She stabbed me. A purple syringe, some kind of knockout drug."

"Must be what they used on Kristen." His sister's smaller body mass might have caused a longer period of unconsciousness.

"Let's keep moving," Joseph urged.

As they followed him, Felicity related what had happened to Flick in the cave, her discovery of the meteorite with the embedded object. "She said it appeared to be of artificial construction and possibly indicative of intelligent extraterrestrial life."

She made the pronouncement with a caution worthy of her scientific background. Despite everything that had happened, Felicity would never go overboard about such things, not until solid proof was obtained and alternate possibilities eliminated. A day ago, Brad would have been skeptical as well that aliens were somehow involved. But now it was just one more item to file in a rapidly expanding weirdness catalog.

Felicity told them about the black goo that had gotten in Flick's mouth, supposedly from a swarm of bats, and how it had altered her personality.

"Not bats," Joseph said grimly. "That had to be Nowhere Man. You must have found his lair."

Brad told her about Big Moxie's recollection of Amos Swanteri's warning, that Nowhere Man was going to fly out of his cave. Individuals would be goo-shooted and become his slaves forever.

Felicity looked pained by the revelation. Brad realized he should have left out the "forever" part.

"Whatever this goo is," he added, "I'm sure there's an antidote."

She nodded, wanting to believe him.

"So we hike to this cave while it's still light out," Brad said. "Before Nowhere Man flies out of there."

"And do what exactly?" Joseph demanded.

"Use your weapon. Finish him off. Better to kill a vampire in daylight while it's still asleep in its coffin."

"Nowhere Man is far more dangerous than some mythic boogeyman."

Brad again sensed trepidation in Joseph's tone. The idea of a confrontation with Nowhere Man clearly frightened him. This time, Brad wasn't going to ignore it.

"He freaks you out. I get that. But why? It has to be something more than just the fact he's a scary dude. I mean, you're a pretty scary dude yourself."

Joseph didn't answer.

"Returning to the cave doesn't sound like a good idea," Felicity said. "We need to rescue Flick and Kristen. If this crack house is in town, and if their gang has been using it all along, we should be able to find someone who spotted the limo or saw them going in and out of the place. Or maybe this will help."

She pulled out a phone. "Found it in the pocket of the big dead guy."

Brad glanced at Joseph. In their hurry to leave the cabin, neither of them had thought to search the bodies.

"Did you check it?" he asked.

"Can't. Password protected. Do you know his name?"

"Kyzer," Brad said. "Not sure of the spelling."

Felicity tried three or four variations, shook her head. "There are downloadable apps for unlocking phones. But there's no service out here, so that's a nonstarter too."

"What about the Swanteri brothers?" Brad asked. "Did they have phones?"

"No. At least not on them. I have an idea. Dad's IT guy at the bank is really sharp. If anyone can break into a phone and do it fast, he can."

Brad nodded. The phone could have important clues, maybe even the location of the crack house. "But if that doesn't pan out, we still have to figure out how to locate the place. And Sindle Vunn could have been speaking in general terms when he said the house was in Gracious."

There were many isolated properties outside the official town borders. Locals often employed a kind of shorthand, referring to the entire region as Gracious. He'd heard the classification "in town" applied to homes and businesses nearly ten miles from Lakamoxin Street and the downtown.

"We're wasting time debating things," Joseph said, picking up the pace.

Brad agreed. Yet he flashed back to Joseph's silence when quizzed about his fear of Nowhere Man. Once again, he had the feeling Dearest Grandfather was withholding vital information.

THIRTY-FOUR

Joseph could almost feel Brad's eyes boring into the back of his head as he proceeded along the haphazard trail. At least it was easy to follow. His own boot prints coming toward him were bold and forceful, indicative of his escalating rage as he'd rushed toward the cabin following that deformed creature's assault. Brad's insistence on sparing the creature had come as a surprise. If nothing else, it could be a sign that his grandson was overcoming his self-centered attitude and becoming more empathic.

And what am I becoming?

An anger burning bright in his youth had been tempered over the decades, first by Isabella's love, and later by simply growing older and attaining a more mature outlook. But one violent act seemed to have shattered those placid years, spewing forth the molten core perpetually bubbling underneath. Nowhere Man's servants, having surrendered to callous evil, certainly deserved to die. But his own emotions and motivations were less than admirable.

I badly wanted to kill them.

Maybe his reawakened fury was for the best. He'd need every advantage if there was to be any chance of saving Kristen – and that despite Silso's warning that the bearer of the first part was beyond his direct help. Yet even if he proved Silso wrong and they succeeded, what then?

Brad was right about him being afraid of a confrontation with Nowhere Man. It was something he'd inherently dreaded since first seeing that winged monstrosity soaring over the mountains of the eidolon. He'd never revealed to SOS or anyone else the chills that coursed through him when he contemplated such a face-off. He couldn't catch specific glimpses of the future the way Kristen could. Nevertheless, the second part somehow enabled him to sense that his ultimate fate was intertwined with Nowhere Man's.

That wasn't all Joseph was holding back. He'd neglected to mention Orjos' stunning revelation upon entering the eidolon this morning and saving Brad from the venting. It was too demoralizing. If his grandson was to become heir to the second part, better for him to believe the future offered hope.

Nowhere Man is boundless, Orjos had explained in his typical haughty tone.

"I don't understand," Joseph answered, hoping the admission would prompt Orjos to expand on the subject.

Of course you don't understand. You couldn't be expected to.

He'd contained his annoyance, tried a more direct approach.

"Let's overlook my ignorance for the moment. All I really need to know is how to kill him."

Orjos responded with a dismissive laugh. *Haven't you been paying attention? You don't kill Nowhere Man. For all practical purposes, he cannot die.*

"Every living thing dies."

That should provide even your feeble mind with a clue. The Pestilence is not alive, not in the sense you perceive life. It is functionally immortal.

"Are you sure we're on the right path?" Brad asked, drawing Joseph from his reverie. There was an undertone to the question, a hint of criticism. An expression of Brad's continuing mistrust.

"It's the way back," Joseph retorted, unable to contain irritation at being challenged.

"Gee Grandfather, absolutely certain of that?"

Joseph knew the revelation was for Felicity's benefit. She was appropriately surprised.

"You're his *grandson*?"

"Yeah, imagine that." Brad unleashed a bitter laugh. "Oh, but here's the kicker. I just found out today. You see, Joseph, he's the sort of family member who likes to keep little details like that under wraps."

Felicity was wise enough not to insert herself into the squabble. Brad went quiet as well. Joseph kept his eyes downward, fixated on his own boot prints marching angrily toward him.

THIRTY-FIVE

Joseph's incessant need to keep secrets was like thrusting a hot poker into an open wound. It was the same crap Brad had dealt with his entire life. Saving Kristen was the only thing keeping his inner turmoil in check, or at least the worst of it.

They emerged from the trail onto the fire lane and headed back toward the main road. The lane was wide enough for the three of them but he and Felicity let Joseph walk ahead. The flanking wilderness made it seem they were in a green tunnel, an effect not as noticeable off-trail, where the woods totally enveloped.

A short time later, they came upon the van. Joseph approached warily. Felicity unslung Hiram's shotgun and joined him.

"Empty," she said, peering through the front window. "The rest of them must have all left in the limo."

"What time is it?" Brad asked. He'd lost track. The meager sunlight that pierced the canopy revealed lengthening shadows.

"Five-thirty," Felicity said, glancing at Kyzer's phone. She'd been checking it from time to time for the unlikely possibility of a signal.

He was surprised it was that late. That meant they only had maybe another three hours until sunset, when presumably Nowhere Man would emerge from his cavernous lair and come for Kristen. Despite Felicity's upbeat attitude – she believed someone in town would know the crack house's location and the IT guy would unlock the phone – there didn't seem to be enough time. A renewed feeling of hopelessness swept over Brad.

A hoot owl drew his attention to the woods. It was curious hearing one so early. Most of the birds were nocturnal. As if to punctuate the thought, the skies swiftly darkened and the shadows grew deeper. Was a storm blowing in?

The chilling answer arrived an instant later. The heavens went pitch black and a full moon with a bluish cast took shape low on the horizon. The canopy acted as a sieve, dicing the moonlight, creating a ground-level panoply of geometric patterns: rectangles and octagons, pentagrams and triangles, all seemingly infused with cryptic meaning.

Brad whirled back to Felicity. She was gone. So was Joseph. He was in the eidolon again, on that upwardly winding path. Somehow, he'd crossed over. As with his previous excursion, he sensed he wasn't alone. A swell of movement surrounded him, drawing closer.

The venting!

They appeared amid the trees from every direction. Most were humanoid, a handful bizarrely not. But even among the humanoid ones, there was enough distinctiveness in size and shape to confirm that many were not representative of anything born on this Earth. Yet as before, the harder he tried focusing on them, the more indistinct they became. And he sensed there were a lot more this time, a throng extending as far as he could perceive into the bizarre wilderness. Their intent was clearer this time. They didn't want to just harm him. They wanted him dead.

The venting relentlessly closed in. He recalled what had happened in his first encounter when they'd come close enough to touch him, how he'd experienced that barrage of negative emotions. He spun in a circle, looking for a break in their ranks. But there was nowhere to retreat.

"Brad, shut your eyes."

The urgent voice seemed to emanate from everywhere at once. Recognition coursed through him.

"Mom?"

"Shut your eyes. Acknowledging the venting makes them more potent."

He did as she asked. But even without looking, some part of him continued to sense they were still coming toward him. He was too freaked out not to look and flashed open his eyes.

"Bradley Van Reed, do as I say!"

Her sternness yanked him back to memories of childhood, to those times she'd hover over him in the living room, hands planted angrily on hips while administering a final warning that it was his bedtime, that he was to turn off the TV *this instant*. Then, as now, her no-nonsense attitude prompted obedience. He pinched his eyes tight. And then the weirdness level reached overdrive as his mother's disembodied voice broke out into song.

It was that lame Beatles-clone ditty, "The Mercy of Gracious," the one weaponized against generations of Gracious schoolchildren in order to inspire affection for their hometown. He remembered Mom making him sing it with her to help him memorize the lyrics for a second-grade class assignment.

"The Mercy of Gracious, yeah yeah; The strength of its bones, yeah yeah;

"Forever calling, yeah yeah; Its wanderers home."

She'd always had musical talent, highlighted by a vibrant lilting voice. The song flowed and echoed through the trees, still defying his attempts to locate a source.

"Follow it," she urged, reverting to a speaking voice. *"Follow its sound."*

"Follow it how? Why? Where are you?"

She went melodic on him again, launched into the second verse.

"The Mercy of Gracious, yeah yeah; Protective and strong, yeah yeah;
"Always pardoning, yeah yeah; The traveler's wrongs."

And suddenly, weirdly – if that word even still had meaning – it was as if Brad was hearing the song for the first time. Music and lyrics, shaped by the warm haze of his mother's spirit, washed over him. He listened with a childlike freshness, acceptance without judgment, cynicism abolished. He followed the song not with his body but with some aspect of a self that long ago had fallen into subliminal depths, a sensory membrane discarded upon the ascent of consciousness and reasoning.

The revival of that primordial means of perception enabled him to sense, simultaneously, what was ahead of him and what was behind him. Time was no longer a one-way stream but an ocean with waves flowing every which way, swamping deeply held notions of temporal direction, revealing past and future as mere aspects of some vaster totality.

His mother segued into the song's bridge, a countermelody of phrasing in a minor key.

"Draw out the evil; Bear true might; Discard all doubts; Forgive all slights;

"Urge they follow; Lead the way; Unite before they're led astray."

He sensed he was moving toward higher ground. The impression emanated from beyond his body, beyond the sensory apparatus constituting human locomotion. His mother began the final verse, a repeat of the first.

"The Mercy of Gracious, yeah yeah; The strength of its bones, yeah yeah;

"Forever calling, yeah yeah; Its wanderers home."

And then the song was over and he felt intense longing, not wanting it to end, not wanting her to leave him. Her final words were familiar.

"Find the third part."

And then she was gone. Solidity returned to his body. He was still moving steadily upward on that path and he sensed the venting still surrounding him. Yet they were no longer quite so close, quite so threatening.

He reached a small clearing at the top of a hill, somehow aware it was a temporary oasis from those spectral beings, shielded against their intrusion. A pair of voices chattered behind him. He whirled, surprised to find himself standing in front of a three-headed creature.

"SOS," he whispered.

The triplet of heads faced outward, equidistant on the thick neck. The chattering voices emanated from the pair facing in his general direction, although separated by a 120-degree arc. The one to his left seemed female, the one to his right male. But when he looked closer, the opposite seemed true. Regardless of their genders, both had pony-tailed hair vaguely similar to his own blond style and color. Their eyes were different from his, however, a deep ultramarine.

He could only see the third head from the back. It had the same light-hued ponytail but drooped forward, either asleep or unconscious. A white gown flowed outward from the bottom of the massive neck, expanding into a conical shape that nearly touched the ground. If the creature had appendages, they remained hidden.

The two heads continued conversing with one another. They were speaking English, and at a reasonable volume. Yet Brad couldn't make out what was being said. Some key element was missing, something that would enable communication, understanding.

The heads didn't appear to notice his presence. He took a step closer and cleared this throat. The thick neck contorted as they twisted to face him.

"What are you doing here?" the one on the right demanded. Its voice, like its features, defied a sexual identity. But there was no mistaking its tone, arrogant and unfriendly.

"It is him," the left head answered, its tone warmer. "The discordant one."

"Very good, Silso," the first head snapped, dripping sarcasm. "Make sure to state the obvious. Otherwise, confusion surely would reign."

Silso took the high road and didn't respond to the derisive words. Something about that head's nature suggested a quiet nobility, the capacity to rise above mundane concerns to look farther and deeper.

"Silso Orjos Sohn," Brad uttered, recollecting the creature's full name from Joseph.

"Look Silso. It talks."

"Be nice, Orjos. We don't want to scare him away." Silso's piercing eyes locked onto Brad. "Can you explain how you entered the eidolon?"

"I'm not sure. Maybe my mother helped?" Had she somehow enabled him to cross over from the real world in the first place, then guided him away from the venting and into the presence of this bizarre entity? An even more tantalizing idea occurred. Could she actually be more than a disembodied voice? Could she still be alive here in this realm?

"Your mother is nothing more than a mechanism for guiding you here," Orjos said, the face morphing into a sneer. "She is dead."

"Which you already know to be true," Silso added, the words tempered with sympathy.

Brad knew it, of course. Mom was gone. Whatever was happening with her voice must have something to do with the Trine and with his memories of her. He recalled Joseph's take on the eidolon, that the great dream forest was believed to be a projection of the three parts, that knowledge acquired here emanated from the Trine itself.

He tried not thinking of Mom, tried concentrating only on eliciting information from the freakish heads.

"Where are the bearers of the first two parts?" Silso asked. "Are they here with you?"

"No... at least I don't think they are." He shrugged. "I can't really say for sure."

"A veritable wellspring of incomprehension," Orjos said, the voice thick with disdain.

Brad grasped something about SOS. Orjos' cynical tone and Silso's upbeat one were exaggerated versions of his own dueling moods, reflections of his own psyche. Sometimes – probably most of the time – he was more like Orjos, angry

at the world and scoffing at its denizens. On rarer occasions
he achieved an attitude closer to Silso's, more balanced and
imbued with caring.

"Did you hope that by coming here we would provide you
with answers?" Orjos snarled. "Did you harbor the naive belief
that we are obligated to assist you in discovering–"

The mouth froze. The Orjos head drooped forward,
unconscious. Silso seemed about to speak when the same
thing happened to it.

The neck rotated 180 degrees, bringing the third head front
and center. The being known as Sohn raised its head and
opened its eyes. Like the other two, it lacked a clear gender. It
didn't speak, just gazed at Brad with a blank expression.

"Hello," Brad offered.

There was no response, no indication the word registered.
Joseph claimed the third head never spoke. Maybe it was a
deaf-mute or had some other kind of disability.

"I'm Brad," he said, pointing at his chest. "You're the one
called Sohn."

Still no reaction. He tried another approach.

"I'm a friend of Joseph's." That wasn't quite accurate.
Grandson, yes, friend, no. It didn't appear to matter. Sohn's
wooden expression remained intact.

"OK, listen, maybe you can understand what I'm saying,
maybe not. If you can and you're just playing hard to get, I could
really use your assistance. I need to save my sister. But first I have
to figure out how to travel back to the real world. Any thoughts?"

Nothing. Brad let his frustration show.

"Fine, be that way. It's been so very nice not talking to you."

He was about to turn away and look for the path down from
the clearing when Sohn's face grew animated and it spoke.

"You wish to take all your troubles, compress them into a
ball and hurl it far away."

Brad wasn't surprised the voice was gender-neutral like
the other heads. But he was astonished to hear his long-time

fantasy vocalized. Although the notion came upon him often, he couldn't recall telling a soul or even uttering it aloud.

"Any idea how to do that?" he asked. "Get rid of all my troubles?"

"Find the third part."

Brad sighed. "You know, I've been hearing that a lot lately. What about something more useful, something concrete. Like how and where do I find the third part?"

"Your sibling will soon face the Pestilence. If you do not go to her aid, it will acquire the first part. The world as you know it will be consumed."

Sohn's words hit like gut punches. "I want to help Kristen, more than anything! But I don't know how to find her. I believe she's been taken to a place called the crack house. Do you know where that is?"

"Find the third part."

Brad's frustration bubbled over. "Look, goddammit, just tell me what's really happening here? What the hell is the Pestilence? What's the purpose of the Trine? What's the meaning of all this crazy shit?"

He wasn't expecting a proper answer, only more mystifying hints. Joseph claimed that was usually the case during his encounters with SOS. It avoided direct assistance, provided only clues and vague suggestions.

But Sohn surprised him. Maybe the anger behind his demands had triggered something. Or maybe Sohn had a different function than its conjoined mates, a different agenda.

It stared off into the distance. When it spoke, its style of delivery was reminiscent of a middle-school science teacher Brad recalled liking, a man whose lectures were offbeat and rarely boring.

"More than a century ago, a repository of emotional detritus crash-landed on your world. The repository was one of millions dispatched into the void by a hyper-sentient civilization far from Earth, a civilization far advanced over your own. They were careful not to launch the repositories near living worlds, knowing there was an infinitesimal chance that one could be captured by a planet's gravity well. Here on Earth, against all odds, just such an event occurred."

"What do you mean, 'a repository of emotional detritus'?"

"A distillation of negative emotions and repressed pains. Fear, rage, loneliness. Frustration, cynicism, inadequacy. Resentment, disgust, helplessness. Quadrillions of corrosive feelings and urges which if not periodically extracted from individual minds would result in violent social perturbations and instabilities."

Brad recalled his initial encounter with the venting, how a mix of just such emotions had overwhelmed him.

"This civilization developed a means for periodically extracting such negativity from its citizenry. This emotional detritus was then distilled into a quasi-physical structure – a repository – and exiled into the void. Periodic removal of the detritus enabled the civilization to concentrate on nobler and more meaningful pursuits, largely freed from their most disruptive emotions."

"The Copernian Ridge meteorite," Brad concluded. "This repository was inside it."

Sohn gave a faint nod.

"And this repository... split open? The emotional detritus got out?"

"Essentially. A fundamental aspect of the detritus is immunity to destruction. That is the reason the repositories are dispatched, hidden within meteors to lessen the chance of other intelligent, spacefaring species identifying them as alien relics. The detritus can never be eliminated, only exiled. Even sending it into a sun or black hole would not result in annihilation and could produce other deleterious consequences."

Brad wondered what those consequences could be. Sohn continued before he could ask for clarification.

"Once the detritus arrived here, there was almost an inevitability that a human would come upon it."

"You're talking about that professor, Summersby."

"The being once known as Summersby was the first to be contaminated. Merely coming into physical contact with the repository was enough. He absorbed a fatal dose of those disruptive emotions – the detritus. The process of transformation took more than a hundred years, during which he hibernated in a cavern. When the process reached its culmination he emerged as the Pestilence, a being embodying all of those disruptive emotions. He is an animated malignancy, doomed to seek power and control as a substitute for what he lacks."

"What does he lack?"

"The élan vital. The essence of what it means to be a living being."

"Nowhere Man," Brad whispered.

"The Pestilence directly spread its poison to others, enslaving them to its will. They were tasked with acquiring the three parts of the Trine by whatever means necessary to prevent it from fulfilling its function. Should the Pestilence ultimately succeed in that task–"

"Wait, its function? What exactly is the Trine?"

"A trimorphic organism engineered to apply temporally unrestricted solutions to detritus containment and banishment."

"Uh-huh. Run that by me again but in English."

"A metaphor may provide clarity. The Pestilence is like toxic waste contaminating the environment. The Trine is the remediation device for cleaning it up. A Trine is incorporated into every repository for just such an unlikely event that occurred here, a meteor impacting and unleashing the detritus."

"OK, it's all starting to make sense... sort of. So you're saying the three parts can destroy Nowhere Man... destroy the Pestilence."

"No. The detritus exists in perpetuity. Therefore, the Pestilence does as well. It cannot be eliminated, only contained and exiled."

"All right, moving on. How come you're telling me all this

stuff? According to Joseph, you and your other heads would barely give him the time of day. Seems to me that if you were more forthright from the start, things would be a lot easier for everyone."

Sohn finally withdrew his gaze from the distance and met Brad's eyes. "The third part will be your guide in answering that question."

"Back to that again, huh? OK, but why three parts? If the Trine is meant to clean up this toxic waste – the Pestilence – why not make things simple and have the remediation device all in one? Give it to some suitable person and let 'em have at it. Easy-peasy."

"Were the three parts melded into a single device and bestowed upon one individual, that person, no matter how well-intentioned, likely would fall sway to its immense power. Such an individual could then become as malignant as the Pestilence."

"Absolute power corrupts absolutely." Brad murmured. "All right, I think I get it. To save Kristen, I have to find the third part. But you said Nowhere Man's going to consume the world. How's he going to do that? What's his ultimate plan?"

"Should the Pestilence acquire the first part of the Trine, it will be used to create an opening between–"

Sohn stopped in mid-sentence. Its eyes closed. The head drooped. SOS dashed away from Brad, gliding across the ground in a way that reminded Brad of one of those maglev trains on a cushion of air. It vanished over the far edge of the hill and descended into the woods. He sensed the venting were moving from its path, as if mandated to provide it an escape route.

Something prompted him to turn skyward. An airborne creature skimmed across a distant mountain range, too far away to distinguish features. But he had no doubt of its identity: Nowhere Man.

It seemed to notice his presence. Changing direction, it flew straight toward Brad. Chills went through him as the shadowy form accelerated. A whooshing sound filled the dark skies, the flapping wings disturbing the air. All too soon it was hovering above the clearing, the wings twitching faintly to keep it airborne.

Little Moxie's description was spot-on. It had an angular face and was hairless, and at least eight feet from head to toes. The wings sprouted from its upper back. The skin was pockmarked and crusted in a black sheen that resembled motor oil. The stink it gave off was reminiscent of something dead and putrefying – he fought the urge to retch. It was hard to believe such a monstrosity had once been a nineteenth-century science professor.

It hung there, eyes that held no light fixated on Brad, an apex predator encrusted in darkness. It spread its wings to their fullest measure, revealing on the underside a network of bloody veins. And protruding from its stomach area was something that resembled a coiled wire.

The creature swept down upon him. He released a startled cry and stumbled backward, instinctively throwing his hands up to protect his face. And then he was back on the fire lane, in that same frightened pose, arms aloft as shields.

"Brad!"

Felicity's exclamation was ripe with concern. "My god, where did you go?"

She stood facing him, Joseph at her side. Brad dropped his arms and tried to still his pounding heart.

"What happened?" she demanded. "You disappeared into thin air."

Joseph nodded with understanding. "The eidolon. You crossed over."

"How long was I gone?"

"Ten seconds maybe," Felicity said. "No more than that. You blinked out. A few moments later you blinked back."

"It was longer... over there."

He told them everything that had occurred from beginning to

end. Felicity and Joseph's expressions ranged from incredulity to shock. Yet when he finished, neither appeared to doubt the veracity of his experience.

"That description of the Trine's purpose," Felicity said. "You said something about it being a trimorphic organism?"

Brad recalled Sohn's exact words. "A trimorphic organism engineered to apply temporally unrestricted solutions to detritus containment and banishment."

"Then the Trine is actually alive. Though obviously not in the way we would define life."

"Yeah, I guess so."

"Temporally unrestricted solutions," she mused. "Do you have any idea what he meant by that?"

Brad shrugged. He wasn't surprised she'd zeroed in on the science-y aspects of his experience.

"And you still don't know how you're able to journey back and forth?" Joseph wondered.

"Not really." He hesitated. "Wait, maybe that's not entirely true. Both times when I crossed over, I was caught up in feelings of despair. It was like I was trapped in a situation I was powerless to change. And when Nowhere Man attacked and I returned here, it was a similar feeling, that there was no way to defend myself, no way I could win."

He faced Joseph.

"I think you were only partly right about the eidolon being a projection of the three parts of the Trine. I think it's also a projection of the Pestilence and the venting." He recalled his mother's singing. "And mixed in with all that are the thoughts and personality of each of us."

Joseph's expression indicated agreement with his appraisal.

Those feelings of despair and negativity that had coursed through Brad during his first passage through the eidolon, when the venting had been all over him, suggested that they had drawn him into the great dream forest, not SOS. Yet maybe it wasn't a black-and-white situation, one or the other.

Maybe some combination of the Trine and the Pestilence-venting was necessary for his crossings. Feelings of despair and negativity pulled him into that realm, yes. But also feelings of hope represented by the Trine.

"The rate that time passed for you," Felicity mused. "It was obviously different here from the way it was over there." She turned to Joseph. "Is that how it is for you?"

"No. Time always seems to pass at the same rate. Twenty minutes there is twenty minutes here. Clearly, there's something fundamentally different about Brad. Not only that anomaly but his ability to cross over in the first place with no apparent means of assistance." A tinge of envy crossed Joseph's face. "And I've been trying to elicit information from SOS since the 1960s. It always refused to explain things clearly or else dodged my questions. And I was never granted a conversation with Sohn."

"Find the third part," Felicity quoted. "You said that those words came from both your mother and Sohn. Obviously it's super important."

Brad shrugged. "No argument. But I still don't have the faintest idea how or why."

"The fact they both suggested it indicates you must know more than you think. Subconsciously, maybe you have a notion how to find the third part, or at least clues to its whereabouts."

"Makes sense," Joseph added. "That could explain why Sohn opened up to you."

Brad didn't doubt their conclusions. But he felt no closer to making sense of it. And Sohn's final interrupted sentence seemed critical as well. If Nowhere Man got the amulet or any other part of the Trine, he'd be able to create an opening. But an opening into what?

An answer seemed on the edge of awareness. Yet he couldn't bring it into focus. In any case, the priority remained Kristen. They had to find her before Nowhere Man came. He recalled Sohn's warning.

Your sibling will soon face the Pestilence. If you do not go to her aid, it will acquire the first part. The world as you know it will be consumed.

"We should get going," he said. "Can't afford to lose the light."

THIRTY-SIX

Felicity found the spot where she'd entered the fire lane and led Brad and Joseph on a short jaunt through the woods. Reaching Flick's Jeep, she drove them farther up the road to where the Nissan was cloaked under a stand of black walnuts. Her intent was to drop the two of them off so they could follow her into town. Brad had another idea.

"I'm coming with you," he announced, turning his back on Joseph.

Felicity thought the tension between the men would spill over. Joseph scowled and muttered something under his breath. Brad had a look she recalled from their dating years, apparent when someone had slighted him and he craved confrontation. Fortunately, Joseph decided against a fight and got into the Nissan. Felicity laid her backpack and the shotgun in the Jeep's back seat and waited until Brad was belted-in beside her before pulling out. A glance in the mirror showed Joseph following at a discreet distance.

She used the first few miles to gather her thoughts and try making sense of the mind-boggling events and revelations that had begun with Flick entering the cave. The rational principles governing the world – guideposts for Felicity's life for as far back as she could remember – seemed in jeopardy of being overthrown by forces of supernatural origin.

She wasn't about to give up on the bedrock of science, however. The fantastic occurrences might defy the limits of rational analysis, but that didn't prove mystical powers were at work. Brad's disappearance into that unearthly realm and his descriptions of what he'd learned there suggested a logical interpretation remained feasible... even if he had gleaned his information from a three-headed creature.

However farfetched, she needed to keep an open mind. Could there exist an interstellar civilization so advanced that it could sequester the worst emotions of its citizens into a geometric object – Flick's pentakis dodecahedron – and launch such repositories into space? Clarke's third law seemed applicable: Any sufficiently advanced technology is indistinguishable from magic. After all, the ascending course of human science and technology on Earth over the last few hundred years bloomed with achievements that earlier generations would have found unfathomable.

But however worthy such ideas might be, they remained limited to intellectual understanding. Beneath all her mental interpretations existed an undercurrent of stark fear. She was worried sick about Flick, about the effects of that mind-altering drug, about what further miseries the woman she loved might be facing.

No good would come from dwelling on such things, Felicity reminded herself. She forced concentration back to the present and glanced over at Brad. He sat rigid, gazing straight ahead. She could tell he was in one of his dark moods. Early on when they were dating and that occurred, she'd go equally silent and wait him out. Later in their relationship, she'd often attempt a more direct approach, try talking him through what was bothering him. On occasion she succeeded, at least to a point. But there was always a deep layer in him that stifled her best efforts to penetrate.

She knew he hated his father, and that his storehouse of buried pains largely resulted from their warped relationship. Brad couldn't forgive his dad for causing the crash that killed his mom. Still, Felicity always suspected there was something even more disturbing going on with him, something he perhaps refused to acknowledge to himself, let alone to others.

Back then, Felicity merely had been attempting to reinforce the bonds between them, build a stronger foundation by pushing him to be honest with her. Now the stakes were infinitely higher. Flick and Kristen and the fate of the entire world might hinge on what she and Brad and Joseph did over the next few hours. Allowing Brad to hide inside one of his moods was no longer an option.

He'd admitted to being caught up in feelings of despair and powerlessness when he crossed to or from the eidolon. That had to be related to his buried pains. His mother and Sohn had urged him to find the third part of the Trine – a critical piece of the puzzle as well. It was all threaded together, connected somehow. And she could no longer be delicate about how she went about unraveling it.

"You need to tell me what's going on in your head," she began, "Tell me what you're feeling."

She wasn't surprised to get a nasty look, his typical first reaction to such probing.

"What am I feeling?" he mocked. "Oh, nothing much, Felicity. What are *you* feeling? Are you having a nice day?"

She'd have to push through the snark and rage. It was probably something she should have made a greater effort to do years ago. Had she succeeded, a lot of heartache for both of them might have been avoided. Nevertheless, one way or another, she needed to make it happen now.

One thing was in her favor. They were a good forty-five minutes from Gracious, which meant Brad was stuck in the Jeep and couldn't partake of his go-to response – running away. When his emotions got disturbed, he'd get up and leave, a maneuver that reached its zenith on their wedding day. A secondary tactic was drinking himself silly. Fortunately, the Jeep was bereft of alcoholic beverages. And if he wanted to escape, he'd have to jump from a moving vehicle. She had no intention of stopping or even slowing down to let him out.

"Tell me more about your mom," she said, "about how she

guided you in the eidolon. It must have been comforting to hear her voice again."

His glare dimmed. Keeping his mother front and center seemed to help.

"That song she sang to you, 'The Mercy of Gracious.' Why do you think she did that?"

"I don't know."

"From what you told me, if I had to guess, I think part of the reason was to take your mind off the threat of the venting. A way to clear your thoughts, which somehow helped you find your way to SOS."

He nodded. "That sounds right."

"Still, I'm thinking she might have had another reason for singing it to you."

"Like what?"

"Remember the first part of the song's bridge? 'Draw out the evil; Bear true might.'"

Brad finished the line. "'Discard all doubts; Forgive all slights.'"

"I've always believed the song is essentially about forgiveness. Do you think your mom might also have been trying to tell you that you need to forgive your father for the crash that killed her?"

She steeled herself for an explosion even while hoping that's how he'd react. Worst case, he'd clamp down on his emotions, keep the pain bottled up.

"What the fuck are you talking about!"

An explosion. Good. That was a healthy start. All she could do now was stay the course and plow through his rage.

"I think you know what I'm talking about. What if your mom was trying to make it clear to you that through forgiveness, you might be able to reach a better place, a clearer state of mind?"

"Keep your psychobabble to yourself! Just because you took a bunch of psychology courses in college doesn't make you an expert."

"Maybe not. But it's high time you talked about the things that have been eating you up all these years."

"Fuck you, Felicity! Or maybe find a man to do it to you!"

That was nasty, a low blow. It got under her skin, instantly stripped away her attempted impartiality.

"Screw you too, Brad! Stop acting like a selfish jerk! Kristen deserves better. Not a brother who's so damn insecure he resorts to childish insults!"

She drew a deep breath, exhaled, struggling to restore a modicum of objectivity. Both of them being pissed off wouldn't help the situation.

"Look," she said, forcing calm. "Just try considering what I'm saying for a moment without snapping at me. Neither of us are super beings, just two regular humans living on a tiny planet on the outskirts of a middling galaxy. We don't have the option of removing our bad emotions and shooting them off into space. The only thing we can do is deal with what we're feeling. And that starts by being honest with ourselves."

He scowled. She pushed on.

"I've got pains too. I struggle with them, same as everyone else does. But here's something truthful about me. Even with everything that's gone down between us over the years, I've never stopped caring about you. That's not to say I didn't want to beat the crap out of you after the wedding fiasco, and probably on a few other occasions too. But deep inside, even when I was angry with you, you were always someone I wished only the best for."

He went quiet for a quarter mile. She was about to resume pushing when he spoke.

"Sorry for what I said… about finding a man. That was shitty."

"Forget about that. Just talk to me, Brad. For once in your life, tell me what's really going on with you."

"I'm not sure I can."

"Just try, that's all I'm asking. Talk about what really hurts, the things that pain you the most."

"What's the point?"

"Because of what Joseph said back there on the lane, that there's something fundamentally different about you. I believe the key to finding the third part and making sense of everything that's happening is buried inside you, buried under a load of crappy things that messed up your life. No matter how hard it seems, I think you've got to dive into that crap to uncover the answers."

Silence again took hold of the Jeep, this time for at least a half mile. Then…

"I hate my father. I sometimes wish I could bring the bastard back to life just so I could kill him with my bare hands."

"Why do you hate him so much?"

"Isn't it obvious? He killed my mom."

"But could there be another reason?"

"That's not enough for you?"

She was encouraged. His voice was calm, the snark restrained. She tried to match the tone.

"Back in middle school, way before the two of us were dating, I overheard you talking one day. You were standing at your locker with some of those guys you used to hang with, and you were telling them how much you hated your father. I was pretty naive at the time. I remember being surprised that someone could feel that way about their own parent."

"So?"

"The thing is, that incident occurred at least a couple years before the car crash. Which means you already had good reason to hate your father."

Felicity saw the telltale signs of rising tension, the narrowing of his eyes, the slow tightening of his fingers. She kept the pressure on.

"Bad things already must have been happening at home. Was your dad hurting your mom?"

"He never treated her right, especially when he drank."

"Was he beating on her?"

"No, not that. Yelling, mostly. Sometimes threats. But as far as I know, he never hit her."

"Hitting you?"

There was a telling hesitation, followed by a too-vigorous shake of the head. That cued Felicity she was on the right track. "Was he abusing you in some other way? Sexually?"

"Only that one night."

The words slipped out of him in a whisper. Felicity knew she'd reached the core of his rage.

"I'm so sorry. That's an awful thing for him to have done."

"I got away from him before anything really bad happened. But just the fact he tried to do it..."

"To his own son."

"Yeah."

He lowered his head. She sensed he was on the verge of retreating into the only solace his pain allowed, a well of dark emotions smothered in denial. For his own sake, for everyone's sake, she couldn't allow him to pull back.

"What exactly did your father do to you. It's important to let it all out."

THIRTY-SEVEN

Revealing his secrets to Felicity wasn't anything at all like Brad imagined. No great weight had been lifted. He felt neither better nor worse, not that he'd ever believed it could be otherwise. She was right, he couldn't take all his troubles, compress them into a ball and hurl it far away. Such a painless option had never been anything more than wishful thinking. Looking at that fantasy from a wider perspective, however, was it possible he'd somehow been infused with the knowledge that an alien civilization indeed had engineered such a sublime solution?

Whether or not that was so, he envied them. To rid oneself of personal misery... how liberated their societies must feel, how unfettered their individuals. Yet that liberty had come at a cost, not to their civilization, but possibly to the peoples of other worlds where a meteorite might have landed. Sohn had explained that the repositories couldn't be destroyed, which made sense. Negative emotions and pains – their residue didn't go away simply because it was felt or acknowledged.

Still, something had changed within Brad. He felt sharper, more enlightened, more attuned to the world. He also realized there remained a critical symbolic door through which he had to pass. He'd been contemplating Felicity's final words to him for the past couple miles.

I know it'll be hard for you but somehow you need to seek absolution. It may mean finding a way to forgive your father for what he did.

Brad suspected she was right, that passage through that final portal meant, among other things, granting absolution to his father. But he just couldn't imagine doing it. Acknowledgment was one thing, forgiveness something else entirely. That portal may as well have been ringed in flames, representing the accumulated years of his seething fury.

Turning away from such uncomfortable thoughts, he abruptly found himself again puzzling over Sohn's final words.

Should the Pestilence acquire the first part of the Trine, it will be used to create an opening between–

Between what? The eidolon and the real world? The more he'd considered it, the more that seemed like the obvious answer. But if so, why would it matter? Nowhere Man could already cross over. Brad was still missing some important component.

"Duck!" Felicity hollered.

He unsnapped his seat belt and slithered to the floor. He'd told Felicity earlier about his need to stay out of sight because of the suspicions he was responsible for the fire. But it hadn't seemed important to worry about yet. They were still a good fifteen minutes from town on a sparsely traveled section of road.

"What's happening?" he whispered.

"Township cop. Parked in the trees, probably a speed trap. I didn't see him in time."

"Do you think he spotted me?"

The wail of a siren provided the answer. Brad grimaced. "We can't be caught."

Felicity stepped on the gas; the Jeep lurched forward. The siren grew louder. She slowed.

"It's crazy trying to outrun him. He'll radio ahead and we'll be arrested for sure. We just have to talk our way out of it."

He considered another option as she eased onto the shoulder. He could leap out, make a dash for the woods.

And then what? Even if he evaded the cops, he'd still be faced with a long hike back to Gracious. Another wilderness trek would eat up the precious remaining hours.

Brad sat up as Felicity cut the engine. The side mirror revealed the cruiser pulling over a few yards behind them. The Nissan came into view. Joseph slowed as he passed, acknowledged them with a glance, then accelerated. It was wise for him to keep going. Getting involved, possibly unveiling the weapon... Brad sensed little good arising from that scenario.

"We might be in luck," Felicity said. "I know this cop. Todd Jablonski. I've waited on him a bunch of times at the bank. I think I know how to buy us some time. Let me handle this."

Her confidence was encouraging. She rolled down her window as the cop approached. He had a boyish face that could pass for a high schooler.

"Hi, Todd," she offered in a friendly voice. "What's the problem."

He ignored her. "You're Brad Van Reed?"

"Yeah."

"You're going to have to come in for questioning."

"Have they found Kristen?" Felicity asked, her tone hopeful.

Todd shook his head.

"We're planning to do exactly that," Felicity explained. "Brad came to me after his aunt and uncle's murder. The fire was set by a man named Sindle Vunn and his gang. They've kidnapped Kristen. We were following some leads out around Copernian Ridge. No cell service there, which is why we didn't contact the police."

Her story was flimsy. Todd looked justifiably skeptical as she continued the mix of truth and lies.

"I know Brad's a suspect but he didn't do it. Given his reputation around town, I insisted he'll need legal representation. We're on our way to my parents' house to consult with my father and then to a lawyer. After that, we'll come in. Meanwhile, you need to alert everyone searching for Kristen that Sindle Vunn is who they should be looking for."

"Two of the kidnappers were in a fight at Moxie's a few days ago," Brad added. "Chief Wellstead knows about them. And the chauffeur, Nidge, he's involved too."

Felicity projected urgency. "It's true, Todd, I swear. Brad had nothing to do with the fire. I'm sure you've heard the stories about our wedding day. Think about it. Would I be helping him if I wasn't totally convinced of his innocence?"

Todd hesitated. "I'm going to have to check with the chief."

"Good idea. But meanwhile, we can't afford to waste more time. You can follow us into town if you like."

She rolled up the window, started the engine and slowly pulled onto the road. Brad watched through the mirror. Todd gazed after them for a moment, then walked slowly back to his cruiser.

"We're lucky he bought it," Brad said.

"We're lucky he didn't spot the shotgun."

The weapon was partially hidden under Felicity's backpack. Had the cop been a bit more observant, he might have made an issue out of it, or at the very least delayed them further with additional questions.

"Dammit!" she said. "I should have asked him about the crack house. If there is one in town, good chance the police know of it."

Excitement surged through Brad. "That's it!"

"What's it?"

"The crack house! It's got nothing to do with drugs! Sohn said the Pestilence wants the first part of the Trine to create an opening. The *crack* is the opening! A fissure in whatever separates our world from the eidolon!"

Felicity looked skeptical. "How can you possibly know that?"

Brad couldn't answer. He knew only that his eidolon conversation with Sohn had somehow jolted his consciousness into perceiving things in a more profound way. "The crack will allow the venting to cross over! That's how Nowhere Man will consume the world. He's going to unleash those creatures on us!"

A chill went through him as he recalled their shadowy forms, groping and choking, wanting to extinguish life. The venting were the embodiment of all the negative and despairing emotions and repressed pains Sohn had referenced. Fear, rage, loneliness. Frustration, cynicism, inadequacy. Resentment, disgust, helplessness.

Brad now perceived the outlines of the process, how the various elements fit together. Nowhere Man was like patient zero in a pandemic, the first one infected. The infection could proliferate by means of the goo, a poison somehow secreted from his body. But that method was limited to direct contact with a victim. However, with an uncountable army of the venting at his disposal, the pathogen would spread unchecked.

Brad could literally *see* it, a future where all life on Earth was eventually overwhelmed by the corrosive feelings cast out by an alien civilization. And Gracious was ground zero for the invasion, which explained why Nowhere Man didn't simply create the opening between worlds out around Copernian Ridge. The venting would need an initial population to contaminate. Those victims would then go out into the world, spreading the disease.

"They'll poison everyone with the most horrible emotions, make them into walking afflictions. It'll be a plague worse than anything the Earth's ever seen!"

Felicity's skepticism gave way to fear. He could tell she was trying to maintain her cool by drawing slow deep breaths, her way of dealing with troubles small and large.

"So, this crack," she said. "Is it going to occur inside an actual house?"

"Yes. Maybe. I don't know." A mental haze descended, blotting further insights. His enhanced consciousness apparently had limits, maybe could occur only in discrete bursts.

"If it is a house, we still don't know it's location, right?"

He nodded glumly. They were no closer to their goal.

True to form, Felicity remained upbeat. "Don't worry, we'll figure it out."

He was glad for her encouragement, glad she had pushed him to open up. Nevertheless, the future remained shrouded in the darkest of hues.

THIRTY-EIGHT

Joseph had been tempted to stop and intervene when the cop pulled them over. But he'd decided it was best to keep going. There was no connection between him and Brad. He wasn't wanted for questioning, so he still had freedom of movement. Under a worst-case scenario, should Brad be arrested or detained, Joseph would drive to police headquarters and use whatever means necessary to free him.

For reasons he couldn't yet fathom, Brad's abilities – passage to and from the eidolon without assistance, conversing with Sohn, his mystifying connection to the third part – made it vital he be present when they confronted Nowhere Man. And if Joseph's worst fears about that confrontation came to pass… well, someone would be there to take up the second part of the Trine and continue the battle. Meanwhile, in the hour or so of remaining daylight, he'd nose around town for information about the crack house.

He headed for the Apex Eatery. Other than Moxie's, which was closed Sundays, it was the best place to pick up gossip. However, the diner was empty except for a boy and girl sitting beside one another in a booth. They were holding hands while taking turns spooning fudge-streaked ice cream from a sundae. The teens reminded Joseph of his own youthful days.

He sat at the far end of the counter, giving him an unobstructed view of the street. If the Jeep drove by – or better yet, Sindle Vunn's limo – he'd spot it.

Donna, the waitress who'd served him breakfast this

morning, pushed through the swinging doors from the kitchen. Despite her age, she often worked twelve-hour shifts – no surprise considering she was part owner of the Apex. Her frequent presence made her especially attuned to the rumor mill.

"I'm shocked, Joseph," she offered with a crooked smile. "Can't remember the last time I saw you in here other than at breakfast."

"Not my normal routine," he admitted. "Anything new on the Van Reed kids?"

"Not that I've heard. Cops are still searching. It's so sad about Nipa and Zack."

"Yeah."

"Coffee?"

He nodded. She retrieved the carafe, flipped over his cup and filled it to the brim. She knew he took it black.

"That rich guy, Sindle Vunn," he said. "Happen to see him around today?"

Donna unleashed a squawk, her signature display of disgruntlement. "I'm sure we're too down-home for the likes of his sort. That creepy chauffeur, though, he's been around a few times. Always orders takeout."

"You saw Nidge today?"

"Not today, no."

"What about his ride? Happen to catch sight of the limo?"

"Not that I recall."

"You're sure?"

Donna frowned. "What's the deal, Joseph?"

"No deal."

"C'mon, it's not like you to be curious about… well, much of anything." Her throaty chuckle was loud enough to distract the teens from their amorous sundae.

"The chauffeur, he owes me money."

The lie wasn't enough to convince Donna. But something in Joseph's urgency prompted her to push open the kitchen doors and gesture to someone. A young man in a chef's apron emerged. It was Rashaad Wellstead, the police chief's son. He was home from college for the summer and working at the diner.

"Joseph's trying to track down that chauffeur," Donna said. "Did he happen to come in earlier when I was on break?"

"Not today," Rashaad said. "Last I saw him was when I made that big delivery. That would have been... Thursday night. He called it in late. Must have been going on eight-thirty, quarter to nine."

Joseph hunched over the counter, intrigued. "Where? Where did you make the delivery?"

"Right to his limo. It was parked on South Third. He ordered enough sandwiches and drinks for five or six people, but it was just him. I suppose he was on his way to a party or something."

"In that block?"

"Don't think so. I remember 'cause it was the same night I had this other delivery just up the street."

"Mrs Druzba," Donna interjected. "She orders late dinners from us a couple times a month."

Rashaad nodded. "Just as I was leaving her place, I saw the limo pulling out."

"See which way it was headed?" Joseph asked.

"Pretty sure he made a right at the corner. West onto Denton Street."

The information wasn't much but it could narrow down Joseph's search. He thanked them, slapped two bucks on the counter and rushed toward the door.

"Don't you want your coffee?" Donna asked.

"Maybe later."

THIRTY-NINE

Felicity's parents would have been furious seeing her with Brad, let alone catching him snooping through their home office. Fortunately, they were in Scotland on a long-planned vacation.

"I know it's here somewhere," Felicity said, rifling through cabinets and drawers in search of the key to her father's desk.

"Why does he keep his rolodex locked up?" he asked.

"Old school. Why do you think he still uses a rolodex?"

Brad ran a finger along the top edge of the bookshelf, feeling for the key. On the shelf below, a three-photo set of Felicity as a teen caught his attention, strikingly beautiful in the stirrups of a black horse. Back when they'd first dated, before she'd grown fascinated by all things astronomical, she'd been big into riding.

The pictures stemmed from the same original image but had been photoshopped into ghostly abstracts, each highlighted in a different muted color. Something about their illusory nature revitalized his augmented comprehension, triggering fresh insights.

It can't be taken, only given. He realized the rule was based on the assumption that the amulet would be captured by a living being. But it suddenly dawned on him that the Pestilence was *not* alive, that it wasn't governed by the rules of organic entities with measurable lifetimes. Did that mean Nowhere Man *could* take the amulet from Kristen?

"Found it!"

Felicity's shout spared him from dwelling on the disturbing notion. She slipped the key from beneath a folder on the credenza, unlocked the desk and retrieved the rolodex. Flipping through the alphabetized cards brought up Lionel "Tenny" Tennison, the bank's information technology officer. She dialed his private number on her father's landline.

"Tenny, this is Felicity Bowman… Yeah, I'm fine. Listen, no time to explain, it's an emergency. I need your IT expertise with a locked phone… uh-huh, got it. We'll be right over."

She hung up. "His place is ten minutes away."

Todd Jablonski's cruiser was parked across the street and the cop followed them to the older development on the north end of town. Tenny was waiting at the front door of his one-story rancher and ushered them in.

"I can't begin to tell you what's at stake," Felicity said, her tone layered in desperation as she handed him Kyzer's phone. "We need this immediately!"

Tenny didn't seem to react to her urgency. Moving slower than Brad would have liked, he ambled to a laptop on his living room coffee table and connected the phone with a cable. Worse, he didn't look like a hacker, at least not the type exemplified in the media, who were usually young, garbed in dark hoodies and either undernourished or overweight. Tenny was in his late fifties, well-tanned and wearing a pink Ralph Lauren polo shirt tucked into white Bermuda shorts. He looked like he'd just stepped off the golf course.

Brad and Felicity moved to flank him so they could watch. Tenny raised his hand.

"No, the two of you wait over there." He gestured to a spot opposite the coffee table where they couldn't view the screen.

Much better, Brad thought. Depictions of hackers usually indicated a certain level of mistrust, if not outright paranoia.

Tenny whipped his fingers across the keys and touchpad. Less than a minute later he handed the phone back to Felicity.

Brad grimaced, waiting for him to admit that the phone couldn't be accessed.

"It's unlocked." He reacted to their surprise with a smug look.

"Thanks, Tenny. You are amazing."

Brad thought of something else. "GPS tracking. There might be a location history on the phone."

"Thought you might want that as well. I checked. GPS wasn't enabled."

Felicity gave Brad a meaningful look. "Or was deliberately disabled."

They headed for the door. Felicity turned back to Tenny. "Might be better for all concerned if no one learns you helped us."

"Helped you with what?"

They waited until they were back in the Jeep to check the phone, ignoring Todd's cruiser parked three spaces away. Felicity looked relieved as she scanned Kyzer's texting history.

"He apparently didn't delete anything. Lots of stuff, going back ten weeks. Must be when he acquired the phone."

Brad waited impatiently as she worked through them.

"Here's one he received this past Thursday. It says 'ch tonight @ 9'"

"That's got to stand for crack house. Who's the sender?"

"Unknown. Maybe from a burner phone that can't be traced?"

"I'd put money it belongs to Sindle Vunn."

Felicity continued scanning the texts. "Here's another from last week. It starts out 'ch tonight @ 10'. But then there are specific instructions. 'From campsite, due north through woods. Back of building, middle door.'"

"Must have been the first time Kyzer was going there," Brad concluded. "Wherever this house is, it sounds like the sender wanted to make sure he wasn't seen entering."

"The closest campsite I can think of is Byer-Raddison Park."

"That's a good six or seven miles from town. Maybe it just refers to a place they've been camping, not an actual park or campground."

She nodded and scanned the rest of the history. "That's it. No further texts with the ch wording."

Brad couldn't hide his disappointment. "Which means we're still nowhere."

"Maybe not. Those instructions. Back of building, middle door. It implies there are at least three doors. That doesn't sound like a regular house."

"An apartment building, maybe? With woods behind it?"

Felicity had obtained the number of Joseph's borrowed phone. He answered on the third ring and she put it on speaker. The two of them recounted the highlights of their encounter with the police and what they'd found on Kyzer's phone. Joseph updated them on what he'd learned at the Apex.

"I've been cruising Denton Street and the surrounding neighborhood," he said. "There aren't any apartment buildings out this way. And the closest woods are where Denton terminates against the mountains."

"Maybe it's not an apartment building," Brad said. "What about that abandoned factory, Eckenroth's?"

Felicity's face lit up. "They had those basement showrooms!"

"Set up to look like someone's house." Mom had taken him there a few times as a kid. He remembered being bored as she'd dragged him through the different suites, each set up to resemble the room of a trendy modern home. And behind the building was a forested hill.

Joseph instructed them to meet him at the corner of Denton and Bell Alley. From there it would be about a half-mile walk. If they drove too close to the factory they might be spotted.

Felicity hung up. Before she could start the engine, Todd's cruiser pulled out, did a U-turn and headed away. Seconds later, another police vehicle pulled up behind them and flashed its lights. Brad checked the side mirror. It was Chief Robin Wellstead's 4x4. She was on the radio.

"I'm open to suggestions," Felicity said.

He was tempted to tell her to hit the gas. But as earlier when they'd been stopped, a high-speed getaway didn't seem like such a good idea.

Chief Wellstead got out and approached the driver's side. Felicity lowered the window. The chief was more alert than Officer Jablonski. Her gaze took in the back seat and Hiram Swanteri's shotgun.

"Both of you need to come in for questioning."

"Is Brad under arrest?" Felicity asked.

"No. But you still need to come in."

"We can't. At least not yet. First, Brad needs to consult with a lawyer and–"

"Officer Jablonski explained all that. He said you were going to your parents' place to talk to your father."

"We just came from there. Dad gave us some helpful advice. He recommended a lawyer. We were just on our way to–"

"I thought your parents were in Scotland."

Brad knew they'd been tripped up. Felicity could claim they'd video conferenced with her dad. But expanding upon the original lie would likely just make the chief more suspicious. The only option he saw was appealing to Robin Wellstead on a personal level. They needed to tell her the truth... or at least a watered-down version of it that didn't involve supernatural forces and end-of-the-world scenarios.

"You need to let us go," he began. "Sindle Vunn and his gang kidnapped Kristen. If we're detained or hindered in any way, she could die."

"They have my fiancée too," Felicity added. "Please. We need to get to them by nightfall."

The sun hovered just above the western horizon.

"We think we figured out where they're holding Kristen and Flick," Brad said. "We don't have time to explain everything.

You wouldn't believe most of it anyway." He recalled what she'd said to him on that night ten years ago, when she'd caught him running away from home. "You once offered to help me if I ever needed it. I'm asking you now for that help."

The chief regarded him with an unreadable expression. "Where do you believe they're being held?"

"That abandoned factory, Eckenroth's," Felicity said. "Possibly in those basement showrooms."

"And you can't call for backup," Brad warned. "If they see a bunch of cops closing in…" He trailed off, allowed the chief to reach her own conclusion.

The chief scrutinized them for a moment, nodded. "All right but we go together. I'll drive."

She opened the Jeep's door before Felicity could object and gestured for them to step out. Brad didn't like it but saw no rational alternative. Felicity reached around to retrieve her things.

"Backpack is fine," the chief said. "And the knife can stay on your belt as long you promise to keep it sheathed. But I'm gonna need that shotgun."

Slipping the weapon from Felicity's hand, the chief guided them to the 4x4 and urged them into the back seat. It was partitioned from the front with a prisoner cage. Once they were inside, they'd be at her mercy. If she decided instead to haul them to headquarters for further questioning, there would be little they could do about it.

The chief noted their hesitation. "Trust works both ways."

Felicity got in first, squeezed over to allow room for Brad. The chief closed the door and went back to the Jeep, retrieving the key fob and locking their vehicle. Returning, she slipped behind the wheel of her 4x4 and tucked the confiscated shotgun into an empty cradle. Starting the engine, she turned to face them.

"Last chance. You sure we don't want to sort all this out over at headquarters first?"

"There's no time!"

Brad and Felicity uttered the words in tandem. Their alarmed expressions apparently were enough to dispel any lingering doubts. The chief pulled away and turned west at the next intersection. It wasn't going to be a quiet ride, however.

"I'll be needing a lot more details from the two of you," she snapped. "So start talking."

FORTY

They told Chief Wellstead just enough to keep her motivated to help and not so much she'd run them in for psych evaluations. The balancing act seemed to be working, at least until the 4x4 reached the corner of Denton and Bell alley, where Joseph sat waiting cross-legged on the pavement. Brad had become accustomed to his bloodied head and an appearance more disheveled than usual. But the chief regarded Joseph with a scowl.

"You're kidding, right."

"We need him," Felicity said.

"Why?"

Brad hopped out, leaving Felicity to generate a believable answer. He outlined the situation to Joseph, who was equally unimpressed that the chief was now involved.

"She thinks she knows where their campsite is," Brad argued. "Turns out the chief followed Kyzer's van there last week while trying to get evidence that they were the ones who dug up my mom's grave. Plus, she might have a way into the factory without being seen." He didn't add that an armed cop could be helpful against what they'd be facing.

Joseph still had doubts. "And just how long can you keep her in the dark about what's really going on?"

"At least until you start impaling bad guys."

Joseph acquiesced and followed the three of them in the Nissan. The chief drove north on Bell Alley, which morphed into a winding country road as it departed town limits. Minutes later they turned onto a dusty lane that doubled back toward Gracious. A quarter mile in, the way was blocked by the limo. No one was around. Joseph eased to a stop behind them.

Brad acknowledged relief. Their hunch about Eckenroth's had been on the money. But with confirmation, a fresh round of fear for Kristen's safety churned his guts.

The chief retrieved a flashlight and a modern, pump-action shotgun from the cargo space. She radioed headquarters but, per Brad and Felicity's insistence, limited the call to reporting her position and informing the dispatcher it was routine follow-up on a case. But she remained unsympathetic to appeals that Felicity be allowed to wield Hiram's shotgun.

"This is a police matter and the three of you are civilians. I can't have you going in there with firepower. By rights, I should make the three of you wait for me here."

"You do not want to do that," Brad warned.

She studied their faces, seemed to grudgingly acknowledge his words had merit. Felicity continued making a case for being allowed to wield the shotgun. But the chief's stance made it clear there would be no compromise on that issue.

"Let's just do this," Brad said, cutting off Felicity in mid-plea. Here under the dense canopy the light was almost gone. Continuing the debate would only waste more time. Felicity wasn't happy but contained her frustration.

They followed Chief Wellstead along an obvious trail. It was littered with discarded food wrappers and beverage cans. The chief possessed Joseph's woodlands skills, moving with stealth while keeping her light beam trained low. They soon reached the campsite. As expected, it was deserted. The fire pit was topped with a spit roaster built from a tripod of branches. Animal bones and refuse were scattered about. At the edge of the clearing, black flies swarmed over a deer carcass.

"How far from here?" Felicity asked.

"Maybe the length of a football field," the chief said. "It's uphill a ways to a ridge, then a pretty steep descent to the factory." She regarded Joseph. "Could be tricky in the dark. Maybe you should wait here for us."

"I'm not an invalid," he snapped. "Worry about yourself, Robin Wellstead. You have no idea what we're facing."

"You're right, I don't. So far these two" – she gestured to Brad and Felicity – "have mostly been feeding me a line of crap. Half-truths and outright lies. So before we go any farther I'm going to need to have matters set straight."

Felicity tried further appeasement. "Chief, this is a unique situation. You just have to trust us and–"

"Enough! What the hell is really going on here? You tell me there are three men holding Kristen and Flick and that their mysterious boss is supposed to show his face at nightfall."

"That's right," Felicity said. "But remember, Flick isn't herself. She's been drugged with some kind of mind-altering compound. And they also have these purple syringes that–"

"So you've said. If everything you've told me is true – which I still figure is a mighty big if – it sounds like we could be walking into a shitstorm. So I want some answers and I want them now. If you don't come clean, I'm calling in the regional SWAT team to handle this. And while they're doing hostage rescue, I'll haul the three of you back to headquarters and we'll hash things out in an interrogation room."

Brad could tell she was serious, just as he'd known it ten years ago when she'd refused to heed his pleas not to haul his runaway ass back to Zack and Nipa's. He nodded to Joseph.

"Show it to her."

Joseph hesitated, then removed the triangle and held it aloft. The chief frowned. "Is that supposed to impress me?"

"No," Brad said. "This is."

Joseph threw the weapon at the ground, shattering it into its component sticks. The sticks leaped into the air, burning embers instantly streaming along their edges. Twirling like high-speed copter blades, the fiery sticks made three swift orbits around the chief's head. Joseph extended his arm, summoning them back. The sticks vaulted across the clearing and reassembled into a triangle in his hand.

Brad had to give it to Robin Wellstead. Other than a slight raising of the eyebrows, she'd kept her cool throughout the demonstration.

The weapon's red glow faded. Joseph tucked it back under his coat.

"So the rumors are true," the chief murmured. "Joseph LeFevre and his voodoo stick."

"You've been talking to Big Moxie," Brad said.

"Among others. I've heard the stories over the years, including those from a few of our seedier townsfolk. Men who said they tangled with you and got their asses kicked by an unnatural weapon. I never really believed them."

"How about now?"

"Does this have something to do with Nowhere Man?" she asked.

"How do you know about him?" Felicity wondered.

"The department's been getting reports about a flying creature scaring the hell out of folks. We've been trying to keep it under wraps so as not to cause a panic. But last night it crashed through the bedroom window of Sue Lynn Everett's son. For whatever reason, it stole the boy's robot companion. The Everett's have a fancy security system. They caught the entire incident on video from multiple angles. I tried telling myself I was watching some sort of Hollywood special effect, that nothing made of flesh and blood could move like that." She paused. "It's not human, is it?"

"Not anymore." Brad gave her a quick recap of events while trying to contain frustration they were wasting more precious minutes. Felicity and Joseph injected details into his story. Robin Wellstead listened patiently, her placid demeanor providing no hint of her thoughts. When they finished, she summed things up.

"So this Nowhere Man, who might well be an undead

immortal being, is going to try taking the amulet from Kristen. And if that happens, a ghostly army from another dimension will invade the Earth."

"And end life as we know it," Brad added. "Don't forget that part."

He wasn't trying to be sarcastic. She needed to understand what was at stake.

The chief craned her neck to the heavens. Twilight was upon them; only the barest trace of blue remained in the open sky above the campsite. Without another word she led them uphill, in the direction of Eckenroth's.

FORTY-ONE

Chief Wellstead turned off the flashlight when they got to the ridge, concerned the beam could be spotted from below. The downward slope was indeed steep, and even with tightly bunched trees offering handholds, challenging in the near-darkness. The chief, Felicity and Joseph navigated it with ease. It was Brad who tripped over a vine and took a wild tumble, rolling to stop perilously close to where the tree line and foliage petered out. Just beyond was a ten-foot drop to the outer edge of the parking lot.

"Goddammit!" Brad hissed. The curse was twofold, directed at his own clumsiness and at having banged his left ankle, which hurt like blazes.

"You OK?" Felicity whispered.

He got up, wincing as he put weight on that leg. Nothing seemed broken. His entire body had been slammed and bruised since the attack on the house. He supposed he was growing acclimated to a constant level of discomfort.

They peered through the remaining border of foliage. Beyond the parking lot, which had weeds spiking from its cracked asphalt, was the abandoned factory. The imposing four-story structure was silhouetted against a backdrop of darkening skies. The moon had not yet risen. A few brighter stars were visible amid a smattering of evening clouds.

Eckenroth's rear flank had to be at least six hundred feet across. Five closed doors were spaced evenly along its length. The ones at opposite ends flanked truck loading docks. Even in the dim light it was obvious from the different style of brickwork and smaller window openings that the left half of the structure was a later addition. If Brad remembered his local history, the right side was the original factory, dating to the mid-nineteenth century. In that pre-electricity era, windows were larger to maximize natural light.

The basement showrooms were located in the newer area, along the far-left side of the building. All of the first-floor windows were boarded up. Those on the upper stories were mostly devoid of glass, no doubt from years of vandalism via rocks and guns. No lights were on. Nothing moved, inside or out.

Felicity panned the scene with her binoculars. "Padlocks on all the doors except for the middle one. But it could be locked from inside."

The unsecured door accessed the newer part of the factory. To reach it they'd have to cross the wide parking lot. If there was a lookout on one of those upper floors, they'd be seen for sure.

Attempting entry from the front of the building, where it butted the last block of Denton Street, was impossible. Although there were no nearby homes, the factory's departing owners, ostensibly to assuage guilt for depriving Gracious of a major employer and community supporter, had agreed to cosmetic upgrades. A facade had been installed across the front and left sides that faced town, cloaking all doors and windows. But Brad had heard that the real reason for the facade was part of a deal with the township, which in exchange for redevelopment rights to the factory assumed all future liabilities.

Thus far, the township had gotten the short end of the stick, failing to attract any new tenants. And no one seemed to have considered that the facade's smooth gray paneling provided an appealing canvas for taggers. At one point, Harry Fenstermacher had stopped selling spray paint to anyone under twenty-one.

"So where's this secret way in?" he asked, still wincing from his bruised ankle.

The chief motioned them to follow. Keeping within the tree line, she headed right, moving parallel to the building along a rudimentary path. They reached an area directly across from the rear corner of the original factory. Brad became aware that the ground beneath them had become unnaturally level and flat. Through the layer of grass and weeds at his feet he could just make out a surface of ancient concrete.

"We're above the factory's original kiln," the chief whispered. She pointed to a brick chimney deeper in the hillside, so shrouded with creeper vines that Brad had mistaken it for another tree. "It's where they fired the pottery in the early years. Later they moved the whole operation inside."

She came upon a steel hatch in the concrete and eased it open. Oil-starved hinges groaned, louder than they would have liked. They froze for a moment but detected no reaction to the noise.

A rusty ladder descended into a well of darkness. The chief handed Felicity her shotgun. Not wanting to risk using the flashlight yet, she lit a match and dropped it into the shaft. The match flickered out halfway down but not before revealing that the ladder touched bottom twenty feet below.

The chief eased herself over the lip. Once secure on the ladder, she motioned Felicity to hand back the shotgun.

"It's an old tunnel," the chief explained. "It connected the factory basement to the original kiln. They used it in winter to keep hot ceramics fresh out of the fires from turning brittle from exposure to sudden cold."

Brad figured the shaft served as emergency access in the event of a cave-in as well as allowing excess heat from the tunnel to escape.

"How do you know all this?" Felicity wondered.

"I was part of the township's safety tour when Eckenroth's was closing. Got a firsthand look at the layout. The tunnel is our best shot. Even if no one's watching from one of those windows, crossing that parking lot would be dicey. From what you've told me of this Sindle Vunn, he sounds slick enough to have planted surveillance cameras or motion sensors."

Brad hadn't thought of that. It made sense, though. The possibility triggered a new worry. He asked Felicity to look at her phone.

"No service," she said.

The chief and Joseph checked their own devices. The same result.

"Must be another jammer," Brad said. "They used one last night at the house."

The chief toggled her radio through multiple channels, grimaced. "I'm blocked too. A hell of a powerful unit to knock out my comms."

She hesitated, then began the descent. "You three wait here. I'm going to check things out."

"We should all go," Brad insisted.

"The tunnel might have collapsed or been sealed off. If it's clear I'll be right back. If I don't return in a reasonable time, assume the worst. I doubt the range of their jammer extends beyond the ridge. Get back up there, call 9-1-1 and tell them to get SWAT out here pronto."

She climbed down before they could mount further arguments, not turning on her flashlight until reaching the bottom. She headed toward the factory. The light from her beam gradually diminished, then disappeared altogether.

The three of them waited, huddled around the hatch. Brad suspected that if things went sour, calling for SWAT wouldn't be a realistic option. By the time a team assembled and made it out here, darkness would have fallen. Kristen's fate and the world's likely would have been decided.

Minutes passed before the chief reappeared at the base of the ladder and signaled them to come down. Felicity and Joseph went first. As Brad was about to step onto the rungs, peripheral vision caught a flash of movement. Something appeared to be ascending into the violet-tinged skies above the most distant mountain range. As he turned toward it, the heavens suddenly went pitch black and the globe of a fierce bluish moon took shape. Before he could even register surprise, everything snapped back to normal, the skies resuming their proper twilight hue.

For that brief interval, he'd again crossed over into the eidolon. And he was certain about what he'd glimpsed. Nowhere Man. He sensed that the creature had emerged from its cavernous lair.

He quickly descended the ladder, trying not to dwell on the incident and the fresh wave of anxiety it brought. He tried estimating how long it would take Nowhere Man to fly from Copernian Ridge to Gracious. Twenty minutes? Two minutes? Then he recalled those differences in the passage of time between the two realms. Bottom line, it was impossible to judge how long they had.

"A portion of the tunnel collapsed," the chief said. "But I think we can get through."

Brad glanced behind them, in the other direction. The tunnel continued deeper into the hillside but was bricked up a few yards in. Beyond would be the original kiln with the overgrown chimney.

Led by the chief, they moved cautiously. The air was damp and slightly rancid. Faint scurrying sounds indicated a rat population. Joseph drew the weapon from under his coat. Felicity rested her hand on the hilt of her knife.

They kept alert to where they were walking, but not for fear of stepping on rodents. The tunnel floor had once anchored a narrow-gauge railroad track for transporting the ceramics back and forth, probably in small carts the workers moved by hand. Although the rails had been removed, some of the decomposed wooden crossties remained, the gaps between them making for awkward footing. Felicity turned on her flashlight, providing a helpful second source of illumination.

They proceeded in silence. Brad couldn't help wondering whether Sindle Vunn knew of the tunnel. If so, had he planted booby traps along it, or somewhere inside the building? Hopefully the chief would spot anything obvious in time, such as a tripwire.

The showrooms were catty-corner to their position, the farthest distance away. Of course, that was based on the assumption that the crack house indeed referred to the showrooms, and that their enemy hadn't chosen some other location within the expansive structure.

Too many unknowns.

They reached the collapsed portion. Erosion must have loosened the beams supporting the roof. Several had fallen in, bringing with them a mound of rocks and muddy dirt. There was just enough space to squeeze by the obstruction single file. Beyond, the tunnel began curving. Its arc was tight, preventing them from seeing more than about fifteen feet ahead.

The tunnel straightened and terminated at a crude wooden door partially sheathed in steel plates. A pair of ancient hinges indicated it opened toward them. The doorknob lacked an adjacent keyhole, which made sense. There would have been no reason to keep it locked. The door was probably just to stop the kiln's heat from being drawn into the factory during warmer weather.

"Let me do it," Brad whispered, reaching for the knob.

The chief stepped to the side and aimed her shotgun at the portal. Brad tensed. If someone was waiting for them…

He gripped the knob, twisted gently while alternately pushing and pulling. The door didn't budge. It must have been padlocked or bolted from the inside. He checked the hinges. The screws were layered in rust. Even if they had a decent screwdriver, removing the door would be a time-consuming project.

"If I shotgun those hinges it'll wake the dead." The chief nodded toward Joseph's weapon. "Any ideas?"

The triangle glowed as Joseph touched two of its overlapping ends to a screw on the upper hinge. The screw turned red, then white-hot. It melted like wax and dripped out of its hole. Joseph repeated the process five more times until both hinges were disconnected from the wood.

Brad again took hold of the knob for what little leverage was available. This time when he pulled, the door moved slightly toward him. While the chief stood with shotgun at the ready, Felicity inserted her knife between the hinges and the jamb. Together with Joseph, they pried it open. It was still secured along the knob side and resisted their efforts. But they got the hinged side separated from the jamb far enough to be able to squeeze through.

Felicity shined her light through the slit. "Some kind of storage area."

She went first. The chief followed, with Brad and Joseph bringing up the rear. The room was long and narrow, the walls covered by floor-to-ceiling shelves, empty except for a few pieces of chipped dinnerware. Broken pottery shards littered the dirt floor.

Another door at the far end was ajar. They passed through it into a long brick corridor filled with cobwebs and strung with a wire from which hung primitive electric sockets. Even if there had been power, most of the sockets were devoid of bulbs. Everything bore a patina of dust. Heavy metal doors flanked both side of the corridor. Brad guessed they led to the newer kilns.

They arrived at a three-way junction. Closed doors marked two of the routes. The third was an ascending staircase. That's where the chief headed.

"Wait," Felicity whispered. "Why are we going up?"

"They built the addition as a separate structure," she said. "It's mainly offices. They wanted the excess heat from the kilns confined as much as possible to the factory area. So they didn't connect the basements and the two lower floors. Only the third and fourth floors cross over."

Their shoes crunched a layer of loose pebbles and dirt on the stairs as they climbed to level three. From there, the chief led them through a series of zigzagging corridors. All were strewn in cobwebs and years overdue for sweeping. Closed doors on both sides led to offices. Some bore department nameplates such as "International Sales" and "Magazine Advertising."

The chief turned a corner and halted. The way ahead was blocked, the hallway an improvised storage area. Old and scarred wooden desks were stacked to the ceiling. Beyond lay a random assortment of junk: grimy sinks and toilet bowls haphazardly positioned. Coils of wire and cabling were strewn across the floor. Clearing a path would be a noisy effort and consume even more time.

"We'll have to go back to the stairs and try the fourth floor," the chief said.

Brad hesitated, staring at the conglomeration blocking their way. Something seemed wrong. Felicity threw him a quizzical look but he couldn't figure out what was bothering him. He shook his head. It was probably nothing.

They trailed the others back to the stairwell and ascended to the fourth floor, emerging into a hallway that was equally decrepit and cobwebbed. But there were hints of a former elegance that was absent below. The floor was thickly carpeted. Fancy ceramic globes suspended from the ceiling had provided illumination and the walls displayed vintage ad posters of the company's various product lines. Most of the artwork had suffered damage, the glass cases fractured, the posters wrinkled and stained. Office doors featured personalized nameplates and titles, and their wider spacing indicated spacious interiors. The company's top executives had once worked up here.

A poster caught Brad's eye, a photo-realistic painting of a 1950s-era mother serving her family a holiday meal on sparkling Eckenroth's dinnerware. The image prompted longing. He flashed back to his mother's voice in the eidolon, guiding him away from the venting and toward SOS, and instructing him to find the third part of the Trine.

He pushed the memories from his mind as they reached a thick portal in the middle of the hallway. Dangling hinges indicated the opening had once been protected by a fire door, marking it as the connection to the newer part of the factory. Inexplicably, the fire door had been removed. As they passed through to the other side, the chief urged them to huddle.

"At the far end of the building is another stairwell," she said, gesturing ahead. "It leads to the basement showrooms. From here on, move as quietly as you can. Our only chance is to surprise them."

Everyone nodded. But it was obvious no one felt much confidence in the plan. Brad couldn't help thinking that somehow, Sindle Vunn had made preparations to deal with intruders.

They kept going. The carpeted floor contributed to a reasonable degree of stealth. An office door on the right was open and Brad gazed in as he passed. On the floor was the outline of where a desk had stood, the spot now bizarrely occupied by a wastebasket topped by a grungy toilet seat. Beyond was a wall of glass that once would have overlooked the western edge of Gracious. It was now obstructed by the exterior facade cloaking the front of the building.

He suddenly realized what had bothered him about the blocked corridor below. Unlike everything else they'd come across on their trek, those desks and plumbing fixtures had been bereft of cobwebs and dust. The obvious conclusion was that they'd been moved there recently. But why?

Before he could contemplate a reason, the scene before him changed. The dim office, illuminated only by back splash from their flashlights, faded to pitch black. A bluish full moon took shape in the air above the makeshift toilet. In front of it appeared the flapping wings of Nowhere Man. The creature was flying straight at him.

Startled, Brad jerked away from the door, bumping into Felicity.

"What's wrong?" she hissed.

In that brief interval, the office looked normal again. But for the second time since arriving at Eckenroth's, he'd briefly crossed over into the eidolon. He didn't know what it meant or what was happening to him. But it was creeping him out.

"We should keep moving," Felicity urged.

He nodded, trying not to reveal how shaken he was. What was happening to him? Had the barrier between the real world and eidolon become porous? Did that somehow portend the appearance of the crack that would allow the venting to invade?

The others had already reached the closed door at the end of the hallway. Joseph was gingerly rotating the knob, the chief again poised next to him with the shotgun. He and Felicity scurried to catch up.

Their delay saved them. As Joseph pushed open the door, a muffled explosion erupted from somewhere beneath. A violent shudder roiled the corridor, knocking Brad and Felicity sideways, dislodging lamps and posters and bringing down chunks of wall. Just beyond their position, ten feet of floor vanished. Joseph and the chief dropped from sight amid a rumbling cacophony of undulating carpet and disintegrating plasterboard.

A choking dust cloud arose from the cavity where the corridor had been. Brad had to wait a few seconds for the worst of it to clear before leaning over the edge.

"Be careful," Felicity warned, grasping the back of his belt in case more flooring gave way.

His footing seemed solid. The explosion had undermined only that single section of hallway. The absence of cobwebs and dust on those desks and plumbing fixtures now made sense. The third floor had been deliberately blocked, forcing them to ascend and cross here. Like rats in a prepared maze, their route had been directed. The booby trap had been set by someone with demolition expertise. The trigger must have been Joseph opening the door.

Through a haze of dust, Brad could just make him out, sprawled face up on the heap of rubble on the third-floor hallway below. Chief Wellstead was face down a few feet away. Neither of them were moving.

The triangle had shattered. Two sticks were in view. The third, along with the chief's shotgun, must be buried in the debris. The chief's flashlight had survived the plunge. Embedded in a clump of plaster, its fixed beam cast eerie shapes in the powdery air.

"Oh god," Felicity whispered, still holding onto Brad but leaning forward enough to see for herself. "We need to find a way to climb down and–"

"No." He shocked himself with the finality of the utterance. "Even if they're alive, we'll have company any minute."

His mind raced with the likely scenario. Kristen's kidnappers would ascend to the third floor to survey the destruction and finish off any survivors. Even if Nowhere Man hadn't yet arrived – a big question mark – that still left three armed and dangerous men to deal with, and possibly a drug-enslaved Flick as well. Weaponless, he and Felicity would be outmatched.

"We have to get out of here," he said. "We have to…"

He trailed off as Joseph opened his eyes and stared up at them. Brad was bewildered to see the smudged and bleeding face break into a smile.

FORTY-TWO

The pain should have been worse, Joseph realized. He could feel blood trickling from his mouth and streaming from his nostrils. The fall had broken bones. Many of them. Considering how he was unable to move his lower extremities, it was likely the injuries had shattered critical vertebrae, leaving him paralyzed from the waist down. The conclusion was inevitable.

I won't be leaving here.

Two concerned faces gazed down at him from the edge of the collapsed hallway above. Despite his dire situation, the fact they had survived prompted a smile. Joseph wanted to tell Brad that it was up to him now, that he alone would have to save Kristen, save the world. But try as he might, the words refused to come. Maybe his jaw was broken. Or maybe synaptic pathways between brain and mouth had been severed, rendering speech impossible.

He couldn't move his left arm. The elbow felt as if it had snapped. But the right arm still functioned. He managed it lift it above his head and hold the shaky forefinger steady enough to point at Brad.

That effort, along with undiluted strength of will, transformed into action. The two sticks beside him rose obediently into the air. The third one squirmed from under the rubble to join the ascent.

The sticks came together into their familiar shape. Joseph watched with satisfaction as Brad reached out for the triangle.

My parting gift. The power and the burden are now yours, Grandson. Use it well.

FORTY-THREE

"We have to go," Felicity whispered, gripping Brad's arm and trying to pull him back from the edge. Even with the weapon in hand he seemed unable to take his eyes off Joseph.

Brad felt his fingers gripping the triangle with more force than necessary. It was a physical reaction, an attempt to hold back a turbulence of emotions.

"Back to that stairway," Felicity urged. "There must be another way across."

It took effort for him to turn away from Joseph. Before he could take a step, harsh noises erupted from the office that had snared his attention moments ago. Shattered wallboard and fractured glass sailed through the open door into the hallway. Something had crashed into the building from outside, disintegrating the exterior facade and interior windows.

It slithered from the office into the halo of Felicity's beam. She let out a piercing scream. Chills coursed through Brad, as they had during his first encounter in the eidolon.

Nowhere Man stood three paces away, silently regarding them with dead eyes, its eight feet of winged malignancy nearly touching the ceiling. The pockmarked skin shimmered like an oil slick. The putrefying smell was overwhelming. Every once in a while, the creature faded away, momentarily becoming a ghostly presence. Brad recalled what Joseph had said, about Nowhere Man not yet able to exist completely in the real world.

Its head drooped ever so slightly. Brad knew its gaze had been drawn to the weapon.

His choice was instantaneous. He was too terrified to even consider standing his ground. Spinning away from the monstrosity, he grabbed Felicity's hand and made her leap with him over the edge and into the pit where the floor had been. There was no time to consider how they might land, whether they'd come down atop Joseph or the chief, or break ankles, knees or ribs upon impacting the jagged pile of rubble.

None of those things occurred. They never landed, at least not in the real world. The transition occurred in midair. They continued falling, but suddenly were thousands of feet above an unnatural forest bathed in the piercing light of a full moon. The canopy of the eidolon was spread out below. They plunged toward it at an alarming rate.

In seconds they reached the treetops. Felicity echoed his own panicked gasp as they braced themselves for what surely would be an agonizing collision. He closed his eyes. Branches swatted him as he fell through the foliage clusters. Yet there was no pain. It was more like the feeling of walking barefoot through tall summer grass, the blades soft and caressing.

He opened his eyes in time for a clearing to come into view. The ground was interlaced with geometric patterns from the filtering moonlight. Rectangles and octagons. Pentagrams and triangles. He sensed the shapes bore hidden significance, like the hieroglyphics of some impossibly strange civilization that the limitations of the human mind were incapable of translating.

They were still falling fast. He knew from Felicity's tightening grip of his hand that she too was steeling herself for a hard impact.

It never came. There was a disorienting moment, as if senses had awkwardly skipped a beat. And then the two of them stood in the clearing, unharmed, their hands still locked together.

Felicity broke away and pivoted wildly, eyes darting into the trees that fell away on all sides from the elevated glade. Brad knew it was the same place in which he'd recently conversed with Silso, Orjos and Sohn. SOS was gone, however. And somehow, he knew that the three-headed entity wouldn't be coming back.

"It'll be OK," he said, trying to calm Felicity before her growing trepidation morphed into panic. He had no idea if his words bore any semblance of reality but they seemed to help. She inhaled and exhaled slowly, her self-tranquilizing inducing a state of calm, at least on the surface.

"I lost my flashlight," she whispered.

"It's all right. We don't need it here."

"Here? Is this...? Are we in the...?"

"Yeah. The eidolon."

Their eyes met. They experienced the same concern simultaneously, wrenched their gazes upward to the canopy through which they'd fallen. If the two of them had crossed over, would Nowhere Man be close behind?

But the winged monstrosity didn't appear, nor did Brad sense the presence of the venting in the surrounding trees. Understanding arrived along with an icy dread. However much the Pestilence might desire the weapon, it already had Kristen and the amulet waiting for it in Eckenroth's basement. As to the venting, they would be gathering in preparation for crossing over into the real world. The crack between the realms was imminent.

The threat jolted him into action. "We have to get back!"

"Do you know how?" Felicity wondered.

He didn't. How the two of them had bridged the realms, as well as his earlier crossings, remained a mystery. All that was certain was that something deep in his subconscious mind was causing an increasingly permeable state between the real world and the eidolon. Yet there must be a way to make the transition a conscious decision rather than being swept back and forth by forces beyond his control.

He recalled his first trip here, how Joseph had employed the second part to facilitate their return. He raised the triangle, willing it to glow and spin with gyroscopic fury, creating a hole between the realms through which they could pass.

His mother's voice interrupted the effort, her tone more urgent than ever as it seeped into him.

Find the third part.

"Goddammit, how do I do that?" he demanded, unable to prevent himself from shouting the words to express his frustration. "Just hearing you say 'find it' over and over isn't helping."

The ethereal voice didn't respond. He met Felicity's quizzical gaze.

"Your mother again?"

"Yeah."

"Still telling you to–"

He nodded, recalling what Felicity had said to him in the Jeep when they were returning to Gracious. Seek absolution. Find a way to forgive his father. Resolving that ancient hurt somehow was crucial to finding the third part of the Trine. But…

"I can't. I can't forgive my father."

"What's stopping you?" Felicity asked.

Anger and pride. Fear and disgust. Helplessness and inadequacy. His very own repository of emotional detritus, a personalized blend of corrosive feelings and urges. Yet underlying those barriers was a singular emotion that he abruptly recognized as the most potent and insidious of them all.

"Guilt," he whispered.

Uttering the word produced an uncomfortable sensation in his guts. He suddenly knew he was on the cusp of some profound revelation. A thing buried long ago was struggling to reach the surface.

"What do you feel guilty about?" Felicity prodded.

A part of him tried resisting and he experienced an all-too-familiar desire to run away. But even if he'd wanted to partake of that time-tested ploy, a process toward greater consciousness had been initiated. It could no longer be halted.

Agony lanced through him, a searing affliction, intense and merciless. He collapsed to his knees. The weapon fell from his hand. He wrapped his arms around his midsection, a last-ditch effort by the flesh itself to deny, contain and repress the truth.

Guilt! He'd borne it for ten years, a guilt that had twisted and warped every aspect of his life, from his relationships with Kristen and Felicity, to how he dealt with Uncle Zack and Aunt Nipa, to his interactions with the world in general. And beneath that guilt were the long-repressed emotions it had served to keep hidden. They burst from his lips amid a cry of pain.

"I never told her!"

"Told her what?" Felicity urged.

"What my father did to me! What he did to me that night, how he'd been prepping me to be a victim of his abuse. I should have told Mom! I should have told her!"

"And if you had?"

"She'd still be alive!"

The insight erupted in a cascade of tears, more real than the unreal ground they fell upon, more substantial than anything in either realm. Had he told his mother, she would have left the bastard, spirited Brad and Kristen away from his malignancy. Had he revealed the truth, the future would have been altered. Mom would have severed the marriage. She never would have been around to get in the car with him on that terrible night years later, never would have become his last victim.

He felt Felicity kneel and wrap her arms around him, trying to bring comfort. He couldn't stop crying even as a part of him knew the tears could be consuming critical minutes.

"I had it wrong!" he sobbed. "It's not my father I need to forgive. It's *me!* I need to forgive *myself* for not telling Mom!"

"You can do it," Felicity whispered. "You have the strength."

Her encouragement helped. He could do it. He had the strength. He could see that now. Mere acknowledgment served to free him from the ancient torment. The guilt and the pain weren't gone, of course. They'd always be there, with an emotional scar forever signifying their underlying presence. But elevating those feelings into consciousness enabled their most debilitating aspects to be absorbed, made part of who he was now, today, in this moment.

He regained control. The tears stopped. Felicity released her grip. He rose to his feet with renewed purpose. Even though events here in the eidolon passed at a different tempo than in the real world, he still had to return to save Kristen in time–

Time! The word reverberated in his head, reactivating that enhanced state of mind and producing another flood of realizations. Becoming conscious of his true self had served to open an even deeper inner pathway. An emotional roadblock had been ripped aside, making possible a more complete and encompassing level of understanding.

He whirled to Felicity, energized by the insights.

"Remember what I told you earlier? About what Sohn said to me about the nature of the Trine?"

Felicity quoted the sentence. "A trimorphic organism engineered to apply temporally unrestricted solutions to detritus containment and banishment."

"Temporally unrestricted solutions! A civilization so hyper-sentient it can manipulate not only space but the very fabric of time! They incorporated that power into the Trine. It's why Kristen can glimpse things that are yet to happen. And I think it also has something to do with how the weapon works."

He recalled his mother singing *The Mercy of Gracious* to him in the eidolon, how in those moments he'd perceived time as an ocean, past and future simply aspects of some vaster totality that normally remained opaque to human perception.

"The first two parts make only partial use of that power. But it's the very essence of the third part!"

Felicity got caught up in his excitement. "So you know where the third part's hidden?"

He didn't. That final piece of the puzzle lay tantalizingly close. Yet an aspect still eluded him, remained just out of reach.

"I don't know where it is. But I think I know *when* it is!"

She looked confused. Not surprising, considering he was equally in the dark. He didn't understand the meaning of that last utterance. It was like hearing a speech given in a foreign language you didn't speak. The words meant nothing, yet the emotion in the speaker's voice struck a chord. All he knew with certainty is that the nature of time and the nature of the third part were intimately connected. Beyond that...

He couldn't waste more time puzzling over it. Even if the passage of time in the eidolon was different from the real world, they needed to go back. Summoning the weapon, the triangle leaped up from where he'd dropped it. He grabbed Felicity's wrist with his other hand.

He raised the triangle. The red glow was instantaneous. Brad knew his control of the second part was as complete as Joseph's had been, maybe even more so. The second part hung in the air, began its mad, gyroscopic dance in three dimensions until dissolving into a black hole enveloped in fiery sparks.

FORTY-FOUR

Joseph heard the commotion above. Moments later, Brad and Felicity were leaping down on him, hand in hand like a pair of wild acrobats. He had no time to react, not that it mattered. His crippling injuries made it impossible to move out of the way.

The heel of Brad's boot was within a foot of his midsection when the pair of them vanished. He barely had time to process that event when a malignant thing glided into the shadows of the floor above.

Joseph had only ever seen Nowhere Man in flight, never upright and immobile, and never from such a close vantage point. Its wings were compressed against its upper back as it gazed down upon him. The eyes were devoid of anything remotely human.

Not alive in the sense we perceive life. Functionally immortal. Joseph idly wondered what that must feel like. Then he realized that even though such a creature was at its core an amalgam of negativity and subjugated pains, the actual experiencing of such feelings would be irrelevant to it.

That should not have been the case for Joseph. In his helpless state he should have been overwhelmed with terror. The ultimate confrontation with Nowhere Man that the second part somehow had enabled him to perceive as an inevitable future was now happening. He supposed the reason for the absence of paralyzing fear was that the fall already had benumbed body and mind, had brought him to the brink of death. It no longer mattered whether mortal wounds dispatched him on the final journey or he perished at the hands of this vile thing.

The Pestilence stepped forward and into the main arc of the flashlight beam lodged in the debris, accenting further characteristics. Oddest among them was a bulky mass centered roughly where a navel would be on a human. The mass slowly unwound like a coiled snake until it was at least two yards in length. Its end drooped over the edge. Black goo dribbled from the tip.

Joseph knew the tentacle was the source of the addictive poison Nowhere Man employed to compel devotion from his murderous servants. At the same instant he realized the creature had no intention of killing him. It wanted to make him into another drugged slave. But why? He was almost gone, of no practical use.

He grasped its reasoning, or what passed for reasoning in that composite monstrosity of dark emotions. The Pestilence recognized him as a bearer of the Trine. It concluded, however improbably, that he might survive death as an adversary in some way, shape or form. Had Joseph still possessed the ability to speak, he would have pointed out the flaws in its thinking, and done so in a tone echoing his disdain for what it represented.

Even with the end at hand, Joseph had no intention of spending his last moments drugged and yoked to such repugnance. He extended the arm that still functioned and clawed at the rubble for anything he could use. His fingers located a jagged clump, once part of the concrete decking separating the floors. A piece of rebar jutted from its end.

Gripping the clump by the protruding bar of steel, he raised the weapon. It felt monumentally heavy – he was weakening fast. But his will remained strong. He managed to suspend it high above his head.

Nowhere Man stepped off the edge. Wings unfurled, flapping to slow its descent. As the creature closed in, its immensity blocked out almost all the light, rendering it an oppressive shadow. But he could still make out enough detail to see the black tip of that appendage angling toward his mouth. A droplet of black goo fell, landed on his chest.

He thought of Isabella and those wondrous days they'd spent together. Their time had been far shorter than what he'd once dreamed, that the two of them would be melded for the better part of their lives. Yet however short its duration, those days of physical and emotional joy had been unimaginably long in terms of their impact on the man he'd become.

I'm sorry, Isabella. He'd failed in his promise to her, that he'd always watch over any descendants who bore the amulet.

A final rumination occurred. The darkest and most unsavory emotions survived death. Was it possible the good ones did as well?

The dribbling tip snaked to within inches of his mouth. He brought the clump of concrete down with all his might on the peak of his own forehead. A moment of intense pain was followed by an inhalation of sweet air scented by cloves.

FORTY-FIVE

Brad felt himself falling into the hole between the realms, this time with a startled Felicity at his side. The opening enveloped them. Violent crackling noises filled his head, followed by a burst of white light that seemed to emanate from his very body.

And then they were back in the real world, completing the leap from the edge of the hallway to the pile of rubble below. He had only a moment to twist his legs away from landing on Joseph. Still, there was no gentle touchdown as in the eidolon. His boots plowed into the debris at an odd angle, causing fresh swirls of dust. The impact broke his grip on Felicity's wrist.

He made no attempt to stay upright, sensing he'd better absorb the fall by rolling onto his side. Pieces of crumpled flooring jabbed at his ribs. He ignored the pain, rose and whirled toward Felicity.

"You OK?"

She'd managed to land on her feet and gave a thumbs up. "Where's Chief Wellstead?"

"I don't know." The chief's disappearance wasn't a total surprise. "I think I moved us forward... forward in time."

The action had been entirely subconscious, another aspect of an expanding relationship to the Trine. Until this moment, he hadn't even been aware he'd done it. Strange new powers continued to develop within him even as their capabilities defied full comprehension. But he understood the rationale behind this one. So did Felicity.

"So Nowhere Man wouldn't land on top of us," she

concluded, not sounding the least bit awestruck. The day's remarkable events had eliminated such reactions.

But how far into the future had Brad shifted them? Had hours or more passed since they'd first leaped off the edge?

Felicity checked her watch. "About five minutes, I think. Ten at the most. But what happened to the chief?"

Brad had no answer. Nowhere Man might have taken her. Or she might have survived the fall, awakened and left on her own. He was more concerned that too much time had passed.

Time! Again the word pulsated through him, taunting him to make a final leap of understanding.

"He's gone," Felicity whispered.

She'd dislodged the still-working flashlight from the debris and was kneeling beside Joseph. His eyes were open but lifeless. In the center of his forehead was a fresh wound, deep and bloody, as if some heavy object had smashed down upon him. The surrounding rubble revealed a bloodstained chunk of concrete with a piece of rebar protruding from one end. Either the debris had fallen on Joseph or Nowhere Man hit him with it.

Brad confirmed Felicity's words by checking Joseph's wrist and neck for signs of a pulse. She didn't say anything, just gently closed Joseph's eyes.

"It's for the best," he said, unable to keep his voice from cracking. Had Joseph lived, all he likely would have had to look forward to was a long hospitalization with little chance for meaningful recovery. Still, that was just a rationalization. Brad felt a sense of emptiness in his guts, a feeling amplified by watching Felicity wipe a tear from her cheek.

There was no time for mourning. They scrambled over the debris in the direction of their original course, toward the stairwell at the far side of the building, the beam of Felicity's flashlight playing at their feet. A closed fire door appeared up ahead. He went through first. A stairwell circled downward in five-step increments. But when they arrived at the first floor, there was no place to continue the descent. The steps terminated at another fire door. Had Chief Wellstead been mistaken? Was there no way to access the basement from this end of the factory?

He pushed through the fire door and they entered a spacious lobby. A reception desk bore an older model computer, cobwebbed and dusty, and with a cracked screen. Double doors across from the desk were boarded up. But the layout jogged Brad's memory. The doors led to the factory's main public entrance, now blocked by the paneled facade. Just around the corner should be an elevator and a wide staircase used by the public to access the showrooms below.

They tiptoed across the lobby and reached the stairs. There were no sounds of activity arising from the basement. Another memory popped into view, of descending the wide steps at a very young age with Mom, holding onto both her hand and one of the flanking banisters.

They reached the midpoint of the stairwell, turned 180 degrees onto the final flight. He recalled the steps opening into another lobby. Just beyond it would be the entrances to the various display rooms of the faux-home.

He froze three steps from the bottom, engulfed by a feeling of terror. He didn't know its origin but feared the worst. Had Kristen been...?

Don't go there, he told himself. *She's all right. Nothing's happened to her*.

Despite his efforts to ignore the feeling, it grew steadily. He was almost too frightened to go on. Felicity moved to his side, whispered in his ear.

"I feel it too. Something horrible in the air... something all around us."

He motioned her to turn off the flashlight. In the utter darkness, the triangle glowed. Its dull reddish hue revealed they weren't alone.

Spectral apparitions ascended from the basement in a kind of slow motion, a boundless horde eerily illuminated by the light emanating from the second part of the Trine. They passed around Brad and Felicity as if the two of them were enclosed in a bubble. He knew the weapon was responsible, that it was serving as a protective shield against the worst of that outflow of negative emotions. But he also knew it could not help the rest of humanity.

Most of the apparitions were humanoid, a few horribly not. A squirmy thing with tentacles floated past on their left. On their right appeared an entity that looked like an upside-down crab.

We're too late. The only explanation was that Nowhere Man had taken Kristen's amulet... or somehow had tricked her into giving it to him. The Pestilence had used the first part to crack open the barrier separating the realms.

The venting had been unleashed. They were on their way up and out into the world.

FORTY-SIX

The fear remained constant and oppressive but Brad forced himself to push on. With Felicity close by his side and her flashlight probing the gloom, they descended the final steps to the basement and entered a semi-circular lobby. The venting continued flowing around them, a wave of limitless proportions, otherworldly and toxic. The second part continued serving as a bulwark, shielding them from the most overwhelming effects. But his hopes of stopping the invasion grew bleaker by the moment. Hundreds of the venting, perhaps thousands, had already crossed over into the world. Even moving at their glacial pace, it wouldn't be long before they found their way out of the factory and began their conquest on the streets of Gracious. The second part was less an obstacle than a tiny island in the path of a tsunami. And yet...

Kristen is alive! It was no longer just a matter of Brad staying upbeat about her fate. Now that the two of them were in close proximity he could literally feel her presence. He sensed the locus of her being, her élan vital. How that was possible he couldn't say. But the perception, flowing across him as a cluster of warm memories of their years together, now guided his path.

She was just ahead and to the far left. Felicity followed him toward the first of the five open doors ringing the lobby. The other four accessed the dining room, living room and patio suites, and the outlet store.

Kristen was being held in the kitchen suite. As they curved toward that portal they moved out of the venting's unrelenting path, bringing immediate relief from that projected gloom. The wave of apparitions emanated from the central portal, along with an unnerving racket reminiscent of violent electrical discharges. Nowhere Man must be in there. Brad wondered if it was some sort of demented cosmic joke that the Pestilence had chosen the *living* room for the crack between the realms.

They entered the darkened kitchen. Felicity gasped. Her beam locked onto three figures standing on the far side of the room beside a countertop of ceramic tiles.

"Kristen!"

Brad was so relieved to see his sister that for an instant he barely noticed her captors. Then his attention flashed to Nidge. The chauffeur stood behind her, the ivory-handled garrote used to kill Uncle Zack stretched between his hands. The wire dangled loosely against Kristen's chest, a deadly necklace poised to end her life.

Kristen's hands were open. The amulet was gone, confirming what Brad already knew from the venting's appearance. She'd been forced or tricked into surrendering the first part.

Yet even with that loss and the threat of the garrote at her neck, she didn't appear afraid or upset. Instead, she projected a mood he'd seen before, a kind of inner calm that came over her when she'd retreated from the world into some private arena. However, there was another explanation for her apparent lack of concern. Maybe she was experiencing aftereffects from the drug they'd used to knock her out. Or worse, maybe she'd been rendered catatonic by the long hours of trauma she'd been made to endure.

The third figure was Sindle Vunn. He stood to Kristen's right. His smile exuded confidence.

"Bradley Van Reed, welcome to the crack house!" His tone carried the flourishes of a mad salesman. He laid a hand on Kristen's shoulder as he spoke. She didn't flinch.

"Are you a betting man?" he continued. "I would think you must be. Certainly the evidence would suggest as much, considering your rather astounding capacity for surviving all manner of hazards. Still, are you confident enough to make a truly momentous wager? Would you be willing to bet that the second part of the Trine can spare your sister before Nidge crushes her larynx?"

Brad kept a poker face but his guts were knotted in fear. He had no idea whether the weapon could be bent to his will fast enough to save Kristen from being strangled.

Sindle Vunn opened his jacket, revealing the holstered pistol. He drew the gun and pressed the barrel against Kristen's head just above her right ear.

"And even if you should succeed in disarming Nidge in time, would you also be able to prevent her demise via bullets from not one, but *two* guns?"

Those last words were a signal. Brad and Felicity turned in surprise as Flick stepped out from behind a tall, glass-doored cabinet to their left. A pistol was clutched in her hand, a Beretta.

Felicity's face melted with relief. "Flick! I've been so worried! We're going to get through this, I swear. Just try to remember who you really are, who I am. Who the two of us are together." Felicity laid her palms over her heart, whispered, "I feel you feel I."

The impassioned pleas produced no reaction. Even if Felicity couldn't perceive it, Brad knew Flick was gone. Like the others, she'd been dispatched to a place where the best aspects of human feeling could no longer register.

Flick raised her arm and aimed the Beretta at Kristen. Sindle Vunn voiced triumph.

"Three means of execution versus what? Your pathetic little dinner bell?"

His laughter filled the kitchen, echoing off the ceramic counters and mock appliances.

"So, Bradley Van Reed, I ask you again. Are you a betting man? If so, what would you estimate the odds to be? More to the point, are you willing to wager your sister's life?"

FORTY-SEVEN

Elrod didn't like what was going on in this pretend living room, not one little bit. He sat in the middle of the sofa, fingers pawing nervously at the cushions on either side, trying to avert his eyes from the gross contortionist act Nowhere Man was performing atop that blue leather recliner. The scene was made even creepier by the shadowy lighting from a bunch of jar candles lined up on the fake media console.

What was happening now was way worse than what had occurred back in the cabin when he'd been forced to serve as Kristen's jailer. At least there a closed door had separated him from demon child. Plus, she was a real person, and deep down likely had appreciated what a helpful friend he'd been for cleaning the floor and getting rid of those shoe spots. But being alone with Nowhere Man, that was a whole other matter.

He wished Kyzer was here. He hoped nothing had happened to him. Sindle Vunn had said that the Kyze-Man and Double Bub should have called by now.

When Nidge's booby trap had gone off, the boss had ordered Elrod to stay put and keep an eye on Kristen while he, Nidge and Flick went upstairs to check things out. Although demon child's hand continued to clutch the amulet, she remained unconscious, face up on the floor, so that hadn't been much of a big deal. But moments later the three of them had come scurrying back into the pretend living room, with the boss breathlessly announcing that Nowhere Man had arrived.

Elrod figured that since he'd gotten used to Double Bub's freakish looks, seeing the savior for the first time wouldn't be all that different. But when that winged nightmare slipped into the living room, he'd found himself leaping off the sofa in a panic.

"Hey, glad to meet ya," he'd babbled, pinning his arms against his legs in a vain attempt to stop his appendages from twitching. "Heard a lot about ya over the years. Well, not really over the years, 'cause I didn't really know you existed until weeks ago. Or maybe it was more like months, I can't remember."

Elrod was aware that what was coming from his mouth sounded stupid but he couldn't stop himself. "When I was a kid, I got thrown into a cesspool so the older kids could see if I'd float, and when somebody finally helped me out, I probably looked pretty much like you do. I mean, not exactly like you do, but all dirty and slimy, at least till I fired up the backyard hose and cleaned all that shit off. Not that you need to clean up or anything 'cause I'm sure you're fine just the way you are."

Nowhere Man didn't say anything, just stared down at Elrod like he was some annoying backyard critter, which made him even more uncomfortable. There was something else disturbing about the winged freak. He occasionally faded away as if he was a ghost.

Elrod's twitching had grown worse and the only thing he could do about it was start babbling again, which might calm him down. But Nidge's menacing glare discouraged any fresh outpourings. Instead, he clamped his mouth shut. Even so, it felt like a jumble of words were still trying to push their way out but couldn't get past his clenched teeth. He'd been mightily relieved when Nowhere Man finally turned away and approached Kristen on the floor.

As the imposing creature bent down over her sleeping form, she'd popped awake. His appearance startled her, and for a moment her face got all twisted and she looked like she was going to start screaming. That made Elrod feel better, knowing he wasn't the only one who found the savior deeply unsettling.

But demon child recovered fast. Instead of raising the roof by hollering and carrying on, she rose and planted herself right in front of Nowhere Man. She'd gazed up at him with an expression that said she wasn't frightened, not even one tiny little bit. For a while they seemed to engage in a staring contest, eyes locked on one another, neither blinking nor turning away.

It was Sindle Vunn who finally broke the silence. But he did it in a weird way. Squinting as if he was facing a bright light and clamping his hands over his ears as if trying to hold back noises only he could hear, the words bubbled from his lips in a disjointed fashion. It was like he was having to translate his thoughts from some foreign language while at the same time a monster truck with bright headlights and blaring horn was bearing down on him.

"The savior wishes... for you to know... he desires your cooperation."

Elrod figured out what must be going on. Nowhere Man was relaying his thoughts through the boss. It must be some kind of mind control or telepathy, like in that movie where the alien talked through the President's mouth. That scene had been kind of scary but otherwise it had been a great flick, with lots of stuff catching fire.

"It can't be taken, only given," Kristen said, not breaking eye contact.

The boss didn't seem to like that response. His squint worsened and he pressed his hands even harder against his ears, as if the telepathy was becoming painful. Elrod hoped all that pressure inside his head didn't cause it to explode on account of him standing close enough to be splattered with brain goop.

"The savior... wishes... a trade."

Kristen looked suspicious.

"Surrender it... and your brother's life... will be spared."

Her fingers tightened around the amulet.

"He is... coming. You must... decide."

Demon child made an odd face, or at least it seemed odd to Elrod. It was kind of like a frown. But at the same time it was also like she was only pretending to be upset.

"You promise not to hurt Brad?"

"The savior... promises."

"And you promise they won't hurt him either?" She gestured toward Sindle Vunn and Nidge.

"The savior... commands it."

"What if they don't listen to you?"

"The savior will tear them to pieces... and consume their souls."

Elrod didn't like the sound of that. He waved his hand, trying to signal to Nowhere Man that he was definitely going to listen.

Kristen seemed to be considering the offer. Still, Elrod had been flabbergasted when she opened her hand and freely offered the scary triangle to the scary savior.

Nowhere Man didn't hesitate. He reached out a claw-fingered hand and snatched it from her grasp. The instant he did, that ghosting effect ended. It was as if possessing the amulet had made his essence fully a part of the world.

And that had been that, the big event accomplished without trickery, torture, bloodshed, or fuss and muss of any kind. Elrod still had a hard time accepting it had gone down so easy-peasy. It reminded him of the time he'd come up with this elaborate plan to steal his mom's best earrings, replace them with fakes and sell the real ones to a local fence for cash to go to the movies that night. But lo and behold, out of the blue his mom had handed him a ten-spot. It was "make yourself scarce money" on account of her having her kinkiest trick coming over that evening, a banker who paid two hundred bucks to lick Rice Krispies out of her stiletto heels while she yelled at him for being a bad boy.

Kristen giving up the amulet was sort of like that. A person went and made complicated plans only to realize they hadn't been necessary in the first place.

But it was what had happened next in the pretend living room that led to Elrod's present state of anxiety. Nowhere Man had released Sindle Vunn from his mind control, and the boss ordered Elrod to stay put while the rest of them departed. He'd begged to be allowed to go with them but the boss refused, telling Elrod that a great honor was being bestowed upon him, as he was to bear witness to the savior's actions.

Elrod didn't feel honored, only freaked out. They were barely out the door before Nowhere Man began his contortionist act on the recliner. Pressing his folded-up wings against the back of the chair, he'd bent over it backwards at such an impossibly sharp angle that his spine must have been made of rubber.

And then that penis thing uncoiled from his belly and rose stiffly into the air, holding its shape the same way Sergeant Apone did when he got excited. But instead of cum, a stream of wap shot from the tip, spouting with such force that it splatted against the ceiling and rained down all over the room. If Elrod hadn't been so befuddled by the whole incident, he might have remembered to open his mouth and try swallowing a hit or two.

Still bent across the chair facing the ceiling, Nowhere Man pitched the amulet into the air. The tiny triangle landed perfectly on the tip of the penis thing. It stuck there like a ring on a finger. Then the penis thing started whipping back and forth, so rapidly that the air itself began sparkling with greenish light and making crackling noises similar to what you heard in an electrical storm. Elrod had never much cared for those sounds and wanted to pick his butt up from the sofa and hightail it out of there. But he couldn't take his eyes off the display and could only sit there pawing nervously at the cushions.

The penis thing abruptly halted its violent motion and

collapsed back onto the savior's belly. But the glowing amulet stayed put, floating above Nowhere Man. The air around it seemed to separate, splitting open into a wide fissure.

Something began pouring out of that crack. Elrod couldn't have said exactly what it was because he actually couldn't see anything. But he could sense it, at least well enough to tell how very creepy and nasty it was. He suddenly found himself dwelling on all the bad stuff that had happened to him in his life and all the bad stuff he'd done.

He wished he could make all the badness go away. But somehow he knew it was too late, and that maybe the real reason he'd been left here was to bear witness to the end.

FORTY-EIGHT

Felicity would save Flick. She told herself that over and over, made it into a mantra. She couldn't envision the entirety of a plan but the first step was clear: take away the Beretta. That was doable. Flick was unaccustomed to handling weapons. The way she kept her arm extended and the barrel trained on Kristen was putting a strain on her upper arm muscles, causing the gun to waver. She should have been gripping the butt with two hands to steady her aim and assuming a more stable firing stance by leaning her weight forward.

Felicity trusted her own physicality, knew she could lunge across the short gap between them and snatch the gun from her hand before Flick could pull the trigger. There was a catch, however. Any sudden movement could set off a chain reaction of events. The chauffeur could strangle Kristen. Or the arrogant one with the big mouth could shoot her.

That meant Felicity dared not act until Brad did. She would bide her time, wait for him to spring into action. He would unleash the weapon's awesome power against the two slimebags and she would disarm Flick, the first step in saving the love of her life from madness.

FORTY-NINE

"Let Kristen go," Brad warned. "If you hurt her, I'll tear you to pieces."

"And consume our souls?" Sindle Vunn asked, amused.

Brad didn't understand the reference. The only option he saw was continuing to make threats. "Before you die, you'll wish for it to be over. You'll wish you were dead. You'll beg to be put out of your misery!"

Even as the words spilled out of him, he knew escalating the confrontation wasn't the way to go. Kristen remained imperiled by Sindle Vunn's pistol and Nidge's garrote, and Flick had the Beretta pointed at his sister. Brad's anger would have no impact, especially upon the pair of stone-cold monsters who'd murdered Uncle Zack and Aunt Nipa, and likely had stolen other lives before bringing their misery to Gracious.

"May I offer a suggestion?" Sindle Vunn asked. His tone was diplomatic, all traces of cruelty veiled.

Brad knew what he was going to say and beat him to it. "I hand over the second part of the Trine. You hand over Kristen."

The smile intensified. "A reasonable way of resolving a precarious situation, wouldn't you say? Our master already knows that the old man was the rightful wielder of your weapon. He was seen with it in the eidolon, using it to rescue you from... well, frankly from a fine mess you'd gotten yourself into. And considering the incident back at the cabin, your attempts to make use of the weapon, it should be quite

obvious to you by now that... how should I put this nicely...
you simply don't have what it takes."

His laughter was light and breezy. Brad knew that even if
such a trade was enacted without a double cross, they and
the rest of the world would be left defenseless against the
onslaught of the venting. Kristen had surrendered the amulet
but he still had the second part, and it was now their only
hope. Yet he still couldn't perceive how he might employ the
weapon to save her life.

"No trade." He tried matching Sindle Vunn's lordly attitude
and exuding a level of confidence he didn't feel. "It's not going
to happen."

"And is that your final say in the matter?"

"Yeah."

"Please, I want for you to be absolutely certain. The most
drastic consequences could arise from your decision."

"If you hurt Kristen, I'll–"

"Of course you will. Your intentions have been rendered
explicit. But before you act rashly, I would only ask that you
carefully consider the situation."

Brad realized something. What was occurring in this suite
was part of a stalling tactic. Nowhere Man must have instructed
Sindle Vunn to keep Brad occupied, involve him in a senseless
debate for as long as possible. Meanwhile, the venting would
continue crossing over, unimpeded.

He grimaced. No more delays. He had to act.

Sindle Vunn seemed to realize Brad had caught on to the
stalling charade and that little would be gained by continuing it.

"Very well," he said, motioning to Nidge. "Do her. Make it
slow and painful."

The chauffeur slipped the garrote up to Kristen's neck,
yanked on the handles. Kristen's mouth opened wide. Her eyes
devolved into agony and terror. Her fingers clawed helplessly
at the strangling wire.

"No!" Brad screamed. "It's yours! The weapon is yours!"

He pitched the second part toward them. The triangle hit the floor a yard in front of Sindle Vunn. It broke apart into the component sticks, their reddish light extinguished upon impact.

"Please," he begged. "Let her go."

Sindle Vunn nodded. The chauffeur relaxed his grip, allowed the wire to droop below Kristen's chin. She clutched her bruised neck and frantically sucked down gobs of air.

Sindle Vunn knelt by the broken sticks, gingerly reached for the closest one. His eyes remained riveted to Brad. "Any tricks and she dies."

There would be none. Surrendering the weapon might be the worst and last mistake Brad ever made. Kristen could be strangled anyway, he and Felicity dying moments later in a hail of bullets. But he'd had no choice. His action wasn't based on rational behavior but on the love he felt for his sister. He'd done the only thing possible to save her life at this moment in time.

This moment in time.

Sindle Vunn's fingers were mere inches from the sticks when his countenance flared with alarm. Lunging upright, he jerked backward so fast he almost stumbled over his own feet. Nidge was retreating too, pulling Kristen along with him. Brad glanced over at Felicity and Flick. They were moving away from him as well, their features warped by astonishment.

"What's happening to you?" Felicity whispered.

Temporally unrestricted solutions.

The phrase coursed through Brad, igniting more insights. The Trine had been created by a civilization able to transcend the conceptualization of time. The first two parts were given to Grandma Isabella and Joseph in the summer of 1966, at their moment in time. And the third part...

It's been given to me. Right now. My moment in time.

No, that wasn't right, not exactly. The third part hadn't been given *to* him.

It *was* him.

I'm the third part of the Trine.

As astounding as the idea was, he knew with utter certainty it was true. The third part had always been within him, a living presence, growing stronger as he edged into maturity. But his personal growth had been stunted, thrown off course by the dark events of his early teens. His father's abuse and his mother's death had combined to pack tons of unacknowledged guilt into a mental storehouse, barricaded against access by barbs of pain. That coalition of repressed emotions had propelled him onto a divergent path, one where bleak, cynical thoughts flayed his spirit, like branches pushed aside only to relentlessly snap back upon him. The events of this extraordinary day, culminating in the sacrifice he'd made to save Kristen – putting her survival above his own – had returned him to the path he was always meant to be on, and exactly when he was meant to be on it.

This moment in time.

He understood, without knowing the specifics, that Kristen had deliberately surrendered the first part. She'd given it up to save Brad, just as he'd surrendered the second part to save her. The Trine, by some expression of its organic wisdom, recognized the selflessness of their acts, that what they had done for one another transcended concerns about absolute power corrupting absolutely.

As staggering as his insights were, they still left him with questions. What did it actually mean to be the third part of the Trine? Why didn't he feel any different? Most perplexing of all, why was everyone still backing away from him?

The answer to the latter question became clear when he caught his reflection. Or, more precisely, the absence of it. In the darkened kitchen, with Felicity's flashlight the sole source of illumination, the angle of her beam rendered mirror-like the glass door of that tall cabinet.

Brad was startled to realize he cast no reflection, or at least not the one he had been familiar with for the past twenty-four years. Instead, staring back at him was a human-sized equilateral triangle. White and diaphanous as a cloud, it slowly rotated in three dimensions as if mounted on an invisible set of axes.

Sindle Vunn regained his composure. He stopped retreating, held his ground. "Cute trick but nothing has really changed."

Yet there was uncertainty in that voice, in Sindle Vunn's stance, in his very essence. Something else had changed within Brad. He'd become hyper-sentient, hyper-alert to his surroundings. The most insignificant details now succumbed to his observation and discernment.

He pointed an accusatory finger at Nidge and was surprised to see his own extended arm and hand. To his own eyes, he looked normal, was simply Brad Van Reed. It was the manner in which others saw him and how he viewed his own reflection that was different.

"Let my sister go," he warned. The words issuing from his mouth were somehow comprehended by the others even though from their point of view he no longer had a mouth.

Nidge hesitated. But then his resolve hardened. A subtle increase of tension in the way the chauffeur gripped the garrote handles revealed his intent. He was about to again pull taut the strangling wire around Kristen's neck.

Brad stopped it from happening. The kitchen suite became a 3D tableau, the five figures robbed of animation, each frozen in their last pose. The power of the third part had enabled him to suspend time.

No, that wasn't right. He hadn't suspended time. A more accurate explanation was that he was momentarily moving without temporal restrictions, unhinged from what was commonly called the fourth dimension. In truth, time was an immeasurable presence whose borders lie at the furthest edges of perception. His unique status was making it difficult to distinguish between moments. Past, present and future were blurring together.

But not so much that he couldn't function. He stared at Nidge's frozen figure, seeking a reason to feel the same pity he'd felt with Double Bub back at the cabin after having detected strains of humanity on those sad and frightened faces. But the chauffeur projected nothing of the sort. A darkness had long ago consumed him, well before he'd attached himself to Sindle Vunn and fell under the sway of Nowhere Man.

Nidge had murdered Uncle Zack. He was threatening Kristen. Brad directed the energy of his thoughts at the three sticks. They elevated off the floor in cadence, a trio of angry twirling batons bathed in crimson light.

He sent the second part of the Trine flying across the room.

FIFTY

Felicity was transfixed, unable to comprehend what had happened to Brad, why an amorphous white triangle marked the spot where he'd been standing moments ago. Only when Sindle Vunn spoke was her attention momentarily drawn to the other side of the kitchen.

"Cute trick but nothing has really changed."

The three sticks vanished from the floor. Defying the laws of motion, the triangle reappeared around Nidge's neck, tight against his flesh like some exotic piece of jewelry. It was as if time had skipped a beat.

The chauffeur managed a surprised grunt. The sticks compressed inward, shrinking the triangle's dimensions, strangling him. The garrote fell from his grip. Fingers clawed frantically at his neck, trying to dislodge the choking collar. His futile efforts ignited the weapon. Burning embers streamed from the sticks, cascading upward. Nidge's face morphed into a cauldron of spark and flame.

Kristen darted away as Nidge gyrated violently across the room, out of control, his head a fiery pillar. Mad with agony, unable to scream, he plowed into Sindle Vunn. The collision knocked the latter man down and sent his pistol skittering across the floor.

Nidge continued spinning, slamming headfirst into the edge of a hanging cabinet. There was a loud thud as he hit. He dropped out of sight behind a kitchen island of marbled-ceramic tile. Smoke from his burning face continued to spiral up from where he'd fallen.

Flick was riveted to the horrifying scene. Felicity knew she'd never have a greater advantage. She pounced, grabbing hold of Flick's gun arm at the wrist, wrenching the barrel upward while simultaneously twisting and squeezing. Flick had no choice but to drop the Beretta.

Yet even disarmed, her fiancée fought back, a drug-addled wildcat of flailing arms and pounding fists. Felicity batted away the appendages, trying to deflect the brunt of the attack while not causing her serious injury.

"Stop fighting me!" she pleaded with Flick. "I'm trying to help you!"

The entreaty went unheeded. Felicity caught a peripheral glimpse of Single Vunn getting up from the floor and staggering toward his fallen pistol.

No choice. She needed to end this fast. Lacking one of those purple syringes, she'd have to put Flick out of commission by more traditional means.

Taking half a step back for a greater swing radius, she clenched her right hand and attacked. Her target area was Flick's left temple between hairline and eyebrows, just forward of the left ear. The fist connected. Felicity had never taken down an actual person this way, having only used the technique against practice dummies in her self-defense courses at the gym. In theory, a strong enough blow to the temple would cause the brain to bash violently against the skull lining, resulting in an immediate blackout.

It worked. Flick dropped, out cold. Felicity had no time to worry whether she'd hurt the love of her life too badly... or done even worse to her. Sindle Vunn was reaching down for the fallen gun.

Felicity snatched up the Beretta. Two barrels pointed at one another from across the room. Their eyes locked.

Sindle Vunn blinked first. Apparently realizing that even winning a gun battle wouldn't spare him from Nidge's fate, he opted for escape. Lunging behind the island, he ducked into a narrow aisle between the dishwasher and a fake stove. Felicity heard a door slam at the back of the kitchen. An access passageway must run behind the display rooms.

Kristen ran toward her brother.

"No Kristen, stop!"

The voice was Brad's even though he wasn't there, only that gyrating white triangle.

"Stay here, both of you."

Kristen halted. For the first time since their arrival, emotion played across her face.

"But I want to come with you," she pouted. "I can help."

"No, do as I ask. Both of you stay here. I'm going to finish this."

FIFTY-ONE

Brad reattached himself to the moment. Relief washed through him and he hunched over, breathing deeply. Existing without temporal restrictions took a lot out of him physically. He felt like someone who'd just run a marathon. He could only attempt the time trick for brief intervals.

He willed the weapon to disengage from the chauffeur's neck. The sticks flew from Nidge's corpse and reformed into the familiar triangle in Brad's hand. He possessed the second part. He *was* the third part. A glance at that mirrored door revealed what others saw: a glowing red triangle magically floating within the borders of an indistinct white triangle, both aswirl in a dreamy dance.

He backed out into the lobby, keeping an eye on Kristen and Felicity to make sure they obeyed his instructions and didn't follow. His sister looked irritated at being left behind. But the two people he cared about most could distract him from his task. Besides, Felicity was armed now. Brad trusted her to protect Kristen in case Sindle Vunn returned or other threats appeared.

Realizing they were staying put, he turned away and headed for the living room. First priority was sealing the crack and stopping the invasion of the venting. To do that he'd have to take the amulet from Nowhere Man, which brought up an obvious problem. The amulet could not be taken, only given. Kristen had willingly surrendered the first part. He couldn't envision a scenario where the Pestilence would willingly return it. There had to be another way.

A voice washed over him. *Join the heads.*

It again sounded like his mother, yet this time he could tell it wasn't. His enhanced consciousness identified the voice as a clever imitation, the tonal style drawn from his own memories. The actual speaker was SOS. The three heads of Silso Orjos Sohn had uttered the words in tandem, their blended voices somehow capable of perfect mimicry. He realized it had been their combination of voices from the very beginning, from that moment in Kristen's bedroom two nights ago when he'd first been instructed to find the third part.

The meaning of the new phrase perplexed him just as the earlier one had initially. *Join the heads.* He guessed he wasn't supposed to take it literally, that it didn't mean he should try fusing SOS's three heads into one.

He crossed the lobby and approached the portal to the living room suite. Once again, he found himself in the path of that endless wave of ghostly apparitions. As on the stairway, the venting passed around him, unable to go through the Trine. And despite their incorporeal aspects, they obviously couldn't pass through solid matter either. Nor could they float freely. Gravity dictated their movements as it did everything else on the planet.

He also sensed that the venting hadn't yet found their way out of the factory. But it wouldn't be long. Soon they'd reach accessible doors and windows, swarm out into the streets of Gracious and ultimately the world.

He entered the living room. Nowhere Man was contorted backward across a recliner, the amulet floating above him within a large opening shaped like a vertical teardrop. The Pestilence was bent over so far that its head was upside down in relation to Brad, which made the creature appear even more hideous. Erratic buzzing noises like overloaded electrical circuits erupted from the crack between the realms, and the amulet gave off the most vivid light he'd yet seen. The green glow easily overwhelmed the meager illumination from a line of jar candles on a media console.

Elrod was the only other entity present, his hands clamped onto the sofa, his face a mask of confusion and terror. It was clear he wanted to run away from the madness but couldn't summon the strength.

The venting poured through the teardrop crack one at a time, falling like droplets of water from a leaking faucet onto the floor beside Nowhere Man. Midair twists landed them upright, or at least it did with those possessing humanoid bodies. The ones with more alien forms dropped onto their clawed appendages or bony protrusions or flailing masses of tentacle. Whatever their configuration, all quickly fell in line with the escaping throng.

Brad finally grasped their true nature. They were representations of individuals – body-image memories – from the multitude of species comprising the civilization that had banished its emotional detritus. Each contained its own unique mix of corrosive feelings and urges, and together they encompassed quadrillions of negative emotions and repressed pains. Until now, the venting had been secured in the eidolon, a penitentiary of sorts, with SOS functioning as warden. Nowhere Man was staging a mass prison break.

The analogy prompted a question Brad hadn't considered. Why had the civilization that created the repositories and the Trine endowed the first part with such power? Why would they craft the amulet so it could serve as the key for unlocking the prison door, creating a crack between the realms that allowed the emotional detritus to escape?

It was another mystery whose solution would have to wait. Nowhere Man finally took notice of Brad's entrance. Performing a twisting midair somersault worthy of a gymnast, it vaulted off the chair and landed upright in front of him less than a dozen feet away.

Brad no longer felt afraid of its menacing presence. But he did feel something. He momentarily couldn't identify the emotion because it was so novel: a fusion of positivity. Optimism, hope, fierce resolve, love for Kristen and Felicity, abiding affection for the world in general. It was what people were supposed to feel, what many of them did feel before life's bleaker emotions infiltrated consciousness and created repressive storehouses guarded by cynicism and doubt.

"Time to end this."

His words elicited a reaction. Nowhere Man's head jerked back, as if surprised at Brad's fearless stance.

"Glad you're reading me, asshole."

He thrust out his free hand and willed the first part to come to him, figuring it was worth a shot.

Nothing happened. He tried anew, this time calling upon the force he'd used to unhinge himself from the temporal flow. Again he reached out his hand. Again the amulet failed to budge. Although Elrod had been rendered a statue on the sofa, Nowhere Man's slight movements revealed that Brad's time trick had no effect on it. And the venting continued pouring through the crack unabated.

He returned to the familiar temporal flow before that out-of-breath sensation could weaken him. Why hadn't the Pestilence tried stopping him? Maybe it knew his efforts would fail. Or maybe the fact he wielded two parts of the Trine was enough to keep the creature at bay.

"Join the heads." This time he mouthed the words, both to inspire his own thoughts toward comprehending their meaning and possibly get a rise out of Nowhere Man, maybe even prompt the creature to reveal some vital clue. But there was still no reaction, nor any welcoming onslaught of inspiration. The stalemate continued, the two of them staring one another down.

FIFTY-TWO

Felicity moved cautiously through the kitchen, Beretta in one hand, flashlight in the other. Keeping an eye on Kristen, Flick and the main entrance, she checked for the presence of additional doorways. There didn't appear to be any other than the one Sindle Vunn had escaped through. She lifted a pair of stylish, Z-shaped chairs from a snack table and propped them at a precarious angle against the door. Should anyone open it from the other side, the chairs would collapse inward with enough noise to alert her to the intrusion.

She returned to Flick and knelt beside her. Again she checked for a pulse. There was no need. It was clear from the gentle rise and fall of her chest that she was breathing normally. But that wasn't enough to alleviate worry.

"You should tie her up," Kristen said, her attention shifting back and forth between Felicity and the lobby with the rigor of a metronome. Her normally placid expression had been replaced by a scowl. She was still annoyed that Brad had ordered her to stay put.

But Felicity knew his decision was the right one. Whatever he'd become, it was likely beyond their expertise to match. Confronting Nowhere Man was something Brad had to do on his own, without his concentration being diverted by worrying over their safety.

Felicity readjusted the inflatable backpack pillow she'd tucked under Flick's head in an effort to make her more comfortable. Her fiancée looked so peaceful, a true sleeping beauty. Kristen's suggestion to bind her made sense and already had occurred to Felicity. She'd been holding off, still nurturing hope that upon awakening, the Emily Flickinger she knew and loved would return from drug-induced enslavement. But in her heart, Felicity knew there was little chance for such a spontaneous recovery. Flick, had she been present, likely would have quoted her the odds against it.

Retrieving a length of rope from her backpack, she cut two short pieces and secured them around Flick's wrists and ankles.

A faint moan came from behind the island where Nidge had fallen. Felicity snatched up the Beretta and flashlight and scurried over to investigate. The chauffeur's face was a charred mass, no longer recognizable as something human. Without a doubt he was dead. The moan must have been one of those normal post-mortem sounds caused by a body's release of built-up gases.

"It's OK," she assured Kristen. "Nothing to be concerned about."

There was no response. Felicity turned around. Kristen was gone.

FIFTY-THREE

Brad still didn't know what to do. Should he again try using the power of the first two parts to draw the amulet to him? Should he launch a direct assault on Nowhere Man?

Fear wasn't holding him back. It was a sense that neither ploy would be meaningful. As for the creature, it was apparent why it wasn't going on the offensive. The stalemate wasn't really a stalemate. The Pestilence was winning simply by Brad's inaction, which was allowing the venting to continue crossing over into the world unimpeded. It was the same stalling tactic Sindle Vunn had used.

So don't just stand here. Do something.

He half expected the voice of his mother-slash-SOS to repeat its most recent instruction. But no words sounded. Maybe its silence was a message in and of itself, that he already possessed all the clues necessary to figure out what to do.

Join the heads. He knew the phrase wasn't to be taken literally, that it was code for something. The Trine, in the guise of Silso Orjos Sohn, functioned mainly to inspire action in others, have them figure things out on their own. SOS was a kind of guidebook, a source of information for those who wielded parts of the Trine. The heads had performed that function with Joseph over the years and now with Brad, although Sohn had never been forthcoming with the original wielder of the second part. Deeper knowledge of what the meteorite contained, and the nature of the Pestilence and the Trine, were meant specifically for Brad, as he was the one embodying the third part. The imparting of such knowledge had been essential to get him to where he was now, in a position to…

Join the heads! So obvious he felt like an idiot for not having not seen it immediately. Bring together the three parts of the Trine!

The amulet had been given to Nowhere Man. It couldn't be taken back and the creature would never surrender it. But there was another option. Brad didn't have to take the first part, didn't even need to possess it. Nothing prevented him from *giving* the second and third parts, inserting them into the crack between the realms so they could link with the amulet.

The part about "nothing preventing him" turned out to be wishful thinking. As he tried flanking Nowhere Man to reach the aerial opening, the creature lunged in front of him, blocking his route. Clearly he wasn't getting past without a fight.

So be it.

Brad didn't know how he appeared in Nowhere Man's eyes, whether he came across as two oscillating triangles or a semi-normal human possessing the second part and somehow embodying the third. Either way, he was about to find out.

Transforming the weapon into a fiery staff, he attacked. Or tried to. Wings flapping, the Pestilence leaped into the air, dodging Brad's blow. It slammed hard against the ceiling, sending a cascade of plaster raining down. Brad split the staff into its components, willing the trio to shoot upward like a line of flaming arrows.

Nowhere Man batted the first one aside, sent the arrow tumbling harmlessly away. The creature twisted its body from the path of the second arrow. But it couldn't avoid the final one. The arrow tore into the creature's left wing. The wing ignited in red flame. Brad couldn't tell if Nowhere Man's shriek was due to pain or rage.

It couldn't stay aloft with a fiery damaged wing. Dropping from the ceiling, it landed feet-first with a muffled crack. Before Brad could regroup the weapon, the creature rushed toward him, a dark appendage sweeping toward his head.

He whipped up his arms up to protect his face. His left forearm took the brunt of the blow. It was like hit being hit by a two-by-four wielded by King Kong. Knocked off his feet, he flew across the room toward the sofa onto which Elrod was latched. He landed back first on the coffee table in front of it, shattering a pattern of inlaid porcelain tiles. The worst pain was a tossup between his battered forearm and the back muscles that had absorbed his touchdown.

He struggled to concentrate his thoughts on the weapon. Too late. Nowhere Man was coming at him. There was no time to get on his feet. The best he could do was slither off the coffee table onto his back and crab walk across the floor. He made it about three paces when a spiked talon raked his upper chest.

The claw pierced layers of clothing, causing a new order of agony. He cried out. His eyes blurred with tears. Through their watery shroud he glimpsed Nowhere Man raising its arm for what likely would be a final strike.

Something else snared the creature's attention. Its head whipped across the room toward the entry portal. Brad followed its gaze. Panic overtook him.

"Kristen, no! Get away from here!"

His sister ignored the plea and took two steps into the living room. Her body assumed an odd pose, torso tilted to one side, head cocked the opposite way. Her eyes grew pinched, lips compressed into a distorted grimace. She looked as if she'd been afflicted by some crippling malady of old age.

A bone-deep rumbling shook the air followed by a thunderous roar. A sinkhole swallowed Nowhere Man, the coffee table and a sizable chunk of flooring, leaving Brad perched inches from its rim.

He rolled away from the edge as fountains of dust spurted from the massive hole. On the far side was the sofa, with Elrod dangling precariously on the lip. More flooring started giving way beneath the couch.

FIFTY-FOUR

Elrod held onto the cushions as the sofa plunged into the pit. But as the couch upended, the cushions came loose, as did his grip on them. And then he, sofa and cushions were falling separately, all heading downward with increasing speed.

He couldn't see the bottom. It was far beneath him and shrouded in dust. Nowhere Man was below him and already passing through the rising cloud. The fire in its left wing had been extinguished but the wing was too charred and full of holes to provide lift. It flapped uselessly. One good wing wasn't enough to keep it aloft.

Elrod continued dropping. There was still no bottom in sight. As the dust cloud enveloped him, he realized there was no way he was going to survive such a long fall. His last hope was that wherever he ended up, it would be a place that had fire.

FIFTY-FIVE

Brad turned back to Kristen. She was just starting to come out of that crunched-up pose, returning to normalcy… if such a thing ever again could hold meaning for their family. He waited for the worst of the dust to settle before inching back to the sinkhole and peering over the edge.

It was deep, well below where the room's dim light could penetrate the powdery air. He couldn't make out the bottom. Ten feet below the lip, the sinkhole had severed an ancient cast-iron sewer pipe. Cloudy water trickled from both ends, creating scrawny waterfalls that fell away into the void.

Brad froze. From far below came movement. Nowhere Man emerged from the darkness, clawed appendages digging into the craggy wall, climbing at a relentless pace. It could no longer fly. But the slower means of ascent would still get it to the top.

He struggled to his feet, fighting multiple pains and a wave of dizziness. He thought he was going to collapse, but hobbled forward. One step became two, then a sequence. The sequence turned into a jog, the jog into a flat-out dash around the edge of the pit.

He reached the leather recliner, ran up it like a staircase, from footrest to seat, from seat to backrest. Compressing his legs as he ascended to that highest point, he launched into the air, arms outstretched toward the crack with the piercing green triangle at its center.

FIFTY-SIX

The ominous rumbling was familiar. Felicity had last heard it yesterday morning in the library's conservation room with Brad, when that sinkhole had opened up under the old jail. She glanced at Flick who remained asleep, the bindings intact.

Racing from the kitchen, Felicity crossed the lobby and entered the living room. She came to a shocked halt beside Kristen.

In the air above a leather recliner was a dazzling light show, green, red and white arcs of flame intermingling to create a rainbow of quivering hues that seemed to perpetually explode in and out of one another. The phantasmagoric display emitted a wavering buzz, like a swarm of bees in an elliptical orbit, alternately approaching and retreating. The light show was so intense Felicity couldn't look directly at it for more than a few seconds. Raising an arm to shield her eyes from the worst of its harshness, she realized a translucent spherical object was at the center of the display. The sphere was composed of smaller triangular faces. It bore the same configuration Flick had discovered in the cave, a pentakis dodecahedron.

Kristen held her gaze steady on the sphere's brilliance.

"You shouldn't stare directly into it," Felicity warned. "You could damage your eyes."

"Uh-uh. It won't hurt us. It only hurts them."

"Them?"

Kristen answered with a sweep of the arm, pointing from the sphere to the portal behind them. Felicity was confused.

"I don't understand what you're–"

"Don't look with your eyes. Look from the inside, not from the outside."

The instruction was vague. Yet somehow Felicity understood. Following the track of Kristen's finger, she experienced that same feeling of unpleasantness when descending the stairwell to the basement with Brad.

"The venting?"

Kristen nodded.

"Something about them… they seem different."

"They're not coming out of the crack anymore. They're going the other way. They're being pulled back into it."

An unfathomable sense allowed Felicity to perceive the distinction. The venting indeed were being recaptured.

"Where's Brad?" she wondered.

Kristen pointed up at the sphere. Before Felicity could quiz her further, movement on the other side of the room snared her attention. The fierce light had been so compelling that until this moment she hadn't noticed the sinkhole that had swallowed a massive chunk of floor. And something was emerging from it.

"Nowhere Man!" she shouted, grabbing Kristen's hand, ready to yank the two of them out of the living room. The creature's hideous head peeked over the lip.

"It's OK, Felicity," Kristen said. "It's not trying to get out, it's trying to stay here. But the Trine isn't three parts anymore. Brad made it into one."

Felicity accepted the answer although she didn't understand it. And she couldn't comprehend how Kristen was staying so calm. But her assessment of what was happening to Nowhere Man was spot-on. The creature wasn't climbing from the sinkhole, it was being sucked out by some invisible force, the same force that drew the venting into the sphere. Nowhere Man clawed and scratched madly at the edge of the pit, trying to latch onto the world, maintain a foothold on something real and physical. But that invisible force emanating from the sphere was stronger than gravity and more tenacious than musculature, human or inhuman, living or dead.

Nowhere Man's grip was broken. Lifted violently into the air, the creature tumbled across the room, arms and legs flailing helplessly. At the moment it disappeared into that tumultuous light show, Felicity sensed that the last of the venting also had been recaptured. She experienced a feeling of lightness, of a crusted gloom having been lifted from the world.

The light show faded. The sphere began pulsating, then gyrating in a manner that defied logical mechanics. It seemed to be spinning in every direction at once, as if possessing an infinite number of axes of rotation.

A roar filled the room. Felicity clasped her ears as the noise gained power, escalating to near-painful intensity. It peaked with a sonic boom she felt all the way down to her bones.

The sphere vanished, leaving nothing tangible in its wake.

FIFTY-SEVEN

Brad existed. He told himself so even though he could sense nothing, see or hear nothing. He'd been uprooted, marooned in a timeless void. Only feelings and thoughts remained, disengaged from anything fundamental, anything real.

Am I dead? Is this what it felt like when life was over? Was this some great beyond, a final state into which the lifeless were consigned? He wanted not to believe his time on Earth was over. But the nothingness seemed omnipresent.

A chill came over him. Were things even worse? Was he now part of the venting?

He glimpsed something in the distance, drifting closer. Recognition came. It was SOS. Yet now, there was but a single head atop that conical body. As its face came close enough to make out details, he sensed aspects of its three distinct selves. Silso's hopefulness... Orjos' doubts... Sohn's curious mix of impenetrability and wisdom.

Come back, a voice urged. *You can do it. Come back.*

At first he thought it must be SOS, again speaking with his mother's voice. But the entity's mouth remained closed as it floated past, ignoring his presence, fixated on some point in the far distance. And the style of speech was different. Stranger still, he began to hear the voice more distinctly and realized it was actually two overlapping voices, both female yet neither his maternal parent.

Kristen. Felicity.

Recognition brought a longing to respond. But he couldn't

discern how. The void seemed to permit only thoughts, not speech.

He felt something. A sharp impact against the side of his face, not overwhelmingly painful but not pleasant either. The sensation took root inside him, led to a resurgence of physicality, awareness of lying on something hard. A floor. A living room. An abandoned factory.

He opened his eyes. It took a moment to focus on Felicity kneeling over him, her features pinched with concern even as her arm was raised to slap his face again. Kristen stood behind her. Whatever emotion his sister might be feeling remained cloaked.

"Bet you wanted to do that for a long time," he whispered.

"For at least two years," Felicity said, her garbled laugh offset by relieved tears running down her cheeks. "It felt good to get you back."

"Where did I...? How did I...?"

"The sphere, it disappeared. We thought you were gone for good. But a few seconds later you fell out of the air."

Brad couldn't remember anything about a sphere. The last thing he recalled was leaping off the recliner into the opening and reaching out to bring his two parts of the Trine into contact with the amulet. After that... the void. Yet he had the impression of other events occurring in that interval, many of them. Perhaps the memories would return. But maybe it was better they didn't.

"I'm guessing I don't look like a giant triangle anymore."

"Thankfully not," Felicity said. "Can you stand up?"

"I think so."

He needed her help. She held onto his arm until the wobbliness passed and he felt strong enough to walk on his own. He went immediately to Kristen, knelt and wrapped her in a hug expressing how he truly felt about her, and that he'd denied the two of them from experiencing for far too long.

"It's over now," he whispered. "We're going to be OK."

She didn't answer. And although her arms encircled him, her response to the hug felt more like a formality, a social obligation.

We've been through a lot. It'll take time for both of us to recover.

"We should get Flick and get out of here," Felicity said. "Sindle Vunn is still on the loose."

Brad doubted the man was hanging around. Just the same, he was reassured Felicity had the Beretta in hand and was keeping alert as they made their way through the lobby and back to the kitchen.

Flick had awakened. Her hands and ankles were bound but she seemed at peace, staring quietly at the ceiling. Felicity rushed to her side, knelt and whispered something in her ear.

Flick didn't react, not even when Felicity cut her bindings and helped her stand. Brad gripped Flick's other arm and the two of them helped walk her out of the kitchen. But it was like guiding a zombie. Maybe Nowhere Man's demise eventually would free her from enslavement, reverse the drug effects.

He badly wanted Flick to make a full recovery, not only for her own sake and Felicity's, but because it provided him with hope that Kristen too could be brought back from an emotional void he feared may have claimed her. He just needed to stay positive. It was well-known that people recovered from traumatic events. All it sometimes took was time.

FIFTY-EIGHT

Brad was content to let Felicity lead them out of Eckenroth's.

"We should go the same way we came in," she said. "They may have planted other booby traps."

Her suggestion made sense. Even though the doors at the back of the building were closer, the longer route was the safer option.

They followed Felicity up the stairwells to the third floor, maintaining silence in case the last of Nowhere Man's servants was waiting in ambush. Flick had fallen into a walking rhythm and didn't need further assistance. But she was still out of it, her eyes vacant, plodding behind Felicity like a dutiful robot. At least Kristen's impairment wasn't as severe. She remained alert to her surroundings. But whatever she was or wasn't feeling remained a troubling question mark.

They came upon the hallway that had collapsed from the floor above. Joseph was there in the rubble, undisturbed. Brad tried not to look at him as they passed. His grief remained too close.

There was still no sign of Chief Wellstead. Either she'd been slain by Nowhere Man or his servants and her body moved elsewhere, or she'd awakened and overcome her injuries enough to make her way out and summon help.

It took several more minutes to reach the old tunnel connecting the basement with the original kiln. Brad was the last one to climb the ladder, an effort accentuating his multiple pains, particularly where the creature had raked his chest with its claw. The wound didn't seem too deep and no fresh blood was leaking through his shirt. But the upward exertion put extra strain on the injury. He was relieved to make it to the top and breathe in the fresh night air.

The skies were clear and filled with stars. The moon had risen, providing a backdrop of natural light that augmented Felicity's flashlight. Now that they'd exited the factory, Brad acknowledged more mundane concerns. They'd survived an unbelievable ordeal but he had no idea what would happen from here on out. He didn't even have a clue where he and Kristen were going to spend the night, let alone where they might live going forward.

Felicity led them along the rudimentary path above and behind the parking lot. Brad was glad she was taking the initiative. He'd begun to realize how monumentally tired he was. Despite the pain from his injuries, it wouldn't have been hard to lay down right here in the woods and conk out.

"Phone should work once we get to the ridge," Felicity said, turning off the path and heading up the forested hill. "If not, we'll use the chief's radio to call for–"

A shadowy figure leaped from behind a tree. Felicity whirled with the Beretta. Too late – a pistol butt cracked the side of her head. She fell. Her gun and flashlight hit the ground, the latter illuminating her attacker in a crooked beam.

Sindle Vunn looked half-crazed. He panned his weapon from Flick to Brad, freezing the barrel on Kristen.

"No!" Brad yelled, lunging in front of his sister as a shield.

"Noble but pointless." A joyless smile punctuated the words. "My initial thought was to just shoot her and see your reaction. A speck of pleasure for an evening that admittedly went sideways. But the order in which you die doesn't really make much of a difference, now does it."

Felicity was out cold. The Beretta was too far from Brad to make a grab for it. Flick was a statue, oblivious or indifferent.

"Don't worry, Brad," Kristen said, boldly stepping out from behind him. "It's going to be OK. Look."

She pointed to the tangled roots at the base of an oak to Sindle Vunn's right. The conviction in her voice was so compelling that the leader of Nowhere Man's servants couldn't help but whip his gaze in that direction. Seeing nothing unusual, he swiveled his attention back to them. His movement was too swift for Brad to even consider taking action.

"He doesn't know," Kristen explained, as tranquil as if commenting on the weather. "He can't see it."

Her freakish self-assurance evaporated Sindle Vunn's smile.

"See what?" he demanded.

She didn't answer, just stared at him with those unflinching eyes. He aimed the pistol at her head, his voice bubbling with rage.

"Tell me what you see, you little bitch!"

"I see your shoo spot. It's your time."

A branch cracked to Sindle Vunn's left. He whirled toward it. The explosive discharge of a double-barreled shotgun unleashing both barrels split the night. The dual splatter of buckshot caught Sindle Vunn in the guts, hurling him backward against the oak. He crumpled onto the nest of tangled roots.

Chief Wellstead emerged from the trees with Hiram Swanteri's shotgun. Her face was bruised and streaked, her uniform splotched and torn. A limp indicated an injury to her right leg.

Brad stared wide-eyed at Kristen. She was as unruffled as ever. He ran to Felicity, who was waking up and clutching the side of her head.

"Are you all right?" he asked, helping her sit up.

"I think so. What happened?" Felicity took notice of Chief Wellstead standing over Sindle Vunn's body. "Where did you come from?"

"Long story."

They stared, wanting more. The chief relented.

"When I came to after the explosion I didn't know where you were. Couldn't do anything for Joseph, he was in bad shape. Do you happen to know if–"

"Didn't make it." Brad said.

The chief noted his pained expression and went on. "I headed out of the factory, made it back to my vehicle and called for assistance and EMS. I grabbed the shotgun and was on my way back when I spotted this piece of crap." She nudged Sindle Vunn's body with her boot. "He was waiting to ambush you. Lucky I got here in time."

"Lucky," Brad murmured, again gazing at Kristen.

"I had an extra flashlight so I left the other one back at the collapse. Figured it could be a beacon if the two of you returned that way."

Sirens sounded in the distance. Helping Brad get Felicity on her feet, the chief noted Flick's vacant expression. "Should she be cuffed?"

Felicity shook her head. "No, she's fine. She's going to be OK."

Chief Wellstead didn't look convinced but turned her attention to Kristen.

"Honey, I'm really glad you made it out of there and that you're safe now. You must have had quite the ordeal. And you know, sometimes when people have really bad things happen to them, their feelings get kind of messed up and they go numb. But that'll pass. We're going to get you lots of help, people you can talk to about what happened."

"They wouldn't understand," Kristen said. "They can't see."

The chief seemed taken aback by her poised attitude. "Maybe not. But it might be good for you anyway. So try to keep an open mind about it."

"They can't see."

Her tone was more insistent. The chief frowned. "Just before I got here I heard you say something about Sindle Vunn not seeing. And something about his shoes, and about it being his time?"

Kristen ignored her and turned to Brad. "We should go to

the hospital. You and Felicity and Flick and Chief Wellstead are all hurt and you all need doctors."

"You're right," Brad said, even while realizing she was trying to evade the interrogation by deflecting attention away from herself. But the chief's advice about having her talk about her experiences and not keep everything bottled up was on the money. Considering the weirdness factor of what had happened to them, traditional psychologists or trauma specialists probably weren't the best options. In fact, maybe there weren't any good options.

The sirens grew more intense. Lights flashed through the trees from below. A line of police cruisers, fire trucks and ambulances pulled into the parking lot.

"Stay put," the chief ordered, wincing from her injured leg as she made her way down the embankment. "I'll get EMS to bring stretchers up here."

Brad didn't know if Kristen was aware of Aunt Nipa and Uncle Zack being killed and their home being destroyed. He was loathe to tell her if she wasn't. Yet it would be even crueler for her to learn of it later from strangers.

"Listen, Kristen, some really bad things happened after you were taken. Aunt Nipa and Uncle Zack–"

"They're dead." She displayed that same eerie calm. He nodded and went on.

"I'm sorry. The house is gone too. But you and I are going to find a new place to live, I promise."

Thinking about the house reminded Brad of something else. "When we were back in the factory and that sinkhole appeared and swallowed Nowhere Man... You did that, right?"

He already knew she had. But as the chief pointed out, prompting her to talk about her experiences was important. And who better than Brad to provide an understanding ear.

"I'm sure glad you did," he continued. "You saved my life. But what's the story with those other sinkholes, the ones at the house and library. Did you make those too?"

"Uh-huh."

"I'm kind of curious. Why?"

Kristen looked momentarily confused. She craned her neck to the starlit heavens as if seeking an answer out there. When she finally faced him again her confident attitude was back.

"Practicing."

FIFTY-NINE

It was a beautiful August morning as they hiked up the hillside above Uncle Zack and Aunt Nipa's property. Kristen had been reluctant to come out here but Brad had gently insisted, telling her it was time finally to get over her trepidation and revisit the place where she'd spent most of her eleven years. Besides, the task he was here to accomplish wasn't something he wished to do alone. It was important for family to be present.

The temperature was in the low seventies. Amid the trees, golden daffodils and rosy snapdragons bristled, vying for their place in beds of lush grass. Woodland scents filled the air, sharpened by yesterday's rain. The ground remained damp, but Brad found a level spot with a good view of the clearing below and unfolded the wide blanket from his backpack. Spreading it, he sat on one end, leaving plenty of room for a gap between them. One of Kristen's latest quirks was wanting always to have space around her, not wanting anyone to get too close.

It was a Saturday, so the construction workers were off. The demolition team had finished earlier in the week and the last burned remnants of the house had been hauled away. The builders had begun prepping the mortared stone foundation. It soon would support its third structure since the 1700s.

Eleven weeks had passed since the fire. Reconstruction had been slowed by bureaucratic entanglements. Although he and Kristen had been named sole heirs in their aunt and uncle's will, sorting out the homeowner's policy and getting the insurance company to issue the check, as well as back-and-forth paperwork with the state to have Brad appointed his sister's guardian, had consumed the months.

"The new house will probably be ugly," Kristen said.

"Nah, it'll look great. They're going to build it from similar plans except everything will be brand new and modern." He didn't have to be prescient to know what her next words were going to be. She'd been hammering them at him for weeks.

"We don't need a new house. We already have a place to live."

They'd been staying in a bungalow on the edge of town, with six months' rent paid in advance, mostly courtesy of Felicity and her dad. The pair had spearheaded a campaign to raise emergency funds for Brad and Kristen, soliciting donations through the bank and via an online fundraiser. Some money also had been brought in by selling Uncle Zack's Chevy Blazer and vintage Plymouth Valiant, as well as tools from the garage.

"You know the bungalow's only temporary," he said. "Besides, it's too small. And didn't you say we should take our time to think about where we eventually want to live and not make any snap decisions?"

"You said that."

"Maybe, but you agreed."

She scowled. Removing a flexible water bottle from her backpack, she squirted it at his face. The act wasn't meant to be playful.

"Thanks," he said, forcing a smile. He was getting accustomed to the challenges of his new role, being both sibling and parent to a strange and precocious tween. Kristen was already well beyond the borders of a conventional life but seemed determined to push the envelope even further.

He wiped his wet cheek and offered her one of the peanut butter and jelly sandwiches he'd brought. She reached out for it but he yanked it away at the last moment, bringing forth another scowl.

"Give it to me," she demanded, her cheeks flaring with anger.

"Only if you promise not to throw it at me. This is a brand-new shirt."

"I'll think about it. I won't make any *snap* decisions."

He chuckled. Her tendency toward sarcastic humor was recent. He wasn't sure whether it was a normal aspect of her development toward young womanhood or a reaction to having been through such a hellish experience. Possibly both. Or, more ominously, maybe it was related to the fact she'd retained some or all of the amulet's powers.

It wasn't as if she'd caused any new sinkholes or forecast the future or pointed out more shoo spots since those fateful events back in May. Still, he was certain her preternatural capabilities hadn't dissipated, that she was simply keeping them under wraps. He couldn't have said how he knew. He just did.

As for his own Trine-inspired powers, they seemed to have vanished the moment he'd united the three parts in the crack above the factory living room. Of course, it was possible somewhere deep inside, he was still the third part, or at least that shadowy capabilities from it still existed, awaiting the right impetus for revival. He fervently hoped not. Still, when passing by a mirror or mirrored surface, he often found himself staring hard.

These days, his only vivid connection with the Trine occurred through his dreams. Sometimes they even provided answers to questions he'd continued puzzling over. In fact, a few nights ago Sohn had appeared in one of them. SOS's third head had dutifully explained why the civilization that dispatched the repositories into space had given the amulet the power to form the crack between the realms.

In retrospect, the reason kind of made sense, although he remained a bit hazy on the logic behind it. According to Sohn, a crashed meteorite that infected someone with the emotional detritus would automatically compel that individual to seek the first part in order to unleash the venting, as well as solidifying the Pestilence's presence in the real world. The first part also was empowered to draw the second and third parts to it. Thus, an opportunity was provided to end the threat of the Pestilence by bringing the creature, the venting and the three parts together in the same place at the same time.

The dream also had served to remind him of the deviousness of those extraterrestrials, as well as their callousness in risking the annihilation of other civilizations by uprooting their darkest and most dangerous emotions and dispatching them into the void. On a whole other level, was it possible they'd been corrupted by their own absolute power?

Brad sighed. Such speculation was interesting but unlikely to generate answers. Besides, thinking about such things for too long tended to give him a headache.

He handed Kristen the sandwich. She slid it from the plastic bag and took a bite while staring down at his truck parked beside the garage. At least she seemed hungry enough not to waste any of the sandwich on sibling-targeted missiles.

Despite Kristen's negative feelings about moving back out here, he'd felt it was important for a new house to rise on the foundations of the old one. There was something right and proper about that, something that honored the memory of Aunt Nipa and Uncle Zack. It's why he'd elected to spend the insurance money on the rebuild. When the house was ready for occupancy, if his sister still felt like the location would stir up too many bad memories, he'd bow to her wishes. They'd sell the property and buy a place elsewhere.

He'd briefly considered relocating them out of state. He and Kristen had driven down to North Carolina in the aftermath of events, a necessary trip to formally quit his job and close out his apartment. Their time away also had served to evade the worst of the media stampede that had descended on Gracious.

Robin Wellstead, with the support of Brad, Kristen and Felicity, and the blessings of a number of prominent citizens such as Felicity's dad, had concocted a story about the "incident" that eliminated all evidence of the uncanny and supernatural.

His sister's kidnapping and the violent deaths of nine people had been reframed for media consumption.

The fabricated story stuck to the truth wherever possible. Sindle Vunn became a crazed cult leader who'd descended on Gracious with his followers. They'd kidnapped Kristen with the intention of holding her for ransom. Brad, Felicity, Joseph and Flick had stumbled upon the cultists on Copernian Ridge. After a deadly confrontation at the cabins, they'd followed the survivors to the abandoned factory. There, with the help of Chief Wellstead, the cultists had been vanquished and Kristen freed. The earlier sightings of Nowhere Man were dismissed as the rantings of the over-stimulated or over-inebriated.

Sue Lynn Everett and her husband had gone along with the charade, deleting the security system video of Nowhere Man crashing through their son's window and stealing his robot companion. Brandon was thrilled to have a reprogrammed and reanimated Wolfie back, and his parents wanted no further disruptions in his life.

If the public ever learned what really happened, Gracious would become a magnet for scientific investigation and a beacon for supernatural tourism. Brad could easily envision the area turning into a version of what Roswell, New Mexico, had become for the flying saucer crowd. None of them wanted that.

So far, the fabricated version seemed to be holding. Most of the media had moved on after a few weeks, although a few tenacious reporters had stuck around. And Brad and the others were still getting calls from publishers and producers offering substantial sums to tell their story. But he figured that as long as the core group stuck together and continued downplaying the incident, the town's notoriety eventually would wane.

There was a wild card, however: Flick. Although her addiction to that mind-altering drug extruded by Nowhere Man turned out to be surprisingly treatable – a cocktail of medications similar to that used for opioid withdrawal – the psychological impact remained harder to address. Felicity hadn't revealed all the details to Brad, but had hinted that Flick's brief interaction with Kristen's kidnappers had badly messed with her head. There may even have been a brief sexual relationship with Sindle Vunn, consensual or otherwise. In any case, she'd been diagnosed with post-traumatic stress disorder.

Still, Felicity's love for Flick remained unwavering. Brad felt confident Felicity would nurse her back to health and they'd eventually marry as planned.

"What's going to happen to those old bones?"

Kristen's question jarred him from his contemplations. "I'm not sure. I suppose that after the coroner finishes the autopsy they'll get buried or cremated."

"Why do you think nobody ever knew they were there?"

He shrugged. The demolition crew had uncovered the human bones while digging up the old dirt floor in the back of the basement near the water heater. The coroner hadn't yet issued an official estimate of their age, but Chief Wellstead was pretty sure from the bits of surviving clothing and shoes that they dated to an era well before Aunt Nipa and Uncle Zack owned the property. With that much time having passed, the victim's fate might never be definitively established.

The bones' discovery had solved one mystery, however. The victim represented the third shoo spot in the house, the one Kristen claimed was different from the others.

Brad waited until they'd finished their sandwiches to remove the heavy white container from his backpack.

"Shall we get to it?" he asked.

"I guess so."

They stood up. He pulled back the lid and gazed solemnly at the lumpy gray ashes.

"Do you want to help scatter them?"

"No."

"Do you want to say anything?"

Kristen shook her head. Months ago at Aunt Nipa's and

Uncle Zack's funeral service, she hadn't spoken either, and that ceremony was for the people who'd essentially raised her. It wasn't surprising she'd have nothing to say about Joseph LeFevre. He'd been a total stranger to her, much as he'd been to Brad up until that last fateful day.

It had taken this long to get possession of the ashes. Bureaucracies moved slowly and Joseph had left no will and nothing in the way of instructions about what to do with his mortal remains. The chief did find a smattering of notes in his apartment that indicated that for years he'd secretly watched over Kristen, and for decades before that did the same for their mother. He would often come out to this very hillside and perform what he felt was his duty, standing as silent guardian amid the trees. It was as good a place as any for his permanent resting place.

Brad upended the receptacle and scattered the cremains. A gentle breeze took the ashes downhill.

"Goodbye, Joseph. I truly wish Kristen and I had gotten the chance to know our grandfather. But I'm glad you were there for us at the end, there when it counted the most."

Shaking a few clingy particles from the receptacle, he returned it to his backpack. He was surprised to see tears on Kristen's cheeks. She hadn't cried at their aunt and uncle's funeral, nor on any other occasion he knew of since the night of the Trine.

She muttered something. Brad didn't catch the words.

"What did you say?"

"Nothing."

She turned away. Brad could only follow her back down to the clearing.

1.

White sky stretched from Wakeman's Edge, across the wedge-shaped valley of Thursdale, to Slapelow Hill. Drystone walls and bare black trees marked the blanket of snow; nothing broke the silence. The only signs of life were a police Land Rover parked halfway up the hill road, and a policewoman in a grey fur hat, peering over the crash barrier.

Ellie crouched and squinted down the slope. The man lay on one side, doubled up around the base of a tree in the beech coppice below. He wore a donkey jacket, jeans and Wellington boots, dusted by the snow that clogged his tangled hair and covered his upturned face.

The air was clear and sharp, the afternoon cold and still.

The two hikers who'd called it in were huddled together in the back of the Land Rover. Only idiots went blundering around the Peaks in this weather; at least stumbling over the corpse had stopped them from getting lost in the snow while Ellie and Tom Graham spent the night out looking for them. Or adding two more bodies to this year's total, because some idiot always thought he or she knew better – especially, for some reason, when it came to this part of the Peak District. It was usually hikers who came to grief, although a couple of years ago some amateur archaeologist looking for the ruins of Kirk Flockton had drowned in the marshes on Fendmoor Heath. Every year, it seemed, there was always at least one.

But a body was a body: somebody's husband, somebody's son. Someone, somewhere, would be missing the poor sod.

Hopefully. There was always the possibility that nobody was, a prospect so depressing Ellie never cared to contemplate it for long. Either way the body would be retrieved, but not just yet. Ellie had no intention of risking a Christmas in hospital by trying to shift the body single-handed. Tom was en route, with Milly Emmanuel; Milly would help her move the body and cast an eye over the scene besides.

Ellie tramped back over to her vehicle. She was a small, sturdy woman in her forties, her dark hair salted grey, and there were days where she felt every one of her years and every degree of cold. This was one of them.

In the Land Rover, the boy was crying, the girl hugging him. Ellie softened a little: they were kids, after all. Seventeen, maybe eighteen at the outside: Richard would be that old now, if he'd lived. Better she was called out for them because of this than because they were injured or dying.

Ellie opened the Land Rover's tailgate, making the kids start at the sudden sound. Knowing she'd be out for a while, she'd filled two flasks before setting off and stowed them in the back; she took them out and shut the tailgate, then opened the driver's door. "Hot chocolate?"

"Please," the girl said.

Ellie handed her a cup. "Careful," she added. "Hot." Which should have been obvious, but she'd learned long ago never to take the general public's intelligence for granted.

The girl cradled the cup and sipped. The boy, wiping his eyes, eyed it with some envy, so Ellie sighed, took the cup from the other flask and poured out a measure for him. "Let's go over it again," she said.

"We weren't going far," said the girl. "I just wanted to show Rick the Height."

Rick: an unwelcome jolt passed through Ellie at the name. Just coincidence, but still unpleasant, after the similarity in the boy's age. The moment passed, and Ellie was glad to see it gone; she leant against the doorframe and breathed out.

"Are you okay?" said the girl.

"Fine," grunted Ellie. The wind was blowing hard along the hill road and making a low, dull moan. She climbed into the front seat and shut the door. "So," she said, "the Height."

"Yeah. You know –" The girl gestured up the road.

"Yeah, I know where it is." Ellie tried not to sound snappish. "Where were you coming from?"

"Wakeman Farm," said the girl, now gesturing down the road.

"Grant and Sally Beck?" said Ellie, then remembered they had a girl away at university. "You're the daughter?"

"Kathleen Beck. Kate." The girl took the boy's arm. "Rick came up to stay. I wanted him to see it."

Ellie nodded. Maybe the girl, at least, wasn't as thick as she'd thought. Wakeman Farm was close by on Spear Bank, which ran from the bottom of the hill road across Thursdale to the Edge. Even that wasn't without risk in these conditions, but it wasn't as dangerous as a longer hike. "You tell your folks where you were going?"

Kate shrugged.

"You need to," Ellie said. "Main roads are gonna be cut off for the next couple of days, and there's more snow coming. You get caught out in it and get in trouble, right now there's exactly two coppers in the area." Or one, if she included Tom Graham.

The girl's story was simple enough. They'd stopped for a short rest, as the hill road was pretty steep; before setting off again, the boy had gone to the road's edge to study the view, and seen something lying in the snow.

"Took me a few seconds to realise what it was," said the boy, wiping his eyes again and giving Ellie a shy smile. "Sorry about that. Gave me a bit of a shock – never seen anyone dead before."

Town lad – a bit soft, maybe, but polite. Well-mannered. The kind you'd bring home to meet your parents.

"Happens sometimes round here," said Ellie at last. "You get used to it. What happened then?"

"Managed to get a signal," Kate said. "So we called it in."

"Lucky again," said Ellie. "Reception's a nightmare round here, specially when it's like this."

She had no idea what else to say, so she looked out through the windscreen. To her relief, an olive-green BMW X5 came round the hill road's bend and drove down towards them. Barsall Village had two full-time officers and one official vehicle, so at times like this Tom Graham's own 4X4 – a seven-seater SUV, no less, a proper Chelsea tractor – was pressed into service; a blue police light had been hurriedly mounted on the roof, but, as usual, he'd forgotten to switch it on.

The BMW halted beside Ellie's, and Tom got out. "All right, Ell. What have we got?"

Ellie trudged over and pointed. "Body, Sarge."

"Oh, yes." He scratched the back of his neck. "You did say."

He looked lost – as usual – so Ellie, once again, stepped in. "The young lady and gentleman over there found him. I thought if you took them back to the station and got their statements, Dr Emmanuel and I can retrieve the body."

"Oh. Yeah. Makes sense." Tom gave the kids an amiable if vacant smile, then frowned at Ellie, or more accurately the fur hat. "For God's sake, will you stop wearing that bloody thing on duty?"

"It keeps my head warm and the regulation cap doesn't. I like having ears."

"I wouldn't mind so much if you'd take *that* off it." He had a point, given that the hat was Soviet-era Red Army surplus, complete with a hammer-and-sickle-emblazoned red star badge Ellie had never trusted herself to remove without tearing a gaping hole. "Ernie Stasiolek's gonna think you're the bloody Stasi one of these days and take a pot at you."

"Ernie Stasiolek's Polish, Tom. The Stasi were East German."

"All right, clever clogs." Tom took a step towards the kids

and called out. "This way, you two. Nice cup of tea when we get in, eh?"

He probably hadn't even noticed the cups they were already holding, but you could never have enough hot drinks on a day like this. The kids followed him back to the X5 as Milly Emmanuel climbed out of it, hidden under multiple layers of clothing culminating in a neon pink puffa jacket and matching ski-hat that rendered her almost globular. She waved to Ellie and waddled over as Tom managed a clumsy three-point turn before driving back up the hill road towards Barsall.

"Afternoon, Constable," she called.

"All right, Doc. Got enough layers on?"

"It's all right for you. My Dad was from Jamaica, remember? I'm not half fucking penguin like you are. So where's the patient?"

Ellie pointed. Milly peered over the crash barrier. "Think we might be a bit late to help."

"What would I do without you?"

"Many a true word."

"Oh, sod off."

"So what's the plan? Please tell me you can call someone in."

Ellie shook her head. "Phone and radio reception's up and down like a whore's drawers and the main roads are snowed up anyway."

Milly groaned. "Don't suppose we could just shovel a bit more snow over him and leave him till the spring?"

"I wish."

"Great. So, heavy lifting duty, then?"

"That and your medical expertise, Doc."

"I'm not a pathologist –"

"You're the closest I've got."

"Fair enough." Milly's breath billowed in the air. "But you'd better have some decent wine in for later."

"Do my best. Got some hot chocolate in the meantime, if you want it."

They got in the Land Rover and Ellie drove down to the bottom of the hill road. She cleared space in the back, spread a blanket out there, folded another over her arm and picked up a small black pack. She opened it and checked the contents – latex gloves, evidence baggies, a pair of small flashlights – then slung it over her shoulder and turned away. Ellie wasn't expecting to find any evidence of foul play – chances were a drunk had slipped and fallen on the path, and the cold had done the rest – but it was best to be prepared.

Milly had already climbed over the crash barrier and was waiting. Ellie climbed after her. Intermittent snow drifted down. Ahead of them a narrow footpath ran along the hillside, past the edge of the Harpers' land, towards the silent trees.

For more great title recommendations,
check out the Angry Robot website and
social channels

www.angryrobotbooks.com
@angryrobotbooks